A GHASTLY CATASTROPHE

ALSO BY DEANNA RAYBOURN

Killers of a Certain Age

Kills Well with Others

Veronica Speedwell Mystery Series

A Curious Beginning

A Perilous Undertaking

A Treacherous Curse

A Dangerous Collaboration

A Murderous Relation

An Unexpected Peril

An Impossible Impostor

A Sinister Revenge

A Grave Robbery

A Ghastly Catastrophe

Lady Julia Grey Novels

Silent in the Grave

Silent in the Sanctuary

Silent on the Moor

Dark Road to Darjeeling

The Dark Enquiry

Lady Julia Grey Novellas

Silent Night

Midsummer Night

Twelfth Night

Bonfire Night

Other Works

For a complete list of Deanna's titles,
please visit *deannaraybourn.com*

To the readers who have been with Veronica since the very (curious) beginning. Ten adventures in, and hopefully many more to come. Excelsior!

A GHASTLY CATASTROPHE

Author's Note

March, 1898
London

It has come to my attention that there has recently been published a work of fiction which appears to take as its inspiration many of the details and events contained within this memoir. How the author may have come to read my own private reflections of the terrible events of that April of 1890, I cannot imagine, but read them he must have done. Otherwise, how could there be so many similarities between his distasteful but commercially successful *Dracula* and my own experiences? I have been advised by counsel not to seek damages in the matter—I am, after all, a private and discreet individual—but I will state for the purposes of this document that Bram Stoker is a thieving blackguard. (I am told that "Stoker" is his own actual surname and not a nom de plume stolen from my inamorato, but I should like to see proof.) In accordance with the rules of honour, I have issued a challenge. Naturally, he may choose the weapon, although I am dearly hoping to display my prowess with a hatpin, unconventional as this may be. I have as yet to receive a reply.

—VS

CHAPTER 1

London, 1890

"Do you want to do the deed or shall I?" I asked as we stared down at the carcass.

Stoker sighed. "I suppose I will." The lackadaisical air he adopted would have been cause enough for concern; the sigh was terrifying. Stoker had always been a man of extraordinary vigour, striding with purpose and energy through all of his endeavours, no matter how small.

But our lives had, in recent weeks, grown very small indeed. Despite a physically hectic and thoroughly enjoyable winter holiday together in the Isles of Scilly,* Stoker and I had returned to a London bedevilled by bad weather and worse moods. After an autumn which had seen us crack our most extraordinary case yet,† the season of mists and mellow fruitfulness had given way to choking fogs and a deep, creeping damp which settled into our very bones. Both of us had suffered through a

* *Any account of this adventure is missing from the papers of Veronica Speedwell but may someday be found.*

† *A Grave Robbery*

series of lengthy colds, snuffling and sniffling until we were quite mad with it. We smelt of mustard plasters and liniments and other assorted unguents. The tip of my nose was, for the whole of March, the unbecoming shade of a ripe plum. Spring was slow in arriving; a series of late frosts blackened and withered the snowdrops, and the daffodils shivered in their pretty yellow caps. It was, in short, a dismal time, and if it had been only the weather and our various ailments to assail us, our spirits might not have fallen so low.

But I was conscious of a new and unwelcome feeling that spring. I had, for the first time since I had made Stoker's acquaintance, experienced ennui. My boredom lay not with him—never think it! He was as engaging and maddening a companion as ever, offering sustenance for both body and mind through a combination of vitality, intellect, and charm that was as heady as it was rare. No, our intimate friendship was as intimate and friendly as it had ever been.

Our regular work was likewise fulfilling. We had been engaged by the Earl of Rosemorran to catalogue his extensive collection with an eye to someday opening a museum. While Stoker and I were natural historians by trade—he a naval surgeon turned taxidermist and I a lepidopterist—we had been given charge of the entire collection with the result that all of our spare hours were spent in study of the various artefacts in our care. From coins to corals, stamps to suits of armour, the previous earls had collected it all, and it was the present earl's task to bring order to the hotchpotch of his forefathers. The collection was enormous and not particularly orderly, but most of the entries were exquisite, chosen with taste and purchased at great expense. (I do not include the present earl's acquisitions in this assessment. Whilst his ancestors applied standards of beauty and worth to their additions, the present earl simply buys what he likes. This accounts for the puppet theatre, the moth-eaten camel saddle we use as seating for guests, and an assortment of prosthetic limbs in questionable states of hygiene.)

The collection had come to be housed in an enormous freestanding ballroom on the earl's estate at Bishop's Folly in the heart of Marylebone. The ballroom—called the Belvedere—was only one of the various buildings that had been placed at our disposal. Stoker and I each had a folly for our private quarters, and an elegant glasshouse had been refurbished for my use as a vivarium where I might breed and study butterflies and their mothy kin. We had been given free rein over the collections, empowered to either deaccession or purchase as we saw fit, and we were beholden to no one for our time. We lived in extraordinary comfort, and we enjoyed interesting work as well as harmony in our own relationship—spiced with the occasional spirited debate when Stoker proved overly emotional. (I have long held that the male is the less logical of the species and have yet to see evidence to the contrary.)

What then ailed us that long and gloomy season, I hear you wonder, dear reader. With so many advantages, we ought to have been content—nay, we ought to have been as happy as angels.

And yet. We did not speak of it, but souls cannot be as linked as ours and have secrets. I intuited Stoker's restlessness as clearly as I felt the itch in my own blood, and the cause of it was the same as my own: we wanted a mystery. It had been nearly six months since our last investigation, and while we were certainly not professionals, we had fallen into the habit of murder—the sleuthing and not the committing, I hasten to add. And we had found it a difficult one to break. How could any mind trained to logic and observation, any person that thrilled to challenge, not find these deductive puzzles utterly intoxicating? They were as delicious to us as the rarest of wines, and we were, quite simply, suffering from the lack of a body.

I stared down at the corpse in front of me, knife in hand.

Stoker's lack of enthusiasm for the present job was not lost upon me. "Oh, let me," I said to Stoker as I bent to my task. Swiftly, the deed was done, and I held the bone out to him.

He curled his littlest finger around the bone and I did the same.

"On three," I instructed. I counted in Latin, and we pulled. There was a moment of hesitation, and then the bone snapped with the larger part resting in my hand.

"The wish is mine!" I crowed. I closed my eyes and made it quickly.

"What did you wish for?" Stoker asked as he helped himself to a drumstick.

"I cannot tell you or it will not come to pass," I reminded him.

Just then, George, the hallboy, entered brandishing a letter.

"Post, miss!" he called as he fought his way through the pack of dogs which we had somehow acquired in the course of our adventures. From Huxley the bulldog to Betony, the enormous Caucasian sheepdog, they represented every possible variation of the canine species. We had lazy dogs and dogs possessed of enough energy to pull a sled of Olympian proportions; we had affectionate dogs and dogs that would very probably stand by and watch us be devoured by Stoker's collection of dermestid beetles. The only thing they had in common was an abiding adoration of George, doubtless because he invariably smelt of interesting things. The boy had come from impoverished circumstances, and it was not until he had come into his lordship's employ that he had known food that was both wholesome and delivered at regular intervals. Still, the habits of the starveling are difficult to break, and George invariably tucked away some portion of each meal against any future hunger. A chicken wing, a bread roll, a sliver of good English Cheddar—his pockets were emptied each day either into his own stomach or that of one of his grateful siblings, but the delectable aromas remained for the dogs to sniff out.

By the time George had fought his way clear of the snufflings of each wet black nose, Stoker had finished carving the chicken and was portioning slices of juicy fowl onto our plates.

"Have you eaten, George?" he asked, poised to serve another portion.

"I have, sir," George said, although he eyed the roast potatoes with avarice in his gaze.

I did not blame him. The potatoes were golden and crisp and piping hot. I plucked one from the platter and offered it. It disappeared with a conjuror's skill into his pocket as he handed over the letter.

"From Mr. Mornaday, that detective fellow," George announced helpfully.

Stoker and I were both eager to instill in George the skills and accomplishments necessary to make something of himself. He was a Cockney child, born out of wedlock to a mother who had repeated the process of giving birth without benefit of a husband several times over. As the eldest, it fell to George even at his tender age to contribute to the household expenses. Lord Rosemorran had employed him as a hallboy whose duties included the running of errands, some of the less arduous of the heavy cleaning chores undertaken by the footmen, and whatever assorted tasks might be reliably handed off to a diligent child. In return, he was paid a modest wage and given bed and board with leave to visit his family often. So long as he attended church once a week and kept himself free of vice, he was assured of a position which might one day lead to his promotion to footman, provided he grew to at least six feet and had shapely calves. Otherwise, he would be turned over to the gardener for training in heavier labours.

Everyone seemed thoroughly pleased with the arrangement—everyone except George. He was an ambitious imp who was determined to rise from the ranks of servitude. By way of his lordship's generous gift of a library for the servants' hall, George had taught himself his letters, believing literacy would be the key to his future ambitions. He had wheedled basic numeracy out of the butler, and Stoker had undertaken to give him weekly lessons in the essential sciences, including geography and astronomy. Stoker was pleased with his progress, saying that he was very nearly ready for the fundamentals of chemistry, but I had my own thoughts upon the matter.

It had occurred to me that a slender and unprepossessing child would make an excellent observer, undetected and underestimated by everyone. A wiry lad, small for his age and agile, George was slippery as an eel when it came to finding his way through the teeming streets of London. There was not a cobbled alley or paved court he did not know; from knacker's yard to noble's garden, he had made a study of the capital, committing its secrets to memory. Each day upon his various errands, I set him a task to develop his powers of observation. I would tell him to find a man with a bowler hat and follow him for thirty minutes to see where he went and give me an account of it. Or he might count the number of butchers in a given street and tell me the price each charged for a Cumberland sausage. On days when the weather was too abominable to permit such excursions, I would give him an envelope or a bit of brown paper that had wrapped a parcel, and ask him for his conclusions about the senders.

"Veronica," Stoker had inquired after one memorable day when George had deduced the contours of a concealed Wardian case from the size of its packing crate, "is there a point to these exercises? These are the sorts of skills one would expect to be mastered by a criminal apprentice. Do you intend to set George upon a career as a pickpocket?"

"Certainly not," I had replied with some asperity. "His talents may be put to excellent use in the pursuit of justice—as have our own," I reminded him.

"How?" Stoker demanded.

"In the course of our investigations, we would often have profited enormously from another pair of eyes, youthful and sharp eyes to keep watch upon suspects and inform us of comings and goings. I am training George to be our assistant."

"Our assistant?" It is seldom that one actually witnesses someone tearing at one's hair, but Stoker threaded his hands through his tousled witch-black locks, tugging in frustration. "Veronica, we are natural scientists. Teach the boy to identify one of your bloody moths, or let me train him to the taxidermic arts, but for the love of all things holy and good, do not think to make a sort of detective of him. We are not the police."

"No, and that is a pity," I told him as I made a mental note to introduce George to the study of handwriting. "If we were the police, there would be far fewer criminals about."

Stoker tugged harder upon his hair, and I let the conversation drop solely out of concern for his follicles. Naturally, I carried on with my plan to instruct George in the detectival skills with the result that he—quite correctly—identified the hand of our sometime partner in the investigative arts, Mornaday of Special Branch.

"Well done, George," I told him. "I imagine you noticed the peculiarity of his 't's."

"That it smells of macassar oil," he said. "I should like some of that. It's how a gentleman ought to smell," he added with a reproachful look at Stoker.

"If you mean to shame Stoker on that score, you shall be a long time at it," I advised George absently. "He will always smell of leather, honey, and good whisky." As these were not unpleasant to me, the reader must not mistake my observation for criticism.

"And glue. And linseed oil," George murmured under his breath. He was not wrong. The tools of Stoker's trade were often to be detected clinging to his person, but I found the combination quite arresting—intoxicating, even.

I skimmed the missive, reading it over a second time as a slow smile spread across my face.

"What is it?" Stoker demanded.

"Mornaday says he will call upon us shortly. And this letter is proof that wishes on a chicken bone may come true," I told him as I pushed away from the table, dinner no longer of any consequence.

George slid smoothly into my chair in my stead, picking up my fork and helping himself to a wing and another roast potato. He eyed the broken wishbone as he crammed a forkful of potato into his mouth.

"Whahdyewhshformis?"

"Chew, George," I instructed as I made preparations to receive our visitor. "And if you are endeavouring to ask what it is that I wished for, I am only too happy to tell you. A body, George. I wished for a body."

CHAPTER 2

Horsefeathers," Stoker said succinctly as he handed the note back with a gesture of lofty disdain. "Mornaday says only that he will call. There is nothing whatsoever about a body. Your rampageous imagination has got the better of you. Again."

I gave him an indulgent smile. I could afford it. I was certain we were perched once more upon the precipice of adventure, and the resulting exhilaration made me generous with Stoker's impatience.

"I know you have never properly warmed to Mornaday," I began.

Stoker made a sound that was a cross between a snort and a heave of unwellness. Naturally I ignored this and went on.

I cleared my throat. "As I said, I know you have never properly warmed to Mornaday, but I think he is quite fond of you."

[NB: Stoker's reply was unsuitable for delicate readers, and I decline to repeat it here. —VS]

"Scoff if you like," I went on, "but you cannot deny there has been real camaraderie amongst us in the past," I reminded him. "And more than once Mornaday has demonstrated himself a true friend and ally. You must admit he has some admirable qualities."

"He had me stripped and searched at Scotland Yard. By seven policemen," Stoker said grimly.

"He applies himself to his work with thoroughness. You have just proven my point."

Stoker growled and the dogs followed suit, setting off a cacophony that made further conversation impossible. He returned to his work in progress—something which entailed a great deal of smelly glue and the occasional flurry of sparks from a welder's torch, all conducted behind draperies he had hung to conceal his latest efforts—whilst I mounted the stairs to the snuggery. This was my favorite part of the Belvedere, comprising a wide gallery that circled the inside of the building. It was lined in bookshelves and stands for Wardian cases and punctuated here and there by alcoves that had been furnished with the haphazard luxury of the Rosemorrans. An archbishop's throne might have a stuffed miniature antelope for a footstool, while a brandy barrel served as a side table. A hammock from the Amazonian rain forests might swing gently over a rug straight from the skillful looms of Anatolia. In one alcove, an elegant Swedish stove had been installed along with a pair of mediaeval X-chairs from a French abbey. The chairs and a camp bed once slept in by Napoléon had been made more comfortable by the addition of numerous cushions fashioned out of various scraps of velvet and satin and kilim rugs, and the whole alcove was illuminated by an assortment of beaded lamps hanging from silken cords. Where others might have placed a birdcage or a bowl of goldfish, Stoker had installed a glass case of the aforementioned dermestid beetles, a particularly nasty variety of insect whose only purpose is to strip the flesh from the bones of other animals. When I had objected, he defended them as tidy, homely creatures, and in the end, I left them. After all, when a man wishes to contribute to the comforts of his home, he must be encouraged, no matter how dire the consequences.

I lit the lamps and the stove and plumped a few cushions, for my own comfort—Stoker and Mornaday wouldn't notice if they were sitting upon one of the thornier varieties of cactus. Various decanters and bottles of libation were always at hand, and I retrieved a tin of Stoker's favorite biscuits in case we had need of a little refreshment while we conferred.

I had just arranged everything to my satisfaction when I heard a tread on the spiral stair—too light to be Stoker or Mornaday. I turned with a smile.

"J. J.!" I exclaimed. The dark red head bobbed into view followed by a slender figure holding her dripping bonnet by its strings. The dogs padded after her, sniffing eagerly. She usually brought some delicacy for them, filling her reticule with anything from bits of cheese to cooked chicken livers.

"It is a filthy night out there," she said, coming near the fire to warm herself. She tossed the bonnet—now much the worse for wear—into a corner where Betony, the largest of the dogs, promptly sat upon it. I almost called her off, but then I realised the dog could do nothing but improve the state of the unfortunate headwear. As a working reporter, J. J. cared little for her appearance and nothing at all for fashion. The bonnet she habitually wore was at least ten years out of date, and even then it had only been suitable for someone living on a prairie.

J. J. settled herself into one of the chairs and propped her feet up on a hassock covered in a scrap of threadbare tapestry. She whistled and Nut, the small pharaoh hound, leapt into her lap to be petted. J. J. crooned a little as she cuddled the dog, and I saw that her eyes, usually bright with mischief, were a little dim. A smudge of ink, the telltale mark of the reporter, stained one cheek and the fingers of her right hand. She had been hard at work, but everything about her countenance said the experience had been unsatisfactory.

A nice cup of tea would probably help, I reflected, but a glass of aguardiente would help more. I poured her a measure of the fiery concoction of fermented sugarcane liquor and handed it over.

"Bless you," she said fervently. She took rather more than she ought to have on her first sip and choked so hard her eyes watered.

"All right there?" I asked as I poured my own glass.

"Never better," she replied huskily. "Except that I have been suspended from the *Daily Harbinger.* My editor has withheld my pay as compensation for damages I caused when he told me I was suspended. And my landlady is not open to a barter arrangement in lieu of cash for my rent. I am therefore, as of tomorrow morning, lacking both employment and a home." With that she downed the last of the aguardiente and held out the empty glass.

"J. J., you really ought to pace yourself with aguar—"

"Pour," she instructed. I did as she told me. Whatever ill effects she suffered would be her business, not mine, and the oblivion she would buy in the interim might do her well.

I refreshed her drink and had just settled in with my own when Mornaday arrived, trailing Stoker. He stopped dead in his tracks when he caught sight of J. J. glowering into her glass.

"What are you doing here?" he demanded.

"Mornaday!" I reproved. "That is hardly a proper greeting for someone who has been our companion in danger and detection." It was also not a suitable greeting for a woman for whom he harboured a tendresse, but Mornaday's gentler feelings were not suitable for general conversation, particularly as they were not reciprocated. J. J. was firmly wedded to her career and had no intention of settling down with Mornaday or any other fellow, a view I heartily applauded, as my own sentiments were strongly in opposition to babies, rose-covered cottages, and any other sugary image of domestic incarceration the mind could conjure.

Mornaday, usually amenable to a gentle correction, did not soften. "I wrote that I was coming specifically so that we would be uninterrupted and alone."

"I do not care what you've come about," J. J. informed him loftily.

"You could be planning the theft of the Crown Jewels from the Tower, you could be plotting to hang the Prince of Wales by his toenails, you could be scheming to steal Her Majesty's pantalettes, and I would not care. Go on. I have business with the bottom of this glass." She tipped it up, sucking out the last few drops of aguardiente with an audible slurp.

"Good god," Stoker said, turning to me. "Does she know what that will do to her?"

"I do not think she much cares," I replied. "She is without home and without employment and therefore in a state of some desperation."

"I am not *desperate*," J. J. corrected. "I am angry. I am angry with them," she added, pointing a wavering finger between Stoker and Mornaday.

"What the devil did we do?" Mornaday demanded.

"Not you fespically," she said.

"I think you mean 'specifically,'" I put in.

"That is precisely what I said, Veronica. Do not interrupt." She turned back to the men. "It is not the pair of you. It is your kind. Running everything from time imm—immem—immemememmorial. Lords of creation, acting as if the rest of us were simply put on God's green earth to serve you."

"Well, according to the Bible, you were," Mornaday said. His tone was perfectly reasonable, but I knew him well enough to realise he was goading her deliberately. J. J. made to stand, forgetting completely that Nut was still happily ensconced in her lap. I hurried to refill her glass before she managed to evict the dog and struggle to her feet.

"Veronica, the last thing she needs is more of that," Stoker said.

"On the contrary," I said, handing over the glass. "The more she drinks, the faster she will become unconscious and we can settle to the subject of the murder Mornaday is so eager to discuss."

Mornaday gave a start. "I never said anything about a murder."

"You did not have to. For you to warn us in writing that you meant to call, you must have a matter of urgent business to discuss. And your business is murder."

"My business is a few other things as well," he protested. "I do investigate the occasional bank robbery or jewel theft, you know."

Stoker poured himself a measure of whisky and handed the bottle to Mornaday. "We do not stand on ceremony here. You know where the glasses are. Get on with it."

Mornaday looked as if he would like to cavil, but Stoker's expression brooked no argument.

"Pay him no attention," I instructed Mornaday. "He is tetchy because he is having difficulty with his latest commission." Upon occasion, Stoker undertook the rehabilitation and refitting of zoological specimens, exercising his mastery of the taxidermic arts for discerning clients who were prepared to pay astronomical fees for the privilege. Other men might have done so for sybaritic reasons, but not Stoker. His needs were modest, his personal luxuries limited in the extreme. But he did harbour an unholy lust for the accoutrements of his trade, and he invariably ran tremendously overdrawn accounts at the various suppliers. The house of Deyrolle in Paris, those purveyors of the most splendid of taxidermic fittings, were forever sending chastening letters regarding the state of his balance in their books. The result was his occasional foray into commissions which were, to put it delicately, beneath his talents. "Or, rather, his lack of one. He is upset about the walrus."

"I am not upset about the walrus," Stoker said, clearly seething.

J. J. blinked several times as if trying to bring Stoker into focus. "What are you stuffing now?"

"It is not *stuffing*," he corrected coldly. "It is mounting. And I am mounting nothing. I have not been invited to participate."

I leant near to Mornaday, pitching my voice to a confiding tone.

"There is a particularly fine walrus, an enormous specimen that has been secured for purposes of display to the general public, but the taxidermists engaged to prepare it have been less than satisfactory."

"They have ironed out all of the wrinkles!" Stoker roared.

"Wrinkles? The wrinkles of a walrus?" Mornaday asked in some perplexity.

"*Odobenus rosmarus*," I explained. "A very large pinniped indigenous to the Northern Hemisphere."

"Veronica," Mornaday said icily, "I know what a bloody walrus is. I have read Lewis Carroll, you know. I am not entirely illiterate."

"Well, then. You may be one step ahead of the taxidermists who have the commission of mounting the walrus in question," I said. "They were presented with only the hide, and they subsequently applied sound if unfortunate reasoning to the task. They have, I am sorry to say, stuffed the skin to capacity, smoothing out all of the characteristic wrinkles of the creature."

"It. Is. Not. Stuffing," Stoker repeated through gritted teeth.

I waved an airy hand. "However it has been done, it has been done badly, and the poor thing looks as if it were about to burst. Most disconcerting."

"It does not bear thinking about," Stoker said. "Mornaday, you had a reason for coming, one presumes?"

"I have and I do. But J. J.'s matter is more pressing." He turned to J. J. "How did you lose your post?"

Her expression darkened and she looked around for the aguardiente, but I had taken the precaution of concealing the bottle behind my chair. "I wrote a story my editor didn't much care for. About a landlord in Whitechapel who takes advantage of his tenants, raising rents on them when they are ill for the sole purpose of forcing them out of his lodgings and into the workhouses."

"Why did your editor object to that?" I asked.

"Because the landlord is his brother. The editor was away, and his assistant approved the piece. It went to print before anyone could stop it. It was a good piece," she added mulishly. "The landlord is thieving scum, and the editor isn't much better."

"But how did you lose your room?" Mornaday pressed.

"I was slightly in arrears from last month, and I had promised to make it up to my landlady." She paused to let a fat tear roll down her nose. It hesitated on the tip, then plopped into Nut's fur. J. J. gave a great sniff and went on. "I would have done, if the paper hadn't taken my last wages to pay for the window I broke on the way out. I had to be escorted from the premises."

"Poor J. J.," Stoker said gently. He picked up his biscuit tin and held it out to her. "Shortbread? Cook's secret recipe. I think there's a bit of ginger in, but I can't be sure."

J. J. accepted a piece and chewed it woefully. "Definitely ginger."

"There is more if you like."

"I ought to eat it, it may be my last meal. I shall have to live on stale crusts and cheese stolen from mousetraps. I will be forced into degrading work like prostitution or standing for Parliament."

"Nonsense," Stoker said. "There will always be food here for you. And you will always have a roof over your head so long as Veronica has a place to live." My mouth dropped open, and Stoker took the opportunity to stuff a piece of shortbread into it as he went on. "Isn't that right, dearest? After all, you have the chapel folly all to yourself, and J. J. cannot take up much room. You will hardly know she is there."

J. J. gave a hiccup. "Oh, that's so kind of you, Veronica! I will be the very best of guests. Quiet as a mouse, I shall be. And I do not snore much at all."

I bared my teeth at Stoker in what a stupider man might have mistaken for a smile. "Not at all, J. J. You are most welcome." Stoker gave me the sleekly satisfied grin of a cream-sated cat. He had got his own back since I had raised the painful matter of the walrus, and he had upped the ante decidedly.

I turned to Mornaday. "Since that is settled, let us have it clearly. Tell us about your body."

"Why do you persist in believing there is a body?" he demanded.

I arched a brow and said nothing until he puffed out a sigh of defeat.

"Very well. There is a body."

It is not my way to crow when I am right, but I must have betrayed my pleasure, for Stoker spoke up. "Do not gloat, Veronica. It is unbecoming."

"I do so love to be right," I replied. "Now, tell us. Who is dead? Where? When? How can we help?"

"The name of the deceased is Maurice Quincey. And he was found in a carriage outside Highgate Cemetery a fortnight ago."

"A ghoulish place to die," Stoker mused. Of all the graveyards in London, none was more magnificent or more atmospheric than Highgate.

"That is not the worst of it," Mornaday said. "Quincey's physician said it was natural causes, that the fellow had had a weak heart and was never going to make old bones."

"You think otherwise?" J. J. ventured. She hiccuped again, but the shortbread seemed to be sopping up the worst of the aguardiente. And the instincts of an investigative reporter are impossible to quash. "Why?"

Mornaday hesitated, then blurted out the answer in a rush. "Because he had a pair of puncture wounds on his neck. They were spaced two inches apart and they dripped blood. It was inexplicable."

"Not inexplicable," I corrected in a thrilled tone. "It was the work of a vampire."

CHAPTER 3

"For the love of bleeding Jesus," Stoker cut in, "there are no such things as vampires."

"This coming from the man who spent months searching the forests of Bavaria for a mythical creature," I retorted.

"It is entirely possible that wolpertingers existed," Stoker protested coldly. "Similar creatures have been sighted in Thuringia and Austria—as far away as Sweden, in fact."

"And so may vampires exist," I said, neatly drawing the conversation around. "Go on, Mornaday."

"Wait a minute," J. J. put in. "I heard nothing about a vampire loose in Highgate. The people have a right to know if some undead creature is stalking the city. Why wasn't the story made public?"

"For exactly that reason," Mornaday answered. "My god, can you imagine the uproar if John Bull caught a sniff of this? There would be pandemonium, utter panic in the streets. No, the circumstances of Maurice Quincey's death had to be kept strictly confidential."

"Was there anything else suspicious about Quincey's death? Besides the puncture marks?" I asked.

"Oh, yes," Mornaday said with a grim smile. "He was—what d'ye call it when the blood has all but drained out?"

"Exsanguination," Stoker supplied.

"That's the one." Mornaday gave a nod of satisfaction. "This fellow was properly exsanguinated he was. Just the bit of blood about his collar and nothing more. Natural causes, my arse!"

"But if Scotland Yard have decided to cover up the true cause of Quincey's death, why bring it to us?" I asked.

"Because there has been another death—not a vampire," he added with firm haste. "But suspicious just the same."

"Suspicious in what way?"

Mornaday paused to consider his words. "Maurice Quincey's closest friend, Jameson Harkness, died a week ago. He fell from the balcony at his home in Surrey. The verdict at the inquest was one of accidental death based upon testimony from his father, Sir Ranulph Harkness, baronet."

Stoker began to look interested in the story. "Sir Ranulph Harkness? Where have I heard that name?"

J. J. waved an arm. "Everywhere, my dear Stoker. There is not a financial plum in London into which Sir Ranulph hasn't stuck his thumb. He is legend."

That much was true. Mornaday had exercised understatement in merely describing him as a baronet. He was far more than that. As chairman of the Balfour Bank, he was one of the foremost financial minds in the City, responsible for advising the Chancellor of the Exchequer and directing the investments of his institution as well as those of the royal family. Born to affluence, he had amassed a considerable fortune of his own, using it to build Rosewood Hall, a Gothic villa modelled after Strawberry Hill that put Walpole's house firmly in the shade.

"How tragic for him to lose his son," I mused. "Was Jameson his only child?"

Mornaday nodded. "He was. Jameson was not yet thirty. He leaves behind two small children of his own and a widow, Araminta Dalziel Harkness. Of the Perthshire Dalziels," he added loftily.

"And what precisely was Sir Ranulph's inquest testimony regarding the death of his son?" Stoker inquired.

"That Jameson fell to his death when a bit of balustrade on the balcony gave way. He said Jameson had gone out to admire the view and leant against the railing, but it had been fixed to a patch of rotting stone and gave way."

"Rotting stone? At Rosewood Hall? The place is scarcely a quarter of a century old," I protested.

Mornaday grinned. "My thoughts exactly. As I say, Sir Ranulph maintains that Jameson stepped out to admire the view whilst leaning against the railing. The whole affair collapsed under Jameson's weight, dashing him to the stone terrace below—a drop of a good thirty feet."

Stoker winced. "An unpleasant way to go."

"You can say that again, my lad. His head was soft as a ripe melon by the time I saw him."

"You saw him? You investigated the death?" I pressed.

Mornaday pulled a face. "I was not permitted to investigate. Sir Ranulph is bosom chums with the acting head of Special Branch."

"Acting head? Where is Sir Hugo?" I demanded.

Special Branch was the division of Scotland Yard tasked with the most delicate of operations—largely the protection of the royal family and the investigation of sensational crimes. Sir Hugo Montgomerie, the official head, was our sometime friend and sporadic nemesis. We had crossed swords with him upon occasion; upon others he had proven himself a true ally. Stoker avoided him like one of the lesser plagues—locusts, perhaps—but I preferred to think of him as a cordial adversary, one who deserved our respect if for no other reason than the fact that he had kept the secret of my parentage when it would have garnered him a fortune if he had sold the information to one of the more sensational newspapers. (The revelation that the Prince of Wales had a semi-legitimate daughter who might reasonably make a claim to the throne would have seeded considerable unrest in the empire, particularly the Catholic bits. Stoker maintained that Sir Hugo kept my secret in order to save his own job, but I liked to think it was because he was a true gentleman.)

Mornaday's scowl deepened. "He is a martyr to his gout. He has gone off to Bad something or other. One of those German places where they dunk you in sulphur water and put you on a diet of boiled potatoes and vinegar. While he is away, Special Branch is being looked after by one Digby Carruthers."

"He sounds as if he should be rowing eights for Cambridge," Stoker said dryly.

"He sounds like a pain in my backside," Mornaday replied with a glower. "He charged me to come with him to Rosewood Hall when Sir Ranulph reported the death. I thought it was finally my chance, that I would enter at the sharp end and really get my teeth into this case. When we arrived, Sir Ranulph was in the process of having the body moved. Claimed it was beneath his son's dignity to lie there in the rain."

"If it were raining, why would he go onto the balcony to admire the view?" I asked.

Mornaday snapped his fingers. "That is precisely what I asked! And as soon as I did, the pair of them looked at me like a spaniel that has piddled on the Axminster. Sent me away with a flea in my ear and told me to stay near the carriage until Mr. Carruthers was ready to leave."

"Your question unsettled them," J. J. mused.

"Bloody right it did. And I was not about to let it go at that. I know the smell of something rotting in the state of Denmark. So I nosed about the house, and in the sitting room, I found Araminta, Mrs. Jameson, the widow. Pretty little thing. On saint," he added as an aside with a waggle of his eyebrows.

Stoker's forehead furrowed. "On saint?"

Mornaday coloured slightly. "You know." He sketched a gesture, arcing his arms into a wide circle in front of his belly.

"On saint? For the love of god, man, are you trying to speak French? Do you mean enceinte?"

"That is what I said," Mornaday told him doggedly. "On saint. Anyway, I did not much want to distress a lady in her condition, so I could only ask a question or two, couldn't I? And apparently, her father-in-law, Sir Ranulph, hadn't had the chance yet to tell her to keep quiet about what really happened."

I leant forward in my chair. "And what *did* really happen?"

Mornaday's mouth thinned to a grim line. "What really happened is that Jameson Harkness opened his morning post, rose from the breakfast table, strode directly onto that balcony, and threw himself off of it."

J. J. gave an impression of almost perfect sobriety as she sat forward, eyes rounding in interest, scrabbling in her pocket for her notebook. "Why? What was in the post?"

"Nothing," Mornaday said with the flourish of a practiced raconteur. He even drew out the succeeding pause to increase the dramatic tension of his narration. "Save this." He reached into his waistcoat and produced an envelope.

J. J. put out her hand immediately, and Mornaday obligingly passed the envelope over as she urged Nut from her lap. "Careful," he warned as she took hold of the paper. "It is fragile."

The envelope held no letter, only a few bits of plant material. J. J. withdrew it carefully, mindful of Mornaday's warning, for the specimens had been dried and were pale and pitiful things, desiccated ghosts of what they had once been.

J. J. held one piece up to the light, peering at the etiolated green stem, the translucent indigo petals. "What is it?"

"Wolfsbane," I said just as Stoker replied, "Monkshood."

We exchanged glances. "Both are common names for the same plant," I told J. J. When flowering, the blooms appeared on upright swords, the petals forming little purple or blue caps that looked like the head coverings of priestly men, hence the name "monkshood." This one had been pressed flat and the color leached so that it was a subdued hue. "The botanical appellation is *Aconitum napellus*. Very common and highly toxic. I would not handle it with bare hands," I advised her. "The poison may be absorbed through the skin."

She gave a start and dropped the pressed flower to the floor, her eyes round with alarm. Stoker extracted one of his handkerchiefs—an enormous red affair with the traditional print of the Indian bandanna—and lifted it, studying the plant carefully.

"Is it really poisonous?" J. J. asked.

"Oh, yes," Stoker assured her. "And well known for being so since antiquity. Persian warriors used to dip their arrows in the milk of the plant before going to war. Farmers in Italy have been known to use it to rid themselves of wild goats who are eating their crops. A particularly nasty way to die."

"But not how Jameson Harkness died," I pointed out. "He was not poisoned, yet he viewed the sight of this plant as a clear warning that his life was in grave peril. Why?"

"Well, if it is as toxic as you say," J. J. ventured, "its very presence in the envelope would be alarming."

I shook my head. "But the average person would not recognise aconite except as a cottage flower, much less grasp the dangers of aconite. Mornaday, was Jameson Harkness a keen gardener? Amateur botanist? Plant enthusiast?"

"None of those things," Mornaday assured me.

"And yet he was terrified by the sight of wolfsbane," I said. "What of the other bit of plant material?" J. J. handed over the envelope, and I extracted the second botanical specimen. It was something different to the wolfsbane, but unfamiliar to me. "Only a few leaves," I observed. "And without bloom or berry, much harder to identify." We passed them around in a gingerly fashion before I put the leaves back into the envelope and set them aside for safekeeping.

"Tell us more about Harkness," I urged Mornaday.

"He went to work in his father's bank in the City, regular as clockwork. He spent his free time attending lectures."

"On what subjects?" Stoker asked, placing the bundled wolfsbane carefully on a side table out of the reach of the dogs.

Mornaday shrugged. "He was a curious fellow, interested in the occult, the esoteric arts. His wife seemed a little embarrassed to say he enjoyed mythology and folklore, and I cannot say as I blame her. Strikes me as a trifle childish. In between sobs into her handkerchief, she pointed me to his bookshelves, and I can only say the books they held were strange."

"Do you recall any specific titles?" I wondered.

Mornaday shook his head. "None in particular, just a load of twaddle. Fairies and talking to the dead and curses. Superstitious this and nonsense that. If it were barking mad, he apparently liked to read about it."

"Any other women in his life?" J. J. queried.

Mornaday rolled his eyes. "I could hardly ask that, could I? You cannot very well inquire of a grieving widow if her husband was in the habit of coming home with his shirttails hanging from his flies and stinking of French perfume. But from what I gather, he was a faithful sod."

Stoker cut in smoothly. "How was Mr. Harkness's demeanour in the last weeks before his death? Did he have any concerns? Nervousness?"

Mornaday turned thoughtful. "According to Mrs. Harkness, he was grieving Maurice Quincey's death. They had been friends since boyhood, so his feelings were naturally afflicted, but Mrs. Harkness noted a curious thing—his grief seemed to intensify with each passing day."

Stoker stroked his chin. "It is not unreasonable that Jameson Harkness would have taken his own life. His best friend had met a sudden and terrible end. He perhaps felt constrained by his life—his first youth is finished, he works for his father in a notoriously dull occupation."

"No one truly loves banking," J. J. agreed.

Stoker went on. "Mornaday, you say he was faithful to his wife, but that does not necessarily mean he loved her. Without a note relating his intentions at the time of his death, we cannot know his true state of mind."

"How do you know there was no note?" J. J. demanded.

"Because Jameson Harkness rose directly from the breakfast table and threw himself from the balcony," I reminded her, intuiting Stoker's conclusion. "Mornaday said nothing about a detour to the writing table. I suppose there is no handy diary to give us a clue as to his state of mind?"

Mornaday shook his head. "And even if there were, I'd not be getting my hands on it. No sooner had Superintendent Digby Up-His-Own-Arse Carruthers discovered me talking to the widow Harkness than he hauled me from the house by my ears. Warned me if I so much as breathed a syllable of what I'd seen and heard, my career at Scotland Yard would be finished and he'd personally have my guts for garters."

"A singularly strong reaction," I remarked.

Mornaday inclined his head. "Precisely what I thought. So I kept a weather eye upon the case. The inquest was held as quickly as the law permits with a jury handpicked by Sir Ranulph himself. Inquests are supposed to be held in public, but this one was run through with a few of Sir Ranulph's men stationed at the door to discourage onlookers. Only his evidence was taken down and the verdict was returned unanimously and without deliberation in two minutes. They've buried him and probably written his death in the family Bible as a terrible accident. That is what the staff have been told, his children. No one will ever know exactly what happened to Jameson Harkness, why the sight of that little flower—" He paused to point at the shrouded bundle of monkshood. "Caused him to experience such a state of terror that he threw himself from a balcony rather than face whatever was coming. Sir Ranulph used every bit of influence, every tool at his disposal, to sweep it under the carpet."

Stoker's brows knitted together. "I cannot fathom a man willing to overlook the murder of his own son simply to avoid a scandal. Surely seeing the murderer hang for his crime would ensure justice is done."

"And yet whatever would be discovered if the crime was made public is somehow worse to him," I added. "Bad enough that he would rather see whoever drove his son to take his own life escape retribution."

J. J. looked up from where she had been scribbling feverishly in her notebook. "And the same was done for Maurice Quincey. Two men, best friends, both dead under mysterious circumstances."

"And both deaths covered up by those nearest to them, the very people who should have been clamouring for justice. But why?"

"That," Mornaday said, raising his glass in a toast, "is what I want you to discover."

CHAPTER 4

"Absolutely not," Stoker said flatly.

"But—" J. J. began to remonstrate with him, but I held up a hand.

"Leave him be, J. J. We will not attempt to persuade him that this investigation is a necessity."

A gleam kindled in Stoker's gaze. "Oh, won't you?" I deduced at once that he was being deliberately provocative. He had been suffering from boredom as acutely as I, and here we had a case dropped in our laps—and not just any case, a case that had it all: Cryptic threats! Mysterious suicides! A touch of the macabre! His refusal was twofold, I decided. First, he would rather set fire to his own hair than willingly do a favour for Mornaday, at least not without extracting the maximum amount of begging on Mornaday's part. Second—and this brought a tinge of pink to my cheeks—Stoker loved nothing more than pricking my temper with an eye to energetically making amends later. (Natural historians classify such behaviours as courtship rituals, but human beings have another word for it.)

Very well. If he wished to play games, he would always find me a willing and worthy opponent. I bared my teeth in a semblance of a smile. "Certainly not. You have stated unequivocally that you have no intention of helping. That is your right, just as it is my right to immediately undertake this investigation on my own. Now, at some point, you may be struck by the notion that in unravelling this mystery, a terrible wrong may be righted and a murderer brought to justice. I beg you, do not regard such a thought. Put it directly from your mind. It may also occur to you that writing this story will enable J. J. to find a new and better post at a significantly more respectable newspaper than the *Daily Harbinger*."

J. J. made a noise of mild protest, and I gave her a pitying smile. "I know you have been comfortable at the *Harbinger*, but you must admit that there are squirrels in Hyde Park with better morals than that filthy rag."

"It was *my* filthy rag," she muttered, dropping her head to scribble again in her notebook.

I carried on speaking to Stoker. "And I insist that you must not consider J. J.'s prospects for better employment. She could always give up journalism and take up another occupation. Perhaps beekeeping. Or casual prostitution. Although I doubt she has the temperament for either—one must be very nurturing to keep bees."

Stoker opened his mouth, but I continued to speak as if he had not.

"And you must not be swayed by any thoughts that this might benefit Mornaday by exposing his superior's actions and leading to Superintendent Carruthers's removal. I mean, the whole affair *reeks* of corruption at the highest levels, but I shouldn't want you to give that a moment's pause. I am certain the status quo must be preserved because the men in power would certainly never *use* that power to cover up their crimes and misdeeds. And you must not consider for a second, not the merest mouse-breath of a moment, that by investigating on my own I might be exposed to certain danger—"

"Enough." Stoker surged out of his chair, scattering dogs as he reached to lift me out of mine, gripping my shoulders so tightly I would later find finger marks upon the silk. His eyes were bright with mischief and something more tender. "If it means enough to you to embark upon that ridiculous diatribe, I will help. The very idea of you haring about London in solitary pursuit of a murderer chills me to the marrow."

I rewarded him with my most dazzling smile. "I knew you would not be unmoved by concern for my safety."

His black brows shot skyward. "Your safety? Veronica, you could take care of yourself when matched against all the demons in hell. I am worried for the murderer."

Mornaday gave a bark of laughter, but I did not care. I bestowed a brief kiss to the tip of Stoker's nose, knowing how public displays of affection unsettle him. He unhanded me immediately and I turned to Mornaday.

"Are there any other facts you can relate regarding either the death of Maurice Quincey or Jameson Harkness?"

Mornaday shrugged. "The only items published in the newspapers were obituaries and they were brief to the point of insignificance, so I did not bother to hunt them down for you."

"Any materials from the coroner? The inquest?" Stoker asked.

"Nothing beyond what I have told you. Only that Sir Ranulph stated he witnessed his son's death, but the widow Harkness let slip to me that her father-in-law was in his study, working. He was there when she ran to find him after Jameson's fall from the balcony."

"A direct contradiction of Sir Ranulph's testimony under oath," I mused. "He must have been desperate indeed to avoid any suspicions that Jameson took his own life."

Mornaday sat forward, his expression solemn. "I cannot stress enough how discreet this investigation must be. If Carruthers catches wind of the pair of you nosing about, it will be my neck in the noose, figuratively speaking. Only a handful of us know what really happened that day, and it would not take him long to come sniffing at my door."

"We cannot question any of the Harknesses, then," I concluded. "What of the Quinceys?"

"The same," Mornaday replied swiftly. "Quincey was unmarried, parents deceased quite some time ago. Maurice's elder brother inherited their father's baronetcy when he was at school, and Maurice was sent to live with an uncle, Everard Quincey. Maurice had precious little contact with his elder brother in the years before his death—exchanging Christmas letters seems to be the extent of their relationship, and he cut himself off completely from Uncle Everard."

J. J. looked up, her interest clearly piqued. "Everard Quincey? I know that name. He is the Bishop of Ludlow, is he not?"

"He is, and very involved in the relationship between the government and the church in his capacity as the spiritual adviser to the Home Secretary," Mornaday supplied. "At least unofficially. The bishop likes to have a quiet word with him about appointments, vetting them for scandal and so forth. Any hint of misbehaviour and a candidate will be struck off the list of potential appointees. The bishop's pet cause is moral rectitude."

"I should like him for a dinner partner," J. J. said wistfully. "That is a man who knows all the most delicious bits of gossip, I should think."

"He is silent as an oyster," Mornaday told her. "Won't say 'boo' to a goose. That is why young Quincey's death was hushed up. No prince of the church wants his nephew's sordid little murder to become fodder for public gossip, especially when said prince's raison d'être is probity."

"So he countenances lies on his nephew's behalf," Stoker pointed out. "That smacks of hypocrisy."

"Not to the bishop, I am sure," I told him. "It is always 'one rule for thee, another for me.'"

Stoker made a low growl in his throat by way of reply. His dislike of the ruling classes—both temporal and spiritual—was born of too close an acquaintance with them. As the third son of the late Viscount Templeton-Vane, Stoker had been perfectly positioned to assess the flaws of nobility and to reject his birthright soundly. He had begun to run away from home at the age of twelve, always being dragged back by his enraged father. He only succeeded in leaving the Templeton-Vane legacy behind when he entered the Navy as a surgeon's assistant. Since his discharge after the siege of Alexandria, he had spent time in a travelling show, established himself as a natural historian of note, and embarked upon the successful investigation of several elusive mysteries. The one thing he had not done was reconcile himself to his own past. It had taken herculean efforts on my part to persuade him even to speak to his brothers again, and their relationships were still fraught with old resentments and grudges that usually spilled over into fisticuffs. I always made a point of keeping a kit of medicaments handy whenever two or more Templeton-Vanes were in the same room.

"There are two other things," Mornaday said slowly. "Bits of gossip that never made it into any of the official reports. They are so insignificant as to be hardly worth mentioning—"

"Mention them," Stoker commanded.

"Very well. First, a boy was seen lurking about when Quincey's body was discovered in the carriage outside Highgate."

"A boy? Was he ever questioned?" I asked.

"He was never found, and I do not think anyone made a particular effort to look. The bishop was on the scene quite early, insisting upon discretion, so letting the boy slip out of sight was a sure way of keeping his name and testimony out of the records."

"Do you have a description of the lad? He shall be impossible to trace otherwise," Stoker pointed out.

"Only that he appeared to be Romany."

Stoker groaned. There was no more elusive soul in the world than a traveller who did not want to be found.

"And the second thing?" I asked.

"Quincey and Harkness attended lectures together. Somewhere in Hampstead. A private society. That is all anyone would say, and I got a flea in my ear for asking."

"Why is that significant?" J. J. asked.

"Because gentlemen of their class would meet at a club," Stoker told her. "They would socialise privately but in Bond Street or similar. A place as far out as Hampstead suggests a specific shared interest that they were not keen to make public." He raised his brows at Mornaday, and Mornaday shrugged.

"The widow Harkness said her husband had a fascination with the occult, but I've no way of knowing if Quincey felt the same."

"So we have two corpses, dead under mysterious circumstances, powerful relatives who do not want these deaths investigated, and our only clue is a Romany boy who may have been seen in Highgate Cemetery," I concluded. I looked around at the trio of gloomy faces and grinned. "This may be our most challenging case yet, but it is also the most intriguing. Come," I said, rising to my feet, "the scent is laid!"

The assorted responses left much to be desired. Stoker was still grumbling, Mornaday was at great pains to remind us that a lapse in discretion would mean the end of his career, and at the mention of employment, J. J. refreshed her glass of aguardiente and took up once more her litany of woes.

"It grows late, Veronica," Stoker reminded me. "I have work, and no doubt Mornaday has somewhere terribly important to be—perhaps his bookmaker's or the physician's so he may be treated for a raging case of boils—and if you do not remove that glass from J. J.'s hand, I cannot answer for her head tomorrow."

"Shall I carry her to bed?" Mornaday asked, his expression hopeful. Mornaday's schoolboy crush on J. J. was as deep as it was unrequited.

"No need," I told him. "Stoker will manage."

"I just said I have work—oh, never mind," Stoker said, giving in with a sigh. He caught J. J. just as her head lolled forwards and the glass dropped gently to the carpet. Rather than cradling her carefully like a child, he hoisted her with all the elegance of a dockworker shifting a sack of grain. Her midsection landed on his shoulder, and he set off, whistling to the dogs as he went.

"Veronica," Mornaday said, "I was wondering about J. J.—"

"Not now, Mornaday. If Stoker reaches my folly before I do, he will give her the bed, and I am *not* sleeping on the sofa."

"But do you think she might be amenable to—" he began.

"No," I said flatly. "Whatever you mean to suggest, I can promise you, this is the worst possible time to woo her," I called over my shoulder to his woebegone face as I hurtled down the stairs after Stoker and J. J.

I caught them up when they were just outside the Belvedere. Something of the brisk night air or the motion caused J. J. to stir. She raised her head and gave me a befuddled look.

"What's happening? What am I riding?" She poked Stoker's backside, the only accessible portion of his anatomy, with a stiff finger. "Why is it so *hard*?"

"That is Stoker's posterior," I told her coldly. "Do try to contain yourself."

"Oh," she replied. Then she dropped her head and resumed her modest coma.

A brief walk brought us to the pond at Bishop's Folly, fringed with reeds and the shrubbery in which Patricia, his lordship's Galápagos tortoise, occasionally marooned herself. When she was unable to extricate herself from the bushes, she would simply wait with mournful cries to be rescued. The effort never took less than six fully grown men, but Patricia never learnt. I was beginning to suspect she liked the attention.

But there was no sign of Patricia that evening as Stoker made his way directly to my folly. Mine was one of half a dozen structures scattered on the grounds of the estate, each built according to the whim of a previous earl to represent a different time and place. Stoker slept in a Chinese pagoda whilst I dwelt in a Gothic chapel that resembled the exquisite jewel box of Sainte-Chapelle, complete with stained glass and star-dusted ceiling. The amenities were a trifle rustic, but I had lived in far more perilous conditions during my butterfly-hunting expeditions around the world. With a comfortable bed, a chimney that drew excellently, and a sturdy bookshelf, I had all that I required in a lodging. There was even a copper kettle, kept bright by one of the housemaids, for tea and basic ablutions, although I availed myself of the folly designed after a Roman bath for more serious efforts at cleanliness.

At my direction, Stoker dropped J. J. onto the sofa, where she began to snore gently.

"I knew it," I muttered darkly. "I shall get no sleep whatsoever with J. J. making noises like a sawmill."

Stoker regarded me thoughtfully, one fingertip reaching out to stroke my collarbone. "You could stay with me."

The offer was not without its inducements—namely a bit of health-giving physical congress guaranteed to warm the blood and quicken the pulses—but I shook my head regretfully.

"I will stay with J. J. should she have need of me. Aguardiente is the greatest of friends when drunk and the vilest of enemies the morning after."

"If you are certain," Stoker said mildly, dipping the fingertip lower to skim the edge of my décolletage.

"Well," I said, swallowing hard and taking a step nearer. "Perhaps I could join you for an hour or two—"

Just then J. J. rolled to her side and made a very specific and most alarming noise.

"Bucket," she rasped.

I had no bucket to hand, but there was a convenient basin, which I held under her as she revisited the aguardiente she had consumed. She heaved for some minutes, each effort more strenuous than the last, until finally she seemed to have completed the exercise. She collapsed back onto the sofa, pale and damply perspiring as she moaned gently.

"Stoker?" I looked up to find the door to the folly wide open and Stoker nowhere in sight. Not even the dogs were there. "Cowards," I said distinctly as I rose to empty and clean the basin. It promised to be a very long night.

CHAPTER 5

J.J. availed herself of the basin twice more before lapsing at last into a sleep so deep I was forced to hold a mirror to her lips to determine whether she was breathing. She was flat upon her back, a small Galápagos tortoise resting on the pillow beside her. I had roused myself just before dawn, as is my custom, and made a quick toilette, dressing in a warm gown of violet twill. The bodice and hem were heavily embellished with black silk passementerie. I had conspired with my dressmaker to create a costume that would serve for working purposes at the Belvedere as well as more conventional activities. The cuffs had been stiffened for holding minuten, the tiny headless pins used by lepidopterists to fix butterflies and moths to cards for display. And deep pockets, useful for killing jars and magnifying glasses, had been inserted cleverly into the side seams. But the bustle at the back was fashionably tiny, and the skirt was elegantly draped to hide the pockets as well as flatter the figure. I could tend my butterflies in their vivarium as easily as I could pour tea for a vicar.

Stoker was already at work behind his curtains when I arrived at the Belvedere, singing a song I suspect he learnt in Her Majesty's Navy, if the subject matter were anything to judge by. I fortified myself with several pieces of hot buttered toast and a pot of tea as I sorted the first post. I had just finished when J. J. appeared, walking slowly with a hand raised above her eyes as if to keep the light at bay.

"Veronica, I have questions," she said in a thick, rasping voice.

I did not look up from the letter I had just opened—a request for an essay to be published in the *Antipodean Journal of Lepidoptery*. "You were thoroughly inebriated, so I permitted you to stay with me."

"I remember a turtle," she managed.

"That was a Galápagos tortoise," I corrected. "*Chelonoidis niger*. Lord Rosemorran purchased him as a potential mate for Patricia, but he is a juvenile—far too diminutive for the task expected of him. Patricia has been known to wear him for a hat."

J. J. edged her way gingerly onto the camel saddle we keep as seating for guests. "I did not think it was possible for a head to ache so badly. I believe I am quite literally dying. If I had anything to leave you, I should make a will and name you executrix."

I put my post aside with a sigh and poured her a strong cup of tea, heavily sweetened. "Drink," I ordered. I retrieved a set of tinted spectacles from the box of oddments Stoker and I kept—various bits of costumery that we used upon occasion to disguise ourselves whilst engaged in surveillance activities. J. J. took them gratefully to shield her eyes from the light. I shoved a piece of dry toast at her and returned to my letters. She had shuddered at the sight of the bread, but I heard crunching a moment later.

When she finished the tea and toast, I replenished both. After the third round, she looked a little less afflicted but still fragile, the perfect state for achieving my aims.

"J. J., you remember that you are no longer employed at the *Harbinger*?" I asked pleasantly.

Her brows snapped together. "I do. I further remember that I shall in very short order no longer have a home either."

I waved a dismissive hand. "I shall speak to Lord Rosemorran about letting you stay—temporarily, mind—in one of the follies. The Bavarian cottage is presently vacant. And you would be neighbours with Spyridon!"

"Who, pray tell, is Spyridon? Another tortoise?"

"How you jape! No, Spyridon is currently in residence in the miniature Scottish castle on the far side of the pond. He is a Greek philosopher and possibly an assassin—I must admit my command of modern Greek is not as thorough as I would like, and one does get a little muddled in conversation with him. Does your head still ache?" I asked as J. J. put her fingers to her temples.

"Not as much as it spins. You mean to arrange lodgings for me next door to an assassin?"

"A *possible* assassin. But he was most helpful in our last investigative endeavour,"* I explained. "Stoker has known him for many years and vouches for his character. He is a little rough around the edges, but nothing you have not seen before."

J. J. shrugged—or winced, it was difficult to tell the difference in her current state. I went on. "I shall settle the matter with his lordship this morning. You can retrieve your things from your landlady and be comfortably ensconced by teatime."

"Provided the old witch hasn't already sold them in the secondhand market," J. J. said darkly.

"If she has, I am certain his lordship could be persuaded to offer a commission or two," I told her, waving a vague hand to indicate the whole of the Belvedere and its eclectic contents. "Stoker and I have been compiling reports on which collections are complete and what pieces are required to round out others. A precís of these reports could be helpful for his lordship's next trip abroad."

J. J.'s expression was one of fervent gratitude, and her thanks would

* *A Grave Robbery*

have been effusive, I think, had a nasty little suspicion not wormed its way into her mind. "Veronica, that is truly so kind—*wait*." She whipped off the tinted spectacles and glowered at me—at least I think she meant to glower. In her depleted state, the most she could manage was a curl of the lip and a small burp. "It isn't kindness at all. You want something. It is to do with Mornaday and his bloody case. What was it again? Vampires?"

"That is unconfirmed," I told her coolly. "It is a case remarkable in its opacity, but there are one or two promising lines of inquiry."

"I remember now. The suicide which was not a suicide and the body which was drained of its blood. You are right—it is a ludicrous case. I do not know what you think I can do about it."

"You were eager enough last night," I prompted. "You made copious scribbles in that filthy little notebook of yours."

She groped in her pocket until she found the object in question. She flicked through the pages, squinting at her pencilled scrawl. "I cannot read this."

I gave her a brief review of the facts as we knew them, and she nodded her head, wincing again as she waved at me. "I seem to recall the *Daily Harbinger* has an extensive archive," I finished.

"And you want me to ferret about for some information about the victims," she deduced.

"Precisely. Gentlemen of that class would not be mentioned in the good newspapers beyond their births, deaths, marriages, and official appointments. We want gossip, some thread we may pluck to learn more about them."

"I am not finding you a plucking thread," she said flatly.

"What changed?" I demanded. "You were keen as mustard last night."

"Last night I was under the influence of imported liquors, which I can only assume are illegal in respectable countries," she returned. She resumed her tinted spectacles and dropped her head onto my desk.

I did not care for this reply—I did not care for it *at all.* An indignant J. J., an incandescently enraged J. J., a J. J. ready to fight for her ideals was a happy J. J. This pathetic wretch before me was a shadow of the woman I had known.

"This will not do," I said sharply. I took up a little silver hammer—once used to strike popes upon the forehead to ensure they were truly dead—and rapped it hard upon the desk. She jolted up, clapping her hands to her head with a moan.

"Veronica, what the bloody—" The rest of that sentence was not worth listening to, and so I did not. I held up a hand.

"Do be quiet, J. J., and stop caterwauling like an offended moose. I have offered you a place to live and a potential story—an excellent tale with great public appeal. In addition to this, you have the opportunity to thwart wealthy men who have conspired to circumvent justice, which—if my memory serves, and it always does—is one of your favourite pastimes. Now, you may feel deflated and dispirited. That is common after a setback of the sort you suffered yesterday. But we are not common, J. J.," I reminded her. "We are better than that. We rise above, and we do what we must because carrying on is what we were meant for. And do not pretend that you haven't the heart for it. I have seen you, too many times, launch yourself into a precarious situation like an avenging Fury, heedless of the cost. You will do it again. And again. And again. As many times as you must because that is who you are."

She sat, stubbornly unresponsive, and I went on.

"Besides, I do not think you have much choice. There are the practicalities to be considered. You are without employment and shortly to be without lodgings. And you have never struck me as the sort of person to save a bit by for a rainy day, so I suppose your supply of funds is meagre at best. It is either this case or the workhouse, and I do not think you would flatter a pauper's smock."

Of course it would never come to that. J. J. and I both knew I would shelter and feed her rather than ever let her enter such an institution. Still, I thought it worth reminding her of the precarity of her situation if only to rouse her mettle. She muttered something wholly rude in my general direction, but I knew it was only the despair talking.

"When you have finished abusing me, you ought to apply yourself to this," I said, handing over the envelope received by Jameson Harkness on the morning of his death. "We have identified the first specimen as wolfsbane, but the second will be much harder. The books here are shelved by subject," I said, pointing to the gallery circling overhead. "Botany is the section on the north side of the building with all the clocks. After that, the *Harbinger* archive, I think."

She considered my instructions, her expression mulish, and I expected her to mount a fresh argument, but suddenly, her shoulders sagged.

"I cannot show my face at the *Harbinger.* They will all know I've been discharged," she said, her tone still woebegone.

"You needn't see the whole staff," I reminded her. "Didn't you tell me the archive is in a different building?"

She brightened a little. "It is. And Barnaby, the fellow in charge of the archive, he has always liked me. And I think he would like to get one over on the editor in chief. He is forever complaining that no one appreciates how difficult his job is."

"There you are," I said briskly. "It is settled. You find us a piece of useful information for this investigation, and I will secure you lodging and a small commission."

She cocked her head to one side. "Board as well as lodging. A lady has to eat. And I suppose it is interesting, the vampire angle of the story. Also the notion of Harkness being driven to his death by something as small and innocuous as a bit of dried plant." She grinned at me. "So I am an avenging Fury, am I?"

"Upon occasion," I told her. "It is a role which suits you. Never forget that. And perhaps next time, not quite so much aguardiente. It does tend to leave one feeling very unsettled indeed."

She put out her hand. "Very well. You have a bargain."

Just then Stoker burst into another verse of his spectacularly filthy song, and I waved J. J. off. "You ought to go before he gets to the chorus."

I had expected the task to take J. J. the better part of a week—the *Harbinger* being a daily newspaper meant the archives were vast—but to my astonishment she appeared late the same afternoon, bearing a slip of paper and wearing a triumphant expression. She was still pale from her encounter with the aguardiente, but even its aftereffects could not dim her victory.

"Huzzah and hurrah," she crowed. "I have a name."

Stoker had emerged from his work begrimed but looking somewhat satisfied, and we had just settled down to a hearty tea of sandwiches and scones when J. J. arrived. Before she would tell us more, she helped herself to a plate and heaped it with food, cramming a roast beef and lettuce sandwich into her mouth as she reached for the scones.

"I did not have time for luncheon," she said, her voice muffled by the sandwich.

I plucked the piece of paper from her fingers and read it aloud. "'Seward Johnson.' Who is this?"

J. J. grinned as she swallowed. "Schoolmate of Jameson Harkness and Maurice Quincey. In the archive, I found a mention of the three of them at an event together. Then I looked up young Mr. Johnson himself. He is the younger grandson of a baronet and has a position as private secretary to the American industrialist millionaire Horace Von Hilsing."

J. J. didn't need to elaborate on the name of Horace Von Hilsing. His was a name as familiar in Cape Town as California. He had patented a special process to smelt steel from pig iron—a formula he had stolen from the Chinese, incidentally. It was a process that Henry Bessemer refined and repatented ten years later, but that decade-long head start had been the foundation of the Von Hilsing fortune, a fortune which had made him extremely influential. Early in his career, he had been known for the lavish entertainments he held as well as the politicians he courted. No amount of money was too outlandish for him to spend if it meant he secured the government contracts he needed to further his aims.

But over the past few decades, he had become something of a recluse. Although he had in his youth travelled frequently, he had settled in London in his later years, preferring to entertain in his own luxurious home on a tiny square so exclusive it had been renamed Steel Square in his honour. Invitations to his dinners were coveted things until word circulated that Von Hilsing had become something of a health crank and limited himself—and his guests—to a strictly vegetarian diet. The fatal blow was when an outraged marchioness claimed he insisted his dinner parties end with brisk walks about the garden and robust exercises on gymnasium equipment. After one too many evenings spent eating parsnip pie washed down with plain milk, the stream of visitors to the grand house in Steel Square dried up. The house was situated just behind the Duke of Wellington's residence at Apsley House on Hyde Park Corner, an address so illustrious even Buckingham Palace could only look on with envy, but nothing could make up for the depressing food and endless discussions of health tonics and physical jerks that Von Hilsing inflicted upon his guests.

J. J. passed around a few cuttings about Von Hilsing, most dating back more than thirty years, the heyday of his international travels and lavish entertaining.

"He is less remarkable than I expected," I observed as I studied a sketch of the millionaire. "He looks distinctly forgettable."

"Disappointing," J. J. agreed. "He is so very *ordinary*. One would like to think of him as having the form of Adonis and wisdom of Zeus to complement the riches of Croesus."

"To what end?" Stoker asked. "Do you have designs upon the poor man? I thought you were completely opposed to the married state."

"I am," J. J. assured him. "In principle. But if an inordinately handsome man expressed a heartfelt wish to lavish his significant fortune upon me, it would take a woman of greater moral fibre than I to refuse him."

They continued bantering for a few moments as I flicked through the cuttings. They were much the same—profiles of the millionaire industrialist and the burgeoning eccentricities his money afforded him. There were no photographs, but many pen-and-ink drawings, one with a set of bagpipes during his attempts to connect with his Scottish roots, he claimed, although one must wonder which part of the Highlands he thought the Von Hilsings had called home. There was a flurry of articles detailing his various purchases of expensive gewgaws—a clock said to have belonged to Louis XIV, a handful of exquisitely expensive jewels, and an elephant purchased off a maharajah on a whim during a tour of India. It was on this trip that he had begun to explore the benefits of eating solely plants and of bending oneself into unaccustomed shapes. That article included an image of Von Hilsing wearing only a bit of loincloth, and I put it firmly aside as J. J. returned to the subject of Seward Johnson.

"The Johnsons are familiar figures in diplomatic circles, particularly with Americans. Seward's mother and grandmother were both American."

"Well, we shall not hold it against him," I said.

J. J. finished her first sandwich and reached for the second. "Would you like to know *where* Harkness, Quincey, and Johnson were seen together?"

"Pray tell," Stoker said as he heaped a scone with cream and jam.

"At a meeting of the Harpocrates Society."

"Harpocrates?" I asked.

"After the Roman god of secrets," Stoker observed.

"That society sounds fictitious," I put in.

"I think it is," J. J. replied. "Or at least very discreet. I scoured the archives, and there is no other mention of it. This bit was in the society column, and I spoke with the reporter who inserted it. He said there was a brief period when he heard a few snippets about the society, but then it seemed to vanish as quickly as it had come. Either it disbanded or they got extremely good about keeping it extremely quiet."

"Was there anything noteworthy about the society?"

J. J. shrugged. "It seems to have been founded by a fellow called Ruthven." She pronounced it in the properly Scottish fashion. *Ri-ven.*

Stoker went on. "There are dozens of Ruthvens knocking about. Anything special about this one? A forename, for instance."

"My source is unfortunately given to a bit of tippling at work. The archive is a solitary and dusty place, and he finds a pint or two of bitters helps the hours pass more swiftly."

"So he was intoxicated when you questioned him?" I suggested.

"Almost entirely inebriated, although I should point out that the average newspaperman is inured to the worst effects of insobriety. In this case, he was recalling insignificant details from the briefest of mentions. I marvel he remembered anything at all."

"Did any of them ask for inclusion in the society column?" I asked.

"No, which is curious for a group that seemed to be open to new members. In fact, there was a polite but very firmly worded request by Lord Ruthven *not* to give any more publicity to the group, as he intended it to be invitation only. It seems Seward's late mother, being something of a social climber, was the one who gave the item to the paper in the first place."

"Why on earth would she think a mention in the *Harbinger* would carry any social cachet?" Stoker demanded with the bone-deep outrage that only a born aristocrat could muster.

J. J. shrugged. "As I said, American. She must not have realised how finely calibrated such things are in England. And before you ask, no, we cannot question her. She returned to New York some time ago and, rather inconveniently for us, died."

"When was the item published in the newspaper?" Stoker asked.

"Just over a year ago." J. J. reached for a fresh sandwich, this one potted shrimps. "Oh, that is *heavenly*," she said after the first bite.

"Cook keeps an herb garden just outside the kitchen door," Stoker told her. "Fruit trees as well, which is why her preserves are so good. She adds a single quince to the orange marmalade, and it really sings. What you're tasting in the potted shrimps is a bit of fennel. An unexpected choice, but the aromatic sharpness is an excellent foil to the sweetness of the shellfish."

"It makes all the difference," J. J. agreed.

I rapped sharply upon the table. "If I might draw your attention back to the investigation?"

J. J. shrugged. "I have told you everything I discovered. Harkness, Quincey, and Johnson all attended a lecture together, and Johnson is currently in the employ of the American millionaire Von Hilsing. I have earned my reward," she added, reaching for a miniature cherry cake studded with almonds.

I rose, dusting the crumbs of a scone from my fingertips as I reached for my cloak. "Come along, then. We must seek Mr. Johnson at once."

Stoker stared mournfully at the lavish trays. "I have only just begun to eat, Veronica. It is teatime."

"All the more reason to go now—Mr. Johnson will be obliged to offer us refreshment, and confidences are always more easily pried from a man holding a teacup. Yes, J. J.?"

She had opened her mouth to ask a question but broke off to stare—in surprise or admiration, I was not certain which—as Stoker crammed a handful of scones into his pocket. "Have you arranged for my lodging?" she managed finally.

"Lord Rosemorran was amenable to your use of the Bavarian cottage, at least for a fortnight," I told her. "It is currently empty, so he is having it thoroughly cleaned and aired today and a few pieces of furniture moved in. It shall be ready for habitation tomorrow, if you do not mind sharing with me for another night."

"Excellent. I have a carter bringing my things in an hour or so. In the meantime, I shall reap my just rewards for a good morning's work," she announced. She opened a chicken sandwich and began to parcel out the roasted meat to the dogs.

Stoker's expression was gloomy as he pulled shut the door of the Belvedere.

"Why are you sulking?" I asked, buttoning my cloak against the spring damp.

"Chicken and chutney sandwiches are my favorite, and she's giving them to the bloody dogs," he muttered.

"No matter," I soothed him. "I shall make it well worth your while later."

CHAPTER 6

Stoker and I travelled—as we often did—on foot, preferring a brisk walk through Marylebone and into the streets and leafy squares of Mayfair to an interminable ride in a stuffy hackney. We located the Von Hilsing house easily enough—it was the only house in the square, the other buildings being given over to Mr. Von Hilsing's mews, guesthouse, coach house, and various other offices. At the arched entrance to the square, a pair of inordinately large fellows flanked the street. They regarded us closely but made no attempt to impede our progress.

"If they are meant to be guards, they are remarkably accommodating," I mused. "They've let us walk right in."

"You realise this call may be extremely ill-advised," Stoker remarked as we approached the door.

"How so?"

"The Quinceys and Harknesses have gone to great lengths to keep the nature of Maurice and Jameson's deaths secret. And Mornaday counselled discretion. By interrogating Seward Johnson, we may be opening a particularly nasty can of worms."

"Interrogating! What a word. I merely mean to ask the man about his dead friends. Besides, worms might be nasty, but they are exceedingly useful. Ask any angler—one needs them to bait a hook."

At the front door, Stoker made use of the brass knocker—an eagle, as one might expect of an American. The door was opened almost at once by a cadaverously thin man with four or five wisps of greying hair combed carefully over his bald head. The butler, I surmised.

"Yes?" His voice was sepulchral as he regarded us with the same enthusiasm a pirate might demonstrate at discovering his wooden leg is riddled with termites. I was dressed neatly in my violet, but Stoker's appearance always hovered on the disreputable, occasionally tipping over into outright shabbiness. Money was not the source of the problem. It was not that he could not afford nice things; it was that he so rarely troubled himself about what he put on, most often reaching for his work clothes without a particle of consideration. Each of these garments, while made of quality materials from distinguished tailors, had been subjected to so much abuse in the course of his activities that they were invariably stained, worn, patched, or faded. It did not matter how expensive or new the article of clothing, he had no care for it. I had once seen him stuff a dead rat—a treat for his ever-voracious dermestid beetles—into the pocket of a new suit. The fact that he had forgot the rat for two days did nothing to improve the suit's condition.

But the clothes were the least remarkable aspect of his appearance. At six feet, he was taller than average, and his muscles were highly developed from the physical nature of his work. His hair, witch black and cut infrequently, tumbled past his collar, brushing his shoulders. He eschewed facial hair, preferring to shave on an irregular basis, which meant his chin was always shadowed. A slender silver scar ran from the line of that shadow up to his eye, the remnant of an old injury that meant he sometimes wore a patch when he found himself fatigued. Coupled with the gold hoops he wore in his ears, it gave him the look of a not altogether unsuccessful Elizabethan privateer.

The butler could not conceal his moue of distaste as he regarded the smear of ink on Stoker's collar. "The tradesman's entrance is behind the house."

Before I could mount an appropriate response, Stoker drew himself up to his full height and gave the butler his most autocratic stare, arching a single brow. His elder brother could not have done a better impression of offended nobility. Stoker dipped his fingers into his pocket and retrieved a card, offering it with a disdainful gesture.

"Revelstoke Templeton-Vane to see Mr. Seward Johnson."

A lesser man would have revealed that the card actually read *The Honourable Revelstoke Templeton-Vane*, but Stoker, for all his bohemian leanings, understood every exquisite nuance of the etiquette of the upper classes. "Honourable" was a distinction that should be printed but never spoken aloud, and the butler was well aware of this. He was too well trained to show any sort of reaction to the information on the card, but I saw the telltale flinch of his Adam's apple and noted the brief flicker of his mouth into a semblance of welcome.

"Of course, Mr. Templeton-Vane. Forgive me, sir, you are brother to the current Viscount Templeton-Vane, if I am not mistaken?"

"You are acquainted with my brother?" Stoker asked in a coolly detached tone.

"Oh, yes, sir. His lordship is a frequent visitor to this house." That information ought not to have surprised me. Tiberius had followed in their father's footsteps as a man of international affairs, some related to business, others to more carnal matters. There was nothing in the household of an aging vegetarian tycoon to appeal to Tiberius's more sensual appetites, but I could well believe he had cultivated Horace Von Hilsing as a useful contact in his dealings.

"In that case, I am certain you will not wish to make me wait any further," Stoker replied.

"Certainly, Mr. Templeton-Vane. Right this way. If you and your companion—" He paused and looked expectantly at me.

"My companion's name is of no consequence to you," Stoker said.

"Yes, sir. If you and your companion would care to wait here for just a moment, I will let Mr. Johnson know you have called." He backed up, gesturing towards a small parlour. A pair of straight-backed chairs stood in the vestibule, but the man was cowed enough not to make us wait in a draught, and I was grateful for it. The house stank of fresh paint, enough that my eyes began to water. Von Hilsing might not entertain much anymore, but he certainly liked to keep his house in proper trim, I observed. We entered the parlour, and Stoker made a flicking gesture of dismissal with his forefinger. The butler scurried away and I turned to Stoker.

"For a man who despises aristocrats, you do an exceptional impression of one."

Stoker grinned, his disdain completely forgot. "I learnt from the best. My father was the greatest snob in existence. He could cow the loftiest butler with a single glance."

I had not met the late Lord Templeton-Vane—he was deceased and the title passed on to Stoker's eldest brother by the time I came on the scene—but nothing I had heard of the man made me regret the omission.

It was not often that we called upon millionaires, so naturally I took the opportunity to survey our surroundings. The room was sparsely furnished with very good pieces, boasting only a few chairs and a narrow sofa with a handful of ornaments scattered on the mantelpiece. One of these was a small statue, a bronze replica of *Liberty Enlightening the World*. I was admiring her uplifted torch and sober expression when the door opened and a slender young man entered. We had seen the sketch of him in the *Harbinger*, and it occurred to me that he might successfully sue the artist for damages. The illustration bore only the faintest resemblance to the man himself. He was, at first glance, unremarkable—middling height, possibly thirty, with sandy hair and blue eyes.

But lepidopterists are keen observers, trained to look beyond first impressions. As I studied Mr. Johnson, I noticed the subtleties of his appearance. Blue eyes may, as in Stoker's case, be remarkable for their sapphirine brightness, but these eyes were an uncommon shade tinted with grey, like a storm on a summer sea. They seemed touched with melancholy, yet I suspected they would brighten when he was interested or amused. He was dressed with the quiet expense of a gentleman who does not care to display his wealth, but the lines of his tailoring were excellent, and a slender band of heavy gold on his right hand was set with a small but handsome gemstone. He moved, like all good employees, on silent feet. When he spoke, his voice was low and melodious but pleasant, the sort of voice one hears from tenors in passably good choirs. He was, in short, the perfect private secretary, a man whose commendably good taste would make him easy to overlook in a crowd. It was only when he drew near that I noted the classical purity of his profile and the superb moulding of his mouth. It was his handsomest feature, and he used it to good effect, almost but not quite smiling as he approached.

He regarded Stoker with curiosity. "Mr. Templeton-Vane, you wished to see me? I am Seward Johnson."

"Yes, Mr. Johnson. I should like to present Miss Speedwell, my associate."

Johnson inclined his head to me, his expression still faintly puzzled as he shook the hand I extended. His was long-fingered, the palm broad and warm. The hand of a musician, I decided, or perhaps an oarsman, although I detected no telltale calluses. "I am sorry, did you have business you wished to conduct with Mr. Von Hilsing? Only he is away at present."

"Away?" I asked. "I thought Mr. Von Hilsing no longer travelled."

The ghost of a smile ripened into something slightly warmer and a little wry—a most attractive smile, I thought. "Mr. Von Hilsing's reclusiveness is greatly exaggerated. He crosses the Atlantic at least twice each year to visit his home in California, and he often spends a week or two on the Continent in service of his health. He has a touch of rheumatism in spite of the care he takes with his constitution," he added in a confiding tone. "Always in search of fads and cures. I am afraid you have just missed him. He left only this morning for France. He heard of a new thalassic spa near Deauville and insisted upon trying it at once. His departure was most unexpected."

That explained the ease of our access to the Von Hilsing house. Security would be slack if the millionaire himself were absent.

"In point of fact, Mr. Johnson, we have business with you," Stoker informed him. Johnson gave a little start of surprise but his expression remained pleasant. If anything he seemed gratified that we wished to speak with him instead of the great man himself.

"Me? I am at a loss as to know what you mean, but I am at your service, Miss Speedwell, Mr. Templeton-Vane."

Stoker opened his mouth to reply, but I cut in swiftly. "You knew Maurice Quincey and Jameson Harkness."

There was a quick, almost imperceptible flinch. The pleasantness faded, replaced by a soberness expected when speaking of the dead. "I did."

"We are sorry for your loss. We understand they were close friends," Stoker said.

"Not close," Johnson said hurriedly. "Our paths crossed from time to time, but I had not seen either one of them for quite a while before their deaths."

"What can you tell us about the Harpocrates Society?"

If I had expected to elicit a gasp, to cause the blood to drain suddenly from his complexion, I was disappointed. His brow furrowed, then cleared swiftly, replaced by something akin to nostalgia. "The Harpocrates Society? I have not heard that name in months. I can hardly recall it, to be frank. I think it was some sort of pet interest of Quincey's. Or was it Harkness? I forget. I attended one lecture and that was the end of it."

"Where?" Stoker asked.

Johnson's pale eyes widened. "Heavens, I'm sure I could not say. Somewhere in Brompton? Or was it Bloomsbury? I think it might have begun with a 'B,' but I really could not tell you. It has been a long time."

"How did you hear about the meeting?" I queried.

He shrugged. "One of them suggested it, but as I say, I forget which."

"And the subject of the lecture?" I pressed.

Embarrassment pinkened his complexion. "I am abashed to say that I fell asleep. I never was very studious. Slept through half my lectures at Cambridge. Frightfully slipshod of me, but this was only a social occasion, after all. Still, not very polite. I scuttled out the first chance I had from sheer mortification at my boorishness."

"We believe the society has something to do with folkloric studies," Stoker suggested.

Johnson nodded thoughtfully. "That sounds about right. Although, as I say, I really can't remember. I am good with numbers, but I am afraid cultural subjects leave me cold."

"Then why did you go?" I demanded.

He gave a warm little smile, and I felt the full weight of his unexpected charm. "Miss Speedwell, I am certain you understand what it is to accommodate the interests of one's friends. We indulge them although we may not share them."

"Can you tell us anything about the other members? Did you recognise anyone?" Stoker's question was so brilliant, I was mildly irritated I had not thought to ask it myself.

Johnson seemed more confident now, on firmer ground. "Alas, no. I cannot recall any introductions being made, and I have a poor memory for faces, which I can assure you is something of a liability in my profession. I am sorry I couldn't be of more help, but I am afraid I really must get on. You wouldn't think there would be much business to attend to with Mr. Von Hilsing away, and yet somehow there is more."

He turned to guide us out of the parlour, the interview pointedly over.

I stopped on the threshold, forcing him to pause. "What can you tell us about a man called Ruthven?"

At the mention of the name, Seward Johnson canted his head as he looked at me, clearly nonplussed. But I noted the speedy little pulse beating in his throat, faster than it had been a moment before, I fancied, and his colour had paled noticeably. "It is a common enough name, Miss Speedwell. Scotch, I think. I seem to remember a Ruthven in the history of Mary, Queen of Scots, but one always seems to forget the history one learns at school. Is that the Ruthven you meant?"

"No. I was speaking of the one connected to the Harpocrates Society."

"Ah. Well, as I said, I went only once and paid little attention to the other guests. If you say there was a Ruthven present, I shall have to take your word for it."

As he led us to the front door, Stoker played the same gambit, lingering on the doorstep for a final remark. "I left my card with the butler. Should you think of anything, please do let us know."

"Of course," Johnson replied. "But I cannot imagine I will think of anything helpful."

Stoker nodded towards a heap of cases which were stacked next to the stairs. "Planning a trip, Mr. Johnson?"

Johnson regarded the cases a long moment, then summoned a smile.

"Not at all. Mr. Von Hilsing often leaves in a terrific hurry with only a valise. I am tasked with sending on his cases, putting the staff on board wages, and closing up the house."

I wondered why Johnson was given such a chore instead of a valet or the officious butler, but Von Hilsing was an American millionaire, I reflected—not a British aristocrat. It was apparent the diligent Mr. Johnson had already begun the task of closing the house, for apart from the butler, no other staff seemed in evidence. No maidservants tip-tapping along, no housekeeper bustling past in rustling bombazine. Not even a boot boy clattering through a back passage to disturb the atmosphere.

"Your household seems a bit at sixes and sevens with Mr. Von Hilsing away. I gather the decorators are in," I observed. Mr. Johnson gave me a quizzical look and I smiled. "The smell of fresh paint is rather distinct."

"Ah! You are an observant lady, Miss Speedwell. Yes, Mr. Von Hilsing likes me to use his time away as a chance to have the paintwork touched up. He cannot abide the odour."

"The whims of millionaires, eh?" Stoker ventured.

A touch of hauteur chilled Johnson's manner, not brusqueness, but a bit of stiffening that hinted at disapproval. "Quite," he said, clipping the word sharply. Clearly Johnson did not much care for any possible disparagement of his employer—or perhaps it was the reminder of his own inferior status he minded. "As I will be leaving shortly, do save yourself the trouble of calling again. I should hate for you to waste a trip."

Stoker gave him a broad smile, the sort he used when he meant to disarm. "Good day, Mr. Johnson. As I say, do get in touch if you think of anything helpful."

I stopped to shake hands again, and Mr. Johnson gave me a cordial bow as we bade one another farewell. We had just stepped onto the pavement in front of the house when the butler appeared, ascending the stairs leading from the basement. He wore a fashionable bowler hat and carried a neat carpetbag.

"Good afternoon," I said cordially. "Going travelling?"

He raised his bowler. "Miss, sir. Yes, I am off to spend a fortnight with my sister in Bristol. Mr. Von Hilsing is very generous about giving time away when he is abroad."

"How fortunate," I said.

"Indeed." He lifted his hat again and sketched a half bow before turning to leave, whistling a snippet of a merry tune.

"Someone is happy to be going on holiday," I remarked as we emerged from the tiny square into a narrow street leading directly to Hyde Park Corner.

Stoker stopped, a smile spreading over his features. "You realise that our genial Mr. Johnson was lying."

"Of course he was lying. I could smell the stink of mendacity upon him," I said with some vexation. Other people's lies never failed to rouse my peevishness. I deplored the lack of honesty in principle, but the greater issue was that untruthfulness wasted a good deal of time. The bulk of our investigations were spent unpicking fact from fib. "He claimed hardly to remember Harkness and Quincey, but that rang of untruth to me. He was polite enough and made cordial responses, but I detected a distinct lack of warmth in the eyes."

"Oh, there was something far more significant than that." Stoker paused, no doubt for dramatic effect, and I tapped my toe upon the kerbstone.

"Well?"

"We appeared, asking questions about a meeting he attended with two of his friends, both of whom have died in suspicious circumstances," he began.

"Yes?" I prodded.

"Yet he never asked us why we wanted to know."

"Damn and blast," I muttered. It was the sort of observation I ought to have made, and it was vastly irritating that Stoker had beaten me to the mark.

Stoker stuck out his arm to hail a hansom. A vehicle of some antiquity drew to a stop beside us, the horse looking as bedraggled as the peeling paint of the carriage. As Stoker handed me in, he had the last word. "Seward Johnson is in this matter up to his well-tailored neck. And I want to know how."

CHAPTER 7

I did not gloat over the fact that Stoker was now thoroughly invested in this mystery. I had believed his cavilling at being asked to undertake the investigation was the merest ploy to rouse my temper, and here was proof of it. Our first day upon the case and he was well and truly hooked.

"We did not ask him directly about Quincey's and Harkness's deaths," I observed as we settled against the well-worn squabs of the conveyance.

"No need. If you were watching carefully, he shied like a pony at the subject."

"How you exaggerate! He scarcely turned a hair," I protested.

"He is a well-trained private secretary reared in diplomatic circles. A blink is the same to his sort as a fully engaged swoon to the rest of us. He was decidedly uncomfortable with the subject of Harkness's and Quincey's deaths. And just the mention of Ruthven's name was enough to distress him. He could not be rid of us quickly enough after that."

"Hm. He was indeed eager to see the last of us. Do you think we have really given him enough of a fright that he will leave town?"

Stoker stroked his shadowed chin. "There is one way to know. I shall send George to do a little light surveillance since you've trained him up.

If Johnson takes to his heels, we shall learn of it sooner rather than later."

"Little good it will do us if he is responsible for their deaths," I countered.

Stoker shook his head. "No, it is nothing to do with Johnson, I believe. At least not directly. He may well be not a guilty man but a frightened one. Guilt and fear often wear the same visage."

Stoker was probably correct in that regard, I decided, but I could not possibly tell him so. A man who is too often allowed to be right develops bad habits, I had frequently observed.

He changed the subject abruptly. "Did you notice the strangeness of the house?" he asked.

"You mean the lack of staff? Curious. I heard no one besides the butler and Johnson."

"Not a peep," Stoker agreed. "The water in the flowers in the foyer had not been changed, and the fireplace had not been swept. The housemaids have been turned out."

"And Johnson was expected to pack his master's bags," I reminded him. "A valet's chore, I thought."

"It is," he affirmed.

"Still, there was the smell of fresh paint. Perhaps the staff have been given a few days' reprieve from their duties whilst the master is away and a bit of decorating is being done."

Stoker made an indeterminate noise deep in his throat, and I carried on. "I am glad you thought to hail a taxi. We do not wish to be late for this evening, and I have one or two things to attend to first."

"This evening?" Stoker's black brows knitted together.

"We have an engagement, dearest. Did you not consult your diary this morning?"

"Veronica, you know as well as I do that I have not kept a proper diary since 1872. Where are we going tonight?"

"The theatre," I said promptly.

Stoker began to glower. "What are we seeing?"

"*The Yeoman of the Guard.*"

"That is not the theatre—it's bloody Gilbert and Sullivan," he retorted. "Why in the name of seven hells are we seeing that?"

"Because your brother was kind enough to secure tickets, and I have not seen Tiberius in several months."

"Why must it be an operetta? Grand opera I could stomach. Even the ballet with all its absurd leaping and lolloping. But for god's own sake, not an operetta." He slumped in his seat, picking idly at a rip in its upholstery.

"I shall be certain to ask Tiberius for tickets to *La Sylphide* next time," I assured him. "But for tonight, I have a new gown and I have requested one of the footmen air and press your evening suit. Of course, if we are going out this evening, we really ought to bathe, but we haven't much time . . ." I let my voice trail off suggestively, and Stoker was quick to catch my meaning.

He sat up and rapped his knuckles on the roof of the carriage. "Double the rate if you can have us to Marylebone in five minutes' time."

"Yes, sir!" the driver cried. He cracked his whip near the horse's ear, and the nag leapt into a trot as nippily as a young pony. Within an astonishingly short period, we were drawing up outside the garden entrance of Bishop's Folly. True to his word, Stoker flung far too much money at the driver and grabbed my hand, hauling me along the path to the Roman bathhouse. He drew me inside and slammed the door closed with one booted foot. I had not even removed my hat before he was tugging at my collar, his lips warm against my neck.

"'I will imagine you Venus tonight and pray, pray, pray to your star like a heathen,'" he murmured. Keats was always in evidence in our more fevered moments.

"I should report our findings to J. J.," I said, a trifle breathlessly.

It took me a moment to decipher his reply, muffled as it was against my skin, and when I did, I blushed for the frankness of it. Needless to say, J. J.'s name was not raised again for the duration of the interlude that followed, and when we had exhausted ourselves in the warm waters of the baths—and followed with a delightfully thorough scrubbing—we went our separate ways to dress for the evening. J. J. was ensconced in my little chapel with several of the dogs, a picture of domestic repose as she lay, stretched on her belly on the sofa, a fire crackling merrily on the hearth, a dog on either side, slumbering peacefully. She wore my best dressing gown, now lavishly smudged with ink and marmalade, I noticed waspishly. She was eating—still or again, I was not certain—helping herself to a tin of miniature lardy cakes I kept on hand for moments of unexpected peckishness.

"We ran Mr. Johnson to ground," I told her as I gathered my things. Gown, stockings, slippers, undergarments, petticoats, shift, evening corset. In the corner stood a panelled screen of Coromandel lacquer—badly damaged or it would have been in the Belvedere itself—and I slipped behind it to dress. Most ladies would have required the assistance of a maid to complete her toilette, but I deplored the necessity of a servant solely to put on one's own clothes, and so the corset and gown had both been designed for simplicity. The corset strings had already been adjusted, and it buttoned neatly up the front, as did the gown. These buttons were hidden behind a tidy little placket of black velvet, the same trimming that was used elsewhere to set off the heavy rose-red silk. Loops of black velvet ribbons were caught up on either side of the modest bustle and secured by bouquets of red velvet roses, and the décolletage was edged in black. The effect was highly theatrical, a perfect choice for our evening, and I rather giddily pinned a surplus velvet rose into my hair. My funds had not stretched to a new evening cloak, so my old thick black velvet would have to do, as would a pair of cast-off kid gloves kindly given to me by Lord Rosemorran's sister, my friend Lady

Cordelia. She had also supplied a reticule festooned with glass beads in shades of black, gold, and pink as well as a pair of black silk slippers, only lightly scuffed. Her lady's maid, Sidonie, had embroidered the toes with roses to cover the marks. I never took significant trouble with my clothes, but Sidonie and Lady Cordelia loved to furnish me with expensive castoffs that were very nearly fresh from the dressmaker's salon.

The final effect was judged "utterly delicious" by J. J., who finally looked up from her notes long enough to survey my ensemble. But if she was impressed by my appearance, she was struck speechless at Stoker's. He appeared on my doorstep to collect me, bringing with him the rest of the dogs to spend the evening with J. J. He was dressed in formal black, the severity of the colour and sharpness of the cut suiting him as few other costumes could. (I make exception for his working clothes if only for the fact that he is often stripped to the waist when he is busy about his labours, and the effect is most arresting.) His hair had been neatly brushed until it fell in a gleaming cascade past his collar, his chin closely barbered for once. He had donned a silk eye patch, and his black alpaca cape was newly cleaned. J. J.'s gaze lingered on the tautness of his waist, tightly encased in a starched white waistcoat.

"Good evening, J. J. I've brought the dogs along to keep you company," he called.

I gathered my fan—black ostrich feathers—and my evening cloak. As I turned to leave, J. J. grasped me firmly above the elbow.

"Veronica," she whispered. "You are my dearest friend, and if you were to die, I should be heartily sorry. I should weep piteous and salty tears of woe. But also, if you perished, I should not wait until you were cold in your grave to leap upon that man."

"I should be disappointed if you did not," I assured her. I closed the door behind me, and Stoker dropped my cloak about my shoulders.

"What was that about? Whispering girlish confidences?" he inquired.

"Something like that." My first loyalty was, of course, to Stoker, but there was something to be said for feminine sisterhood. Besides, if I told Stoker exactly what she had said, his blushes would last until we reached the theatre.

As it was, we were very nearly late, delayed by an overturned cabbage cart, the vegetables bouncing around the road and causing all sorts of mayhem. We hurried into the Savoy Theatre, its incandescent lamps dazzling in the gloom of the evening. A mizzling rain had begun, and the drops shone like diamonds in the lights. Tiberius had not waited for us; he was comfortably ensconced in his box, idly thumbing through the programme.

"You are late," he said by way of greeting. This was directed at Stoker. To me he issued a fragrant kiss upon the cheek and a murmured compliment that was very nearly indelicate. He guided me to the little gilt chair next to his so that I might have an unobstructed view. A coupe of champagne was put into my hand and a box of chocolates opened for my delectation. I took a violet crème and savoured it as I sipped my champagne.

"The curtain is still down," Stoker pointed out as he took a seat behind us. "How can we possibly be late?" He was given champagne as well, but the chocolates were just out of his reach. I noticed him gazing longingly at them and passed him a handful of rose crèmes.

"You are late because I have missed Veronica and wished to enjoy her company for something more than the approximately thirty seconds we have before the curtain goes up," Tiberius said. The words were waspish, but there was no real heat in Tiberius. If Stoker were a tiger—energetic and powerful, Tiberius was a lion, lazy and luxurious, a sybarite to his very bones. As the eldest son and heir to the Templeton-Vane title, he had always known his destiny was to let others do for him, and he excelled at delegating everything, including emotions.

I sipped at my champagne and studied the programme. A freshly printed slip of paper had been inserted into the front cover. "Oh, look! An understudy is playing the role of Colonel Fairfax. I am sorry to see it. I was rather looking forward to seeing Courtice Pounds in the role. I hear he is most engaging."

At this remark, Tiberius spilled a little of his champagne, but before I could pursue the question of what had disturbed him, the curtain rang up and the operetta began. The score was ambitious and surprisingly melodic, a love story with farcical elements, although the silliness of the typical Gilbert and Sullivan fare was muted.

As the performance went on, I noticed Tiberius seemed, for once, rather unsettled. His customary languor had deserted him, and although he sat with his usual easy grace, there was a tautness about him I had not seen before. Behind us came a series of gentle snores, and I knew Stoker had fallen asleep and would likely slumber through the entire affair. It was better than the alternative, I decided, which would have entailed a running commentary of rude remarks and the occasional guffaw of laughter at inappropriate times. With Stoker enjoying his nap, I settled back to watch.

When the intermission came, Tiberius turned to ask how I liked the show.

"Very much," I told him truthfully. "I do not despise comic operettas as much as Stoker does," I said with a meaningful glance to where Stoker's head was nodding low upon his chest. "And this one is surprisingly touching."

"Are there any performances in particular that merit praise?" His question was too decidedly casual. I realised at once he had taken a personal interest in a member of the cast, and it only remained to discover which. I scanned the listed performers and smiled.

"The understudy playing the role of Colonel Fairfax in place of Mr. Pounds," I said promptly. "He is a very handsome young man, don't you think?"

"Is he?" Tiberius murmured. "I hadn't noticed."

"Liar." But my smile was genuine as I pitched my voice to a confiding tone. "How long have you known him?"

"The acquaintance is of relatively short duration, but I must confess, he is unlike anyone I have ever met," Tiberius said.

I briefly touched his hand with my own. "I wish you every happiness."

For a moment he said nothing, a sure sign that he was experiencing some surfeit of strong sentiment that he had no wish to acknowledge. Then he cleared his throat. "Well, I suppose happiness is what we all want, although how you have managed to find it with that . . ." He paused to indicate his slumbering brother with a pointedly raised brow. "Is something I shall always find a puzzlement. A woman of your taste and sophistication lavishing yourself on a man who is barely civilised," he added in a tone of purest lament. "Help me to understand."

I smiled. "I could scour the pages of our greatest poets for the rest of my days and never find the proper words. How does one explain the attachment one has to one's own breath? One's own pulse? It is simply there. And if it were not, one would cease to exist. I could no more live without him than I could live without my own heart."

"My god," Tiberius said softly. "He is undeserving of such loyalty."

"He is also listening," Stoker said, stirring in his chair. He gave me a smile of such breathtaking devotion that my corset felt suddenly too tight.

Tiberius raised an imperious hand. "I beg you, no romantic histrionics."

"Then perhaps you would care to distract us with a bit of assistance," Stoker suggested.

The upraised brow climbed higher still. "I am listening."

"We paid a visit today to Steel Square," Stoker began.

"Ah! And how is our Yankee millionaire?" Tiberius inquired.

"Absent," I put in. "He is apparently taking the waters at a spa near Deauville. Thalasso therapy."

"That does not surprise me," Tiberius returned. "He is concerned with his health to the point of obsession. It makes for a mightily uncomfortable evening."

"The butler indicated you were a caller," I told him.

He shrugged one elegant shoulder. "Not for some months. I was interested in his thoughts on Russia—he did quite a bit of business there during the reign of Alexander II, and we compared notes on the present tsar. He put me in the way of a few new contacts I had a mind to cultivate for an investment opportunity. But I soon gave it up."

"Why so?" I asked.

"Veronica, when one has spent the better part of a meal pushing legumes around one's plate as one's host discusses the frequency, appearance, and heft of his bowel movements, one is not minded to repeat the process."

"How very unsettling," I said, suddenly wishing I had not eaten quite so many chocolates, as they churned uncomfortably with the champagne I had drunk.

"There is another matter," Stoker said. "We find ourselves in need of a bit of information, and it occurs to me that no one in London has a wider acquaintance than you."

Tiberius preened. "It is unlike you to resort to flattery, brother, but I am, as you say, widely acquainted."

"I do not suppose you happen to know any Roma?" Stoker ventured.

Tiberius considered this. "Signal for more champagne and let me think."

Stoker did as he was bade, lifting a finger to the waiter to indicate we wished to refresh our libations. A fresh bottle was opened and the wine poured, icy and coruscating, the straw-coloured bubbles dazzling in the theatre lights. Tiberius took a sip, then snapped his fingers, the sound muffled by his gloves.

"Ah! I have it. You will recall the Marches?"

Stoker paled beneath his sun-bronzed skin. "With appalling clarity."

Tiberius grinned and turned to me to explain. "The Earl March has ten children, mad as hatters, the lot of them. They have been famously eccentric since Moses kicked the bulrushes in his cradle. But they compensate for their oddness by being highly entertaining. I was at school with the eldest, Viscount Belmont—a frightful prig, I really cannot stand the fellow. He is the only one of the lot who behaves with anything like decorum, which makes him comparatively dull. But his sister, Portia—Lady Bettiscombe—is utterly enchanting. I might have offered her my hand once except she will insist upon carrying around a flatulent pug of great antiquity."

"Wait, we have met Lady Bettiscombe!" I turned to Stoker. "At the tableaux vivants at my club last autumn." Some months previously, we had been persuaded to take part in a charitable enterprise at the Hippolyta Club, known affectionately to us members as the Curiosity Club. It was open only to females of original mind, and the tableaux had been staged to raise funds to educate promising young scholars. Stoker and I had been posed as Samson and Delilah in honour of the painting of the same name by the Basque artist Errazquin. "We were part of a collection of biblical figures," I prodded Stoker. "She was dressed as Eve, and her pug wore a sort of velvet tube to play the serpent in Eden. Do you recall?"

Stoker shuddered. "I do. That animal emitted the vilest odours imaginable. I have never smelt anything like it, and I work with dead things."

"How did you not recognise her if you know the family?" I asked.

He gave a shrug. "I have not seen any of the Marches for well over a decade and I'd no idea she married a fellow called Bettiscombe."

"In any event," Tiberius said, collecting the threads of the conversation, "Portia was nearer my age. Stoker was forced to attend dance lessons with one of the younger daughters, Lady Julia." He turned to his brother. "I seem to recall she broke one of your toes during a particularly spirited polka. And luckily for you," he added, raising his glass to Stoker, "dear Julia was widowed a few years ago. That dreadful Edward Grey dropped stone dead in their ballroom in front of all of their guests. It was the talk of the social season."

"How does that help us?" I asked.

"Because sweet Julia—she really is an exceedingly pretty woman, all of the Marches are handsome, you know," he added as an aside, "has recently taken a second husband. The private inquiry agent who investigated Edward Grey's death. Apparently he suspected Julia at first, which is a delicious sort of irony given the fact that he ended up marrying her. And before you ask, this aids you because Julia's new husband is a half-Romany fellow by the name of Nicholas Brisbane. He ought to know how to find the information you want. I shall arrange a meeting."

"That would mean speaking to Julia," Stoker said faintly. "I do not want to speak to Julia."

"Why?" I teased. "Have you not recovered sufficiently from the broken toe? What else did she do? Make you hold her hand or talk about hair ribbons?"

"Worse," he said, his expression woeful. "I cared only about my animals and climbing trees, but Julia, well, she rather liked me."

"Did she write you violently passionate love notes?"

"Veronica, we were eleven. Besides, that I could have endured. No, she waited after the lesson the week before Christmas and assailed me under the mistletoe. She kissed me."

I tipped my head to the side. "Do you mean that this Julia Brisbane, née March, was your first kiss?"

"Unless you count my dog Pomona, then yes."

"Then I cannot wait to make her acquaintance," I said with a smile.

CHAPTER 8

Tiberius was as good as his word. The following afternoon he sent a short missive. *All is arranged. N&J joining you for tea.* It was scrawled in his elegantly fluid hand, and there was a postscript. *Come to dinner next week. I want you to meet him.*

There was no need to elaborate on who "him" might be—the actor who played Colonel Fairfax, the heroic tenor of *The Yeoman of the Guard*. He had performed splendidly, and during the curtain call, I noticed him dart a quick glance to our box, his gaze lingering just a moment longer than necessary on Tiberius. The young actor had blushed charmingly before withdrawing with the rest of the cast.

"It is no easy thing to step in at the last moment for so beloved a performer as Courtice Pounds. He did superbly. Shall we go backstage and congratulate him?" I asked gently.

"I think not," Tiberius said with a tired smile. "One must be discreet about these things. Not so much for my sake—I could easily leave the country if needed. But his is a promising career. I'll not have it damaged on my account."

I let the subject drop then, but I was pleased when the dinner invitation followed so swiftly. Stoker's relationship with Tiberius might be fraught, but mine was deeply satisfactory. I informed Stoker of the invitation, and he gave a slow nod.

"You approve?" I ventured.

"It is not for me to approve or disapprove of anything that brings him happiness," Stoker said simply. "My brother's business is his own to mind. But if this new fellow of his sings at us at the dinner table, I will leave before dessert."

"Do not threaten things you will never carry out. You have far too impressive and demanding a sweet tooth to forgo dessert for any reason," I observed. "Did you not enjoy his performance?"

"His performance was fine," Stoker said as he thumbed through the rest of the post. "It was the operetta itself I objected to. I far preferred *Ruddigore*." Our last outing to the Savoy had also been in Tiberius's company, and it had been to see *Ruddigore*, perhaps the darkest of Gilbert and Sullivan's works.

"Oh!" My exclamation was involuntary and so loud it caused Stoker to drop the periodical he was holding.

"What is the matter?"

"You mentioned *Ruddigore*, and I've just remembered the plot. It centers around a vampire—*a vampire named Ruthven*."

Stoker considered this a moment, then shrugged. "A coincidence."

"I do not like coincidences," I told him in a waspish tone. "Particularly when it is a question of murder."

"We do not yet know if it was murder in Jameson Harkness's case, even in the broadest sense of the word," he reminded me. "And the very notion of vampires abroad in London is so utterly ludicrous as to be impossible." I said nothing, and he rolled his eyes heavenwards. "You have already decided, haven't you? My god, Veronica, the staggering illogic of your mind astounds me. There is a curious mark on a dead man's neck and a vague, possible connection to a man named Ruthven, and Gilbert and Sullivan wrote an operetta about a vampire named Ruthven, therefore—"

I waved him to silence. "Yes, yes. I hear it. It does sound absurd when you insist upon phrasing it thusly."

"You mean truthfully?" A mischievous light danced in his eyes, and a tiny smile tugged at the corner of his mouth. Whilst they added to his allure, they also fired my irritation.

"Just because it sounds unlikely does not mean it *is*," I began.

He gave a hoot of laughter. "You are really going to justify this ludicrous theory that Quincey was attacked by a vampire, are you?"

"Yes, and what's more, I am going to prove it," I said stubbornly.

He laughed again, sobering only when he saw the pugnacious tilt of my chin. "Very well. It has been a while since we wagered," he said, touching the guinea coin attached to his watch chain. It had been our habit in the first few investigations we had undertaken to stake the coin on the outcome. It had passed back and forth until Stoker had laid claim to it permanently by having it fixed to the chain of his watch. If I won it back, I decided, I should make a hatpin of it.

"I shall take that wager," I said, thrusting out my hand.

He shook it, still smiling. "I shall enjoy impoverishing you just a little."

I made no reply. The proof of the pudding should be in the eating. Thoroughly piqued, I took myself off to the alcove we had organised as a sort of reference library. Shelves standing nearly twenty feet high filled the gaps between the columns, and neat brass rails had been fitted with rolling ladders for ease of access to the books. It took a dozen trips to find everything I wanted, but at last I had amassed a stack of materials upon my desk. A visit to the file cabinets produced a few slender files to add to the reading I meant to do. I spent the afternoon immersed in folklore, geography, religion, funereal customs, botany, gardening, and superstition—anything I could find related to vampirism, no matter how tangentially. I learnt of the strigoi, the undead who walked the forests of Transylvania, as well as the restless corpses that stalked nearer to home. To my astonishment, I found newspaper clippings in our library describing the ceremonies by which these revenants might be banished back into the grave.

And I discovered that these rituals were still being carried out in places like Styria, the Balkans, even Greece. The most recent of the cuttings was dated less than a decade past. The stories spoke of tiny mountainous villages terrorised by those the villagers claimed did not lie easy in death. It might have been the butcher's uncle or the farmer's daughter who crept from their graves, bringing illness and eventual death to their loved ones. The vampires seemed always to begin with their own kin, making targets of those whom they had most loved in life. Harrowing stuff, enough to make the hairs upon the back of one's neck stand up—and hardly what one expected to find in modern newspapers. It seemed astonishing that people who had seen the arrival of steam trains and electric lights could be so backwards in their thinking, but then I realised these outbreaks of vampirism always occurred in the most remote areas, where life carried on much as it always had. They were agrarian villages, the people devoted to their crops and their livestock and subject to the vagaries of nature, dependent upon the caprices of things that were inexplicable to them save by superstition. There was no germ theory to explain contagion, so they clung to the idea of pestilence passed by the undead who rose from their graves in search of fresh prey. There were no modern technological marvels to exorcise these unholy creatures, only the same customs that had always been used—holy water, burial with bricks in the mouth, stakes through the chest. Or, in the most vicious cases, opened graves and dismembered corpses burnt on a cleansing pyre. When I discovered that the victims of the alleged vampires were often made to drink the resulting ashes in a glass of water, I closed the last book with an audible snap. I had taken copious notes, and since I had exhausted and disgusted myself with my studies of vampires, I started in on the wolfsbane, beginning with several books on folklore and herbal medicine and ending with my favourite florilegium.

Stoker had been correct. Wolfsbane, I read, had been used since antiquity as a defence against wolves. Where they ravaged livestock and villagers, wolfsbane had been the most effective deterrent. The toxin had been distilled from the flowers and stem; even the roots were poisonous. When the decoction was complete, it had been smeared on arrows and spears in preparation for the hunt. The wolves died in agony, I read with some distaste. But wolfsbane had its uses. The purple-blue flowers were strikingly pretty, growing as they did on upright spears some three feet high. In small doses, the crushed blossoms or dried root might be used to ease pain and inflammation, to settle nerves and give rest. But the line between palliative and poison was thin as a cobweb. A pinch too much and the patient would never waken.

In the language of flowers, it was more often called by its gentler name of monkshood, the blooms resembling the habits of holy men. Curiously, it could symbolise purity and respect, although these meanings seemed to have fallen out of favour. The most common connotation was a simple one: death. Little wonder Jameson Harkness had reacted with such terror when the flowers were sent to him. But were they an accusation? Or a threat?

I turned again to my florilegium, reading the final sentence of the entry with interest. An alternate meaning: *A deadly foe is near.*

I had just jotted this last bit of information when I realised it was time to feed my butterflies. I tidied away my papers and hastened out to my vivarium, an elaborate, fairy-tale structure of scrolling ironwork and glass. It had been designed by the same hand that had created the Crystal Palace and reflected the same grandeur and elegance. It had fallen to disrepair by the time Stoker and I moved to Bishop's Folly, but Stoker had persuaded Lord Rosemorran to restore it and fit it with steam heat to serve as a home for the colonies of butterflies I wished to rear. My work had once entailed travelling the breadth of the world to secure the most exotic and elusive specimens both to study and to sell to avid collectors. But I had never been fond of the killing jar, and by breeding my own specimens, I could harvest them once they had perished of natural causes—a much more civilised way to carry out my researches and provide trophies to collectors. I arrived that afternoon to find the emerald swallowtails I had been so carefully nurturing were beginning to emerge from their chrysalides.

I sat quietly under the palmate leaf of a luscious frangipani to watch. It is always a thing of miracles to see a butterfly emerge from its silk-spun home. There is a stirring, a faintly disturbing pulsation of the walls of the chrysalis as the butterfly begins to challenge the parameters of its prison. The weak spots will give way, and the husk breaks apart, leaving the imago hanging by its feet, its wings damp and useless. This is when the creature is most vulnerable, for any opportunistic bird might snatch it away.

But there were no such threats in my vivarium. Instead, the butterfly rested, gathering its strength until at last it felt ready to venture a stretch, unfurling first one wing, then the other. The colours were invariably dulled and darkened by the dampness, but as the wings dried, the hues grew in vibrancy until the whole structure glowed like a lamplit jewel. Once dry, the butterfly would give a little shiver of pleasure, at least I liked to think that was what they felt. It would shudder and raise its wings, stepping daintily away from its perch to launch itself into the air for the first time. This was always a heart-stopping interlude, the pure anxiousness of discovering whether this small, infinitely delicate creature would find its strength and bear its own weight upon those gossamer wings. When it did, it was the most glorious phenomenon to witness. I never tired of that moment when determination met ability and the butterfly was able to do the thing it could never have imagined as it crawled and crept, bound to the earth in its caterpillar form. Gravity was no longer its mistress as it gently flapped its way from leaf to leaf, testing its limits and finding with each thrust of the wings that it could do still more, fly still further.

I watched for hours, enchanted, playing a small game with my butterflies. I stood perfectly still, my arms upraised and a ripe little loquat on each finger and a few in my hair. The butterflies circled my head, eventually landing to feed. More joined them until at last the entire colony had settled on me, flapping in my hair, on my gown and fingertips.

Just then George appeared, leading a couple. "Begging your pardon, miss. But these people say they was invited."

"Dash it!" I muttered. In the excitement of the afternoon, I had entirely forgot the appointed meeting. "George, go tell Cook we shall require tea in the Belvedere at once."

"Yes, miss." He darted off, giving the pair of guests a look of circumspection as he left. George was nothing if not diligent in his scrutiny of strangers, although what he saw in this pair to kindle his wariness, I could not imagine. They were dressed expensively, but with a quiet luxuriousness. The lady's mantle was trimmed in the finest astrakhan, and a clever little hat to match was perched atop her prettily dressed chestnut hair. Her eyes were green and gleaming with interest, and her fair skin rosy from the cold. Her companion was tall, with the sort of olive complexion that would tan handsomely if he were to go abroad in strong sunlight without a hat, I imagined. A few fine silver threads wove through his black hair, but his jawline was as strongly etched as a man of twenty-five. He was perhaps forty, his wife a decade younger, and they were an exceedingly striking couple. The fact that she was the daughter of an earl had given me pause—aristocrats are some of my least favourite people—but her smile was genuine and her manner warmer than mere cordiality would dictate.

I did my best to provide them a better welcome than George had. I smiled broadly. "Good afternoon," I called. "Pardon the confusion, only I've just had several *Papilio palinurus* emerge from their chrysalides, and it's terribly exciting."

"So it would seem," the man said, a small smile playing about his mouth. His companion stepped forwards, holding up her hand. Instantly, one of the emerald swallowtails darted to her, landing on her outstretched finger.

"Oh!" She gave an exclamation of delight. "Its little feet feel like feathers."

"Only mind you don't touch the wings," I warned. "Even a brush of your hand will cause the scales to fall from the wings and it will no longer be able to fly."

"How fascinating," she breathed. The butterfly, perhaps sensing the appreciativeness of its audience, flapped its wings slowly, permitting her a perfect view of its glorious colouration. A few of its friends decided to inspect the gentleman, landing on his head, perhaps attracted by the scent of bergamot I had noticed emanating from his person. No sooner had one taken up residence on his nose than the door to the vivarium opened again and Stoker appeared, shirt agape and heavily streaked with ink and a few other unspeakable substances. His hair was more than usually unruly, and his sleeves were rolled past the elbow to reveal the heft of his forearms.

"Veronica, what in the name of the oozing wounds of Christ—" he began, but stopped as he caught sight of our visitors. The woman broke into a broad smile.

"Hello, Revelstoke."

"Julia March," Stoker said in a wary tone.

"Not anymore," she said with a twinkle. "I should like to introduce you to my husband, Nicholas Brisbane. Brisbane, this is Revelstoke Templeton-Vane, but I have only just remembered he does prefer to be called Stoker."

The menfolk exchanged greetings in the fashion of predatory cats, eyeing one another in a mood of cool assessment. Lady Julia turned to me. "You must be Miss Speedwell. I am Julia Brisbane. I understand you would like our help."

"Indeed we would, Lady Julia."

"Tiberius did not say what you required, but he did indicate it was a matter of some importance."

"The greatest importance," I assured her. "It is a matter of murder."

CHAPTER 9

"My god, Veronica, is that really necessary?" Stoker demanded.

To my surprise, Brisbane merely smiled. "If it is truly a question of murder, best to know up front."

"You seem decidedly unimpressed by the notion," I told him.

"My husband and I have made something of a habit of murder—the investigation of it, I should add, not the committing," Lady Julia corrected hastily.

I stared at her in astonishment. "I have said the same thing, *precisely* the same thing, about Stoker and myself."

Lady Julia grinned. "I think we shall get on famously. Did I hear mention of tea?"

I hastily encouraged the butterflies to move along. Only the one on Brisbane's nose seemed reluctant to abandon its perch, but I coaxed it with a bit of fennel—emerald swallowtails are exceedingly fond of fennel—and it settled down happily to feed. Once the butterflies were cleared, I led the way to the Belvedere. The Brisbanes regarded the place with visible curiosity, and several minutes were spent explaining the work we had undertaken as well as the plans for the museum Lord Rosemorran intended to establish in due course. Lady Julia seemed particularly taken with the caryatids and a suit of Japanese armour, drawing herself only reluctantly, I thought, back to our discussion.

"But that is not why you've come," Stoker said, bringing the conversation to a close. A footman had arrived with the tea things in a large hamper and departed again. I busied myself in setting out the food whilst our guests made themselves at home. Lady Julia took the camel saddle, and her husband arranged himself atop a plaster replica of the Venetian lion of Saint Mark. The wings were broken off, affording him a more comfortable seat than he might otherwise have had.

"Yes, we hear from Tiberius you have a murder on your hands," Lady Julia said in some excitement. "Tell us everything."

I poured the tea and handed around the plates while Stoker began the narrative. With a few judicious additional comments from me, the story was soon told. He described Jameson Harkness's sudden suicide as well as the discovery of Maurice Quincey's body outside Highgate—and the unusual markings found upon it. He also shared our experience calling upon Seward Johnson and our conviction that the fellow knew more than he was telling.

"We have no idea of where to find this Ruthven character or how to locate the Romany child," Stoker finished.

"Ruthven," Lady Julia said, furrowing her pretty brow as she looked at her husband. "I know several Ruthvens."

"Are any of them vampires?" I asked.

Stoker choked on his tea, and Brisbane tipped his head thoughtfully. "Vampires?"

"Maurice Quincey was found with puncture marks in his neck," I reminded him. "Furthermore, I have discovered a literary link between the name 'Ruthven' and vampires."

"Veronica, we are not basing an investigation on the libretto of a bloody—" He darted a hasty look at Lady Julia and flushed to the roots of his hair. He muttered an apology, but I noticed Lady Julia's swift grin.

"You mustn't mind Stoker," I told her. "He spent considerable time in both a travelling show and Her Majesty's Navy, and I am not certain which is responsible for his deplorable vocabulary."

"Most likely it was his brothers," she assured me. "I have five of my own, so I know whereof I speak." She turned to Stoker. "Carry on, please. And do not worry about my delicate sensibilities. I am no longer the hothouse flower of my youth. I have been hardened by my experiences into Amazonian strength, I can assure you."

Stoker shied like a pony and looked to Brisbane, who merely shrugged and crossed one long leg elegantly over the other. "God knows I have tried to protect her from herself, but in the interests of preserving my own sanity, I have given up trying. She has lately taken to experimenting with explosives. She blew up our house a few months ago."

Lady Julia puffed out a sound of indignation. "How you exaggerate! I blew up one room, and it was not even a very large one. As you were saying, Stoker?"

Stoker looked bemused but made a manful effort to carry on. "I was saying that we cannot build a case for vampirism based upon the lyrics of Gilbert and Sullivan."

"*Ruddigore*!" Lady Julia exclaimed delightedly. "Oh, how I enjoyed that show. Brisbane loathes operetta, but I do love it, and *Ruddigore* is a particular favourite of mine. And in that show, Sir Ruthven Murgatroyd is indeed the vampire. In fact, there is a whole line of vampiric Murgatroyds. How clever you are, Miss Speedwell."

"It is not just Gilbert and Sullivan," I said, producing the notes I had compiled earlier. "In 1816, Percy Shelley, Mary Shelley, and Lord Byron took a villa at Lake Geneva. The weather, I have discovered, was foul—1816 was known as the 'Year Without a Summer' after a series of volcanic eruptions in 1815, notably Mount Tambora, altered the climate patterns, resulting in extensive rainfall and much colder temperatures than was the norm. To pass the time that Byron and Shelley and their guests were forced to spend indoors, they embarked upon a competition to write ghost stories. We all know, of course, Mary Shelley's contribution."

"*Frankenstein*," Brisbane put in.

"Exactly so. Now, at the same time, Byron scribbled a bit of a vampire story that was eventually published as a fragment. But a fourth member of their party, Byron's physician, John Polidori, published a full novel, also a vampire story. And his vampire, modelled on Byron himself, was called Lord Ruthven, a name borrowed from Lady Caroline Lamb's own skewering of Byron in her novel *Glenarvon*." I produced another page from the file. "After Polidori's vampire story, the name 'Ruthven' runs through European literature for the rest of this century—always associated with a vampire. France, Sweden, Germany, all of them have vampire tales featuring a Lord Ruthven as a character. He has been the focus of multiple operas and plays, even Alexandre Dumas wrote of him!"

"What are you suggesting, Miss Speedwell?" Brisbane asked.

"I do not yet know. A natural scientist's method is to gather information before forming a hypothesis," I told him.

"Very wise," he replied.

"And thoroughly misleading," Stoker put in. "Veronica, you will see 'a' and 'b' and hypothesise an alphabet."

"'A' and 'b' are the foundational material of the alphabet," I retorted. "You have simply proven the validity of my method."

"I have proven that you sometimes strike it lucky. Like those prospectors in the Yukon who put a pan into a river and come up with gold. Most often, they have only mud to show for their efforts."

"Mud! When I have just comprehensively demonstrated to you—"

"Comprehensively! You have demonstrated nothing but your own not inconsiderable stubbornness—"

Our ripostes had overlapped, perhaps a trifle more animatedly than we had realised, and I suddenly noticed the Brisbanes watching us with open-mouthed interest.

"I do apologise," I told them.

"I am terribly sorry," Stoker began.

To my surprise, Lady Julia looked at her husband, who was smiling broadly, and at the sight of his face, she laughed. "I know precisely what you are thinking, my love." She turned her attention back to us. "You sound exactly like us when we are in the throes of an investigation. There is nothing like murder to heighten the passions."

Her complexion pinkened delectably, and I realised then that the Brisbanes had much the sort of relationship that Stoker and I enjoyed, a partnership of equals based upon mutual understanding and affection, with a healthy dose of intellectual curiosity and physical attraction added to the mix. A heady brew indeed.

I cleared my throat. "To my point, I am not necessarily saying this Ruthven character *is* a vampire. Only that—"

"Balderdash! You wagered only today that a vampire must have been involved—" Stoker countered. But the door opened then and the dogs rushed in, all seven of them. They were in a state of excitement, tails upraised, barking and howling and romping rampageously. For some inexplicable reason, they made a beeline for Lady Julia, upsetting the tea things to get at her. As one, they leapt up, noses twitching as they made directly for her décolletage. I was certain that they meant her no harm, but the mere sight of them as a pack in full cry was enough to stir Brisbane to action in aid of his spouse. It took several minutes to extract the lady from their hairy attentions, but at last Stoker was able to lure them away with cake. I helped Brisbane to settle Lady Julia on her camel saddle once more, brushing the worst of the dirt and dog hair from her gown.

"I am terribly sorry," I told her. "I cannot think why they were so fixed upon you, Lady Julia."

"I can," she said, her voice burbling with laughter. She reached into the neckline of her gown and drew out a bundled handkerchief. She opened it carefully to reveal a pair of bright, bead-like eyes staring back at me. Its mouth was open, its teeth small and sharp as needles, prominently on display as it chittered a scolding in my direction.

"This is Snug," she informed me with the same cordial ease she might have made any introduction.

"A dormouse! How very unexpected," I said. Impulsively, I pulled a tiny grey velvet mouse from my own pocket.

"This is Chester. Not so animated or adorable as your little fellow, but he has great sentimental attachment for me." Chester was my constant companion and had been since my father slipped him into my cradle shortly after my birth. The fact that my father had failed to recognise my existence afterwards did not allay my pleasure in the gift. It was to be supposed that being the Prince of Wales did take up much of his time, even if he were inclined to acknowledge his semi-legitimate daughter.

But I revealed none of that to Lady Julia. Her eyes shone as she regarded my little treasure. "How very enchanting! And what exquisite stitching on the nose."

"He was very nearly lost at sea once," I told her. "Stoker restitched him. He has exceptional skills with a needle." I turned to her dormouse, putting a fingertip to its head. It was inexpressibly soft. The gesture seemed to agitate the tiny creature more, for it turned and applied those needlelike teeth to my appendage.

"Snug, that is very rude," Lady Julia scolded. "It is my turn to apologise for my pet. He is an incorrigible little beast, but I dare not leave him at home. My raven might eat him."

"You keep a raven?" I asked in delight.

"That is as nothing to a March," Stoker told me darkly. "Her sister Portia wore a snake as a bracelet to dance classes."

Lady Julia grinned as she replaced the dormouse into her décolletage. "You were an utterly abysmal dancer, Stoker. Two left feet wading through treacle." She leaned closer to me. "It did not stop me from forming the most tremendous attachment to him. I used to doodle the words 'Lady Julia Templeton-Vane' in my notebook."

"Did you indeed?" Brisbane's black eyes gleamed dangerously, and I thought then that the lazily sophisticated posture he adopted was perhaps more of a mask than I had understood.

"I was *eleven*. The following month I had a passion for our new footman," Lady Julia assured him. "But my heart truly belonged to no one until I met you, beloved."

Her smile was pert, but the one he returned was so full of adoration, I felt a tug at my heartstrings. "You were saying about your raven?" I prompted.

"Grim, he is called. He was a Tower raven, but one of my brothers won him in a wager, and we could not return him without causing a terrible dustup, so it was decided we should just quietly keep the fellow."

"But surely the Tower knows how many ravens they have," Stoker protested. "Didn't they notice you'd taken one?"

Lady Julia shrugged. "He was stolen from the Tower by someone else, so there was nothing to connect us to the matter, and besides, I cannot think the Tower ravens are *happy* there. It is rather bleak and so very exposed, right on the river. That sort of dampness isn't good for ravens, you know, to say nothing of keeping such a creature at sea level." She returned her gaze to me. "Ravens like altitude."

"I think, my darling," Brisbane said indulgently, "we ought to bring the discussion back to the matter at hand." He turned to me. "I do believe your theory about this Ruthven having a vampire connection is intriguing, Miss Speedwell." I preened a little as he went on. "But without more information, I think your best course of action is to pursue the boy who was witness to the discovery of Mr. Quincey's body."

"Do you have connections within the Romany community to whom you might recommend we speak?" Stoker asked.

Brisbane's smile was thin. "Not if I wanted to keep my skin. And you'll not get within fifty feet of an encampment without someone to vouch for you." He sighed and set down his teacup with a gesture of resignation. "So we had best be on our way."

"Now?" Apparently I had been right to suspect that Brisbane's posture of languor was a ruse. He was clearly a man of action.

"My dear Miss Speedwell, there is no time to lose. As you said yourself, it is a matter of murder."

CHAPTER 10

The Brisbanes had left their conveyance in the drive, and it was arranged that we should meet them there in order to travel together to Hampstead Heath. There was often to be found an encampment of Roma upon the heath, and usually one of considerable size, Brisbane informed us. It was the logical place to begin our search. He escorted his lady out as Stoker put on a fresh shirt—he keeps several at hand in the Belvedere—and I pinned on a hat and buttoned my coat.

"I like them," I told him, tweaking the collar of his coat to lie neatly.

"I noticed. Do not become chums with Lady Julia," he warned.

"Whyever not?"

"Because one minute we're sleuthing out murderers and the next we're receiving dinner invitations and exchanging Christmas gifts."

"It is permissible to have friends, you know."

"One does not befriend Marches. One observes them at a distance. Like animals in a zoological garden."

"Piffle. Eccentricity is what makes people interesting. Besides, Brisbane is not a March," I pointed out.

"Even worse. He is a private inquiry agent, which means he has made a profession of the very activities from which I try so desperately to dissuade you. I am afraid he will encourage your worst tendencies."

"Or are you ever so slightly threatened that there is another man about who demonstrates your better qualities but with vastly superior tailoring? I smell the sulphurous whiff of jealousy."

"Jealousy! That is the most insulting—"

"Perhaps not jealousy," I conceded. "It may be nearer the thunderous clash of antlers between stags forced to occupy the same territory. Although now that I think on it, stags are not half as protective of their domains as *Panthera pardus pardus*. The African leopard—"

He stopped my mouth with a kiss that permitted no rebuttal. When he drew back, he kept a finger under my chin, tipping my face up.

"Your ability to construct an argument out of nothing but thin air and the desire to hear yourself speak ought to be studied by professors of rhetoric," he replied.

I gave him a benevolent smile. "Thank you, my darling."

"That was not a compliment."

"Wasn't it?" I returned his kiss heartily, and just as things began to take an interesting turn, I stepped back and adjusted my hat. "Come along, dearest. We mustn't keep the Brisbanes waiting."

The Brisbane carriage was as discreetly luxurious as the couple's clothing. Every comfort had been anticipated and addressed, from the compartment in the floor which emitted a gentle heat thanks to the hot bricks stowed within to the thickly padded seats upholstered in dark green velvet. Brisbane gave a series of instructions to his driver, then assumed his place next to Stoker, facing backwards so Lady Julia and I might have the pleasure of sitting together and the comfort of facing the horses. Our chatter was inconsequential stuff—Brisbane asked a number of thoughtful questions about my work as a lepidopterist while Lady Julia and Stoker exchanged snippets of gossip regarding various mutual acquaintances. With such pleasantries, the journey passed swiftly, and in a remarkably short period of time, I felt the carriage swing upwards, mounting the climb that carried us out of the city and onto the heath.

The afternoon light had faded to the gloaming, an evocative Scots word that so poetically describes the time between sunset and nightfall. The greying skies added to the atmosphere, as did the soft smoky pillars rising in the distance and smudging the edges of the trees and rocks.

"Cooking fires," Brisbane said. He called up to the driver. "Stop here." We alighted and took stock of where we were. It seemed impossible that the heath should feel so much like the wildest of open countryside when London carried on with its hustle and bustle only a short distance away. We were perhaps a mile as the crow—or the raven, in Lady Julia's case—flew from Highgate Cemetery, and I made a note that Stoker and I should pay the place a visit whilst we were in the vicinity.

"This way," Brisbane said with a nod of his head in the direction of the smoking fires. I was conscious of a rising excitement in Lady Julia, and as we walked, she slipped her hand into her husband's, murmuring something in his ear. He smiled in response, stroking the back of her hand with his thumb. They were clearly besotted with one another, and I was happy for them. Such elaborate and public displays would never have suited me, I decided, and I had just about persuaded myself to believe it when I felt Stoker's arm close about my waist.

"Stay near," he said. "There are dangers about."

I felt a flutter of feminine gratification that he wished to take care of me. This was immediately surpassed by irritation that he thought I could not take care of myself.

"Stoker, I am perfectly capable of dealing with whatever menaces we might face," I reminded him.

"I know. I am counting on you to protect *me*."

I turned to remonstrate, but there was a gleam in his gaze, and I puffed out a sigh instead. "You really are the most enraging, incorrigible, frustrating man I have ever known."

He said nothing but tightened his hold on my waist, and those feminine feelings recrudesced, not least because he was close enough that I could detect the warm, leather-book and honey smell he so often carried upon his skin.

We caught up to our companions, and I was fascinated by the change in Brisbane. At the Belvedere, his manner had been quietly composed, his gestures elegant. Here, he strode, his shoulders broader, his chin thrust forward imperiously, as if daring anyone to cross him. His head did not turn, but his eyes roved constantly, taking in every detail, it seemed. We passed the long line of horses, staked and eating contentedly of their evening meal. Steam rose from the pails of warm mash provided by boys who moved down the row, feeding and stroking the animals. Horses were the life's blood of the Roma, providing them transportation and money, and they were accordingly treated like kings. A few young men hovered at the edges of the encampment, keeping watch, but Brisbane moved through unchallenged, and we soon reached the circle of vardos, the elaborately painted wagons which clustered about the campfires. They were decorated in the colours of jewels, the trim picked out in rich gold paint which gleamed in the firelight. Smoke filled the air along with the appetising aromas of cooking meats. Large cauldrons hung from iron supports, their contents bubbling away, and spits for rabbits and chickens and the occasional duck turned slowly, fat dripping into the fires. Tending each fire was a dame, her skirt looped up over her petticoats, her sleeves rolled to the elbow. About her feet there was invariably a child or two and often a basket holding a swaddled babe. On the steps of several of the vardos were older women, swathed in shawls and puffing on long-stemmed pipes. They fixed us with steely stares as we approached.

"Where are the menfolk?" I inquired of Brisbane.

He nodded to the far side of the camp where several groups of men were clustered. Some were drinking, some eating, others working with their hands to mend china or whittle, but most were engaged in some form of entertainment. I saw one clever fellow juggling fire while a companion scraped away on his fiddle. There were outsiders mingling with them, throwing coins in payment for their amusements. One vardo had been set a little apart from the others and bore an elegantly lettered sign—MAGDA WHO SEES ALL. Above this proclamation was the image of an enormous eye, an unsettling thing but one from which it was impossible to look away. Brisbane strode directly to this wagon, but a tall, skinny fellow in a rusty-looking bowler hat stood outside the door. He put up a quelling hand to Brisbane.

"I am sorry, but she is with a customer. You must wait your turn, sir."

He smiled thinly, showing a gold tooth, and Brisbane replied in a lilting language I did not understand.

"Romani," Lady Julia murmured to me as the bowler-hatted man answered Brisbane. His expression was not particularly friendly, and Lady Julia continued to explain, sotto voce. "Brisbane is half-Romany. His mother was a member of this particular clan, but his father was an outsider, a Scotsman. His mother left her people to marry him. That sort of thing is viewed as a tremendous betrayal, you see. Brisbane is not accepted as a fully fledged Rom although he is fluent in the language. Outsiders are not permitted to learn it, so his command of the tongue is a signal that he is one of them, even if they do not wish to acknowledge him." I understood that sort of liminal existence well, I reflected. Half of one, neither of either. Never completely accepted into the world of one's parents and so one makes one's own way, laying the stones for a path not yet trod by another. It was a lonely existence sometimes, and I was fiercely glad for Brisbane and myself that we had found partners to understand us—partners who were, in their own way, like us, struggling against their birth. Stoker and Lady Julia may have been born aristocrats, but blue blood did not flow easily in their veins. They had, each of them, cast off many of the privileges of their station for something altogether different. Their comprehension might be sometimes imperfect, but that it existed at all was something miraculous.

Brisbane had continued to speak to the fellow in their ancestral tongue, and the man unbent enough to indicate we should wait a little distance away, where a few felled trees had been laid to provide rough seats. We did as we were bade, settling ourselves to wait. The fellow must have given instructions to our refreshment, for in a few minutes, a young girl appeared, heavy black plaits swinging to her waist. She offered a tray set with small, beautifully coloured glasses filled with cider.

"From Kentish apples we scrumped," she explained in English. Brisbane handed a glass to me.

"Roma often pick fruit as seasonal employment. Kent is a favourite for hops and apples, and you'll taste no cider better than that pressed from apples scrumped by a Romany lass."

The girl smiled broadly, revealing two deep dimples in her cheeks. She was dressed in layers of bright fabrics, crimsons and deep greens, and her waist and ears were laden with heavy jewellery fashioned from gold coins.

"Her dowry," Lady Julia explained as the girl moved away. "Everything they own, they must be able to carry away, sometimes quite quickly."

"Because they cannot always plan their travels," I mused as I sipped at my cider. It was robustly redolent of sweet, ripe apples, fruity and richly fermented. I made a note to drink slowly.

"They are among the most hated of groups in England even now,"

Lady Julia said with a tightening of the lips. "They are dependent upon public land or the kindness of landowners to find a place to stay for even a single night. There are many doors firmly shut to them simply because they choose a different way of life. It has always been thus for them in England."

"I used to hear stories when I was a boy," Stoker put in. "Father always allowed them to camp on our property—he said it brought good luck. But there were plenty who chased them off and spread rumours about what they got up to. Vicious things were said of them, when all they wanted to do was trade horses and make a little money mending copper. The worst they ever did was steal a chicken or two, and any village lad had done the same or worse."

"There are still laws on the books which permit a gorgio to turn out the cooking pot of a Rom to make certain there are no English babies being boiled," Brisbane said with a curl of his handsome lip.

"That is appalling," I said stoutly. "Inhumane."

"But for centuries the English have regarded the traveller as less than human," Brisbane pointed out. "When one fails to recognise the humanity in others, it is easy to make villains of them."

"What is a gorgio?" I asked.

"It is the Romani word for an English person, someone not of the blood," Lady Julia explained.

"And a poshrat is a half-breed," came a voice behind us. We turned as one to see an older Romany woman approaching. She was heavily wrapped in shawls. One of these—gossamer fine and shimmering with silver threads—was draped over her head, the deep fringe rippling as she walked. Like the younger woman who had served us cider, this one wore finery, but amidst the gold coins were pearls at her throat and ears, enormous, perfectly matched spheres of nacreous grey. They were spectacular and must have been worth a queen's ransom. Fortune-telling, I decided, must be far more lucrative than I had thought.

"Magda!" Lady Julia leapt lightly from her perch to embrace the woman. "How have you been?"

"Keeping well, although there is a rheumatism in my knee," was the answer. The woman looked intently into Lady Julia's eyes. "You have a new happiness. A child, I think."

Lady Julia blushed becomingly. "It is not what you think."

"A child born, a child found, both may bring joy," Magda replied with a shrug. She turned to Brisbane, lifting her chin. "You have not greeted me, poshrat." The word might have meant half-breed and may have carried some vaguely derisive connotation in their language, but I sensed no real insult. Instead, Magda regarded Brisbane with respect and perhaps something like affection.

"Magda," he said, inclining his head politely. "We have need of you."

She raised her arms heavenwards, the shawl making wings of her outstretched limbs. "When do you not? Come, children. Mother Magda will tell all."

CHAPTER 11

Magda invited us all into her vardo, a cramped arrangement, for numerous pieces of furniture had been fitted inside, and there was even a small stove crammed into one corner. Its brisk fire pumped out tremendous warmth, and I imagined the wagon would be cosy even in the iciest of winter winds.

She made a brusque gesture of hospitality, and we seated ourselves around a small table that had been covered with a piece of carpet. Arranged atop were the tools of Magda's trade—a pack of well-worn cards, a teapot, and a small glass orb.

"Which do you prefer?" she inquired. "The cards? The crystal ball? The tea leaves? Or perhaps you would like the palm?"

Without waiting for a response, she reached for my hand and turned it over, tracing the lines of the palm with careful scrutiny. "You have known many lovers," she began.

I snatched my hand back as I heard a repressed choking sound from Stoker. "Thank you," I said with a cool smile. "But we have come on a different matter."

She smiled and sat back in her chair, waving an airy hand. "Fortunes first."

"Oh, for heaven's sake, Magda," Lady Julia muttered. She thrust out her hand, palm up.

"I have read yours," Magda reminded her. "More than once. You want to know your future? Look no further than the man," she said, gesturing to Brisbane. She paused meaningfully.

Lady Julia sighed and turned to me. "Magda has already read for me, and she will not read for Brisbane. It is not the usual custom to read for another Rom," she explained. "Romany folk prefer to read for gorgios."

I had just reconciled myself to being the subject of Magda's reading, when to my astonishment, Stoker sat forwards. "I will do it."

Magda inclined her head. "Very well, lordling."

"Lordling?" Stoker gave her a curious look.

"I know a man brought up in privilege when I see one." It might have been a guess or it might have been a calculated deduction. Stoker's clothes, after all, were expensively made even if he had treated them appallingly. His teeth were excellent—another sign of wealth—and his vowels were elegant. He might present a figure of a man a little down-at-heel, but to a close observer, it would be obvious that he had enjoyed at least proximity to money. A parlour trick, I thought. Clever, but not difficult.

Magda surveyed the items before her, considering them each in turn and muttering to herself in her own language. At last she reached for the deck of cards.

"I rather thought the tea leaves—" Stoker began.

She waved again, sending her shawls rippling. "It is not a matter of choice, lordling. The crystal ball shows me pictures when it wishes. The leaves speak when they have something to say. Now it is the cards who want to be known."

Magda rose and adjusted the lamps so her face was in shadow. "Light must not fall directly upon me when I read the cards," she explained as she resumed her seat. She opened her hand flat in front of Stoker. "You must cross my palm with silver."

"I think you've already been paid. Handsomely," Lady Julia said with a sternness I had not yet heard in her. She was looking hard at the pearls Magda wore, and the fortune teller smiled, stroking the gleaming jewels.

"A gift for my old age. They have nothing to do with this gentleman. And the cards will not speak unless my gifts have been paid for—by him," she added firmly.

Stoker fished in his pocket and withdrew a worn silver florin, placing it gently in the wrinkled, outstretched palm. Magda's fingers closed about it, and when she opened her hand again, the coin had disappeared—probably into her lap, but the effect was good. It added to the otherworldliness of the experience, and I had to admire her showmanship.

She turned her attention to the cards then. They were well used with the ragged softness of much handling. She began to shuffle them slowly, dividing and riffling and reassembling the deck over and over. As she shuffled, she closed her eyes, murmuring again in her own tongue. After seven shuffles, she cut the deck in half and gave this portion a partial turn, then shuffled three more times. Then she tamped the deck together and pushed it towards Stoker.

"Shuffle them with the left hand," she told him. "Four times."

"Why the left?" I asked softly.

"It is the hand of destiny," she explained. "The right hand is that of reason and the mind. The left is connected to the heart." In the gloom, I saw Lady Julia touch her wedding ring reflexively. A slender band of gold, worn upon the finger whose vein is said to run directly to the heart.

Stoker did as Magda told him, shuffling the cards slowly. When he finished, they were stacked neatly in the middle of the table.

"Knock on the cards as if upon a door," Magda instructed.

"How many times?" Stoker asked.

"As many as you like. It is your conversation with the cards, not mine."

Stoker curled his hand into a fist and rapped three times in quick succession. Magda retrieved the deck and held it in her hands, head tipped as if listening to a faraway voice. She then gave a nod and began to deal out the cards.

She dealt five of them face down in the shape of a cross and then spread her hands. "This is the Cross of Destiny. It will tell you about your future, and it will reveal things to you that you cannot yet imagine. It is not for you to understand everything now. But you will remember these images and the things you have heard, and when they come to pass, you will recall what was said here."

She touched the first card but did not turn it over yet. "These are Romany oracle cards, first drawn in Bohemia. Each bears an image that will seem obvious to you. And it bears a title, also obvious. But look closely. They may call memories to the surface. Perhaps strong emotions or fantasies, even. Whatever the card represents to you is unique. There is no one else on earth who could look at these five cards and have the same reaction. So, let us begin."

She paused and took a deep breath, blowing it out slowly through pursed lips, all the while stroking the first card lightly with her fingertips. She turned it over. "This card represents the present. It is the Sweetheart."

The image on the card was of a slender, elegant woman dressed in an old-fashioned yellow gown, a red mantle draped over one arm. She held a letter, no doubt a billet-doux, in one hand, smiling as she read its contents. Stoker flicked a glance to me, a tiny, knowing smile on his lips. Almost immediately, Magda turned over the second card with a brisk snap.

"The past," she told him. "Sorrow."

Another lady in yellow, this one with a blue cloak. She stood in a posture of abject despair, weeping over a letter. She was obviously meant to be a general representation of the emotion of sorrow, but I could not help remembering Stoker's former wife, a woman of incalculable cruelty who had brought him nothing but pain.

"And the third?" Stoker asked tightly.

Magda reached for the card. "The near future." She turned it over. Unlike the first two, this did not feature a figure, but instead a disembodied hand holding an envelope inscribed with a name and address, the writing illegible. In the background was a room with cheerful blue curtains and a tall vase of pretty pink flowers. "The Letter," Magda intoned. "A communication of great significance will come to you. Very soon."

I repressed a sigh. With a deft bit of sleight of hand, any moderately skilled person could have arranged these cards for any client, although even that small bit of effort was not necessary given Magda's performance. Her instructions, the comment that any interpretation might be placed upon the cards, was sufficient to suggest that whatever the querent read into the meanings must be correct and the cards themselves were vague enough to permit the desired conclusions. The Sweetheart card might refer to a current attachment or merely the desire for one, a nearly universal experience. And who among us has not had a heavy share of sadness as depicted by the card of Sorrow? One could read any grief, large or small, in that image.

As for the Letter, the London post was delivered a dozen times a day, bringing with it scores of missives of every description. Bills, invitations, appeals for money, introductions, offers of employment, cheques for services performed, chatty communications from friends near and far. We received all of these and more on a daily basis. Any might be considered a letter of great significance to a mind already primed to expect it. As much as I wanted to believe in the possibility of receiving glimpses into what was yet to come, I feared Magda was a charlatan. Not that I blamed her, of course. She was a woman who had need of funds to support her family, and fortune-telling was a decidedly lucrative endeavour when undertaken by a clever practitioner, which Magda undoubtedly was. She had set the scene perfectly.

But one might have expected a trifle more drama to heighten the atmosphere, I thought as she turned over the fourth card.

"Misfortune," she intoned gravely—and with a bit of understatement. The image was not so much one of misfortune as that of frank catastrophe. A burning building, utterly crumbling to ruin, with a man falling from the top of it. Another man stood at the bottom in the helmet of a member of the fire brigade, pointing a hose at the conflagration, but the jet of water was utterly helpless against the roaring flames. Utter destruction was at hand.

"Magda." Brisbane's voice held a warning tone. She shrugged in response.

"The cards show what they will. I am only a messenger."

"Show me the last," Stoker commanded.

She turned it over with a decisive snap. The background image was of a deep blue sky. Across the sweep of white and pink clouds flew a winged creature with a flowing white headdress. It carried a scythe, a skull neatly tucked behind the crook of its elbow. The expression on the creature's face seemed almost fond as it regarded this memento of mortality.

"Death," Magda said in a tone that I might have described as gloating.

"Well, that went all to hell rather quickly," Stoker said in an attempt at levity. Magda waved a finger in his face, her expression severe.

"Mock the cards at your peril. They offer you their gifts—a warning of what will come if you do not heed. Misfortune and death."

I waited for her to tell him he was cursed and to offer to lift the bane for a price, but she made no such overture.

Stoker's tone gentled. "I meant no offence. Truly."

She regarded him thoughtfully for a long moment, her head tipped to the side, almost as if she were listening once more to a faraway voice. Then she nodded, seemingly in agreement. She reached into her pocket and withdrew a slender leather thong. From it hung a small bone-white stone with a hole straight through the middle. She held it out to Stoker.

"A rock?" Stoker asked. "For me?"

"A hagstone," she corrected. "Taken from the shores of the sea in a place where the magic is old and never forgot. It is the strongest luck. Put it on."

Stoker did as she instructed, slipping it over his head. As the hagstone disappeared into the neck of his shirt, Magda gave a little nod of satisfaction. "Wear it always," she told him. "Do not remove it for any purpose whatsoever."

"For how long?" Stoker asked.

"Until the danger is passed. You will know when it is safe to remove it."

"Thank you," he said.

He reached for his pocket, but she made an abrupt gesture of dismissal. "Keep your money. You have a pure heart, and pure hearts must be protected."

Stoker flushed crimson, but he looked pleased just the same. I leant near. "Vampires are not to be entertained as real, but a protective talisman is logical and scientific?" I murmured.

"Do not be rude to our hostess," he said back through gritted teeth.

"Just admit you are as susceptible as the rest of us to superstition," I replied.

Magda gave me an impenetrable look. "You see more than you admit, lordling. Remember my words, and the stone will protect you." Stoker touched the talisman through the fabric of his shirt, and Magda inclined her head before turning to Brisbane.

"Now we eat."

This was apparently the etiquette of such situations, for Brisbane did not attempt to dissuade her. She went to the door and issued a series of instructions. In a very short time we had been supplied with bowls of stew and hunks of bread. A thin film of grease puddled atop the surface of the stew, issuing forth a rich, appetising aroma. There was no butter for the bread, but it was freshly baked and delicious. I dug my spoon into the stew, noticing only after I had taken a bite that Lady Julia was watching me in amusement.

"What?" I murmured. "Have I committed an offence?"

"Quite the opposite," she replied. "The Romany like a stranger who appreciates their delicacies."

"Delicacy?" I stared down at the dark broth swimming with chunks of meat and vegetables.

"Hotchi-witchi," Magda informed me.

"Hedgehog," Lady Julia added.

"Oh," I said in some surprise.

"Poaching laws have always been strict," Brisbane explained. "They do not dissuade the opportunistic and the hungry, but Romany have learnt to supplement with smaller game—rabbits, squirrels, and hedgehogs to name a few."

"I think it is delicious," Stoker stated, scraping the bottom of his bowl.

Magda gave him a fond smile. "You must have another portion. Keep up your strength, lordling." This time the nickname seemed affectionate, and she ladled out another serving of the stew, taking care to give Stoker the best bits. As they ate, Stoker and Brisbane described the boy we were looking for to Magda, who listened attentively, her gaze fixed upon Stoker's face. She nodded several times and they fell into a quiet, intent conversation. After a few moments, she rose and went to the door, speaking rapidly to the bowler-hatted fellow, who was still lingering outside. When she returned, she gave Stoker the last of the bread, pressing it into his unwilling hands with a gesture of finality.

Lady Julia leaned near to me. "I have never seen Magda quite so accommodating, especially to a gorgio. She worked in my household for some time and still only barely tolerates me."

"Stoker has a curious effect on women of all ages," I told her. "Female creatures of every variety, in fact. They swarm to him like the proverbial moths to his particular flame. I have learnt to expect it."

Her smile was rueful. "I have much the same trouble with Brisbane. I do not doubt his loyalty for a minute, but his previous entanglements have occasionally proven to be excessively annoying."

"I could write a novel about the depredations of Stoker's former wife, and people would think it the grossest exaggeration," I confided.

Lady Julia's eyes narrowed. "Brisbane had a lover in his past who wanted to kill me."

"So does Stoker!" I exclaimed in an excited whisper. "It is consoling to speak to someone who actually understands my situation."

We glanced to where our menfolk were sitting in animated conversation with Magda, the old woman's face agleam with fondness for them both.

Lady Julia sighed. "It is the price one must pay for loving men of such extraordinary talents."

"If only they were not quite so heedless of their own well-being. Does Brisbane do thoroughly reckless things?"

"He once leapt blindly off the roof of a building at full pelt," she told me. "Stoker?"

"Threw himself into the sea to swim an impossible distance to fetch help when I was stranded on a rock being submerged by a rising tide."

"And is he, in spite of this habitual imprudence, almost insultingly obsessed with your own safety?"

"It is a source of constant conflict between us," I assured her.

"Brisbane treats me as if I were made of spun glass," she replied.

"And ought to be wrapped in cotton wool and locked in a box? I am familiar with the mood."

"He is illogical to the point of hysteria about the matter," Lady Julia said. "Just because I have occasionally found myself nearly incinerated. Or exploded. Or poisoned."

"Or drowned. Or carried out to sea and thrown overboard. Or shot," I added, thinking of my own near brushes with death. "What they fail to realise is that these situations have not been of our making. They have been entirely the fault of the criminals we have been pursuing. And furthermore," I added, warming to my theme, "we have indeed faced deadly peril upon numerous occasions; but *we have survived them all.* Would it be so dreadful to actually give us credit for those accomplishments? No, they would rather hover about like overattentive nannies."

"Men," Lady Julia said darkly.

As if sensing our scrutiny, Brisbane and Stoker turned as one and looked at us.

"Stoker," Brisbane said suddenly, "the women are talking. And I do not know about you, but my ears feel distinctly singed."

"As do mine," Stoker agreed. He looked from Lady Julia to me. "What have you two been saying?"

"Nothing of importance," Lady Julia hastened to assure him. She turned to Magda. "Do you know the boy we've come about? The one who may have witnessed a crime?"

"He is a poshrat, like this one," she replied with a nod towards Brisbane.

"He has only half blood?" Lady Julia asked.

Magda shrugged. "His father was one of us, but he married outside of his clan—a thin little gorgio girl who died in childbed her first winter travelling. The boy's father died not long after."

"He is orphaned?" Stoker asked in real concern. His heart was always softened at the thought of any child in peril. Many was the time he had pressed the last coin in his pocket upon a street urchin begging for the price of a bit of bread. And more than once he had handed over a pound note—a veritable fortune—when he had nothing else at hand. "How does the child get by with no family?"

"How do any of us?" Magda returned with a short laugh. "By our wits."

There was a scratching at the door of the vardo, and Magda smiled. "There he is now."

CHAPTER 12

Brisbane reached to open the door and a boy appeared, slender and small, perhaps eight years old, although it was almost impossible to say with certainty. His physique was slight, but his eyes had the watchfulness of experience, and I fancied not much escaped his notice. He was dressed in clothing that was worn but scrupulously clean, the mark of someone who cared for him.

"Thomas," Magda said firmly, "these people wish to ask you questions. You will give them the truth."

He made a swift reply in Romani, and Brisbane answered him back in the same. The boy's expression was one of frank astonishment as Brisbane explained to the rest of us what he had said.

"Thomas wished to know what business Magda had with gorgios, and I requested he speak in English out of courtesy to the rest of you." He made a further remark to Thomas in their language, and I heard the word "poshrat" again, this time delivered with a smile and a gesture towards himself. No doubt Brisbane was attempting to win the lad's confidence by sharing the fact of his own mingled ancestry. The boy continued to look wary but nodded and waited expectantly. Brisbane looked from me to Stoker and made a gesture of encouragement.

"Thomas," I said gently, "you sometimes go to Highgate Cemetery, do you not?"

"Sometimes." His gaze slid from mine, and I realised extracting information from our young source was going to prove a delicate matter. No doubt, like most Romany lads, he spent his time bent upon activities that would earn him a coin or two. And no doubt these activities occupied an area of rather dubious morality.

"I presume you go there to make money?" I suggested.

He shifted and Magda jerked her chin at him, silently ordering him to respond.

"Flowers," he muttered finally. "I collect flowers from the graves, miss."

"To what purpose?" Lady Julia asked.

"To sell," was the blunt reply. "I cut them and tie into nosegays and sell them to passing ladies."

"How very enterprising," I remarked in perfect sincerity. It was a little distasteful to think of him selling grave offerings to the unsuspecting, but one had to admire his entrepreneurial spirit.

He grinned at me, showing a smile missing two front teeth. "I make good money," he assured me.

"I can believe it. Although I suspect the groundskeepers at the cemetery do not approve?" I ventured.

He shrugged one skinny shoulder. "They chase, but they are slow."

"You must be a very observant young man," I told him. "To elude the groundskeepers and the constables? As well as the people who are laying the flowers at the graves."

"I know where to hide," he said. "Many such places in Highgate."

"You must also see interesting things from your hiding places. Did you see a carriage not long ago—a carriage with a dead man?"

He nodded, his eyes widening. "Yes, miss. The carriage is at the kerb for such a long time, I think it is waiting for something. But there is no driver and no horse. So I think perhaps it is empty, and if it is empty—" He broke off with another shrug.

"If it is empty, perhaps there might be something worth taking inside?" I asked.

"Opportunities are gifts from the gods," he answered solemnly. "One must take them or the gods will think you are ungrateful."

The child referred to the gods, but Magda had a crucifix in her caravan, and I had seen candles dedicated to Saint Sara-la-Kali. I realised then that the Roma must wear the religion of their adopted country lightly even as they held firmly to their much older traditions. How very callow we seemed as a nation in comparison! Our Anglican church had been in existence less than four centuries, but the Romany had been worshipping the dark-skinned Sarah at her shrine in the south of France for two millennia.

"But rather than something to sell, you found a dead man," I said.

Thomas nodded, his face clouded. I reminded myself that for all his worldly-wise maturity, he was still a child of tender years. "Tell me about the carriage."

"It were nice enough. Private, but with no markings. Black, the trim picked out in dark green. One of the windows were down, which was what drew my attention, it being such a cold morning."

He paused a moment, then began to speak again as if reciting, slowly and with precision. "He was dressed well and a gorgio. He was the age of that man, I think," he pronounced with a nod towards Stoker. "He was neither thin nor fat, neither tall nor short. His hair was light brown. He were clean enough, close-shaven, but the smell was terrible. His eyes were closed. He looked peaceful, and I thought he was asleep—that is, I thought he had been sick from taking too much wine and were sleeping it off."

"How was he positioned?" I pressed. "What was his physical attitude?"

"Relaxed, miss. Lying back, he was, with one hand to his chest. No ring upon it, or I'd have—" He broke off, colouring slightly.

"Naturally you would have taken it," I suggested. "If a man is careless enough to sleep in public, he must be reconciled to losing his valuables."

A ghost of a grin touched his mouth. "Exactly that, miss. As I say, I looked to his hand, but there were nothing on it, and I might have had a go at the cufflinks but that I saw the—" He swept a finger to his neck, indicating where the puncture marks had been.

"Go on," I urged.

"Two holes, small ones, in the neck. And blood, staining his collar."

"What did you do?"

"I heard the constable coming on his rounds, so I leapt from the carriage, and I ran, miss."

"Very sensible," I told him. "What did you do then?"

"I went into the cemetery, to a place I know where the constable cannot find me. I waited a long time, and I was afraid."

"Afraid the constable would find you this time?"

"No, miss. Afraid the demon that had killed the man would come for me as well."

"The demon? What demon?"

He turned to Magda and rattled off a lengthy sentence in his native tongue. She questioned him sharply, but he pressed his lips closed and would say no more. Magda muttered, then turned to us.

"He saw someone in the graveyard. A witch, he says."

"A witch! Why does he think she was a witch?" I demanded.

Magda shrugged. "She was dressed all in black."

"It is a cemetery and black is the colour of mourning," I reminded her. "Every woman who goes there is dressed in black."

Thomas burst out with another stream of Romani. Magda listened attentively, then translated. "He says she watched him leave the carriage and enter the graveyard. When he noticed her, she put a finger to her lips, a warning to keep his silence."

"Can he describe her further? Any distinguishing marks or peculiarities?" I pressed.

Thomas considered, then gave Magda a rapid answer, his hands sketching the air above his head.

"Her hair—it was very black, as black as night, he says. And she wore it piled up on her head in an old-fashioned style."

"Where did she go?" I asked.

Thomas shook his head, his reply a mumble.

"He did not see her again," Magda explained. "He ran to his special hiding place and waited until he thought it would be safe to leave."

Brisbane, who had been content to let me lead the questioning of our young witness, leant forwards suddenly and fixed the boy with a piercing gaze. "What did you take from the dead man?"

Thomas shied like a frightened pony. "Nothing," he said flatly, but he would not look Brisbane in the eye. Brisbane leant nearer still, pitching his voice even lower. There was no menace in it, only a calm evenness that was somehow worse than any threat might have been.

Thomas started to speak again, but Brisbane shook his head slowly, allowing a small smile to form. Beside me, Lady Julia gave an involuntary shiver.

To my astonishment, the boy reached into his pocket and retrieved something. He threw it in Brisbane's direction before bolting from the caravan. Brisbane caught the object neatly in one hand. The door banged closed and Stoker rose to give chase, but Brisbane waved him off. "The little devil is frightened enough. Besides, if you were to give chase as a gorgio, there would be a dozen Romany men standing between you and the lad even if you caught him."

He opened his hand to examine the object Thomas had thrown. It was a small bag sewn of printed fabric, an old scrap of cotton, perhaps, or a bit of calico, held fast with a knotted drawstring of plaited thread. Brisbane opened the bag to peer inside, but did not disturb the contents. He passed the bag to Magda, who scrutinised as he had done—by sight only.

They exchanged a few words in Romani before Brisbane nodded. "What is it?" Lady Julia asked her husband.

"We call them putsi," he explained. "Many traditions have them. The bag is a sort of amulet, apotropaic in nature. Such bags are filled with any number of things meant to convey luck. The string was knotted seven times, which is also significant. Thomas would have recognised the purpose of the bag when he found it on the dead man. Taking it was not meant to bring him profit," Brisbane finished. "He would have kept it for the sake of the protection it offered."

"Precious little protection it offered to Maurice Quincey," I observed.

Magda had been peering into the bag as we spoke, careful not to disturb the contents. "It is not good to trifle with another's magic," she said, reknotting the bag and handing it back to Brisbane. "Particularly a witch bag."

"A witch bag?" Brisbane asked. "Are you certain?"

She nodded. "There is a small medal inside—the front has the image of a man with a cross and a raven."

"Saint Benedict," Stoker said suddenly.

Magda gave him a look of approbation. "You know your saints."

"I know this one. My mother wore a medal of Saint Benedict until she died. It was buried with her."

"What is the significance of Saint Benedict?" Lady Julia asked.

"The reverse of the medal," Stoker explained. "It always has a series of letters." He broke off and screwed his eyes closed as he thought. "VRSNSMVSMQLIVB," he recited.

"What is that? Some sort of code?" Lady Julia's nose wrinkled up in charming perplexity.

"It stands for the Latin '*Vade retro Santana! Nunquam suade mihi vana. Sunt mana quae libas. Ipse venena bibas!*'"

"'Begone, Satan! Never tempt me with your vanities! What you offer me is evil! Drink your poison yourself,'" I said slowly. "A rough translation but near enough, I think."

"It sounds like a prayer of exorcism," Lady Julia replied.

"That is precisely what it is," Stoker told her.

"Such tokens are created with an eye to protecting one from malevolent spells," Brisbane added. "Many Romany make and sell them."

"Is it possible to trace this one?" I asked.

Brisbane glanced at Magda, who shook her head. "No. The fabric is not remarkable, it may have come from anywhere. And the contents are what one would expect to find in a bag for protection—dried vervain and a small iron nail. There is the medal, which is common enough, as Stoker says. Also inside is a bit of salt and the foot of a black rabbit. Anyone might have made this."

Stoker turned to Magda. "You are certain it is not one of yours?"

She sniffed. "I prefer peppermint to vervain."

"I wish Thomas had not left us so abruptly. I was not finished questioning him," I protested.

Magda waved a hand. "It is of no consequence. He will say nothing more to you. He is frightened."

"Magda, I assure you, we would protect him from whoever murdered this fellow," Stoker told her.

"You cannot protect him from forces beyond this world," she said, crossing herself.

Lady Julia emitted a little sigh of exasperation. "We came for the name of a murderer, not talk of demons and witches."

"You came for information and you have some," Magda reminded her as she pointed to the charm bag. "The man who carried this was afraid of some malevolent creature. God help you if you find him."

CHAPTER 13

With no more to be gleaned from the formidable Magda, we took our leave then. She handed Stoker the putsi, pressing it into his palm and folding his fingers closed around it.

"You should carry this," she instructed.

"That is very kind. But you have already given me an amulet of protection," he reminded her, touching the hagstone through his shirt.

She canted her head, raising a brow at him. "Do you think you have enough good luck to turn up your nose at more?"

He laughed and raised her hand to his lips, pressing a courtly kiss to the back of it. "Thank you, Magda."

"You will come again, anytime you wish," she instructed. She flicked a glance in my direction. "Do not feel obliged to bring the woman."

He laughed again and we left her then. I took the opportunity to ask Lady Julia where she had met Magda.

"Oh, she was my laundress for a time. Romany women will sometimes take on domestic service, usually to supplement their earnings, but in Magda's case, I think it was simply to avail herself of the opportunity to sell her charms and potions to a captive audience. She was forever telling my friends they were cursed and she would happily remove the malefic influences for a small sum." She paused to smile. "But I never begrudged her. I think she was fascinated by how the gorgios live and wanted to try her hand at it. Do you know, it was the first time she slept under a roof that didn't move!"

"Did she enjoy it?" I asked. We had moved back through the circle of vardos and were making our way down the line of staked horses. One or two of the animals raised their heads as we passed, and one whickered gently by way of greeting.

"For a little while," Lady Julia told me. "But she found our domestic arrangements unhygienic and was happy enough to leave us." She pitched her voice to a confiding tone. "She could not bear the fact that we had an indoor water closet. The Romany do not think it clean to attend to one's private business in the same building where one eats and sleeps. When the Romany camp by a river, they are extremely strict about which items are washed upriver and in which order. They are far cleaner than we, I assure you."

I did not doubt it. It was an endless battle to try to keep George the hallboy even halfway clean, and he had access to as much hot water and soap as he could use. Yet young Thomas, orphaned and running wild, had appeared without a speck of grime upon either his person or his clothes.

Just then, I heard Brisbane's name cried out, and an enormous bear of a man stepped out of the flickering light of one of the campfires. He hailed Brisbane with a wide grin, his teeth gleaming white in the black bush of his beard. Brisbane returned the affection of the greeting, and they exchanged an embrace embellished with claps to the back and light punches to the belly.

"Oh, dear," Lady Julia murmured.

"What is it?" Stoker inquired.

"It was too much to hope that we would be able to slip away without his kinfolk learning we were here," she said. Several other men came forwards, each calling greetings in mingled English and Romani. Brisbane turned and grinned at his wife, gave us a quick salute, and was borne away by the crowd. Lady Julia shrugged her shoulders apologetically. "They have not always been welcoming, so we are grateful a rapprochement has been reached. They will expect us to stay for some time—perhaps the night. And there will be more food. *Much* more food. If you don't want to sleep on a pallet in someone's vardo, you will leave now," she warned. "Take our carriage. Just send the driver back."

I was sorely tempted to accept the hospitality of the travellers, but I thought of J. J. back at Bishop's Folly, no doubt still recumbent in her misery.

"We will leave you with our thanks," Stoker told her.

She smiled her singularly charming smile. "I am only sorry it was not more informative." She pressed my hand. "Do say you will come to dinner soon. I must see more of you both!"

Before I could reply, she was off, folded into a group of Romany women who exclaimed happily upon seeing her, chattering like so many brightly plumed birds as they welcomed her.

Stoker looped his arm through mine. "I know you would have liked to stay, but I have had my fill of sleeping in wagons."

I grinned. "I seem to recall sharing a wagon with you for a short period. It was most illuminating." In the course of our first investigation, we had been forced to seek sanctuary with the travelling show that had once been his home.* It had been my introduction to the itinerant life, and while it had forged an immediate intimacy between us—one cannot share a small sleeping space with a man without *learning* things—it had not been precisely comfortable.

"I was thinking of J. J.," I told him. "She oughtn't to be left alone whilst she is feeling so lowly."

---

* *A Curious Beginning*

Stoker rolled his eyes. "She is indulging in a fit of the morbs, nothing more. She is capable, resourceful, and clever. To hear her speak of her lodgings, they were truly dire. She is better off away from them. Moreover, she was utterly wasted writing for that rag. I wouldn't use the *Harbinger* to wipe dog muck from my boots."

This was patently absurd, as I had seen Stoker satisfy his prurient curiosity on more than one occasion by indulging in a quick flick through the pages when he thought himself unobserved. But as it happened, I agreed with him. J. J.'s lodgings had been catastrophically uncomfortable, fit more for the habitation of mice and the occasional enterprising rat rather than a human. And her position at the *Harbinger* had always been at the whim of the editor, a capricious and vicious man who had not deserved to make use of her talents. J. J.'s current misfortunes might well be clouds lavishly lined with silver, if only she could be persuaded to view them as such.

We had come to the end of the encampment, the campfires and calling voices left behind. The warmth of the little settlement, however temporary, had been real, fashioned out of their own will and their meagre resources. It was something of a marvel.

"It has been my first time in a proper Romany camp," I said. "What do you think of them?"

He shrugged. "They pass through and they take nothing, at least nothing that is of importance. Whatever is essential to them they carry always—their family names, their traditions, their language. Whatever customs we try to impose upon them, they make a pose of accepting, but they do so only as far as necessity demands. They are always and authentically themselves. There is much to admire in that."

"Indeed." I fell silent then, brooding a little. As if sensing my mood, Stoker nudged my arm.

"Penny for them."

"I was merely reflecting on the fact that however interesting this interlude has been—and however glad I am to have made the acquaintance of the Brisbanes—our outing has been singularly unproductive. We are no closer to finding this mysterious Ruthven character than we were before—to say nothing of the Harpocrates Society."

We continued walking, Stoker silent as I carried on, indulging in a modest rant. "We know only that Maurice Quincey was afraid of someone, afraid enough to purchase a charm against magic, but that tells us nothing of significance. We cannot question the families of the men who were murdered, for fear of offending them or compromising Mornaday. Young Thomas is too afraid to tell us more, even if he knows anything, which I seriously doubt. And you . . ." I paused to nod towards his burgeoning collection of talismans. "Are apparently marked for death, which I find a trifle unsettling."

"You? How do you think I feel? I am the one who is doomed," he returned with a lightness of tone I could not quite match. I was a rationalist, a woman of science, and yet there had been something deeply affecting in the experience in Magda's vardo. There was much for which science could not yet account, and I was not so foolish as to dismiss the possibility of things beyond my ken. After all, would not a mediaeval peasant find it astonishing that we could be inoculated against smallpox? Explain to a person of that limited understanding that there were organisms too small to be seen with the naked eye that were responsible for disease, and they would think you possessed—or mad, at the very least. And yet we now understood the theory of germs and that handwashing was a critical component of proper hygiene. Would science someday be able to explain the existence of creatures that had only previously been discussed in terrified whispers? Were there such beings as vampires, nourished by blood and cursed to walk in darkness?

We had reached the carriage by this point and Stoker handed me in, calling instructions to the driver. We settled ourselves, and Stoker interrupted my mental peregrinations. "We did discover something," he said as the driver sprang the horses.

"What is that?" I demanded.

"Thomas described the scene in the carriage in detail. The one thing he did not remark upon was an excess of blood."

"Of course there was no excess of blood," I said. "The body, according to Mornaday, was fully exsanguinated."

"Yes," he returned in a tone of exaggerated patience, "but where was it? If Quincey had been killed by means of the wounds in his throat, he would have been soaked in gore. Thomas himself could not have escaped slipping in the stuff. The quantity necessary to drain a man of life would remain puddled for quite some hours, even if the weather was chilly, as Thomas remarked. It would be thick and sticky, but it would not be dry. It would have marked Thomas's clothes, and more importantly, it would have been a gory and memorable sight for the boy. He would not have forgot so significant an image."

"Again, Mornaday said there was no blood," I replied.

"*Then where did it go?*" Stoker asked through gritted teeth. He held up a quelling hand as I opened my mouth to reply. "Do not, I beg you, invoke the notion of vampires again."

"A vampire would account for the lack of blood," I muttered.

"It bloody well would not!" he thundered. "What we can deduce—as scientists and people of actual logic—is that Maurice Quincey was killed elsewhere and then put into the carriage. That is all."

"You cannot know—"

"I bloody well can!" he roared.

The driver rapped on the roof of the carriage. "Everything all right, sir?"

"Perfectly," Stoker returned tightly. "My companion is merely being entirely irrational in the application of reason."

"Aye, 'tis often the way with ladies," the driver agreed.

"It most certainly is not," I said, thrusting my head out of the window to be heard a little better. "Mr. Templeton-Vane is the one refusing to keep an open mind about a line of scientific inquiry."

"Scientific?" Stoker gave a shout of laughter. "It is superstitious nonsense of the sort I cannot believe you are entertaining for the briefest of moments. It is utter and complete *bollocks*."

"Language, Stoker," I chided. I turned back to address the driver. "I do apologise for his vocabulary. He tends to get a little heated when discussing science."

"Think nothing of it, miss," he said, touching the brim of his cap. "I've heard plenty worse and no mistake."

"From Mr. Brisbane?" I ventured.

"Lady Julia, if I'm honest, miss," he replied.

"How very unexpected." I settled back into my seat and regarded Stoker. "At least your profanity is keeping good company. I suspect it is the refuge of the noble class if you and Lady Julia are both in the habit of improper language."

"Do not derail this conversation," Stoker said, his gaze agleam with mischief. "You distinctly said that vampires might possibly exist."

"This is not new information," I returned waspishly. "I said so earlier."

"And I admit I had hoped you spoke in jest. I cannot take you seriously if you continue to claim that this Ruthven character might be an actual vampire. What next? Ghouls? Werewolves?"

"Shall I bring up the wolpertinger *again*?" I asked.

"By god, I do love it when you are in a temper," he said, reaching for me with purpose.

I clicked my tongue at him and held up a hand. "Not now, dearest. We have arrived."

Pleading a need to see how J. J. was getting on, I bade Stoker a good night and left him looking hungrily after me at the door of my little folly. J. J. had already turned in for the night, availing herself of my bed with assorted dogs piled hither and yon. I crept about quietly, poking up the fire and changing into my nightdress and a dressing gown. J. J. was snoring gently, but I was too restless for sleep. I had carried down a stack of books from the Belvedere, and perhaps they would prove a cure for my wakefulness. I wrapped a quilt about my shoulders and settled onto the sofa. My earlier researches on vampirism had been fruitful, but I was certain there was more to know—more that might help me persuade Stoker to at least consider the possibility of the existence of a creature beyond our understanding.

The first book was a slender volume of the folklore of Styria complete with harrowing illustrations of the damage a motivated vampire could inflict. There was even a chapter detailing precisely what one must do to send the revenant back into eternity. I skimmed that bit and reached for the next book. This was Roumanian, thick with phrases from that tongue—words such as "strigoi" and "pricolici" that defied my attempts at pronunciation. The heaviest of the volumes was an antique copy of *The Glory of the Duchy of Carniola*, a first edition published in 1689 in High German. From what I could gather—my command of German was almost nonexistent and I read with a dictionary in hand—there had been four volumes of the *Glory*, and we had only one in the Belvedere library. But the book contained the earliest information I could find about vampires, relating the story of a stonemason who terrorised his family and village for sixteen years after his death. The villagers twice attempted to kill him by stabbing him with a hawthorn stick, hawthorn being frequently used against witches and other powerful creatures. But both times the stick had failed to penetrate the undead flesh, leaving them with no option but to decapitate the supposed vampire. Only then did peace settle upon the little town.

I could well imagine a mob of villagers, stakes and pitchforks in hand, torches lighting their path as they made their way to the graveyard, determined to put down this murderous fiend once and for all. He would be pale, of course, from his nocturnal habits, and he would smell of decay from his coffin bed. He would be confident of his powers, I supposed. He had eluded all threats for well over a decade, striking fear into the hearts of those who would see him banished into the netherworld. By night he held sway over their village, creeping from house to house. It was said if a householder heard a knock at the door, they knew the strigoi had come for them. Did he ever speak? I wondered. Or did he assault them in merciless silence? And did they crow with bloodlust as they took his head? Or was the relief at the end of their misery heralded only by a wary stillness lest they awaken other restless spirits?

I could hear the steps of their roughly shod feet as they entered the graveyard, leather soles scraping on the stones, the thunk of graveyard dirt being shovelled away, the grating rasp of the coffin lid being pushed aside. They would have tightened their scarves over their mouths and noses, those villagers, careful not to let the poisonous night air into their lungs. And when at last they had uncovered the monster, the scarves would have muffled their gasps of horror. Which of them had been brave enough to strike the first blow? A strong lad, coming forward with the eagerness of youth? Or had it been a sturdy farmer who had withstood a dozen years at the plough? Or a housewife, forearms made taut from the toil of drawing water from the village well and kneading bread. She would have knowledge, a housewife would, of how to decapitate from years of putting chickens into stewpots. Or perhaps it was the blacksmith, hands toughened at the forge and muscles bulging as he bent to his work, sawing furiously through sinew and bone until he rose with that terrible trophy in his grasp, the vampire's head borne aloft for all to see. I could picture it as clearly as if I had been there in the crowd, waiting for the creature's reign of terror to be brought to its grisly end, heart in my throat as the dark deed was done. I would have raised my torch in triumph, a palpable and exquisite relief coursing through me as I shouted my approbation. But just then the head swung in the blacksmith's hand, its face swivelling towards me. The mouth opened and the tongue, black and swollen, came out as the sightless eyes stared into mine. I screamed, but the tongue kept coming, the tip of it touching my cheek as I continued to scream, louder and louder—

"Veronica!" One of the villagers had me by the shoulders, shaking me hard, and I opened my eyes.

"J. J.?" I blinked several times, bringing her into focus, a bright nimbus of light about her head.

"Yes, it is J. J.," she said. "You were having a dream. A dreadful one from the sound of it," she said. "Get *off*." This last was said to Betony, the Caucasian sheepdog that had been licking my cheek. The dog obediently left off its washing of my face, and I sat up, groggy and dazed from the dream. The hearth was cold, the fire having long since died, and morning sunlight streamed through the stained glass of the chapel windows, scattering patterns of blue and red and gold across the floor.

"No wonder you had a nightmare," J. J. said, surveying the books scattered around me. Several were open to gruesome illustrations of vampire stories. "These are foul."

But I noticed she set to leafing through them just the same. There was a pot of tea, and I poured a steaming cup as much to banish the remnants of the dream as to warm myself.

"Any luck last night?" she inquired.

"None to speak of," I admitted. "We found the boy, but he told us nothing of significance. The only new piece of information we acquired was the fact that Maurice Quincey was afraid, deeply so. He carried a sort of talisman in his pocket—proof against witches."

"Witches? I thought we were hunting a vampire," J. J. said, tapping one of the books.

"We are hunting nothing at present," I said in some annoyance. "The trail has gone cold, and the game is no longer afoot but rather resting comfortably in some quiet burrow, away from our gaze. What have you discovered in your researches?"

She shrugged. "Nothing of importance. I have asked every one of my contacts about the Harpocrates Society, and there is not the slenderest thread to pluck. One or two have heard rumours about it, but they all come down to the same thing—a private club, entry strictly by invitation, and an emphasis on perfect secrecy. It seems impenetrable."

"That is that, then," I sighed.

"Are there no clues we can chase?" she asked.

"None," I assured her morosely. "The case, such as it is, seems to have ended as suddenly as it began."

To my astonishment and horror, tears filled her eyes. She dashed them away with the back of her hand, turning aside. I had so seldom seen her give way to the softer emotions that I hardly knew how to respond. The loss of her livelihood and her home, undesirable as they had been, had clearly devastated her. And with this investigation—the only prospect she had for rescuing her career—at a standstill, hope must well and truly have seemed lost.

I reached to comfort her, my fingers on her sleeve.

"J. J., we will find something, I promise you."

She pulled her arm away, but not ungently. "I am sure I do not know what you mean. I merely have a bit of dust in my eye. You really ought to clean better in here, Veronica. Your housekeeping skills are atrocious."

She gave a deep sniff and began turning pages again. I sighed. She might not wish to surrender to her despair, but I could smell it just the same. I rose. "I am going to dress and go to the Belvedere for breakfast. I will see you later." J. J. made a flapping motion with her hand, her eyes fixed firmly upon the page.

As I dressed, I reflected on the problem before us. "How do you find a vampire?" I muttered to myself.

But in the end, it was the vampire who found us.

CHAPTER 14

The breakfast things had just been cleared and Stoker and I had settled companionably to our respective jobs when George appeared with the morning post.

"Late today," Stoker called.

"Sorry, sir," George replied, his cheeks full as a chipmunk's. "Cook made jam tarts." That was a sufficient explanation for any tardiness. Cook's jam tarts, with exquisitely light pastry and filled with her own plum preserves, were one of George's favourite indulgences, his enthusiasm matched only by Stoker's.

"I hope to heaven you've brought me one," Stoker told him.

George grinned and reached into his pocket, offering a squashed tart on a grubby palm. It looked almost indecent, but Stoker was not fussy. His own hands were already smeared with two colours of ink and dotted with tiny feathers. He opened his mouth and George tossed the tart in an arc that went only a little wide. Stoker stretched to the side and caught it midair, downing it in a single bite as I flicked through the post.

The envelope was on the top, a heavy thing of expensive paper with the watermark of an exclusive London shop that catered to the most illustrious of clients. The handwriting was elegant and old-fashioned, each letter precisely perfect—a distinctive hand, to be certain, but an unfamiliar one. It was addressed to both of us, so I reached for the Nepalese kukri I was currently using as a paper knife and slit the envelope. There was a single piece of card inside, the paper formally printed with a coat of arms impressed on the top of it. I read the words twice over, scarcely believing my eyes.

"What is it?" Stoker asked, rubbing the crumbs from his mouth on his sleeve.

"It is an invitation."

"We do occasionally indulge in a social life," Stoker said dryly. "Why do you look so amazed?"

"Because our host is Lord Ruthven himself." I held up the card for his inspection. "He wishes us to call upon him late this evening."

The missive was short and direct.

My dear Miss Speedwell and Mr. Templeton-Vane, I hope you will forgive my forwardness in presuming an acquaintance when we have not been formally introduced. I further hope you will oblige me by calling upon me at my home this evening at ten o'clock. Yours most sincerely.

Unlike the fluid and elegant hand of the note itself, the signature was bold, slashing capitals. RUTHVEN.

"Someone knows their *Debrett's*," he observed as he turned from the card to the envelope, noting that it was properly addressed to Miss Veronica Speedwell and the Honourable Revelstoke Templeton-Vane.

He handed the card back, and I read over it for a third time, attempting to parse some hidden meaning from the scant lines. Was it a challenge? Or lure to a trap? "He specifies ten o'clock. A curiously late hour for visitors, and you notice he does not ask us to dine with him."

Stoker grinned. "Of course not. Vampires do not eat dinner, and they famously do not rise before sunset."

I met his smile with a mirthless one of my own. "Jest if you wish, but we are going. This is our one and only clue."

"And you mean to walk directly into the home of a man who might be a murderer simply because he requests it? I should expect nothing less of you, my dearest."

I replaced the note into the envelope and gave my attention to the rest of the post as Stoker made to return to his work. Almost as an afterthought, he turned back, mischief tweaking the corners of his mouth.

"Oh, and mind you wear a high-necked gown, Veronica—for protection. Your neck is utterly delectable, and I wouldn't want Ruthven getting ideas."

J. J. was naturally put out that she could not accompany us, but as I pointed out to her, the invitation was formal and clearly addressed only to Stoker and to me. We left her in the Belvedere, surrounded by stacks of files and books, and once more in the company of the dogs, looking even more disheveled and woebegone than she had the previous night.

"The longer she spends with the dogs, the more she comes to resemble them," I told Stoker as we left Bishop's Folly. "If we do not soon find her some useful occupation, I fear she will begin to grow fur and scratch fleas."

Stoker made no reply. He fairly vibrated with anticipation, and it occurred to me that for all his insistence that vampires could not possibly exist, he possessed enough imagination to at least wonder if he might be wrong. The possibility that we were striding into the lion's—or vampire's—den with the potential to be torn apart simply added a fillip of enjoyment to my evening. There is nothing like the chance of a bloody death to heighten one's appreciation of life and one's senses. As we travelled north—to a neighbourhood adjacent to Highgate Cemetery, I noted with interest—I observed that the evening air had never smelt so pungently of coal smoke and the effluent of horses; the pall of soot hanging in the air had never presented such a picture of shifting veils. My blood thrummed with delight, and I wondered idly if it were the sort of thing a vampire could hear. I was immensely glad I had—in *spite* of Stoker's advice, not because of it, I must insist—dressed in a high-necked gown of dark violet velvet. About my throat I had knotted a narrow black silk scarf. I tried to offer the same to Stoker, but he waved me off with a snort of derision.

"Very well, but if you find yourself with fangs embedded in your carotid artery, you have only yourself to blame," I warned him.

"My carotid? Surely a vampire would strike for the jugular," he argued. "It is, after all, more conveniently located for quick exsanguination."

"But the carotid carries fresh blood," I reminded him. "I expect a vampire would wish for the most nourishing variety of food. Most creatures do."

Stoker stroked his chin thoughtfully. "If they feed solely on blood, then they would be classified as carrion eaters—and carrion eaters do not take their nourishment fresh."

"Carrion eaters! What tosh. The Desmodontinae are not classified as carrion eaters."

He regarded me with an expression of utter amusement tinged with reproach. "You have been reading up on vampire bats. Veronica, really."

"One must know one's enemy," I replied loftily.

"I would dearly love to hear more about how you have prepared to fight an undead revenant, but it appears we have arrived."

. . .

The house was—at a guess—late Tudor in style, built of dark grey stone and festooned with stonework embellishments including a pair of melancholic-looking carved dogs perched above the porch. But if I had expected something more Gothic and sinister, I was disappointed. A heavy veil of ivy shrouded the walls, but the path was neatly swept, and there was not a cobweb to be seen. The hedges were tall but orderly. I confess the house was something of a letdown after I had spent the drive allowing my imagination to have free rein. Where were the turrets, high and pointed as a witch's hat? Where was the moat in which something unspeakable stirred from slumber? And where was the stout door, deep in shadow, that opened of its own accord as we approached? The front door of this house was thrown open, to be sure, but a woman stood in the pool of golden light of the entry. She was dressed all in black, her hair so pitilessly dark it must have been dyed. It was coiled high upon her head, giving her extra height, for she was not a tall woman. But she carried herself well, and her gown, old-fashioned and unusual, heightened the impression that she was a creature out of step with time.

A lady dressed all in black with her raven hair piled atop her head—surely this was young Thomas's graveyard witch! I trod gently on Stoker's toe to alert him to the significance.

"You came," she said by way of welcome. Her mouth curved into a small smile, but whether it was sincere or at our expense, I could not say.

"We did," I returned robustly. "But I am afraid you have the advantage of us."

I waited for her to give her name, but instead she merely widened the smile, showing small, pearly teeth. "Indeed I do. Follow me."

She turned and led the way into the house, and when the door closed behind us, there was a note of finality I did not like.

Much of the interior of the house was in shadow, for few of the lamps had been lit, and those that had were heavily shaded. I was conscious of the warmth of the house as we moved further inside. The walls were hung with dark red wallpaper and between the colour and the heat, it felt as if we were moving into the heart of a living thing. We passed several closed doors before coming to one which she threw back with a theatrical gesture. To my surprise, before us lay a conservatory. Fashioned of delicate ironwork and set with glass panels, it was much warmer than the rest of the house, and that was an impressive feat considering the heat we had already encountered.

"I hope you do not mind the temperature," the woman said as she led us into the conservatory. We passed through a curtain of palm fronds and found a little clearing where a table and chairs of iron had been grouped. A few scattered cushions of dark red silk softened the seats, and she waved us towards them. "I am afraid his lordship is sensitive to the cold, and of course, it would not do my plants any good to be touched by frost." She gestured towards the towering foliage that surrounded us, waves of greenery of every variety. There were plants with broad fronds that dipped their lacy palmettes towards the ground and plants with luscious flowers bursting into bloom and lending spicy-sweet scent to the humid air. There were trees lifting slender trunks towards the roof and shrubs which reached serpentine fingers to vine across the floor. The effect was one of chaos and beauty in equal measure.

The woman seated herself on one of the iron chairs, arranging her skirts in a graceful pool of ebony at her feet. On the table before her was a tea service with an elegant Chinese motif. It was a play upon the willow pattern usually rendered in blue. This was glazed in blood red and featured the image of an aristocrat, perhaps even an emperor, standing in a solitary pose on a bridge beneath the gracefully bent arms of a willow. Below him, a female figure floated in the water. The figure was too small to see whether she were alive or dead, but I fancied I knew the answer to that. Above the gentleman and his lady flew a bird of prey, circling the scene, perhaps in anticipation of its next meal. In the background, an elegant pagoda was in flames. Every image was one of catastrophe or woe. To the side of the tea table, a small paraffin stove held a steaming kettle of brightly polished copper, lending an air of refined domesticity to the scene. Behind our hostess, an unusual plant rose towards the ceiling, its stems laden with creamy white bells as long as my hand, each petal gently pointed at the end. It looked a rapacious thing, fairly throttling the lesser plants that had the misfortune to grow near it.

"I see you are admiring my devil's trumpet," she said, touching one fingernail to the petals.

"It is a handsome specimen," I told her honestly. A flutter of something ghostly white in the shadows caught my attention then. It was a wing, almost as large as my hand. As it flapped past, I saw the distinctive markings of deep chocolate brown.

"*Thysania agrippina*!" I exclaimed. They were a rare sight in these islands, being native to the neotropics. I had never seen one in person, but Lord Rosemorran had a first edition of Maria Sibylla Merian's *Metamorphosis Insectorum Surinamensium* from 1705 in which the moth was described for the first time in a scientific publication. (It was an excellent book, although I far preferred her wonderfully titled *The Caterpillars' Marvelous Transformation and Strange Floral Food*.)

"The white witch moth," our hostess said, giving me a look of grudging admiration. "You know your moths, my dear. These are my particular delight. They emerge every evening about this time. That is why this is my favourite spot to take tea."

She moved gracefully amongst the tea things, filling the curious pot with several spoonsful of tea leaves—a mixture of the expected *Camellia sinensis* as well as other less obvious things, dried bits of berry and leaf and even a twig or two. Over this she poured the steaming water, gently swirling the teapot before setting it down to steep.

Only then did she look up, a tiny smile playing once more upon her lips. "I have been very rude, forgive me. Miss Speedwell, Mr. Templeton-Vane, I have been asked by his lordship to make you welcome until he is available to receive you. I am Asphodel."

I felt my brows rise towards my hairline. "Asphodel? Like the flower?"

She inclined her head, and I noted once more the theatricality of her gestures. "Precisely, Miss Speedwell. You are very well-read."

I smiled modestly at the compliment. "The meadows of Asphodel are well-known to any student of the mythology of the Greeks. They comprise part of the dominion of Hades, Lord of the Underworld. I believe these meadows are where the ordinary folk dwell after death. Pity there are no heroes for you in that realm."

Stoker must have sensed something of my instinctive antipathy for the woman, for he cleared his throat, drawing her attention to himself.

"This is a charming spot for tea. How clever of you to think of it."

The smile deepened, and I no longer saw the resemblance to a cat. She was more vulpine in appearance, I decided. "I am never happier than when I am with my plants. I am a veritable daughter of Rappaccini," she added with a sly look in my direction. Perhaps she meant to test her conclusion that I was well-read, but I would give no quarter. I bared my teeth at her. "From the story by the American author Nathaniel Hawthorne," I returned. "About a woman who has been reared on her father's most venomous plants and is therefore immune to their toxins. But I seem to recall that even her breath was fatal to others. Difficult to make friends in that case, I should think."

She leant nearer to Stoker. "You need have no fear on that score. Does my breath seem poisonous to you, Mr. Templeton-Vane?" She moved closer still, her décolletage spilling from her neckline as she parted pillowy lips to blow out a soft exhalation against his cheek. I saw the curls at his ear ruffle gently, and he flushed.

"No, no—quite sweet," he said, not meeting my gaze.

If Asphodel and I had been sparring, that would have been a palpable hit, I conceded. I decided to defer any sort of further engagement in hostilities and nodded towards the teapot. "I think it has steeped long enough."

It was unconscionably rude of me to hurry her along, but I was in no mood for pleasantries over the tea table. I was too impatient to meet the man who had invited us here, and this enforced interaction with his—associate? guest? inamorata?—beginning to strain my nerves.

As if sensing my mood, she poured out the tea, handing me a cup that steamed fragrantly. I took an appreciative sniff, letting the perfumed warmth of it settle into my bones.

"That is the jasmine," she said, watching me closely. "It is meant to calm the nerves."

I sipped, and the heady floweriness of the aroma became the taste upon my tongue. "There is black tea for hospitality and robustness of flavour. There are rose petals for calmness and green tea for serenity. And a few other things besides, but you cannot expect me to give up all my secrets," she said, passing Stoker a cup of his own.

"Do you always blend your own teas?" Stoker asked politely.

"I make more than teas," she assured him, and somehow it sounded faintly salacious when she said it.

She poured a final cup for herself, but I noticed there was no fourth.

"Lord Ruthven does not take tea," she said, noticing the direction of my gaze.

"Does he prefer stronger libations?" I asked innocently.

"The strongest," she said with a strange little laugh.

She turned to Stoker. "Tell me, Mr. Templeton-Vane, about your work."

I was surprised at the directness of her request, but Stoker obliged her, describing his various commissions as a natural historian specialising in the restoration of mounted specimens.

"The taxidermic arts!" she exclaimed, eyes bright. "How fascinating. Have you been following the story of the walrus? Highly passionate discourse around such an exotic creature."

She could not have introduced a more alluring subject to Stoker if she had tried. "The fellows responsible for this particular disgrace ought to be horsewhipped," Stoker said fervently. "Imagine dealing such disrespect to an animal as majestic as *Odobenus rosmarus*. And do not get me started on the travesty they have made of his mystacial vibrissae."

Asphodel seemed vaguely confused at this, and I decided to offer her at least a token bit of assistance.

"The whiskers," I murmured.

"The whiskers," Stoker affirmed. "In the case of the walrus, it is believed that, as with domesticated and wild cats, they can aid in helping the animal to orient itself, but it is entirely possible they serve another function—that of detecting the presence of food. The walrus, you see, is the only carnivorous—"

He might have gone on in this vein for some time. (I have known Stoker to converse heatedly on the subject of capybaras for fully two hours, and he is much fonder of walruses than capybaras.) I would have let him hold forth on the grounds that it would serve our hostess right for playing up so shamelessly to him, but just as Stoker began to expand upon the subject of carnivorous pinnipeds, Asphodel looked up sharply, her expression instantly softening to one of devotion. When she spoke, her voice rasped a little, as if her throat were choked with emotion. "He is coming!" she said in a thrilled whisper. And as she set her cup down, I noticed that her hand trembled.

I had heard nothing of his approach, and neither had Stoker, I thought, for he was mid-sip and forced to hastily set down his cup. There was no footstep to be heard, no susurration of breath, no sound of human movement at all. He was, one moment, not there, and then suddenly he was in evidence, sheltered by the tallest of the trees—a figure dressed entirely in black, a deeper darkness than the shadows in which he stood.

"Good evening," he said, stepping forwards and into the low light. "I am Ruthven. Welcome to my home."

CHAPTER 15

As entrances go, it was a fine one. Any tragic actor would have been proud of it. To move with such grace and silence into the pool of light to command our attention—Edwin Booth himself could not have done better. But it was not only Ruthven's gestures which drew our gaze. The man himself was of intriguing appearance. To begin with, his complexion was pale as a new moon with a curious quicksilver quality to the skin. The eyes were dark and piercing, the lashes very thick and black. His hair was the same impenetrable ebony as Asphodel's, and he was likewise dressed in shades of deepest mourning with a magnificent ruby pin adorning his black silk cravat. Only the white of his shirt stood out, crisp and clean and perfectly pressed. I could not imagine Asphodel bending to the more demanding tasks of domestic work, and I realised I had thus far seen no servants, heard no signs of those who must cook and wash and lay fires. It was a curious omission.

Before I could ride this train of thought much further, Lord Ruthven approached us. He put out a hand to take mine, and I was astonished to find that his flesh was icy cold, the fingertips nearly blue. "Miss Speedwell," he murmured as he bent over my hand. He did not touch it with his lips but released it almost immediately before turning to Stoker.

"And Mr. Templeton-Vane. How kind of you both to answer my invitation. I hope it did not cause you to disarrange your plans."

He settled himself in the empty chair, crossing one long, elegant leg over the other. He had not looked at or spoken to Asphodel, but something in the air had changed, and I fancied they were able—as were Stoker and I—to communicate without words.

"Not at all," I assured him. "We were most interested to make your acquaintance."

"How very kind," he murmured with a smile. He flicked a glance to Asphodel, who sipped demurely at her tea. "I hope Asphodel has made you welcome?"

"Quite." If the word was a little clipped, Lord Ruthven seemed not to notice it.

"Has she taken you on a tour of the conservatory?" he inquired.

"There was no time, my love," Asphodel answered. "I had only just got to the serving of tea. You were early."

He spread his hands in an elegant gesture of apology to us. "I hope you will forgive my little eccentricities, but I do not receive guests during daylight hours."

I did not look at Stoker, but I could feel his interest pique. "Do your hobbies keep you busy?" he asked our host.

Lord Ruthven gave a light laugh. "Hobbies! What an excellent sense of humour you have, my friend. No, it is more that my health is somewhat demanding. I find that if I sleep during the day and am awake at night, I am much more—" He paused and turned his gaze deliberately in my direction. "Energised."

Asphodel stiffened like an offended cat, but his lordship ignored her. He also swiftly changed the subject, giving his attention to Stoker. "I understand you are curious about the Harpocrates Society."

"Who told you that?" Stoker returned swiftly.

"I have friends"—again that airy, dismissive gesture of the supple hands—"everywhere. Tell me, is it true? Do you wish to know more of what we do here?"

"I am curious," Stoker said. His posture was relaxed, but it was the ease of a predator just before it pounces on an unsuspecting creature.

"Excellent! You are a man of science, I understand. Naturally you are aware that there are many mysteries that human intelligence has not yet learnt to penetrate."

"Many," Stoker agreed.

"But there are those gifted few who sometimes are privileged enough to see a little more than others, to pierce the veils that separate our world from the rest."

"The rest?" I asked. Lord Ruthven did not address his reply to me, continuing to speak only to Stoker.

"Surely you realise there are worlds beyond our own?" he challenged.

Stoker's expression was cool. "Do I?"

Lord Ruthven smiled, and I noted he was careful to keep his lips pressed together. Did he wish to conceal something curious about his smile? Long, pointed canine teeth, perhaps? He went on, his tone amiable. "Of course you do, my friend. You are an intelligent man, a fellow of rare perception. You have sensed at times that there is more to life, more to know than just what we can see and hear and touch." He paused and flicked those remarkable eyes in my direction before returning to stare once more at Stoker.

"Perhaps," Stoker said slowly, as if conceding the point. "One cannot explain away everything with science, however much one would like to."

"And you wish to know what is unknowable, do you not? To have your preconceptions challenged, your ideas tested? To strip away what has been inculcated in you through education and expectation and reveal what is new and beyond the bounds of understanding?" asked his lordship in a voice of seductive encouragement. "Would you not like at least a taste of that?"

"Certainly," Stoker replied.

Throughout this exchange, Asphodel was silent, sipping her tea and watching the two men spar. "And now you would like to experience for yourself what may lie beyond the senses, what truths may be revealed." He broke off suddenly. "But your cup is empty! Asphodel, you have been remiss," he chided gently.

Asphodel moved forward, skirts rustling softly as she poured a fresh cup for Stoker. "Drink it while it is hot," she urged.

My own cup was nearly empty, but no one seemed distressed by this in the slightest. Instead Lord Ruthven continued to speak as Stoker drank his tea. His voice was low and melodic, a beautiful instrument he had learnt to play like a virtuoso, pitching it into an intimate timbre that might have lured nightingales from the trees. As he talked, he toyed with the pin in his cravat, a ruby of impressive proportions. It gleamed in the lamplight, conjuring shimmering scarlet sparks as he twisted it.

"A pretty stone, is it not?" Ruthven asked Stoker, drawing his attention to the pin.

"Remarkable," Stoker said in a low, slow voice unlike his own.

"I am glad you like it. You will find much here to like, my friend. There is nothing here to alarm or discomfit you. In this house are only comrades, those of like mind. Do you understand?"

"I will find friends here," Stoker replied in the same odd voice.

"Many friends," Ruthven agreed. "And the first of these is myself. We will be very great friends, you and I. And you will be friends with Asphodel as well. She is a woman of great power. She can help you."

"What sort of power?" I put in sharply.

Lord Ruthven made a dismissive, quieting gesture towards me with his index finger, and Asphodel grinned at me, saying nothing.

"Asphodel can help me," Stoker repeated. He put a hand to his collar, tugging it free and flinging the starched linen to the floor. "Hot in here," he mumbled thickly. Stoker shrugged off his coat and began working the buttons of his waistcoat, his eyes never leaving the subtle circular motions of the ruby tiepin.

"I think that perhaps is quite enough for one evening," Lord Ruthven said.

"I have only just begun," Stoker protested.

I moved to Stoker, who had removed his waistcoat and was pulling his shirt free from his trousers. "Stoker, really," I hissed, gathering up his discarded clothing. His shirt was over his head then. He had not bothered to unbutton it, instead yanking it up and around his head until it came free with a decisive ripping sound. "It has buttons, you know," I told him severely.

Bare of chest, Stoker began to wander the conservatory, pausing to sniff the occasional flower. He plucked one particularly lush lily and stuck it behind one ear like a Spanish dancer.

"I am terribly sorry," I began.

Lord Ruthven's smile was close-lipped and not particularly warm. "Think nothing of it," he said in a mild tone. "But I do think it best if you see him home now. You will have to come another time."

As I struggled to keep up with Stoker, my gaze fell to the teapot. I whirled on Lord Ruthven.

"What was in the tea?" I demanded. "And why isn't she feeling the effects?" I added, pointing to Asphodel.

"There was nothing in the tea apart from a little mugwort," she said, widening her eyes. "It heightens awareness."

"It seems to heighten nudity," I retorted. Stoker had divested himself of his trousers and was wandering about in his underdrawers, for which I was entirely grateful. He had been known, upon several occasions, to forget them entirely. "Stoker, come along," I said, tugging at his arm. I thrust his garments towards him, but he seemed not the slightest bit interested in taking them.

"Veronica, please. I am having a conversation," he said sullenly.

"With a moth. That is a moth to whom you are speaking," I informed him.

"It is a very clever moth," he replied. "He is talking about Pythagoras."

Ruthven rose and came to me, his demeanour apologetic. "Forgive me, dear lady. I merely wanted to give him a taste of what we do here at the Harpocrates Society, although I admit I have never seen quite so extreme a reaction. You see him there? He believes he is having a conversation with a moth. What does the moth say? What will Mr. Templeton-Vane remember? He will emerge from this state with a new perspective on . . . something. On everything! A new idea, perhaps. A fresh way of seeing the world. His senses are heightened, his awareness utterly free—like a child's. He is discovering what it means to be liberated, my dear."

"You dosed him without his knowledge or permission," I replied in an acidulous tone.

"I asked him if he wished for a taste of knowledge," he reminded me. "And his reply was definitive. He did not hesitate. That is the sort of spirit we want in a man who is a member of our club."

I paused, realising that whatever I said next might jeopardise our entire investigation if I did not handle myself with care. "Forgive me," I said through tight lips. "Of course you are correct. I was only surprised."

"Naturally," he said soothingly. "And he will be perfectly fine, my dear. He will awaken without even so much as a headache from this experience. The only lasting effect will be a determination to repeat it, to learn all that he can of the mysteries of the arcane. But for now, best to take him home and let him sleep it off."

Stoker's conversation with the moth had ground to a halt—probably because the moth had flapped away—and he was staring at his hand in rapt fascination. "Asphodel, will you lead our guests out?" Ruthven asked. If I was surprised he did not guide us himself, I refused to show it.

His lordship bowed deeply to me as I bundled Stoker out of the door and down the hall, hard upon Asphodel's heels. "Give him water with a little bicarbonate of soda mixed in," she advised.

I could not trust myself to muster a civil response, so I said nothing. At the front door, Stoker assumed his trousers only with the greatest difficulty. I helped him into his shirt and coat, but they were hanging open, shirttails flapping as we took our leave.

"There is an entertainment the night after tomorrow," Asphodel told me. "His lordship will wish you to come."

"I am surprised, given how this evening's call has transpired," I told her.

Her smile was indulgent. "Lord Ruthven and I do not judge others. Life is far too long, we find."

"How very kind," I said stiffly.

She bowed once and closed the door on us. I helped Stoker to the carriage and settled him against the squabs, exhaling a breath I did not realise I had been holding. He turned to me, his gaze fathomless in the dark.

"Give me your flask," he ordered in a perfectly clear voice.

"Stoker! You are lucid," I marvelled. I retrieved my flask of aguardiente and handed it over.

"Not for their lack of trying," he said shortly. "Bastards." He turned out his trouser pockets, searching for something. "Eyeball, string, penknife," he muttered as he sorted through the detritus of his pockets. I was not surprised that he had upon his person a glass eyeball for fitting to one of his mounts; I was rather amazed he only had one. "Ah!" He pounced upon a little paper twist with a cry of satisfaction.

"What is that?"

"Salt," he told me. He emptied the paper twist into the flask and shook it vigorously. "Bottoms up," he said, downing the lot in a series of deep gulps.

"But will that not make you—"

Before I finished the question, he was opening the carriage window and leaning out. The sounds of violent retching followed. He repeated the process twice more until there was nothing productive left to be done.

"I think that is the worst of it," he said, lapsing back against the seat. His face wore a faintly greenish hue, but his respiration was strong and his breathing steady. I put a fingertip to his wrist. His pulse beat as rhythmically as ever.

"Are you entirely finished?" I asked.

He gave me a thin smile of purest malice. "My dearest Veronica. I have only just begun."

CHAPTER 16

Stoker strode into the Belvedere with the air of a man who was basking in triumph. J. J. was still tucked into the snuggery, stove warm and dogs scattered about. There was a smudge of ink on her nose, and she was surrounded by piles of newspapers.

Stoker immediately went to the little cupboard where we kept our more robust libations. (It had once been the prie-dieu of a Venetian priest, ornately decorated and fitted with a cabinet for holding prayer books and the like. We had filled it with intoxicants and Stoker's invariable supply of nibbles for when he felt peckish.) He pulled out a bottle of very old whisky, the shreds of the label faded and scarcely legible.

"What has happened?" J. J. demanded.

"What makes you think anything has happened?" I asked in a tone that was far too casual to have fooled anyone.

"Stoker is half-dressed and drinking directly from a bottle of aged single malt. Even for the pair of you, that speaks to an unusual night out." She put aside the newspaper she had been reading and looked from one to the other of us with an expectant expression.

"Stoker was the victim of a glamoury," I began. Stoker broke in rudely with a snort so loud he woke two of the dogs.

"A glamoury? Are you entirely bereft of your senses?" He turned to J. J. "I was drugged by Lord Ruthven and his pet witch. And then he attempted a spot of mesmerism."

"It might have been a glamoury," I said sulkily.

"What is a glamoury?" J. J. asked.

"It is a technique of the more accomplished—"

"Do not say 'vampires,'" Stoker warned. "I shall not be responsible for my actions if you do."

"Revenants," I said instead.

"That is just a synonym for 'vampire,'" he returned. He rummaged in the prie-dieu until he found a tin of crumbling shortbread.

"You have just been violently ill," I reminded him. "Is half a pound of butter really the best remedy?"

"It has ginger in it, the best remedy for an unsettled stomach," he answered, shoving a large piece into his mouth.

"Why were you ill?" J. J. demanded.

As Stoker was still chewing, I answered for him. "Because he took steps to rid himself of the substances Lord Ruthven's associate dosed him with. Mugwort, she said." I turned to Stoker. "You realise that Asphodel is surely the witch young Thomas said he saw in the cemetery when he discovered Quincey's body? That puts her definitely at the murder scene."

He waved a hand. "Immaterial. The boy is a child and a Rom. His testimony would never see the inside of a witness box. It is enough that we know the connection. And you are precipitate, my love. It is possible she is not the woman he saw."

I made a frankly scornful noise. "I cannot accept that mammoth a coincidence. Not only does she look like a witch, she likes to ginger up the tea with a bit of hallucinatory herbs."

"Did she not dose you as well?" J. J. inquired with a look at me.

"She did not," I assured her. "Stoker was the sole recipient of their attentions."

"What then?" J. J. prompted.

"What then?" I echoed. "Then Stoker began to remove his clothing and we were asked to leave."

J. J. dropped her head, and her shoulders began to shake as she emitted a rusty grating sound.

"Is she having a fit of some sort?" Stoker asked me.

"I believe she is laughing," I told him.

After a moment she lifted her head, tears streaming from her eyes. "You disrobed? How far?"

"To his drawers," I told her as Stoker blushed a delectable shade of poppy red.

"I had to create enough of a scene that they would want me gone so I could get rid of the bloody stuff she put in the tea," he protested. "Besides, I wanted them to believe I was under the effects of that damned tea and Ruthven's mesmerism."

"But you were not," J. J. pointed out. Confusion clouded her features. "Why weren't you? If Asphodel dosed the tea, you ought to have been influenced by it. But you say you were lucid at all times."

"I sipped a bit to be polite, but it tasted like pond water and I could tell something was amiss, so I chucked it into the nearest potted palm when Asphodel looked away," he confessed. "I learnt a bit of legerdemain in the travelling show, and I continue to be astonished at how often it proves useful."

"If it was so awful, how did you drink it?" J. J. asked me.

"It wasn't," I told her truthfully. "It tasted of jasmine and perhaps a little cinnamon. I cannot imagine how she—" I broke off, suddenly understanding precisely how Asphodel had dosed Stoker's tea when she and I had drunk from the same pot and been entirely unaffected. "Of course!"

Leaving J. J. and Stoker staring after me in puzzlement, I descended to the main level of the Belvedere. It took me nearly a quarter of an hour to find what I sought. I rummaged through trunks and crates, scattering excelsior hither and yon, but at last I pounced with a cry of triumph. I carried my trophy upstairs and unwrapped it from its silken shroud. Inside lay a porcelain teapot glazed in a rich shade of cinnabar, the handle and lid figured in the shape of a coiled dragon. I made my preparations with my back turned to the others, then presented the pot with a flourish.

"Behold a wonder of the ancient world," I said with a touch of theatre.

"Veronica, that is a teapot," Stoker said.

"A very special teapot," I told him. "I discovered it a few months ago when I was working on a collection of artefacts the last Lord Rosemorran had shipped from China." I retrieved two cups and set them in front of the pot. "Watch closely," I instructed. I raised the teapot dramatically and poured. I had not wanted to wait for water to boil, so out came a stream of the whisky, smelling richly of peat bog and smoke. "Whisky," I said to J. J., holding the cup out for her to sample.

She sipped and choked instantly. "Yes, yes, it is." She thrust the cup back into my hands.

I handed it on to Stoker, who also sampled it and nodded. "Whisky."

I selected a second cup and once more raised the teapot. "This teapot has not been out of your sight," I reminded them. I began to pour into the second cup, but this time a clear spout of pure water came forth.

J. J. stared in open-mouthed astonishment. "What on earth—"

"Oh, that is clever," Stoker said with a short laugh.

"How is it done?" J. J. asked.

I would have stretched the moment just a little, preening over this successful piece of sleight of hand, but Stoker began to explain at once. "Ah, see where the spout has a bit of porcelain running down the middle? The teapot has two chambers inside. Whoever is pouring is able to control what is poured through manipulating holes—probably in the handle," he added. He proceeded to launch into a technical discussion of the surface tension of liquids, and I saw J. J.'s eyes begin to glaze.

"I liked it better when I thought it was magic," she said ruefully. She looked like a child at the circus who has just discovered the coin that the conjurer drew from behind her ear had been hidden in his sleeve all along.

"There is no such thing," Stoker said flatly. "And for all your willingness to believe in this nonsense, Veronica, you have just proven it. Asphodel cast no spells upon me, and Ruthven did nothing of note."

"He did attempt to put you into a trance with his ruby," I pointed out.

"By virtue of the same parlour tricks that charlatans have been using for a century. It is no more than a party entertainment. Any fool can dazzle the eyes with a piece of jewellery and murmur a few words in a soothing tone."

"Then why does it work?" I challenged.

"It did not work on me," he retorted. "I was pretending only because I realised what was expected of me. As soon as I realised the tea was foul, I knew she had dosed me. And then when Ruthven launched into that ridiculous performance with the ruby, I knew they were watching for a reaction of some sort. I was, at all times, entirely in possession of my wits."

"You will concede that mesmerism exists," I began.

"To a point," he ground out. "But only because most folk are deeply suggestible. Tell them what they want to hear and they are already inclined to believe you. People who visit such mountebanks are no different than those who consult spiritualists in order to speak to the dead. They believe spirits are conjured during séances because they *want* to believe. The rest is just smoke and mirrors."

"You seem persuaded enough by Magda's abilities," I reminded him.

"That is different," he returned.

"Why? Because she is Romany?" I challenged.

"Yes. We will never know the full truth of their lived experience. How can we say for certain they do not have certain abilities the rest of us lack?"

"So you do admit that some people may have powers beyond—"

"I never said that. I merely said—"

"You absolutely did! And may I point out that this is the *rankest* hypocrisy—"

"How did Ruthven know to invite you?" J. J. shouted suddenly. Her question, intrusive as it was, headed off the argument before it gained momentum.

"Seward Johnson," Stoker and I replied in unison. I carried on with the explanation. "When Stoker and I questioned Mr. Johnson at Mr. Von Hilsing's house in Steel Square, it must have put the wind up him. He went directly to Lord Ruthven and told him what we were about."

"You cannot know that," she protested.

"It is the only logical conclusion," Stoker replied. "Mornaday was excessively discreet in his handling of this case, and he calls here socially. Even if he were being surveilled, which is so improbable as to be very nearly impossible, there is no reason for anyone to suppose he engaged us to look into Harkness's and Quincey's deaths."

"Murders," I murmured.

Stoker rolled his eyes heavenwards. "You can hardly call Harkness's death a murder. The man flung himself from a balcony."

"After he received a threat in the post," I reminded him. "A bit of wolfsbane, whose implication was clear—his fate was to be the same of Maurice Quincey. Furthermore, if Harkness had not thrown himself from a balcony, he may very well have been exsanguinated just like Quincey. *That* may be the doom he feared so deeply. Furthermore, I believe the wolfsbane sent to Harkness was more than just a threat. I think it was a hint to what had befallen Quincey."

"I thought Quincey was drained of his blood," J. J. countered.

"He was," Stoker put in succinctly.

"But one isn't simply drained of blood," I replied. "Remember that Quincey bore no large wound upon his body, only the small puncture wounds in the large blood vessels of the neck. The exsanguination would have been a slow thing and an altogether impossible one without the heart to pump the blood out."

"Surely he would have fought, attempted to stanch the flow," J. J. said.

"Not if he were sedated," I said in a triumphant voice. "And wolfsbane makes an excellent sedative. If he were dosed with it, he would have been compliant when the punctures were made."

"And would therefore have put up no sort of struggle as his blood was drained away," J. J. concluded. "It makes a ghoulish sort of sense."

Stoker yawned broadly. "But without a shred of proof. That is enough of wild speculation for one night. My head feels as if it were being pounded by a thousand tiny hammers, and these flights of fancy are not helping." He rose and snapped his fingers at the dogs. "Come, beasties. It is the bed for us."

He left us then, looking hardly altered from his usual self—no thanks to Asphodel and her contemptible teapot. "Poisonous woman," I muttered. "Literally."

"I am sure Stoker will admit your theory is possible," J. J. said.

"Stoker will admit nothing unless it suits him. He is a man and therefore susceptible to irrationality. It is not his fault," I assured her. "I think it has something to do with an excessive amount of testosterone."

"Test-testrone? What is that?"

"Testosterone. It is a substance found in the testes of castrated chickens and most likely in the testes of human men as well. Studies have only begun to explore its significance, and I am not deeply familiar with the work," I admitted. "But it purportedly explains why geldings are much more tractable than stallions."

J. J. considered this a moment. "Does that mean eunuchs would be more peaceable than intact men?"

"What an extraordinary question. I suppose so, given the relative behaviour of barrow and boar, steer and bull, capon and rooster. The removal of the testes appears to alter the tendency towards excitability and aggression in the unneutered of the species. And before you ask," I said, holding up a quelling hand, "the hypothesis cannot be tested upon human men for reasons of ethics."

"Still, it is an interesting question," J. J. mused. We both fell silent then. I could not answer for J. J.'s thoughts, but mine were deeply involved in considering the political machinations of various harems throughout history—a train of thought which would likely disprove the notion that eunuchs were more biddable than men who carried the full complement of organs with which they had been born. I had just moved on to the notorious antics of the Baroque castrati when J. J. interrupted my reverie.

"Do you really think Asphodel poisoned Quincey with her trick teapot?"

I shrugged. "She may have sent him a poisoned tea cake, for all I know. But I am persuaded she was responsible for his death, and I am even more convinced that wolfsbane was the source of the poison."

"How can you be so certain?"

"Because tonight in the conservatory at Lord Ruthven's house, I noticed something that Stoker did not, growing just beside the door—an enormous *Aconitum napellus*. A wolfsbane plant large enough to poison an army of men."

CHAPTER 17

The next morning, Stoker seemed hardly the worse for wear after his brush with Asphodel and her noxious brews. If anything, he seemed a little livelier, with a brightness to his eyes and a freshness to his complexion that had me almost considering selling mugwort as a health tonic. I had, naturally, consulted several herbaria to make certain he would suffer no lasting effects from the dose and taken pains to reassure him on the point.

"It is said to help with sleep and strengthening the liver in small doses," I told him. "Although in larger amounts, it is an hallucinogen, which is precisely what Asphodel and Ruthven intended, I believe."

"I sicked up most of what little I drank," he reminded me. "It was rather a clever idea, to get me to ingest a substance which would heighten the otherworldly effects of the atmosphere and then have Ruthven start his routine of parlour tricks. Either of them alone wouldn't have been nearly as effective, but in combination, they might well have caused a suggestive sort of person to fall completely under Ruthven's spell."

"To what end?" I asked. We were at the breakfast table—or what passed for the breakfast table in the Belvedere, namely a repurposed sarcophagus onto which had been placed various covered chafing dishes which rested on vessels of recently boiled water. The arrangement kept the food hot on its journey from the main house. I toyed with a few pieces of toast, breaking them into bits to butter lavishly and then feed to the dogs, but Stoker had already heaped his plate twice over with eggs, kedgeree, sausages, and the honeyed cinnamon buns Cook sent down solely to assuage Stoker's sweet tooth.

"Ah, that is no great mystery," he said as he speared a crispy sausage. "Ruthven clearly wants to recruit me for the Harpocrates Society. All that talk of broadening my consciousness and bestriding the world—that is the same sort of talk you hear from any gentlemen's club of newly made men."

"Newly made men only?"

He chewed thoughtfully at his sausage as he nodded. "Newly made men are the only ones who care about such things. Old families want to sit quietly by the fire and indulge in their pet interests—coins or stamps or Pompeiian pottery. For proof you've no further to look than this place," he added, waving his fork about. "Generations of Rosemorran earls filling up this entire building with things that have taken their fancy. Some of it is valuable, I will grant you. But more than half is utter rubbish. Do you think the earls cared? No, they bought what they liked because it was pretty or because it was unusual or—perhaps more importantly—because someone else wanted it. They did not care in the slightest about making their mark on the world because, by and large, aristocrats never do. Their marks have already been made. They inherit enormous houses that their great-grandfathers seven times back nearly bankrupted the family in building. Their only hope is to die without letting the place completely fall down around their ears. New money puts in a pond or a sculpture gallery or tears the thing down and rebuilds it entirely. Old money is content to *sit*."

"You have persuaded me," I told him.

"And that is why," he carried on as he reached for a cinnamon bun, "I am convinced Ruthven is an impostor."

"An impostor? Just because he is ambitious? I said you had persuaded me, but you go too far."

With a smile of purest delight, he reached behind him for a familiar book and opened it to a page he had marked with a desiccated lizard.

"Is that . . . *was* that a chameleon?" I asked, plucking it out with two careful fingers.

"*Brookesia superciliaris*," he said cheerfully. "A brown leaf chameleon from Madagascar. Poor fellow must have wandered into one of the crates being packed up and come here as a stowaway. Somewhere along the line, he was flattened. Makes a handy bookmark though, and you will find *here*," he said, tapping the page with a forefinger, "the entry in question."

The volume was a comprehensive compendium of the aristocracy of the United Kingdom with notes regarding Ireland and the Channel Isles, I saw. Stoker had pointed out the entry headed LORD RUTHVEN. I skimmed it quickly. "'A peerage of Scotland from 1488," I said. "In abeyance several times, occasionally coupled with the lordship of Gowrie.'" I read on. "'Currently vacated.'"

I looked up to find Stoker smiling into his buns.

"The title is not extant," I summarised. "It went extinct when the last Lord Ruthven died in 1853."

"Which means?" he said coaxingly.

"Which means our Lord Ruthven is indeed an impostor," I admitted. "Hell and damnation." I did not know which I found more irritating—that Stoker had thought to investigate the man's credentials by the absolute simplest means possible or that he had been right and his lordship was a fraud.

"Very well. I concede."

Stoker paused with a cinnamon bun halfway to his mouth. "I beg your pardon?"

"I said I concede."

"I do apologise, but I am afraid my hearing is not what it used to be. Could you repeat that, my love?"

I threw the sugar spoon at his head, but he caught it, laughing.

"So you believe the Harpocrates Society is behind this?" I asked.

His expression turned thoughtful. "It is a possibility to which one might take a fancy. For all his correct vowels and courtly manners, Ruthven—for so we must call him until we learn a better name—strikes me as neither to the manner nor manor born."

"How frightfully lofty you are," I exclaimed.

"I am nothing of the sort." He managed to look a little wounded. "I am perfectly happy to make my acquaintance wherever I find agreeable folk."

"But you are keenly aware of the difference between a gentleman of established blood and one whose wealth has come only recently. How do you account for that?"

"Devil if I know," he said, furrowing his brow.

"I think it is a matter of upbringing rather than innate knowledge," I told him. "If one looks at the theories of Descartes—"

"Do not quote Descartes to me over the breakfast table, Veronica. I'll not have it," he warned. "French Aristotelians lead only to indigestion."

"Aristotelians indeed! Just because Descartes—" He interrupted me by putting his fingers in his ears.

"Very well," I mouthed with a sigh. He dropped his hands with a grin and I went on, avoiding the subject of Descartes altogether. I was tempted to make reference to Francis Galton, but I thought this might send him entirely round the twist, so I kept my remarks carefully neutral. "I simply believe that because your father was an aristocrat and related to other aristocrats and entertained aristocrats, you were frequently exposed to their company. You learnt their manners and airs, their little tricks of pronunciation and deportment. And very likely you learnt all of this without ever being aware of learning it. It was inculcated with mother's milk, I daresay. And such frequent and repeated exposure to a certain set of rules and habits and affectations has rendered you sensitive to their effects even still. You yourself make use of these little intricacies when it suits you. Consider how you managed to so skillfully lord it over the butler in Von Hilsing's house—you cowed him with nothing more than a superior manner and exaggeratedly correct vowels, even while wearing a threadbare shirt and in desperate need of a good barbering. Blood may not always tell but upbringing does."

"Possibly," he said thoughtfully.

"And that is why Ruthven has struck a gong with you as an impostor. There is something in his air, in his manner of delivery or comportment, that does not coincide with your picture of how a true gentleman ought to behave. Although, your instinctive mislike of him as one of your own fails to take into account a vital piece of information. You have failed to consider the differences in Continental manners," I added.

"Continental! You think that jackanapes is European? He is as British as you or I," Stoker said with a decisive snort.

"You were the one who referred to his courtly manners," I reminded him. "And there was a slight suggestion of something of liquidity in the vowels, a certain relaxation of the tongue into the back of the mouth when pronouncing the letter 'L.'"

"Could we have rather less discussion of his lordship's tongue?" he asked as he pushed his plate away. "I find that has as dampening an effect upon my appetite as Descartes."

I smiled at him and plucked the last sausage from his plate. "As you like, my darling."

. . .

I have often maintained that waiting is the truest test of one's character. Whilst I occupied the following hours with work—my emerald swallowtails were coming on nicely, and the article I had promised the Society of Lady Aurelians for their summer number would not write itself—Stoker frequently interrupted his activities behind the curtain with muttered diatribes sprinkled liberally with profanities.

"Why the bloody bollocking hell I am stuck into this nonsense when there are proper specimens I could be fu—"

"Dearest!" I called, putting down my pen as I recognised the futility of attempting to work when he was in such a mood. "I think a little fresh air would do us a world of good."

He required no further inducement. Before I could enumerate my reasons—or my intended destination—he had flung aside his tools and snatched up his coat. I took a moment longer to ready myself, but we were soon striding along the London streets. The afternoon sun slanted over the rooftops, gilding everything to a prettiness that might not stand close scrutiny but was nonetheless pleasing to the eye. The chestnut sellers were about, hawking their fragrant wares, and if the aroma was somewhat overpowered by the scent of the horses' arisings, I did not much mind. The flower sellers were clutching their bouquets, armfuls of apple blossom and cherry blossom jostling with the first peonies. Stoker flung one a tuppence, collecting a nosegay of tiny, perfect white blooms, which he presented to me. The miniature flowers were clustered along slender stems, dangling like pearls between the ensiform leaves of deep, glossy green. I promptly took one sprig to thread into his buttonhole and sniffed appreciatively at the others.

"Lily of the valley! How lovely," I said, admiring the way the little flowers perched *en tremblant* upon the stems. "Curious that it should symbolise happiness when it is so very lethal."

Stoker's gaze narrowed. "You have been at your florilegium again."

"I may have dipped into a page or two this afternoon," I admitted. "Between tasks."

He flicked the sprig in his buttonhole with a finger, sending the little spray of flowers bobbing. "Exactly how lethal?"

"So lethal merely ingesting the water in which the flowers have been held is enough to induce fatality."

"Jesus!" Stoker plucked the stem from his buttonhole and watched as it flew in a graceful arc into the gutter. He reached for my bouquet, but I held it away.

"I seldom receive flowers from my inamorato," I informed him. "I shall thank you to leave them be."

"At least you are wearing gloves," he said darkly as he scrubbed at his own hand with his handkerchief.

"Never mind," I soothed. "You are a man in the prime of his life. I have no doubt your constitution can withstand exposure to a little lily of the valley."

We walked a few more steps before he turned to me, his tone deliberately casual. "And if one were to experience the effects of exposure? How precisely would they manifest?"

"Through loss of consciousness or irregularity of the heartbeat," I said promptly. "Do tell me if you are feeling faint so that I may catch you."

We walked on, threading our way through the teeming city streets. The air was brisk, but there was the promise of spring ripening on the wind. I would have given my best net to have been in the countryside proper, striding about on the chase for the first butterflies of the season to emerge. I may have given up the hunt for specimens to kill, but I still longed for the thrill of the pursuit itself. One may admire what one does not seek to own, I reflected. And it occurred to me then that our forays into detection had neatly dovetailed with the ending of my travels. Was

I chasing murderers as a substitute for hunting specimens? Had I unwittingly traded the field work of a lepidopterist for that of a detective?

"Is it a tasty one?" Stoker asked mildly.

"Is what tasty?"

"The problem you are currently chewing over. I am familiar with that face—it means you are wrestling with a conundrum, usually of the philosophical variety. What is it this time?"

"I was merely pondering the fact that we began our investigative exploits just at the time that I gave up travelling abroad on butterflying expeditions."

"And you are wondering if the two are connected?" he suggested as we dodged an omnibus to cross the street.

"Are they not? They have much in common. The excitement of the chase, the uncertainty of success, the thrill of the victorious outcome."

"The loss of a particularly desirable specimen," he added. "We have not always been successful."

"True. But this is a discussion best had another time," I said. "We have arrived."

We stood in the road, as near to the spot where Maurice Quincey's body had been discovered as we could manage. This bit of Swain's Lane, a narrow and nondescript street, passed between two portions of Highgate Cemetery at the only spot where they overlapped, the east and west sections being entirely separate.

"East or west," I asked Stoker.

"West," he said promptly. "It is the oldest bit."

I turned left and led the way some yards down the street to where a pair of tall iron gates stood. I was pleased to find the gates were closed but unlocked. We tarried a moment, taking in our surroundings.

"Well, this smacks of morbidity," Stoker said as we peered through the gates. The word "cemetery" often conjures images of tidy churchyards, the dead tucked into neat rows like so many parishioners in their pews. Even if the monuments and gravestones are varied, there is usually a sort of orderliness to a well-kept cemetery.

Highgate was nothing like this. To begin with, it was vast, some fifteen hectares—nearly forty acres for this encampment of the dead. The west portion contained two of the great landmarks of the cemetery, the Egyptian Avenue and the Circle of Lebanon. The Egyptian Avenue comprised sixteen vaults of great exclusivity, allowing the rich to be buried as they lived—largely away from anyone else. It featured an inverted torch, a symbol of eternal life and a curious one, I thought. The fastest way to put out a torch was to turn it upside down and smother the flame. But I did not make my observation aloud. Stoker was always of uncertain temper in a graveyard, no doubt because his beloved mother resided in one.

We moved through the Circle of Lebanon, with its crescents of crypts surrounding a cedar of Lebanon of tremendous antiquity, some two centuries at least. Its spreading branches carried shade into the furthest edges of this part of the cemetery, and I was happy to pass into the next part, where the various shrubs and bushes provided abundant habitat for birds and squirrels. They sang and chattered and hurried about, no doubt attempting to secure titbits for their suppers before night fell. I had thought we departed in good time, but inside the cemetery it was much darker than I had anticipated even as the sun still shone upon the street outside. The warmth of its rays did not seem to penetrate the cold, ivy-crept stone of the various monuments and mausolea. Mosses and lichens carpeted the pathways and dressed the statues, from the slumbering cherubs to the elegantly veiled pleurants, the elaborate weeping ladies who decorated the richest tombs with their graceful, tearful sorrow.

"What are we looking for?" Stoker asked, his voice scarcely above a whisper. There was no one about, but I understood the inclination to keep one's voice low. It was not the living we were afraid to disturb; it was the dead.

"I do not know," I admitted. "I wondered if there might be some sign of Ruthven and Asphodel's activities here."

"Because of what Thomas said? About the woman in black?"

"A woman who might well have been Asphodel, here in the same place Quincey's body was found. You must admit it is a clue," I replied, recalling his earlier obstinacy on the point.

"It is not a clue," he countered. "It is a bloody cemetery, Veronica. They are full of ladies in black. They are called widows."

"I still think the possibility of a connection must be investigated," I told him. "Asphodel and Ruthven may well get up to some dark mischief in this place—mischief which ended in Quincey's death."

"Here? When they have the whole of their house to devote to whatever nefarious activities they wish?"

"But how much more effective rituals and ceremonies would be here!" I said, leading the way off the main path and onto a much narrower, more secluded walk. "The house is evocative, yes, but *this* is truly atmospheric. And why was Maurice Quincey found just outside if there is no connection to the cemetery itself? He did not live anywhere near. No, I am convinced Asphodel and Ruthven have been using Highgate as a scene for their intrigues."

Stoker gave a grunt that I interpreted as agreement, and we continued on, taking another little path that branched off, and then still another. We had twisted and turned our way into the beating heart of the cemetery, and as we emerged into an open space, I noticed something unexpected and slightly ominous.

"The birds have gone silent," Stoker said suddenly.

"It does not feel particularly welcoming," I replied. When one has hunted butterflies as extensively as I have—and particularly if one is female—one develops a sixth sense for places that are insalubrious, to say nothing of the downright dangerous.

This place was something else entirely. If I were a superstitious person, which I am most decidedly *not*, I would have shivered and peered behind me, waiting for the trailing, slithering step of something not dead, but not entirely alive. It was a place for hauntings, where the angels that wept over lavish tombs might turn their heads ever so slightly to watch one pass.

"Veronica, are you quite all right?" Stoker's voice was mildly amused.

"Yes, of course. Why do you ask?" I inquired, my own voice determinedly hearty.

"Because you are clutching me so tightly you have bruised my arm," he returned.

I pried my fingers free with only a little difficulty, but just then a sound came from behind us—a sort of scuttling, scuffing, dragging noise that sounded like nothing of this earth. I sprang into action, instantly ready to do battle on Stoker's behalf.

"Behind me!" I cried to him, thrusting him backwards with one hand whilst I reached for my hatpin with the other as an ancient battle cry I had learnt from a Scottish entomologist issued from my lips. In the course of accomplishing these actions, I planted my booted foot upon the nearest headstone and launched myself into an arc towards our attacker, flinging my body between Stoker and danger, determined to battle the culprit with all of my strength. I struck my other foot directly into the miscreant's midsection, forcing him to the ground, supine and gasping for breath as I landed atop him, neatly straddling his rib cage, my feet hooked about his hips, rendering his legs immobile. His bowler hat had settled over his face, shielding his identity, and I gave no quarter. The hatpin was poised at his jugular, and I pricked him gently to show that I meant business.

"Reveal yourself, devil!" I cried.

"For the love of bleeding Jesus and all his seven saints," came the muffled response from inside the bowler.

Stoker dropped a restraining hand to my shoulder. "Rise, dearest. You have just assaulted a friend."

And with that, Detective Inspector Mornaday of Special Branch, Scotland Yard, pushed me away, rolled to his side, and was lavishly sick in the grass.

CHAPTER 18

Really, Mornaday, I have apologised several times." I attempted but was possibly unsuccessful in keeping the waspish tone from my voice. "But you really ought to have declared yourself."

Mornaday was frankly aggrieved. "I have already explained that I was doing surveillance." His own voice was rasping—due to the effects of the stomach acids in his effluvia washing over his vocal cords, naturally. I handed him my flask of aguardiente to wash his mouth, but that brought on a fresh bout of heaving. "God, must you look to poison me as well? Is it not enough you have assaulted me and broken a rib and damaged my manly bits?"

"You do not know it is broken," I replied. I was speaking of the rib. The subject of Mornaday's manly bits was not one I cared to address in any fashion. Stoker generally enjoyed any calamity involving Mornaday, but he turned a hand to the fellow's aid, probing at his side to palpate the injuries he claimed to have sustained. I noticed he too ignored the question of Mornaday's bits.

"Well?" I demanded when Stoker had finished.

Stoker shrugged. "Possibly. It is easy enough to crack a rib when one is accosted in such a fashion. But I felt no displacement."

Mornaday gave him a black look and kept a hand pressed to his side. "I have been wounded. Grievously," he said in a very good impression of a sulk. "And I shall never father children. I hope the pair of you are quite happy with yourselves."

"Why were you skulking about behind us?" Stoker inquired. "Veronica is right, you know—far better to have let us know you were there instead of frightening Veronica when she was already seeing ghouls behind every shrub."

"You mistake the careful attention of a trained scientific observer for nervous trepidation," I assured him. "I was merely being cautious out of a desire not to compromise any evidence we might discover."

"What evidence?" In spite of his purported injuries, Mornaday perked up, shoving his bowler to the back of his head and taking a proper sip of the aguardiente, his disdain for the stuff forgot. He choked only a little this time and handed the flask back to me. "Bracing," he said with a cough. A bit of colour returned to his cheeks, and I suspected he was not as badly injured as he liked to believe.

I took a little nip of my own before replacing the flask. "That is what we are here to find out." I quickly related the little we had learnt from Thomas and our visit to Ruthven's house as well as our current line of inquiry. "Given young Thomas's sighting of a woman who might well be Asphodel, we hypothesise that the location of Maurice Quincey's body relative to the house of Lord Ruthven may not be coincidence."

"The cemetery lies between," Mornaday said, grasping at once the implication.

"And Highgate is the perfect spot for dark rituals involving revenants," I added.

Mornaday looked a little less certain at this suggestion. "That is a bit of a leap, logically speaking. And what do you mean by 'revenant'?"

"Murder investigations are not solved with pure logic," I reminded him. "They require imagination, particularly when the murderer is a vampire."

"The murderer is not a vampire," Stoker said through gritted teeth.

"A vampire," I carried on as if he had not spoken, "with a witch for an accomplice."

"A what now?" Mornaday asked in bewilderment.

"And Asphodel is not a witch," Stoker continued.

"Then what," I asked, pointing with a triumphant finger, "is that?"

Both men followed my gaze to a wide circle just beyond the line of graves where we had been standing. It had been cut crudely into the mossy ground, the rich velvety green churned up with some rough blade. Inside the circle was a series of symbols, each more arcane than the last, laid out in heaping lines of black grains. At the centre was a headstone of some antiquity, the letters long since worn smooth, the grey stone weathered and darkly streaked, stained in some places, and dark, greasy puddles marred the surface. It looked—nay, it *was*—a pagan altar.

"My god," Mornaday said, crossing himself swiftly, and this time there was no intended blasphemy in his speech. It was an invocation to his deity.

We advanced together to study the circle, careful not to disturb the signs and sigils which had been so deftly arranged. Stoker bent to put a forefinger to the black grains and touched the tip of his tongue to them.

"Salt," he said in some surprise.

"Salt is often used in conjuring," I remarked. "Although black salt is an unusual touch, I think."

"Can you identify the markings?" Mornaday asked.

Stoker and I studied them for some minutes, then I shook my head. "They are unfamiliar to me."

"Just a jumble of alchemical symbols," Stoker put in. He pointed out a few of the more noteworthy examples. "Most are based upon actual scientific glyphs."

"Scientific whatsits?" Mornaday's expression was befuddled.

"Glyphs. Symbols meant as a sort of notational shorthand. They indicated planets, chemicals, different compounds. They were popular with alchemists once upon a time, but they've largely fallen out of favour."

"Why were they used?" Mornaday pressed.

"Convenience, mostly. A little line drawing of a triangle surmounting a double-armed cross takes up far less space in a notebook than writing out the word 'phosphorus,' for instance," Stoker explained. He gestured towards the symbols on the stone. "But these are sloppily rendered for all the care in the execution itself. They've missed out the details. There is Mercury, you can see by the little horns atop his head. But the bottom is wrong." The symbol to which he pointed was based upon a circle. Atop this was a curved line, giving the impression of a head with a pair of horns. The body was formed by a simple cross. "The crosspiece ought to be straight for Mercury, but this is tipped like an Orthodox cross. And there is the glyph for antimony, similar to Mercury, but this one is even more incorrect. It ought to have little curved arms reaching upwards, yet it has asterisks, like stars."

"What does it mean?" Mornaday pressed.

"Whoever laid these signs had an imperfect grasp of chemistry or thought to impress other people by making something that looks far more accomplished than it actually is," Stoker replied. "It is nonsense."

"This is far from nonsense," I said. I had moved to the gravestone to study the makeshift altar. The puddles on the top proved to be wax from black candles. But the other stains were suggestive, dark reddish brown and heavily streaked on the stone. I bent near, pulling off my glove to scrape at the stuff with a fingernail. When I had collected enough of the dried matter, I dropped it onto a page torn from the notebook I carried in my pocket. A drop of the aguardiente to moisten it, and it came to life, deep red against the white of the paper.

"Blood," Mornaday said.

I gave it a deep sniff. Even with the potent fumes of the aguardiente, the ferrous scent of the blood was unmistakable. "It is."

"Something was sacrificed here," he said, turning slowly to take in our surroundings.

"An excellent spot for it," I told him. "The cemetery is locked at night. One presumes there are watchmen, but with the enormity of this place, it would be easy enough to elude them."

"And failing that, a guard could be bribed or frightened to silence," Stoker added.

"How do you know they were here at night?" Mornaday asked.

Stoker pointed to the waxen spots before I could. "Every headstone here has marks of candle grease. They would not require such illumination by day."

Mornaday turned once more in a circle. "My god, what abominations have happened here."

"Perhaps nothing more sinister than the killing of a cockerel," Stoker said. "There is not enough blood in those stains for a human."

I hated to admit the truth of it, but he was correct. The streaks I had discovered were insufficient for the sort of blood loss Maurice Quincey had sustained. These definitely suggested occultish happenings of some sort, but they did not include the murder of a human.

Stoker, nose lifted like a bloodhound on the scent of a rabbit, took a turn about the clearing, pushing aside bushes and peering under broken gravestones. After several minutes of this—with the necessary swearing and imprecations after pricking himself on thorns—he gave a cry of triumph.

"Come and look," he said, holding back a shroud of ivy tendrils. They had formed a sort of veil obscuring a broken bit of wall, and at the base of the wall was a rusting grate. From below was the sound of rushing water, flowing fast.

"One of London's buried rivers," I guessed. I remembered all too well what had happened the last time Stoker and I had been forced to explore one of these endangered tributaries, and I was not eager to repeat the experience.* Having a rat land in one's décolletage is a distinctly unsettling encounter.

"I would have to compare it to a good map to be sure, but at the very least, it is part of the sewer system," Stoker said. "But look there."

He pointed to the rust patches on the grate, and with a horrible certainty I knew then.

"That is no rust," Mornaday said, turning away with a slightly greenish cast to his face.

"No," I agreed. "I believe we shall discover that that is the blood of Maurice Quincey."

---

* *A Treacherous Curse*

CHAPTER 19

When the invitation finally arrived, I had nearly given up hope. Several rounds of the post had come and gone with George delivering his usual complement of envelopes and circulars. Bills, invitations, missives from friends—none were welcome to me when I was in a froth of anticipation over further word from Ruthven and his consort.

"It will come when it comes," Stoker said mildly as he flicked through his own letters after tea.

"I am sure I do not know what you are talking about," I replied coolly. "Look, here is an invitation to speak in America including my passage and a handsome fee. It is from the Society of Gentlemen Lepidopterists of America."

"Are there gentlemen in America? I hadn't noticed," Stoker returned. "Ah, a postcard from Figgy Tiverton. She continues well in her studies and has decided to pursue a career in Egyptology. I suppose she has it in the blood. But she may change her mind. I think last month she said she wanted to be a botanist."

Ordinarily, I would have responded with alacrity to any communication from the young friend whose paths had crossed ours in the course of our third investigation,* but not this time. Instead I pounced upon an envelope headed in a now-familiar hand. "It is here!" I tore it open with my fingers instead of the kukri, so impatient was I to read the contents. "Ruthven has written at last! His lordship requests the honour of our presence at a danse macabre at his home tomorrow evening. Rather late tomorrow evening," I added. "Festivities begin at midnight."

"The witching hour," Stoker pointed out.

"Attire is formal and masked," I told him, passing over the piece of card. It was weighty stuff, decorated with a border featuring skeletons leading a line of well-dressed people in satins and velvets, feathers in their hair and jewels at their throats. I had seen such images often enough in the Rosemorran Collection. The present earl's grandfather had had a morbid streak, delighting in the hunting down of memento mori. Anything featuring a skull was fair game, and one corner of the Belvedere was stuffed to the rafters with paintings of skeletons, hair jewellery, and an enormous tapestry featuring Death playing the pipe to lure victims into the grave. Thankfully, moths had been at it, nibbling away the most gruesome bits.

I turned back to the invitation. The envelope had been sealed with scarlet wax, and the impression in the wax was of a wolf or large dog. From the wax hung a narrow fold of black silk ribbon, a nicety one did not often see any longer. It was an old-fashioned embellishment, a detail straight out of a Jane Austen novel.

"Nouveau riche," Stoker murmured with a moue of distaste.

"Hold your prejudices," I said. "And drag your formal suit out of mothballs. We have a ball to attend."

Stoker's suit did not smell of mothballs but cedar and lavender, a much more acceptable fragrance. George helped Stoker to hang it in

* *A Treacherous Curse*

the shrubbery, where the fresh spring breezes might blow some of the staleness out. The only difficulty they anticipated would be if Patricia the tortoise took a liking to it and decided to gnaw at the cuffs.

For myself, I had nothing suitable and was forced to borrow my finery from Lady Cordelia. She was flushed with triumph, having recently published a paper on Boolean algebra. Or Bodleian geometry. Or Baconian trigonometry. I confess, I was not listening when she attempted to explain, mathematics being a subject for which I have little aptitude and less interest. But she was pleased with the reception of her work because it caused her to receive a few pieces of hate mail from the male mathematicians she had criticised. "One is not considered a proper mathematician until another mathematician has threatened to horsewhip you," she had told me.

As a result of her good humour, she was only too happy to make a loan to me of an appropriate costume for Lord Ruthven's ball. It was scarlet—not a colour I usually chose given the violet hue of my eyes—but it seemed to suit the occasion. The skirts of the gown were unfashionably wide, but all the better for dancing, as Lady Cordelia pointed out. She was a trifle slimmer than I through the bosom and waist, but her lady's maid, Sidonie, achieved wonders with a bit of judicious easing of the seams and some aggressive lacing of a borrowed corset.

"Barbarity," I muttered, but I could breathe well enough thanks to Sidonie's clever fingers.

"It makes for a prettier line," Lady C. told me serenely as she smoothed a crease from the skirts.

"I suppose. But you must admit it is a gross miscarriage of justice that gentlemen do not have to submit to the same tortures," I protested.

"Have you ever worn a starched collar?" Lady C.'s gaze met mine in the mirror and she smiled. "And I remember Aunt Wellie telling me of her papa's getting ready for a ball—so vain that he insisted upon padding his calves, gluing a bit of horsehair to his scalp to cover his bald spot, and wearing a coat two inches too small so that his shoulders would seem wider. That sounds decidedly painful."

"I hope he split his seams," I replied. Recalling my earlier precautions when visiting Lord Ruthven, I tied a wide black velvet ribbon about my neck. Stoker might have established that his lordship's bona fides were false, but that did not mean he was not a vampire. In fact, it rather argued *for* the matter, I decided. If one outlived all one's friends and acquaintances, one would eventually have to assume a new identity, and what better than a title which had fallen into extinction?

"Veronica, you look like a kitten ready for judging in a village fete," Lady C. protested. "You cannot possibly go out with a *ribbon* tied about your throat. That has not been the fashion for more than a hundred years." She referred, of course, to the habit of stylish ladies to go about with a slender red ribbon at the neck during the French Revolution—*à la victime*, they called it, in reference to those who had shaken hands with Madame Guillotine. Ghoulish, in my opinion, but handy for my purposes.

"I like it," I said stoutly. Lady C. did not need to know that I wore it because it afforded me some slight protection against a potential vampire. I bent to lift my skirts, tucking a nicely sharpened stiletto into one of my garters.

"Veronica, really," Lady C. chided.

"I must be prepared for all eventualities." My stoutness of heart extended to protecting Stoker at all costs, and I did not trust Asphodel and Lord Ruthven any further than the tip of my nose.

"You expect violence in a ballroom?" Lady C. settled her black velvet evening cloak over my shoulders.

I turned, whirling the cloak into an ebony wing. "My dear Lady Cordelia, I have learnt to expect violence everywhere."

. . .

Stoker, to his credit, was ready on time and had secured the use of Lord Rosemorran's private equipage for the evening.

"Are you sure his lordship does not require it?" I asked as he handed me into the elegant carriage.

"He is spending the evening with a new batch of stamps directly from the Philately Society. He shall likely not emerge until morning," Stoker assured me.

His gaze gleamed in the dim light as he looked at me. "Magnificent," he breathed, touching his nose to the curve of my ear.

I swallowed hard before swatting him away with my fan. "Behave yourself. I must arrive uncreased if I am to play the part of a lady."

Stoker laughed and quoted a saucy bit of Scottish poetry about roving hands, but kept his own sturdy grip to himself for the rest of the journey. We arrived just before the stroke of midnight to find the house illuminated from rooftop to cellar, every window shimmering with a soft golden glow. We could hear music, but the strains were not a modern dance tune. The melody was quite different; even the instruments seemed unfamiliar, although after a moment, I could pick out the throaty cries of the violins and a tuneful cello.

"Folk music," Stoker said. "From the wilds of Austria, I think. Perhaps Bavaria. Someplace with lots of trees and mountains, at any rate."

"All the better to set the scene," I observed. The front door was open, a portly gentleman in black and silver livery standing in attendance. He put out a hand for our invitation card, and as I produced it, I ventured a question. "Are you a regular member of staff?"

"No'm," he said, looking about furtively. "Engaged for the evening from an agency in London."

"How many of the house staff are in residence?"

He shrugged. "No idea, ma'am. If they've staff, we haven't seen 'em."

He stepped back, a clear indication that we were to proceed inside, and I darted a glance to Stoker. "Did you hear? No regular staff that they know of. Curious for so large a house, don't you think?"

"Do you expect Lord Ruthven cleans the house with vampire powers? Or perhaps Asphodel bewitches the silver free of tarnish," he suggested.

"Mock as you wish, but it is strange, and that which is strange must be explained," I returned mildly.

A powder room for the ladies had been set up in a small parlour just off the front hall. and I paused long enough to hand over my cloak and tuck an errant lock of hair into a pin. Other ladies were busy powdering noses or having loose hems whipped. One was considering her posture in the mirror, but I required no such assessment. When Lady C. had been otherwise occupied, I had slipped a series of minuten inside the décolletage of my gown. The merest slouch would set one to pricking a tender spot if I were not careful. But it was worth the risk to my own flesh to have another weapon to hand besides my stiletto. I only regretted I had not dressed my hair with a particularly lethal Spanish comb I had recently acquired. I was very much looking forward to stabbing someone with it.

Toilette complete, I tied my mask into place, admiring the effect. It was a half mask and not likely to hide my identity, but it evoked images of carnival balls and Venetian debaucheries, and I was determined to enjoy myself.

Refreshed and ready for the evening's entertainment, I emerged from the powder room to find Stoker settling his mask into place.

"Having a nice time?" I inquired.

By way of reply, he grabbed me firmly above the elbow and towed me towards the ballroom. Before I could register my protest, he murmured into my ear. “I have just seen a man I would swear is Seward Johnson going into the ballroom.”

“Johnson! He claimed he had no knowledge of Ruthven and no contact with any member of the Harpocrates Society,” I said in some irritation. We had suspected he was the source of Ruthven’s intelligence about us, but it was vexing to have it confirmed. It was always so irritating when handsome young men were discovered to be liars.

“What is your plan, dearest? Do you mean to confront him in the ballroom?” I asked as I tripped against him. He stopped short, one strong arm circling me as he set me firmly on my feet again.

“My apologies, my love,” he told me. “You are right. I ought to be more circumspect. We have all evening to approach him.”

“Indeed,” I said, tugging at my dress and twitching my mask back into place. To the casual observer, it would seem as if I were tweaking my appearance, but really I was making certain my weapons were still secured, ready for action should I have need of them. I stepped in front of Stoker, squaring my shoulders as I took in our surroundings with a swift glance.

“You are twitchy as a cat,” Stoker said, a tiny smile playing about his mouth.

“The saying about pots and black kettles comes to mind,” I replied. “I mean to keep a careful eye upon you tonight. I will not dismiss the possibility that Ruthven means you some mischief.”

“Ruthven merely wishes to recruit me for the Harpocrates Society,” he countered. “Doing me an injury would hardly further that aim.”

“Asphodel, then,” I conceded. “I mislike how she looks at you.”

His dark, velvety brows rose heavenwards. “How does she look at me?”

“As if she were a devout Catholic beholding a succulent beefsteak on a Friday afternoon,” I replied darkly.

"You think she has designs upon my person?" he asked, his mouth twitching further still.

"Do not be so quick to discount the notion," I warned him. "She would not be the first."

"There have not been so very many," he said, lowering his gaze to look demurely through his lashes at me.

"There have been more than I should care to count. But if she thinks to make a mischief here, she had best be on her mettle," I told him.

He turned then to look me fully in the eye. "Veronica, can it be—are you *jealous*?"

"The word, I assure you, is not to be found in my vocabulary."

"Oh, that lofty tone might fool someone who does not know you as well as I, but I know jealousy when I smell it." He had broken out into a full grin at this point, his teeth gleaming whitely against the rosy hue of his lips.

"I cannot imagine what you are talking about." I lifted my chin and took his arm as we approached the door to the ballroom. "Come along, Stoker. To battle!"

CHAPTER 20

When most readers encounter the word "ball," they perhaps imagine the sort of decorous Regency entertainments where matrimony was the aim of all who attended. Such affairs were conducted according to certain rules of decorum, and these rules were applied with a rigidity that would have done a mediaeval convent proud. But those were the balls where debutante virtue was guarded, where virginal young misses were presented to society for inspection and interrogation with an eye to marrying them off to the appropriate suitor.

This evening was a different matter entirely. To begin with, there was no liveried majordomo at the door, announcing guests as they arrived. There was no hierarchy of ladies' maids arrayed outside the door, waiting to administer smelling salts and burnt feathers to heads giddy with the waltz. There was no battalion of chairs circling the room for the chaperones to sit in stoic stiffness, only their feet tapping out the rhythms of glories long past. And there was considerably more nudity.

Not *nakedness*, dear reader. Do not imagine anything so crude. But there were entertainers of every variety, most in costumes which presented bared legs, dressed only in tight-fitting stockings or perhaps with undraped backs that undulated with muscle. That was just the women, balancing on balls they moved across the marble floor or contorted themselves into impossible shapes. There were long ropes of silk hanging from the ceiling, each ending in a bar or hoop bedecked with flowers, and from these hung more shapely young women, moving their limbs gracefully in time with the music. Their male counterparts were likewise athletically displayed, most naked to the waist, exposing pectorals and latissimi dorsi of which they ought to have been rightly proud. (Of their iliac furrows I say nothing, but it may be inferred they were extremely pleasing to the eye.)

Some of the young men were also engaged in the acrobatic arts, but a few were eating fire or juggling balls of mercury glass in which reflections gleamed from the light of a thousand candles. No modern gaslight for Lord Ruthven! No, this ballroom and its décor might have been drawn directly from the pages of a Renaissance volume, all lushly draped fabrics in the rich colours of all the jewels of Araby. Along one side of the ballroom were ranked tables heaped with a veritable cornucopia of ripe fruits, delicate pastries, and enormous slabs of roast meats, some still oozing pinkly onto their platters. Another table held libations, great crystal bowls of bloodred punch with tiny glasses. In keeping with the theme of the ball, the servers were all dressed in black costumes as tightly fitted as a second skin. Onto these had been painted the bones of the human body, perfectly articulated, and in the dim light of the ballroom's edges and against a backdrop of heavy black cloth, they gave the faintly sinister suggestion of dancing skeletons.

"How very original," I said faintly.

"Whatever you do, do not eat or drink anything," Stoker ordered.

"You think they would poison their guests?" The notion was startling and not one I had considered.

"I think they would certainly introduce intoxicants of the more exotic variety," he said dryly. "Something to induce euphoria or perhaps even hallucinations. It would heighten the effects of the entertainment, make everything seem even more otherworldly."

"One of these days, we shall really have to find proper friends," I told him.

Stoker made no reply, but a seriousness had settled over his features as he surveyed the scene. "Let us dance," he said, taking my hand and leading me into the fray.

On the dance floor, several dozen couples were moving to the tunes being played by an orchestra which sat in the gallery above. The musicians were dressed like the servers, in skeletal costumes, and the conductor wore his with particular élan, leaping about as he waved his arms in a grotesque imitation of the danse macabre.

"Do you think our host had to pay them extra to wear the skeleton suits?" I asked as Stoker swung me expertly into a waltz.

"For the next six minutes, I do not wish to think of our host or his accursed entertainment," he said, his lips brushing my ear as he bent his head to mine. "I want only this."

He wove us neatly between a pair of laggardly couples who seemed to be struggling with the steps. We swept around and around, our feet keeping time with each other in that peculiar synchrony that Stoker and I shared. We did not often dance together, but every time we did, I was reminded afresh how neatly our minds paired, how unique was our communication that required no words. We moved as one, circling and sweeping, arcing and whirling until the candle flames streamed like banners past my eyes and the colours of the draperies and the other gowns melded and broke and melded again like the breaking images in a kaleidoscope. The orchestra increased the pace, the conductor now almost frantic in his gestures, whipping his musicians into a frenzy. Stoker also quickened his pace, guiding and holding, leading and commanding as he matched the rising tempo. To the unobservant, it might occasionally appear that I took the dominant role in our relationship.

That, of course, was entirely inaccurate. Stoker more than held his own, particularly when it was a matter that demanded bodily engagement. Whilst I was quicker to give voice to my thoughts, Stoker often expressed his through his sheer physicality. For a strong woman, a woman of determination and courage, there is no greater pleasure than giving oneself up fully to another when there is perfect trust.

And so I surrendered to his lead, flowing and following in the steps of the dance as they turned sinuous and sensuous. I do not know how long we waltzed—it seemed hours, but there were no clocks in the ballroom, and for the duration of our dance, the candles never seemed to burn lower. It was as if time itself had stood still, rooted into one moment and content to remain, captured as if in amber, perfect and unchanging. I was vaguely aware that other guests had stopped dancing, edging away to watch us as we swept past them, our gazes locked as tightly as our bodies, admitting none other to our enchanted world. Around and around the floor we moved, the dance spinning out like a fairy tale without an ending. The notes rose higher still, flames that burnt out of control, leading us higher and faster, my skirts whipping out behind us in a rippling froth of scarlet silk. The conductor fairly leapt as he urged his musicians to greater speed. The fingers of the violinists flew on the strings, their bows screaming a tune born of hellfire. The violins shrieked as strings snapped under the strain, each dying in an eldritch wail that echoed through the ballroom.

And still we danced on as if bewitched, until at last, the music reached its thunderous crescendo and then the tune died away, each instrument falling silent until only a single violin was left to play the final mournful notes. The passion of the piece had burnt itself to ash, leaving only a curious despair behind—despair and a terrible, heart-aching longing that could only be expressed in a single, quavering note held impossibly long until at last it too ceased with all the finality of a passing bell.

For a long moment there was no sound in the ballroom when the music had died away. Stoker and I had finished in the center of the room, our feet positioned on a black star inlaid in the middle of the dance floor. I felt as if I were only recently come to earth, born afresh in some new knowing after the reckless destruction of that dance.

"Veronica—" he began.

"My dear! How exquisitely you dance." Our host materialised at my elbow, one cool hand slipping around my arm where my glove ended, laying bare my flesh.

I turned my face towards him, reluctantly drawing my gaze from Stoker. "Good evening, Lord Ruthven."

It was no guess; he was the only man in the ballroom not wearing a mask. He was dressed head to toe in black, the jacket of heavily figured silk in an extraordinarily elegant cut which suggested something decidedly not European. The collar of the jacket was quite high in the style of the maharajas, and the tails of it reached almost to his knees. He wore no medals or other embellishments, only the jewelled ruby stickpin, now fitted neatly to his jacket just below the collar, and a ring on his right hand, a signet of some sort in heavy, antique gold.

"You look terribly distinguished," I told him. "You will put our English gentlemen to shame." It was a gambit to see if he would admit to not being English, but he did not rise to the bait. He merely smiled, keeping his lips pressed together in the peculiar way he had.

"How very kind you are, my dear. Welcome, both of you, to the Danse Macabre, the spring celebration of the Harpocrates Society. Come, Miss Speedwell, you must give your host a dance," he said, his grip tightening just a fraction as he turned, whirling me away from Stoker. He gave Stoker a nod, as if to acknowledge a gentlemanly exchange of property, and I was not surprised to see Asphodel sidling up to Stoker as we moved away. She was dressed in black, a little sombre for such an occasion, but the fabric was satin, the sheen brilliant under the lights, and the deep darkness of the colour set off the pale alabaster of her skin to stunning effect. She had piled her hair high upon her head, baring her shoulders. The neck of her gown was cut quite low, and upon her breast she wore a curious, magnificent jewel, an enormous, elaborate pendant of gold worked with enamelled figures and set with the largest gem I had ever seen—brilliantly green—and several smaller but no less superb stones.

Surely the centrepiece of the pendant could not be an emerald, I thought, twisting to get a better look, but Lord Ruthven swept me into his embrace. I felt a thrill of some unidentifiable emotion as that cold hand moved from my arm to my waist. I rested one hand lightly on his shoulder; the other was clasped in his, his bare palm pressed to my glove, his fingers curled around my hand in a grasp that was a little tighter than necessity demanded.

"I hope you are enjoying yourself in my home," he said, dipping his head near to mine.

"It is certainly a unique entertainment," I replied. "Are all of the guests members of the society?"

"Yes."

"And we the only outsiders! How privileged we are," I murmured.

His smile was close-lipped and inscrutable. "We are a most exclusive group, Miss Speedwell. We do not often extend invitations to new members, but your Mr. Templeton-Vane is an intriguing gentleman. To say nothing of his companion," he added with a deepening of the smile.

Suddenly, he gave a signal to the conductor, a deliberate inclination of the head, and the orchestra began to play—a slow, stately melody with the cellos very forward and, to my surprise, an organ. I had not seen such an instrument, but the deep wail of the pipes was unmistakable. The effect was otherworldly and majestic, like a dance in hell. Slowed down, the steps of the waltz fitted the tune better than I might have expected, and we crossed the ballroom in long, lazy arcs of movement, tracing curves with our feet that mimicked the shapes we made together as he bent me backwards over his arm at the end of every measure. Each time he raised me up, he drew me a little closer, until at the furthest end of the ballroom, he was holding me tightly against his chest. The tempo was not swift, but the constant turning meant I lost sight of Stoker and Asphodel. I did not think they were dancing—indeed few people were, preferring to watch their host as he led me about the floor.

And then, so suddenly it seemed like a conjuring trick, we were entirely alone. He had whisked me through one of the hanging panels of black fabric and into an alcove beyond. "Come with me," he murmured in a tone which was neither urgent nor commanding, but simply stated, as if he knew I would not resist him. One has only to read any novel of manners to understand that leaving a ballroom with a stranger is one of the grossest violations of propriety for an unmarried lady.

But I was no lady, and if there was any opportunity to learn more about our host and his mysterious origins, I meant to take it. He kept my hand held fast in his, and I noticed his was warmer now. Had he drawn vitality from his nearness to me? I wondered.

He moved with his usual lazy grace through the little alcove and into a passageway beyond. Here the music was muffled and the laughter and chatter of the guests almost undetectable. He led me around the corner and to a small staircase. At the top of this was a door, shrouded in shadows and with no doorknob. He pressed the panel, and it opened slowly to his will. Beyond there were more shadows, and it took me a moment to realise we were in what appeared to be a private suite. The room we had emerged into was neither boudoir nor study, but some amalgamation of both. There was no proper desk, only a slender writing table, and a long, low divan stood in place of the more expected reading chairs. A small marble table next to the divan held a short stack of books and a curious statue of a wolf worked in pierced brass. I saw with surprise that the statue was gently smoking, a thin ribbon of grey trailing from the beast's open mouth. Incense, I realised, and not the sort one smells in church. This was heavier and headier, somehow carnal, bringing images of tumbled beds and unwashed sheets to mind. Bookshelves lined one wall, the volumes dotted here and there with framed pieces of art—mostly landscapes of mist-shrouded mountains and the occasional stormy seascape. Against one wall stood a dressing table with various grooming implements, including an expensive set of brushes and telltale bottles capped with golden lids. Through the open door I caught sight of a bed, old-fashioned with four posts and heavy draperies of dark green. The bed itself was fantastically carved with mythical beasts, things with horns and leering eyes, and I turned my gaze primly away from the horrid faces.

Lord Ruthven did not seem to notice my distaste. He waved me to a seat upon the divan. "Be comfortable, my dear," he urged. The settee was deep and piled with plush cushions, the fringe six inches deep. I perched upon one corner, careful to place a pillow between myself and the rest of the divan. His mouth twitched, and I fancied he was resisting the urge to smile.

"Are you afraid, my dear? Do you think that I bite?" With that he opened his mouth, snapping his jaws sharply before giving a hearty laugh.

"Not at all," I assured him.

He did not sit, but stood, a little too close so that he loomed over me. "I must ask you to take wine with me. Something very special from Hungary. Wait here."

I watched as he moved into his bedroom, his back to me as he rummaged in a cabinet of bottles. I occupied myself by glancing at the dressing table, studying the various bottles and jars arranged there. When I had taken the measure of them, I turned to the little marble table next to the divan. At the top of the stack of books was a slender volume bound in green cloth—an old and indifferent translation of *The Iliad.* I flicked it open idly and saw that it was stamped with the name of a school. LITTLE SAINTS, SRY. I closed it swiftly, just as he reappeared. He collected glasses and opened the bottle of wine, pouring us each a small measure.

"Slowly, now," he cautioned. "It is potent stuff."

I hesitated and he smiled his close-mouthed smile. "You do not trust me after what happened the last time."

"I believe that if one puts one's hand into the fire a second time, one deserves to get burnt."

He laughed then, a surprisingly normal sound. He took a sip from his glass and handed it to me, taking mine instead and sipping from it as well. When he had done so, he held them both out.

"There, now I have drunk from both. You may choose which glass you wish for your own."

I did so and drank, letting the wine roll over my tongue. "If it is Hungarian, I presume it is a Tokay, but it is not as sweet as I would have expected."

"Ah, you see why it is so special!" he exclaimed in pleasure. "Everyone knows that the wine of Tokay is sweet, even cloying. But to find a variety that is dry, that arouses the palate, that is true enchantment. It is the unexpected which is always most bewitching, do you not think?" He looked meaningfully at me over the rim of his glass.

I sighed. "Why have you brought me here?"

He spread his hands, the gold ring glinting in the light. "You are a most arresting woman, Miss Speedwell. Why wouldn't any man wish to get you alone?"

I set down my glass and gave him my most severe look. "Lord Ruthven, this will not do. You are putting on a pretense of seduction, but you have no intention of trying your luck with me. I have been the subject of so many attempts, I am perfectly acquainted with what it feels like when a man has succumbed to my charms. You, my lord, have not. Now, let us dispense with the theatrics, and you will pay me the compliment of rational conversation. Why have you *really* brought me here?"

To my surprise, he let out a sharp bark of laughter, perhaps the first real display of emotion I had seen from him. "Forgive me, my dear. But that was so delightfully frank."

"You prefer to play games, but I did not come to fence, my lord. I am afraid I have left my foil in my other gown."

He lifted his glass in a toast to me. "Very well. I do not say you are correct, but you may ask what you like. I promise to answer honestly."

It occurred to me then that I was likely never to get so good an opportunity as this to question him closely, perhaps to learn the truth about him and his enigmatic Asphodel. It was dangerous—reckless, even. But I was determined to try.

"What is your relationship with Asphodel?"

He seemed surprised at the subject I chose, for his face opened a little, the heavy brows lifting and the eyes widening as he considered his reply. "She has been my companion, my sustenance. We are two intelligent and—if I may be so appreciative of my own charms—attractive people. We understand one another, Asphodel and I. We are not like other folk."

"That I can believe," I said, picking up my glass once more. The wine was delicious, perfectly balanced between the first burst upon the tongue—a tart, crisp edge—and a delicate sweetness that lingered upon the palate. At least he had not attempted to fob me off with cheap wine, I reflected. That was a point in favour of his character.

He went on. "You and Mr. Templeton-Vane would understand this better than most, I believe."

He watched me over the rim of his glass. His posture was casual, but his gaze was taut, assessing.

"Yes, we are unconventional ourselves, so we would never judge you upon that score," I said pleasantly.

"Unconventional! How modest of you, Miss Speedwell." A lightly mocking note had invaded his speech. "But you are far more than that. To be unconventional is to be perhaps a trifle out of the ordinary, not even approaching the bounds of eccentricity, I would argue. But you and Mr. Templeton-Vane have transgressed far beyond such labels. Society would say you are living in sin. Debauched. Depraved." With each word, he leaned a little closer, his gaze never leaving mine. "They will never understand you, you know. They will never appreciate your true gifts, either of you, because they cannot see beyond the tiny prisons they have made for themselves."

"'They'?"

He spread a hand in a sweeping gesture. "They! The great and good of England, the Empire, the world! The folk who would judge you for your behaviour when they possess not a tenth of your talents." His voice rang with emotion, but as he leant nearer still, he pitched it lower, confiding. "My dear, I understand what it is to be a victim of their petty cruelties, assaulted by their tyrannies, they who cannot do what you do, who can never be what you are. Those people out there are bereft of imagination, of vitality, of everything it means to be truly alive. They walk through their lives like ones asleep—not dreamers, for dreamers have vision and poetry and mysticism. These poor sheep are sleepwalkers, their minds and senses dulled to every experience, to every truth. They would rather live in the dull and lukewarm middling of existence than to know despair or ecstasy. They breathe, they move, they speak, but they do not *live*."

"You make a powerful argument, my lord," I said evenly, but there was something appealing in his words. I had often felt the truth of his sentiments, that the majority of folk were too busy with the minutiae of merely existing to reach for the sublime.

"I make a powerful argument because I understand what it is to be stood outside, nose pressed against the glass, a cold and unkind wind tearing the flesh from one's bones, when you would give all that you possess, your very heart's blood, just for a little kindness. And that is when deals with the devil are made," he said, drawing out the syllables in a whisper.

"Have you made such a bargain?" I asked.

He smiled his mirthless smile. "Some things cannot be discussed."

"You promised to tell me the truth," I reminded him.

"And it is the truth that I cannot share everything with you just yet," he replied smoothly.

"Sophistry, my lord! Were you educated by Jesuits?" I teased.

"Ha! No, my dear. I only know that I must protect myself and those who depend upon me."

"Such as the members of the Harpocrates Society?"

"Precisely so." He inclined his head. "Everyone you saw downstairs is a member—at least prospective. I am very proud of my little collection of souls, you know. I have gathered about me men of talent, of vision, men who have the ability to see beyond this world and its puny limitations. With them, everything is possible."

"Men only?" I widened my eyes to show that I meant no offence in the challenge.

"Ah, my dear Miss Speedwell! How I lament that we live in a society which does not adequately value the talents of its women. It is our men who have been educated, raised with purpose, and given privilege over their sisters. Perhaps one day that will change, but for now—" He broke off with a shrug, then went on. "Still, women find a place here. Not as members of the society, but as—"

"Handmaidens?" I suggested.

"Helpmeets," he corrected. "I could not have achieved everything I have done without Asphodel's assistance."

"Assistance, but not partnership?"

He shrugged. "Asphodel's talents are suited to supporting mine. She understands her role."

I wondered if she did. In my experience, gentlemen often take such matters for granted. But I did not ask. Instead, I tried a different tack. "My lord, why did you want to see us? What do you want of us?"

He put his glass aside and reached for mine, setting it on the little table so that he could take my hands in his. His skin was warmer now, almost hot against mine. "I wanted you to come to me. And you have."

"To what purpose?" My voice was a little lower than intended, a little breathier. The incense, I thought vaguely, filling my head and befuddling my senses.

"To take the measure of you. I felt instinctively that Mr. Templeton-Vane would be a worthy addition to the society. But you were the real surprise, Miss Speedwell."

Earlier I had expressed doubts about the sincerity of his seduction, but the mood had decidedly changed. His dark gaze was locked onto mine, his hands holding mine fast as his thumbs began to rub gently at the pulse in my wrist, slow, mesmerising circles of flesh upon flesh as he stared into my eyes. "How could I have expected such a woman existed? And yet here you are. Alone in my rooms. With me. Your heartbeat is quickening—can you feel it? Can you feel the slow stirrings in your blood? I can smell it, you know. I can smell the blood as it leaves your heart, full and rich." He lifted one of my wrists to his nose, his nostrils flaring as he sniffed deeply. "Such delicate skin! But look at the blue rivers that flow just underneath, rivers that could give life to me. Do you understand, my dear?"

"Yes," I said slowly. We both rose then, and with a single savage gesture he kicked the table from between us, the glasses shattering on the floor in a puddle of spilt wine and broken glass. He moved to grasp me tightly against him, my hands cupped in one of his. Then he took the other and stroked a finger down my cheek, ending with a sweep of the thumb just below my lip. He moved his hand to my neck, turning my head gently as he dropped his mouth to touch his lips to where the pulse beat in my throat.

"Veronica," he whispered against my skin. "Tell me what you want and I will give you everything."

"I want—" I paused, breathless with the sensations of his kisses against my skin.

"You want," he prompted. He nipped at my throat, lightly grazing his teeth over my flesh.

"I want to know precisely what Asphodel is doing to Stoker and why you are trying to distract me from it," I said as I stepped back, setting the sharp point of a minuten to the tender skin of his inner wrist and jabbing hard. "Now."

CHAPTER 21

Lord Ruthven could not have been more surprised if I had conjured myself into a cobra and bit him.

He leapt backwards, clutching his pricked wrist to his mouth and sucking gently at the beaded blood. "What the devil—"

"I did tell you I can always tell when a man is feigning interest. Your attempts at seduction were ham-handed, sir, and your attempts at mesmerism hardly better. Now, where is Stoker? Do not make me repeat the question again, or I will resort to a nastier and far more lethal weapon than the one I have already used," I warned him.

His expression turned at once sullen. Gone was the sophisticated gentleman with the polished performance of a practiced seducer. In his place was a sulky man who played a very sore loser. He snatched a handkerchief from his pocket and wrapped it about his wrist, stemming the blood.

"You have assaulted me," he said petulantly.

"I have merely hoist you with your own petard," I corrected. I nodded to the jewel in his coat. "That is a very clever pin, my lord. I note especially the filigree work of the setting. It is quite elaborate and very curiously done. I must say, I have never seen another like it. I imagine the way those two prongs there are configured, they would inflict an interesting mark upon the unwary and incurious—a mark that would look very much like a bite from a mouth with a pair of sharp fangs."

His marble-pale skin flushed angrily, but when he spoke, his voice was under control once more, mellifluous as a song. "I understand that even the most delicate of creatures may lash out when frightened. You have no need to be frightened of me, Veronica. I will never do anything against your wishes."

He was staring warily at the pin I still held in my hand. Assured that he would attempt no further intimacies, I slipped it neatly into my bodice.

"Are you always armed?" Now that I no longer threatened him, he seemed amused by the incident. No doubt he surmised that he had been taken by surprise and that I should be unable to best him a second time. I was content to let him believe it. Men, in my experience, are easiest to confound when they underestimate one.

"It has often been necessary in the course of my travels to defend myself. I like to be prepared." I smoothed my skirts and resettled my mask over my features.

"I imagine you do," he replied. "But it is not necessary here. I want only to be your friend."

He was giving me a piercing look from beneath his velvety brows again, and I sighed. "Please do stop attempting to mesmerise me. It is rather annoying, you know."

His lordship puffed out a sigh of exasperation. "You really are the most provoking woman," he muttered.

"It will not surprise you to learn that this is not the first occasion I have heard such a thing—nor are you the first man to think it," I told him. "Now, where might I find Stoker and Asphodel? And what plans does she have for him?"

He shrugged. "The conservatory, I should imagine. It is her domain and she prefers to entertain there."

I moved to the hidden door above the little passageway, intending to return the way we had come. He gestured towards the main door. "Go that way. Across the hall and down the stairs. You will recognise the direction from your first visit."

"Thank you." I paused on the threshold, glad of the fresh air in the corridor beyond, which came as a tonic after the incense fog of his private chambers. "What did you actually hope to accomplish here tonight?"

I rather expected him to invoke the notion of challenging my perceptions and broadening my experiences again, but instead he spoke plainly. "I hoped to persuade you that Mr. Templeton-Vane would make a valuable addition to our little society. I hoped to make a friend of you."

I stared at him, so perfectly suited to the theatricality of the setting—all shadow and glamour and dark allure. "You have a very peculiar way of making friends, my lord."

With that, I turned and left him. In the hall the sounds of the jollity on the floor below were clear, the music a spirited polka whose jaunty notes were embellished by the bellows of laughter and shrieks of enjoyment from the guests. Clearly the more restrained activities such as dancing had given way to other forms of entertainment I could not have possibly anticipated. I had just reached the bottom of the stairs when an arm snaked out and a firm hand clasped about my wrist. Before I could employ my minuten, Stoker loomed out of the darkness.

"Do not even think about stabbing me," he warned.

"I should not dream of it," I replied, discreetly slipping the pin back into my gown. "What is all the noise about? And where have you been?"

"Someone let a baboon loose in the ballroom," he said, never breaking stride as he towed me towards the front door.

"Heavens! Is it tame?"

"I have no intention of waiting around to find out," he replied. He paused long enough for me to collect my things from the cloakroom, and then we were off again, at such a cracking pace as I had not moved in a very long time.

"Stoker, I am wearing a very tight corset and very wide skirts," I reminded him. "A trifle slower, I beg you."

He checked himself then, matching his steps to my own, and I accordingly sped up a little to accommodate him in turn. It was not until we were safely ensconced in the Rosemorran carriage and on our way back to Bishop's Folly that he heaved a sigh of relief.

Or perhaps he was simply trying to clear his lungs, for he lowered the carriage window with a decisive yank and stuck his head outside, drawing in great breaths in spite of the mizzling weather that had descended. When he pulled his head back in, tiny drops of mist spangled his black hair like so many diamonds.

"Better?" I asked in some amusement.

"I swear that woman nearly asphyxiated me," he grumbled. "Some devilish variety of incense, the likes of which have probably never been smelt outside a Cairene brothel."

I raised a brow. "Have you been in a Cairene brothel?"

"Ask me no questions and I shall tell you no lies," he quipped.

"Hm. And where was the gentle Asphodel plying her charms? The conservatory?"

"Yes. Whilst she waxed on about moon moths and fate and other such nonsense. Paragraphs of tripe."

"Lord Ruthven was engaged in his own variety of blathering," I remarked. "He too had recourse to incense. I cannot understand what grudge these people have against fresh air."

Beside me, Stoker bristled. "And where was he burning his incense for you?"

"His boudoir," I replied, thinking hard. "Or whatever gentlemen call the room next to their bedrooms. A dressing room, perhaps? There was a table for his grooming impedimenta."

"Indeed." The word was ground between molars that were firmly clamped together. I sighed. It was not like Stoker to be jealous, but then I had not found myself in such proximity to an attractive man's bedchamber since our relationship had established itself as one of perfect intimacy. I dearly hoped he was not going to be tiresome about such things, particularly given my own complete lack of envy no matter how trying the circumstances.

"I do not like to admit it, but I believe you were correct," I began.

Stoker sat very still, his eyes closed. He drew in a deep, steady breath, then expelled it through lightly pursed lips.

"Whatever are you doing?" I asked.

"Savouring," he told me. "I so seldom hear those words that their appearance makes a noteworthy occasion."

"Ass," I said, giving him a push.

He looked at me, grinning. "Go on. You were about to lavish praise upon me and extol my many virtues including perspicacity and intelligence. Do not stint, Veronica. Use every large word you know, the more syllables the better."

"I shall ignore your flagrant attempts to wheedle flattery from me, and confine my remarks to the facts. Whilst I was in Lord Ruthven's dressing room, I discovered a few items of note."

"I'll wager you did indeed," he said in a tone of such aridity it would make the Sahara seem lush. I ignored this as well.

"To wit," I began, ticking off the points on my fingers, "he keeps a bottle of hair dye on his toilet table. Very dark hair dye."

Stoker shrugged. "Men may be as vain about their fading looks as women. Perhaps he simply wishes to keep a few grey hairs at bay."

"Vampires do not age. Second"—I held up another finger—"he has face powder of a very pale hue with a sort of pearlised finish. A liberal application of this would account for his pallor."

"And a vampire does not need assistance in appearing bloodless," he put in.

"Precisely. Furthermore, and thoroughly damning in my opinion, there is a looking glass over the washbasin where his razor reposes. What possible use could a vampire have for a looking glass if he casts no reflection?"

Stoker began to speak, but I carried on. "The use of that heavy incense suggests a need to overcome the senses with tricks and flummery instead of a real ability to hypnotise, although I will credit him with an uncanny ability to hold a person's gaze. But worst of all, I think, is his stickpin."

"His stickpin? You object to his choice of jewellery?"

"The piece is a little florid for my taste, but that is not my objection. It is that the setting around the gem has been worked into two sharp points. It would require an attentive eye—the eye of a natural scientist," I added modestly, "to detect it, but I noticed it as soon as he drew near enough for my examination."

"Of course he did," Stoker muttered.

"Attend to the matter at hand," I urged. "The stickpin was cleverly designed to inflict a pair of wounds—punctures spaced almost precisely as far apart as the canine teeth. If he applied that pin to a person's neck whilst they were otherwise occupied, it would leave a highly suggestive mark, one that would almost certainly persuade the victim that a vampire had been at work."

"'Otherwise occupied'?" His voice had taken on a strangled quality. "How might one be otherwise occupied whilst Lord Ruthven is busy ramming a brooch into one's throat?"

"The activity would have to ensure that Lord Ruthven's proximity was extreme," I reasoned. "And that a certain contact between his person and the flesh of the neck was to be expected. Furthermore, the contact might lead to moderately painful sensations as well as pleasurable ones in order to ensure his victim would not pull away. That would obviously suggest activities of an amorous nature. In short, a passionate embrace in the course of which Lord Ruthven may distract his victim with caresses so arousing that his victim does not put an end to them until he has accomplished his task of inflicting the injury with his stickpin."

"Thus ensuring that when the victim notices the pain or even the blood, they would naturally conclude they have been attacked by a vampire."

"Precisely. And as the bite cannot be a fatal one, it is presumed he must be looking for some other result from the interlude."

Stoker tipped his head thoughtfully. "No doubt a modest bite—coupled with the heightened atmosphere of his home, his attempts to make himself appear otherworldly—would persuade his victims that they are now in thrall to him. It is a bit of theatre to act as the coup de grâce to the rest of his amateur dramatics."

"Yes, it all makes perfect sense if you consider him a consummate performer and nothing more. There is the greasepaint in the form of the powder and hair dye, costuming in garments that appear exotic to the average Englishman, and even effects of lighting and setting to heighten his performance."

"To say nothing of his little affectations of character," Stoker added. "I think you have worked it out marvellously well, my love. Shall I conclude you are coming to the realisation that vampires do not exist?"

"One cannot draw that conclusion definitively," I returned. "One can only surmise that Lord Ruthven is not one."

"Veronica, there are no such things as vampires."

"Do stop gritting your teeth. You will wear them down to nubs," I warned. "Besides, it is the soundest scientific reasoning to entertain the possibility that vampires *might* exist. I can only say with increasing certainty that Lord Ruthven is most likely not among their number."

"How?" he demanded. "How can you claim it is sound scientific reasoning?"

"Starfish," I replied promptly. "The echinoderms of Asteroidea. You were a naval man, certainly you are familiar."

"Yes, Veronica. I am familiar with starfish. I grew up on the Sussex coast, remember? Every boy who wanders English beaches knows starfish."

"Then you know what happens when a limb is lost."

"It is regenerated, but I fail to see—oh, for the love of bleeding Jesus, you are not actually suggesting that a man might regenerate his entire body."

"Of course not. The human animal is far too complex an organism for that," I assured him. "But it is possible that the consciousness may regenerate."

"It bloody well is not. Consciousness is—"

"Choose your next words carefully," I told him. "You are about to be dogmatic on this subject, and I would remind you that we know comparatively nothing about consciousness. It is a universe yet uncharted."

"That it is," he allowed, "but we can agree, I believe, that it is thoroughly unlikely that consciousness would leave upon death and reappear, bringing with it the ability to live forever in some liminal state that is neither entirely dead nor alive."

"One may be in such a liminal state when one is comatose," I reminded him.

"When comatose, a person is literally *unconscious*," he returned with an air one would hate to describe as smug. (But one would be sorely tempted.)

"That is open to debate. There are cases where patients have awakened from apparent oblivion only to recite remarks made in their presence when they were senseless. In those cases, physical life was not extinguished, and consciousness was imperfect but it was in some sense present."

"That does not answer my point about eternal life," he reminded me.

"Perhaps vampires do not enjoy *eternal* life," I temporised. "Perhaps it is only extended past its natural expectation. Consider Patricia. Her kind live to be well over a century, more than two!"

"Again, a Galápagos tortoise is not the same as a human being," he said patiently. "Humans are far more complicated a mechanism."

"All the more reason to suppose there is still much we have left to learn. Surely you can admit, we have not even begun to plumb the depths of what it means to be human! Only a handful of years ago, we did not understand what a germ was or how it might live inside a body, inflicting infection. The most erudite men of science believed that miasmas and evil humours were responsible for our afflictions. Now we know better. Do you really mean to say that you are so arrogant that you cannot concede the slightest possibility that something beyond our understanding may yet exist in the human experience?"

He opened his mouth, then snapped it closed again. When he spoke it was a hoarse rasp. "There. Are. No. Such. Things. As. Vampires."

I waved a hand. "We shall make an agreement not to agree."

To my surprise, Stoker resisted the urge to nettle me further. "You realise what this means? The diminutive nature of the stickpin?"

"That it could not have been the instrument of violence used against Maurice Quincey," I said grimly.

"Indeed. A pin such as you describe would cause as much blood to flow as a paper cut. In order to drain Quincey's body entirely, something much larger would have been required to puncture his jugular, particularly because if he were drugged—which I suppose he must have been in order to have been murdered so viciously with no marks upon him—the pulse would have slowed."

"And thus the blood would have flowed more slowly," I concluded. "Excellent point."

"My medical training does occasionally come in useful. Surely we have learnt something this evening. Why are you so bedevilled?"

"I am not bedevilled. I am thinking." I did not care to share my thoughts with him, largely because of the wager we had made. It was more than a mere guinea—it was the principle of the thing. Let a man best you once, and he just might try to make a habit of it.

CHAPTER 22

The next morning, having ensured J. J. and Mornaday were both au courant with the latest developments, slender as they were, I settled to work cataloguing a recent arrival—a case of southern birdwings. *Troides minos* is a truly striking species of butterfly, and these displayed remarkable variety in both size and colouration. As I immersed myself in the study of these most graceful of creatures, Stoker busied himself with his "secret project." Naturally I had not the slightest interest in penetrating his furtive business. Despite what others may say behind my back and—upon occasion—directly to my face, I am not a naturally inquisitive person except where my own work is concerned.

But I will admit to a *wisp* of curiosity given that a mantle of embarrassment seemed to settle over his features whenever he prepared to disappear into the private studio he had constructed within the Belvedere. He volunteered no information and it was beneath my dignity to ask, so when he presented himself a short while later for elevenses with a bared torso liberally streaked with glue and bits of long white fur, I said nothing. I merely extended a cup of tea, dark as treacle and heavily sugared, just as he liked.

"Thank you," he grumbled, plucking the cup from the saucer by the rim. He drank half of it down in a single gulp and crunched his way through two ginger biscuits with considerable annoyance.

"Everything all right, dearest?" I inquired, careful to keep my gaze fixed upon my case of birdwings.

"I am perfectly contented with my work," he assured me. But the deep flush to his cheeks told another story. I was fluent in the language of Revelstoke Templeton-Vane; indeed, I would have challenged anyone to read it with more ease or competency. While I might not know the particulars of his irritations regarding this current commission, I understood the remedy well enough. I would admit to a curious inability to settle properly to my own work that morning. Something about the Danse Macabre tickled the back of my mind, a glimmer of an idea that refused to form itself into a definitive thought. It was annoying in the extreme, and the more I attempted to follow it, the more quickly it eluded me.

With a decisive gesture, I pushed aside the teapot. "I propose a journey. Sponge the worst of the grime from your person whilst I feed the dogs, and then we shall embark."

"I have work—" he began, but his heart was not in it, and I grinned.

"Consider yourself abducted."

Two hours later we were comfortably ensconced in a private compartment on the express train into the heart of Surrey. Arriving at the station and securing our tickets had taken more time than expected, with the result that we almost missed the train altogether, and it was not until we were safely aboard and churning our way out of the smoke-strangled streets of London and into the brisk spring breezes of Surrey that I explained our destination.

"Little Saints?" Stoker asked, reaching for his tin of honeycomb. He crunched into a piece with no regard whatsoever for his teeth—a habit that would have seen my aunts into fits of hysterics—and cocked a brow at me curiously.

"There was a book in Lord Ruthven's dressing room marked with a stamp from Little Saints, a boys' school. I found reference to it in a copy of Lord Rosemorran's *Historic English Schools for Gentlemen Scholars*. It is a modest establishment, founded in the last century in Peasgreen, a village some two miles from Guildford. I am certain we can hire a station fly, or failing that, a short walk in the bracing spring air will be healthful for both of us."

"And what do you propose to do at a boys' school?"

"I do not know precisely," I admitted. "I came away without a firm plan. I was rather hoping you might devise one."

He sighed. "Shall I trot out the family name again? It is a useful one. I could claim to be scouting schools for my brother's eldest son."

"Your brother does not have a son," I reminded him.

"Not Tiberius—Rupert."

I made a point of never committing to memory the names or ages of the offspring of my acquaintance, largely because I was not interested in the slightest, but also because the ages changed with startling swiftness. No sooner had I dutifully admired an infant through gritted teeth than it had learnt to crawl and was terrorising the family pets. After this came walking, a frankly horrifying stage where one could no longer simply put the child down and it would stay put. How mothers and nursemaids managed was a thing I should never understand.

"Ah. I remember now. He has three, does he not?"

Stoker nodded. "The eldest is fourteen and enrolled at Rugby, where one imagines he is being flogged and bullied on a regular basis, just as the rest of us were."

"Barbarous," I murmured.

"Most boys' schools are. But it is expected of a Templeton-Vane." He had told me little of his educational adventures, but I knew enough to realise it was not a happy subject for him. "Perhaps the headmaster will see us, although it is highly irregular to simply appear without a letter of introduction or prior arrangement."

I waved this away, but as we stood outside the gates of Little Saints some time later, it occurred to me that I oughtn't to have dismissed his reservations quite so quickly. The walk from the train had been so lovely, passing through fields dotted with dog violets and lesser celandine and little patches of wood thick with bluebells. The air was so fresh and sweet that I drew in great lungfuls of the stuff, feeling reborn as I walked, arms swinging freely, my stride lengthening as my muscles stretched themselves. It had almost been a pity to reach the school, but the shouts of youngsters as they went about their sporting games struck our ears long before we arrived at the gates. These structures were tall and not particularly forbidding, but they were stoutly locked. Apparently the headmaster of Little Saints was taking no chances of his charges escaping. Or of intruders gaining ingress. A small gravelled court divided the gates from the school, both of them bordered by the playing fields. In the distance was a small pond and beyond that a prettyish sort of wood where I imagined the pupils took nature walks. The school itself had most likely been a house at one point; it had a cosily domestic air courtesy of the warm red bricks of its façade, and the heavy stone lintels over the windows gave it a sleepy look. Thick vines of creeper spread across the walls, and the whole effect was one of smug, snug superiority.

Unexpected visitors excited some interest, for a few of the lads paused their efforts to hurl one another to the ground or fling a ball about—I confess I did not pay much attention to the objective of their game—and one, a tall, whippet-thin boy of perhaps sixteen trotted towards us, tucking in his shirttails and wiping the streaks of fresh sweat from his face. He smoothed his hair and smiled politely as he reached us.

"Good afternoon. Might I be of assistance?" His vowels were carefully modulated—too carefully, I thought. This was no aristocrat's son, but perhaps a banker's boy or a prosperous merchant's heir. He was not born to the caste of the bluebloods, but I had no doubt he would eventually marry in. His games kit was of good quality and showed no sign of having been altered to accommodate a growing lad. He had clearly been furnished with new clothes for the Easter term when many boys had to make do with what they had been given at the start of school in the autumn or perhaps an elder brother's castoffs. As he was expensively presented and with the air of wary confidence that new money brings, it was a simple matter to deduce his father had made a fortune and only recently.

I smiled, but it was Stoker who spoke. "Good afternoon. What is your headmaster's name?"

"That would be Mr. Garvey, sir. Mr. Thomas Garvey."

"I should like to speak with him. Now, if it is convenient." He extracted a somewhat battered card from his notecase and passed it through the gates.

"I shall take this to him directly, Mr. Templeton-Vane," the boy promised. He trotted off in the direction of the school itself. A very few moments later, he returned, looking a trifle abashed. "I do apologise, sir, but headmaster is giving the Latin lesson this afternoon. Our regular Classics teacher is abed with a touch of gout. I daren't interrupt Mr. Garvey."

"A stickler is he?" Stoker asked with a cordial smile. The boy grinned but quickly thought better of it, mastering his reaction with smooth courtesy.

"Mr. Garvey is an excellent headmaster. He brooks no slackness, sir."

"I expect he does not. Well, we shall call again when we have made arrangements beforehand. Thank you, lad."

"Thank you, sir. Madam," he said, bidding us farewell with the most delightfully courtly bow.

"We ought to have got that boy's name," Stoker said as we walked away. "I suspect he shall be prime minister one day."

"Or at the very least, chairman of the Bank of England," I agreed. "How vexing though that the headmaster was not to be disturbed! A wasted trip."

Stoker slid an arm through mine, drawing me close. "Was it really?"

I surveyed the sweep of the fields, now touched with the gold of the lowering sun, and I returned his smile. "I suppose not. Let us return to Peasgreen and wait for the train. I saw a pretty little tea shop just past the station."

We were soon obliged with seats at a tiny table—far too diminutive for Stoker's muscular bulk—and a tea set that might have done credit to Lady Julia's dormouse. The cups were approximately the size of thimbles, and each held but a swallow of tea. The cakes were no larger than a sixpence, and Stoker regarded the sandwiches mournfully.

"I have seen more substantial portions in Lady Rose's dollhouse," he said, referring to Lord Rosemorran's youngest and most chaotic child.

"At least we shall not be forced to make the return journey on an empty stomach," I reminded him.

He emptied the entire jam pot—all two teaspoons of cherry preserves—onto a scone the size of a matchbox. "Hardly better than empty," he grumbled. "Perhaps you were right and this has been a wasted journey."

"I do wish we had been able to speak to the headmaster," I replied as the waitress—a pretty, robust young woman with dimpled pink cheeks—delivered a fresh pot of tea. Her dress was of spotted dimity with an old-fashioned muslin fichu concealing the greater part of an exuberant bosom that gave the impression of being imperfectly restrained.

"Headmaster? Would you be having business with Little Saints, then?" she asked. It was rudely inquisitive of her to insert herself into our conversation, but one must always make allowances for differences in customs when one travels—Surrey being practically a foreign country in my opinion. Furthermore, I had often observed that girls who worked in tea shops were incapable of serving cakes and tea without a generous side helping of gossip.

"We did, but the headmaster was unavailable to speak to us." I was the one who replied, but her eyes were firmly fixed upon Stoker, a discernible rose blush rising in her cheeks.

"Oh, aye? Giving the Latin lesson, no doubt," she told him. She made no acknowledgement of me, and I resigned myself to being perfectly invisible through the rest of the exchange.

"You are remarkably well informed," Stoker told her with a smile so charming it ought to have come with a stern warning from the authorities about its effects upon impressionable young women. I could practically hear the girl sigh before she gave a little giggle.

"Thank you, sir. I am a great one for noticing things," she murmured. She looked down, then peeped up again at him through her lashes.

"For god's sake," I muttered.

"Eat a scone, Veronica," Stoker said, shoving a buttered tea cake into my hand. He turned back to the girl. "We were very disappointed not to speak with Mr. Garvey. Has he worked there long?"

"Oh, not more than two years," she told him. "But if it is school business you're about, you'll not find better than Mr. Baddlesmere. He be the retired headmaster, worked there forty year or more."

"Now, that would be useful," Stoker said, and she beamed with pleasure. "Where might we find Mr. Baddlesmere?"

"Just a step down the way, sir. The street do bend around the church, and just past the churchyard is Bee Cottage. That is where you will find him, tending his bees most afternoons. You cannot mistake it. There is a great skep on the gate," she told him.

He flashed her another winsome smile. "Thank you. You have been very helpful indeed."

"Not at all, sir," she said with an audible sigh.

I placed a few coins on the table and rose, pulling on my gloves. "Come, Stoker. There is not much time before the next train."

He stood, giving the girl a courteous nod and she bobbed him a curtsy. I fairly pushed him out the door.

"I hadn't finished my lardy cakes, you know," he said somewhat regretfully.

I cocked a brow at him and turned towards the church. "It was most definitely time you finished something."

CHAPTER 23

Bee Cottage was, as the tearoom waitress had told us, unmistakable. It might have begun life as a modest dwelling of simple proportions, but the years and someone's fancy had altered it extensively. The roof was low and thatched and neatly trimmed, while the rest of the place was an exercise in whimsicality. There was not a right angle or plumb line to be found; every window was aslant, every wall askew. It rambled from side to side and front to back with haphazard additions and little pockets of gardens, each embellished with some small feature—a tiny pond shimmering with golden carp, a cherry tree thick with pale blossoms, a copper statue of a philosophical frog. An enormous sculpture of a bee skep sat in pride of place upon a plinth next to the gate, and vines of wisteria lay heavily over the lintel of the front door, each raceme crowded with fragrant purple petals. Gentle blue forget-me-nots jostled the earliest pink blushes of the peonies, and through all came the steady hum of bees working the newly budded flowers. It was a distinctly peaceful place, every element, higgledy-piggledy as they were, working harmoniously with the rest.

There was no reply to my brisk knock at the door, and I had almost resigned myself to a second disappointment, when Stoker cocked his head. "Do you hear something?"

Without waiting for a response, he headed around the nearest corner of the cottage, following a narrow path that wound through a little shrubbery that would in summer, I guessed, have been thick with roses and delphiniums. Never one to be left behind, I followed hard upon his heels, and I heard what had attracted his attention—the gentle buzz of beehives. On the other side of the concealing shrubbery, we emerged into a sort of clearing. Here the noise was fairly thunderous, the source a selection of hives that throbbed with activity. Tending them was a tall, gaunt figure who puffed fragrant smoke towards the agitated creatures, soothing them with the heavy, soporific clouds. It was a scene familiar to any apiarian, but what made it so extraordinary was the fact that the figure was enveloped in an enormous nightdress, folds of white linen encompassing it from neck to mid-calf, revealing lower legs encased in thick woolly socks, gaiters, and heavy brogues. Atop its head was a headdress shaped like a great horned moon, the two points rising up from just above either ear. Over this had been draped a long, thick veil of pink tulle, vast swathes of it that were knotted at the waist to provide a sort of protective cocoon for the beekeeper. He wore spectacles with thick lenses and a pair of long leather gauntlets that stretched to the elbow.

Stoker stood, mouth agape at the utterly mad figure before us, but I smiled in delight. Here was an original personality indeed. I called a "halloo" over the noise of the bees—a nearly deafening roar this close to the hives. The figure swung about, clouds of smoke swirling around the veils and horned headdress and giving the appearance of a sort of wizard, sprung from the pages of a child's storybook.

"Hello to you!" he called. "Do not mind me. I'm only setting a new queen for this hive. Won't be a moment. Wait inside the cottage lest you get stung. They're a trifle fractious at present."

He waved us towards the rear door of the cottage, and Stoker and I obediently retreated. Inside, the house was as rambling and curious as I had expected. Every surface was stacked with books or papers or some interesting oddity. A window ledge held a collection of plants in various degrees of health; a fat, lazy goldfish swam in a glass bowl resting on a harpsichord. A Persian pipe stood on the hearth, and the armchair beside it was heavily draped in assorted kilims from Turkey. I seated myself to wait whilst Stoker made a study of the bookshelves.

"I do not believe it," he said, extracting a heavy volume and blowing it free of dust. "He has a first edition of Heughmann's *A Study of Mammalian Anatomy*, volume one. Do you realise how rare that is?"

"Is it?"

"Heughmann only ever wrote the first volume," Stoker said, thumbing the pages with considerable excitement. "It was intended to be a comprehensive study of all mammals, but he only made it as far as Bactrian camels."

"Why?"

"He was kicked by one and lost his nerve," Stoker said, turning the book to display a watercolour of an enormous furry camel with two humps. I had always been a great admirer of Bactrian camels—they are far more comfortable to ride than the decidedly ill-tempered and more common dromedary—but before I could express my sentiments, our host appeared, still garbed in his outlandish costume and rubbing his hands together as he gave a jovial exclamation.

"Visitors! One does so enjoy visitors. I put out a bottle of plum wine this morning and biscuits," he said with a nod towards a low table where a dusty bottle of purple wine and a biscuit tin reposed.

"This morning?" I asked. "How did you know—"

"The bees," he said, laying a finger to the side of his nose in spite of his veils. "The bees know all and tell me most."

He glanced to Stoker. "Admirer of Heughmann, are you, my lad?"

"Indeed," Stoker told him. "I find his detailed studies of mammalian circulatory systems to be some of the finest I have ever seen. Although I must take exception to his thoughts on aardvarks."

Before Stoker could furnish us with those thoughts, I turned to the gentleman beekeeper. "We ought to introduce ourselves. I am Veronica Speedwell, and this is Revelstoke Templeton-Vane."

"Templeton-Vane! Never say you are the fellow who fitted up the water buffalo Lord Maysbury keeps in his entry hall?"

"I am," Stoker said modestly.

"Good god, man, you are legend!" He strode to Stoker and pulled off one of his heavy gauntlets, thrusting a bony hand to grasp Stoker in a violent handshake. "Professor Charles Winthrop Baddlesmere. Batty Baddlesmere, the boys used to call me when I was headmaster," he said with a grin.

"One wonders why," I murmured. But the professor's hearing was excellent, for he turned and blinked at me, his eyes wide behind his thick spectacles. "Oh! My costume. Quite unusual, I admit. But all chosen with great care to provide protection from the bees when they are in a temper."

"Not from a conventional supplier of equipment for beekeepers, I presume," I said with a friendly smile.

"No, indeed! Every bit of this was got from the church jumble sale. The amateur dramatic society donated costumes, you see. They had just done a cracking *Richard III*, and these horned headdresses were quite the fashion for ladies in the Middle Ages. Most perfectly Plantagenet, one might say. The nightdress was a castoff from the vicar's wife—a lady of robust proportions, as you can see. And the veils were from last year's May Day celebrations. The parade for the queen of the May featured pink tulle clouds to disguise the hay wagon she rode in. Very effective it was too." With each mention of a garment, he cast it off until he was standing before us in a set of ancient breeches and his shirtsleeves and braces. He pulled on a strange, voluminous knitted garment—the sort of jumper a fisherman might wear if he were fond of stripes—and settled into his chair with an expression of delight. "How wonderful indeed to have visitors. Miss Speedwell, if you would oblige by pouring out the plum wine, and Mr. Templeton-Vane, if you would be so kind as to hand round the biscuit tin, we can get properly acquainted. Do you mind if I smoke?"

The next few minutes were passed in supplying ourselves with little glasses of plum wine and plates of honey biscuits while the professor used a small pair of tongs to pluck a coal from the fire and apply it to his Persian pipe. Soon the room was filled with the scent of apple-laced tobacco, and from another room a cat appeared, fat and sleek and with a face that looked as if it had been pushed against a window for too long. She gave us a cool, assessing gaze, then leapt upon her master's knee to regard us with the disdain of royalty.

With his pipe in hand and cat upon his lap, the professor turned to me, his eyes brightly inquisitive. "I say, Speedwell! That name is familiar. Are you perchance a relation to the V. Speedwell who wrote so forcefully on the subject of the carnivorous habits of the male common buckeye butterfly for the *Quarterly Journal of the Butterfly Enthusiast*?"

"I am the author," I said with a modest smile.

"How very fortuitous! I was just about to compose a letter to the editor upon the very subject. I am afraid I take the opposite view entirely, Miss Speedwell. One cannot say definitively that the male of the species is the only one inclined to eating carrion. In fact . . ."

Those words, as the astute reader will have realised, were an invitation to a spirited discussion in which the professor and I proceeded to quarrel genteelly for the better part of half an hour. The mantel clock was just chiming the hour when Stoker roused himself from the slight doze into which he had fallen.

"My god, are the pair of you still at it?" he asked, rubbing his eyes. "Have you not finished yet?"

"Very nearly," I promised him. "I have almost persuaded the professor that the effort involved in securing a selection of imagoes of *Junonia coenia* would be well worth it given the variety—"

"Ah, but *is* it?" the professor began, rubbing his hands together gleefully. "If you will but attend my argument more closely, Miss Speedwell, I think you will find—"

"Enough," Stoker pleaded. "I beg you both. Before I must do myself a mischief with the fireplace poker."

"Oh, very well," I said with little grace. I turned to the professor with my most charming smile. "You have not inquired as to the purpose of our call."

His bushy white brows rose skywards, and he gave a great laugh, startling the cat. "So I have not! I was that delighted to receive callers. Very well, why have you come? Wait! Wait a moment. Such a wonderful argument as we have had leaves a body hungry. We must have sustenance! I shall cut sandwiches and then you will tell me your meaning in coming to see me."

He rose, popping the cat to his shoulder, and left us, the cat's tail waving jauntily in the air as they went. In a very few minutes he reappeared, a plate of thickly cut sandwiches in hand. They were all ham, and the bread was spread with the finest new butter and he did not stint with the slabs of cheese nor with the liberal applications of a truly excellent chutney. Stoker applied himself with a tiny moan of pleasure, and I admit to enjoying one or two myself.

As we ate, the professor turned his bright-eyed gaze upon us. "Now then. The purpose of your visit." He broke off pieces of ham, little titbits for the cat, who accepted them as daintily as a princess grooming herself thoughtfully between bites.

"This afternoon we paid a call at Little Saints, but I am afraid we were unable to secure a meeting with the headmaster," Stoker began.

"Ah! Well, Mr. Garvey can be a bit high in the instep," he said with a rueful look. "A good enough fellow, to be sure, but he feels the weight of his office very heavily indeed."

"Did you not?" I asked him. "Being headmaster, responsible for the shaping of so many young minds, their characters and their futures. It is a formidable task."

"Formidable but rewarding! And one must never forget to have a sense of humour about the business. A bit of levity now and again can accomplish more than all the sermonising in the world, particularly with boys. What business did you have with Garvey that you think I could accomplish in his stead?"

The eyes were suddenly shrewd, and I realised then his attitude of bonhomie was—although in no way false—not the complete picture of the man. He was sharp as a new pin, perceptive, and discerning, as he would have to be in order to run a school with any degree of success.

"We are looking for answers, Professor. We have encountered a man who we believe has a connection to Little Saints, but we cannot say what it may be," Stoker explained.

The professor rubbed his hands together. "A mystery! Say on, dear fellow."

"The man calls himself Lord Ruthven, but we know this to be a pseudonym. He is perhaps forty, possibly a little less. He uses hair dye to conceal a few grey threads, we believe. He is almost exactly of my height, although a little slighter of build. He has very expressive dark eyes and is conversant in Latin, I think. And he has made a careful study of mesmeric tricks."

The professor, who had been shaking his head at the beginning of the description, suddenly looked alert. "Mesmerism? A nasty business sometimes."

"How so?" I asked. "I thought the point of hypnosis is that it cannot persuade someone to perform an action against their character."

"In theory," he said, stroking the cat thoughtfully. "In practice?" He shrugged. "I have seen too many attempts to circumvent that limitation to think the activity a healthful one. It cannot be moral to seek to overthrow the free will of another human being."

"Can you think of anyone who fits that particular description?" Stoker asked. "I know it is vague, but perhaps there was someone connected with Little Saints? A pupil?"

"A teacher," the professor corrected. He pushed the cat gently off his lap and went to one of the overflowing bookshelves beside the fireplace. He ran a crooked forefinger along the volumes until he came to the one he sought. He removed it and blew gently, unsettling a modest amount of dust. The cat sneezed, almost pointedly, and removed herself from the room. The professor thumbed the book for several pages, stopping at a photograph. He passed it over to us, and we saw the image was of a group of young scholars, the entire student body of Little Saints, it seemed. Arranged in the front, on a long bench, were the faculty, dressed in their formal robes of academia. Directly in the center, in pride of place as headmaster, sat a younger version of the professor, his beard grey rather than white. And at the far end, in the most junior seat of the staff, an unmistakable and familiar face.

"That is he!" I cried. "That is Lord Ruthven!"

"No, my dear," corrected the professor. "That is Miles Hegarty."

CHAPTER 24

"Who is Miles Hegarty?" Stoker inquired.

The professor paused to relight his pipe, and after several deep puffs, he settled back into his chair, the smoke wreathing his head like a sinuous grey crown. "A man of more imagination than intelligence, I should say. A mediocre teacher and a fine cricketer."

"What did he teach?" I asked.

"Literature, early modern with an emphasis on Shakespeare and the Elizabethan poets and the occasional lecture on Restoration dramas."

"A theatrical curriculum," Stoker observed.

"Not as theatrical as he would have liked," the professor returned dryly. "More than once I interrupted his lectures to find him entirely off-topic, discussing folklore and superstition. It was a passion of his, almost to the point of mania."

"Any subjects in particular?" I queried.

"Anything that might excite a boy's fevered imagination, my dear. Elusive mountain cats of Scotland, German giants, Irish faeries, Cornish pixies. Dragons, wyverns, werewolves, the fellow collected everything he could on all of the most fantastical creatures as well as the local practices that would keep them at bay."

"What of vampires?" Stoker asked.

"Vampires! Oh, my, yes. He did speak of those. Had rather a pretty collection of books from the more easterly lands of the Austro-Hungarian empire. He was forever begging the language master, Mr. Tudor, to translate for him."

"Could we speak to Mr. Tudor?" I asked eagerly.

The professor waved a hand, disturbing the circling smoke only slightly. "Emigrated to Canada last year, I'm afraid. He always meant to strike out for the wilderness, but I shouldn't be surprised if Hegarty's constant demands didn't hurry him along. Of course Tudor only spoke German dialects with a smattering of Hungarian, but Hegarty was forever turning up crumbling little volumes of ancient Roumanian or Serbo-Croat. There were some lovely fairy tales among them, but he was far more interested in having the books about vampires translated. They do not call them that, mind you, not over there. But it is the nearest word we have in English. Tudor didn't have the stomach for it. He preferred Bavarian romantic poetry, and started ducking into the cloakroom whenever he saw Hegarty coming his way. He did it so often, the rumour went round that Tudor had a cold in the bowels, and the school nurse insisted upon dosing all the boys with castor oil as a preventive measure." He pulled a face at the memory, and Stoker smothered a laugh.

"Do you know where Miles Hegarty came from?" he asked as he reached for another sandwich.

The professor thought a moment, then shook his head. "Somewhere in the Midlands, I should think. I have a vague recollection that he was a Leicester man, but it has been a while and my memory is not what it was."

The cat reappeared and settled herself once more upon her master's lap. He fussed over her for a moment, rising to pour out a saucer of tea to which he added a drop of milk. "She does like her tea," he said by way of explanation as he placed the saucer on the floor. The cat leapt up with the grace of a dancer, placing dainty paws on either side of the saucer as she lapped at the libation.

"Where was I?" the professor asked as he resumed his seat once more.

"Telling us what you remember about Miles Hegarty," I prompted.

"Ah, yes. He was, as I say, an indifferent teacher. He might have inspired the boys to a good measure of learning if he had been enthusiastic about his subject, but he found Shakespeare and Spenser a little quotidian for his tastes. He only taught them because it was mandated by the curriculum. He preferred the later dramatists, although even those paled to his folkloric studies. Unfortunately, as often as I pointed out to him that our leading universities do not place value in such subjects, he persisted in including them in his lectures. I was forced to ask him to leave at the end of the first year."

Some small shadow passed over his face, and I leant nearer. "Was there something more?"

"I shouldn't like to gossip," he hedged.

Stoker placed his cup and saucer on the table and folded his hands, almost in a gesture of supplication. "Professor, we would not ask if it were not important."

"How important?"

"If I told you it was a matter of life and death, that would not be too far an exaggeration," Stoker told him.

"Ah," was the professor's only reply.

"You do not seem entirely surprised," I remarked.

He thought a long moment before he replied, considering his words carefully, it seemed, choosing each one with purpose. "Some people have a charisma about them, a quality that draws people near. In olden days, folk called it a glamoury, an actual charm worked to make one attractive to others. The trouble is that such a quality may be misused."

"Did Miles Hegarty have such a quality? Did he misuse it?" Stoker's queries were gentle, and the professor nodded.

"I believe so, although I could never prove it. I dismissed him, quite rightly, because he failed to adequately prepare his pupils for the subject he had been engaged to teach. But I will admit to a deep and abiding relief the day he left Little Saints. It was as though a cloud had settled over our happy little school. And when he left, the sun shone once more."

"How did he misuse his influence over the boys?" Stoker asked.

"Not in a meddlesome way," the professor returned swiftly. "I do not mean anything of *that* sort. And I even hesitate to mention it as there was never any behaviour on his part to which I could point with conviction."

"We are not in a court of law," I said softly. "We do not require proof. In fact, the thoughts of a shrewd and perceptive bystander might be more helpful to us."

His smile was self-deprecating. "Well, I do not know about shrewd, but one does gain a certain perceptiveness when one runs a school for boys, a sort of sixth sense when trouble is about." He paused, puffing quietly on his pipe and watching the smoke drift lazily overhead. "It was nothing more than conversations, really. Little conferences between Hegarty and some of the boys that would abruptly break off when I happened upon them. The boys looked furtive when he was around, as if they shared some great secret and mustn't be found out. It was the choice of boys which I noticed as well."

"Was there something they had in common?" Stoker helped himself to the last sandwich as he awaited the professor's reply.

"Indeed." He tipped his head, studying Stoker from scuffed boots to tumbled hair. "You might look a ruffian, but I know a public school boy when I see one. Eton or Harrow?"

"Rugby, and only for a bit," Stoker admitted.

The professor grinned. "It is the vowels, you see. One never mistakes the vowels. But if you have been to a proper school, you understand how the factions work, the little cliques that form."

"I imagine they are the same everywhere," Stoker said. "Senior lads ride roughshod over the younger boys. There are always a top tier of little autocrats who lord it over everyone else and are rivals to one another even if they put on a show of friendship at times."

"Precisely." The professor nodded, lazily dispersing the little cloud that had settled over his head. "The sons of dukes are never so precious about their rank as the sons of baronets, and knights are the absolute worst. Where was I? Ah, Hegarty's little pets. He had a penchant for singling out the boys who were most socially distinctive in their year. More than once I saw the most illustrious youths disappearing into Hegarty's rooms for an informal social gathering."

Stoker dusted the crumbs of the sandwich from his fingers and gave his belly a happy little pat. "I presume such fraternisation with teachers is not forbidden at Little Saints?"

The professor waggled his hand back and forth. "It is not forbidden but neither is it encouraged. We expected the schoolmasters to know favouritism is a dangerous practise. It can very easily stir up resentments amongst the boys who have not been befriended. And it often leads to the boys who have been so favoured thinking far too highly of themselves. Beyond that, if the parents catch a whiff of those sorts of goings-on, they invariably complain, and then all the devils in hell cannot mend the matter. Still," he added with a sigh, "it is impossible to make a formal policy and to enforce it. Lads are always popping in and out of their tutors' rooms for extra instruction in a thorny subject or for a dressing-down for some infraction. To chase them all down and make certain they were all attending to school business every minute of the day was far more than my time was worth."

"Why would Miles Hegarty make a point of singling out the most socially prominent pupils?" I wondered.

"It sounds as if he were collecting trophies," Stoker suggested.

The professor nodded. "My thoughts exactly. It is distasteful to think of it, but it did occur to me that Hegarty was not above currying favour with the boys whose prospects were the most promising. Perhaps with an eye to angling for an invitation to a country house or some introductions that would provide him with a more lucrative or prestigious post. It is not unknown for schoolmasters to enter private employment as tutors, and while the remuneration is not much better, the circumstances are indeed an improvement. One lives in decidedly more luxurious conditions than a schoolmaster's lodgings, and there are other perquisites—travel being the first."

"The more interesting question," Stoker said, rubbing his chin absently, "is why the pupils were spending time with Hegarty. Forgive me, Professor, but Little Saints is a small school."

"You mean we are not distinguished," the professor corrected, his eyes fairly twinkling as Stoker coloured slightly.

"I meant no offence."

"None taken! We make no future titans here. We boast no prime ministers amongst our alumni, and our ducal progeny are all third sons or lesser," he said, tapping the embers from his pipe onto the hearthstone. "No, Little Saints has no pretensions. It is a good school, even an excellent one, if one judges only on the strength of its curriculum and the character of the young men it sends out into the world. It is the very place to get a thorough grounding in ancient and modern languages, literature, mathematics, and various sciences. We may even distinguish ourselves in our departments of philosophy and history. But what we cannot do is pretend to compete on the grounds of exclusivity. We have taught the odd lordling now and again, but ours is not the name on a nobleman's lips when he is looking to send his son off to be educated. Our masters vary, accordingly, from adequate to gifted. Hegarty was nearer the adequate end of that spectrum. He taught and he breathed life into his subjects for his pupils, but he never did any proper research, never broke new ground. His heart was never in his work. I smelt the stink of ambition about him, as if Little Saints were merely a stepping stone on his way."

"What was his way, do you think?" I asked. "Where did he mean to go?"

The professor shrugged. "I could not say. But I think it was this undefinable suggestion of moving into more elevated circles that fueled the boys' interest in him."

He broke off, pressing his lips together, his gaze shifting slightly.

"There is something more," I said softly. I moved a fraction nearer to the professor. "Sir, if you know something, however insignificant, please tell us. It might be relevant to our inquiries."

"I do not see how it could be," he said, the smile back in evidence once more. "I am being very silly, the whole thing was simply a jape. I did not take it seriously at the time, and I put even less weight upon it now. I have only just remembered a rumour that went round during the spring term, right about this time, if memory serves."

Stoker's gaze sharpened. "What rumour?"

The professor seemed not to have heard him. He chuckled a little and continued on his narrative. "People say girls are illogical creatures, but I shall tell you it is nothing but a calumny. Boys are by far the most hysterical when they get an idea, and the way they gossip! The fishwives of Billingsgate market might learn a trick or two from a pair of schoolboys. The tall tales they will invent and then swear it is the Lord's own truth. Blasphemous little scamps, the lot of them."

"What rumour?" Stoker pressed.

The professor blinked suddenly, drawing himself back from his reminiscences. "Oh, a bit of nonsense, a story the older boys put about to keep the younger ones in check, no doubt. But they did say that Hegarty was—pardon me for laughing, but you will see the absurdity when I tell you—that Hegarty was a vampire."

The professor was wrong, I reflected. It was not funny in the slightest.

CHAPTER 25

Stoker and I took our leave of the professor much later than intended. After we concluded our discussion of Miles Hegarty, Professor Baddlesmere encouraged us to meet his bees and after that prevailed upon us to partake of a light supper.

"It is only a bit of ham and egg pie my housekeeper has put by—today is her day out, you see—but she does make a very good pie, and you would be most welcome."

It occurred to me that the professor might have been a trifle lonely, but that thought was a fleeting one, banished by no fewer than three guests stopping in during the course of our evening together. The daughter of the local big house called to ask if the professor would make a foursome for whist the following day; the doctor came to say he had finalised arrangements for a walking tour of the Lakes for the summer and wanted the professor to accompany him. And the vicar appeared with a question about a Latin phrase meant for Sunday's sermon.

"Ah, I did not realise you have guests, Charles! I shall leave this with you and be on my way," the vicar said with a cordial glance in our direction.

"Not at all," Stoker said, rising from where he had been comfortably resting after consuming an enormous quantity of ham and egg pie, a salad of early cress, a plate of roasted vegetables and potatoes, several slices of cold beef, and half a basin of rice pudding. "We must take our leave if we are to make the last train to London this evening."

The professor turned to the vicar. "These two have come about Miles Hegarty."

"Ah! Rackety fellow who thought he was a vampire?"

The professor tutted at him. "Now, Clarence, do not spread fancies. Hegarty did not think he was a vampire—some of the lads did."

The vicar bristled. "And bloody stupid they were about the whole thing." He turned to us. "Took me the better part of a term to convince them there are no such things as vampires and that he could not enslave their souls. And I still do not think they were really persuaded. They humoured me and seemed to believe he was human enough, but I still say if Hegarty had told them to leap from a cliff, they'd have made fine lemmings of themselves."

Stoker opened his mouth to speak—he is forever correcting people who misunderstand the complex social behaviour of lemmings—but I headed off any possible lecture on the subject with a quick question of my own. "Pardon me, Vicar," I said. "But the boys were really so easily persuaded as to his abilities?"

The vicar smiled. "You must not have brothers, my dear. There is no soul on earth as gullible as a schoolboy who has been told a grisly story. They are ghouls, the lot of them. Ghosts, goblins, faceless wraiths—they sup it with a large spoon, believe you me. The nastier the tale, the quicker they are to believe, and the harder to wean from it."

"Only two or three of them were really convinced," the professor put in. "But the reverend is correct. Those who believed were difficult to sway. And in the end, one cannot control what they believe, only what they repeat. We saw to it they did not influence the other boys, and with Hegarty gone, the matter seemed to resolve itself, and I thought no further upon it."

"You were right to send him away," the vicar said suddenly, his mild expression suddenly sober.

"Because he was a disruptive presence?" I asked.

"Because when he was at Little Saints, I had a feeling of great oppression," the vicar replied.

"It was lumbago," the professor put in dryly.

"It was oppression," the vicar corrected with an unexpected firmness. "My spirit felt the weight of it, in a way I could not articulate even if I wished to try. I have seldom been in the presence of something truly dark, but I can say without reservation that Miles Hegarty had no light in him."

A heavy silence fell until the hour chimed from the mantel clock and we rose.

"Thank you," Stoker said. "You have been most helpful, gentlemen."

"We really must go now," I said, shaking hands with both of them. It was fully another quarter of an hour before we made it through the door—the professor insisted upon presenting us with a jar of honey from his bees and an extra wedge of pie wrapped daintily in a napkin. "In case you feel peckish on the return," he said to Stoker.

The result was that we had to run for the train and very nearly missed it, flinging ourselves into our compartment just as the train was gathering speed, pulling away from the platform and leaving Peasgreen behind.

"A most productive visit," I said, settling happily into the seat across from Stoker.

"Except that I have sat upon my pie," he said with a mournful look into his pocket.

"You have eaten enough pie to credit a regiment," I told him.

He fixed me with a reproachful look. "Veronica, one can never have too much pie."

In that, I reflected, he was entirely correct.

It was past midnight when we stumbled into Bishop's Folly, but the lamps still burnt in the Belvedere, and I realised J. J. would want an accounting of our expedition. To my surprise, Mornaday was there, regaling her with stories of the cutpurses and footpads apprehended during his early days at the Metropolitan Police. The dogs—all seven of them—were comfortably scattered about, some on laps, some on the floor, all of them asleep, paws and noses twitching gently. J. J. was smoking a pipe and Mornaday had removed his shoes, the better to mend one of his socks, lending a note of gentle domesticity to the scene.

"How very enterprising, Mornaday," I said, taking off my coat. "I had no idea you knew how to darn."

"Taught at the knee of my mammy," he said, thrusting the darning needle with its load of wool once more into the fabric of his sock. "But you've no proper darning egg, so I had to make do with this," he added, pulling an ovoid shape from inside his sock.

"That is the fossilised egg of a creature I believe to be archaeopteryx, although I have yet to prove it," Stoker told him severely. "And worth more than the whole of your person." He plucked it from Mornaday's grasp and replaced it with a gutta-percha ball of some antiquity.

Mornaday studied it carefully. "This looks ancient too. Is it very valuable?"

"Considering the fact that it is used as a shuttlecock by his lordship's children when they play at badminton, I should think not," Stoker informed him.

"What have you discovered?" J. J. demanded. She looked faintly desperate for news, but that was to be expected. Listening to Mornaday's tales of derring-do whilst watching him darn a sock of dubious cleanliness was enough to challenge the sangfroid of any woman.

"That Lord Ruthven is most certainly a fraud," Stoker said in some satisfaction. "He is a former schoolmaster by the name of Miles Hegarty, once engaged as a teacher at an establishment called Little Saints in the village of Peasgreen in Surrey. He was discharged more than a decade ago for exerting an unhealthy influence over some of the boys there. Apparently, he had them convinced he was a vampire."

Mornaday guffawed, but J. J.'s expression was thoughtful.

"Vampires sell copies," she said sagely.

"You cannot write of this for the newspaper," I reminded her. "At least not yet. Too much remains to be discovered."

"And even when it is finished, I'll thank you not to start a vampire panic in the capital of the British Empire," Mornaday returned tartly.

J. J.'s features rearranged themselves into a picture of wounded loftiness. "I wouldn't dream of such a thing."

Stoker gently cleared his throat. "As I was saying, Hegarty was apparently practising and perfecting his tricks upon the schoolboys of Little Saints until his dismissal."

"To what end? Seems a dangerous sport for no better reward than a bit of pocket money," Mornaday remarked.

"But schoolboys have affluent fathers," J. J. pointed out. "Perhaps he thought to influence them to perform a little pilfery in their homes and bring him the spoils."

"Entirely possible," I said graciously, although I confess I was slightly annoyed that neither Stoker nor I had considered such a thing. "But you forget one significant fact about schoolboys: they grow up. Perhaps he thought to parlay their connections into some advantage for himself once they were established in their careers."

"A tenuous motive for ensorcelling young minds," Stoker put in.

"Perhaps it was simply meant as a bit of entertainment," Mornaday suggested.

"Or perhaps he is the sort of person who enjoys having a hold over others," J. J. said.

"And possibly all of these motives and more," I said. I turned to J. J. "Did you ever discover the other plant that was included with the wolfsbane in Harkness's missive?"

J. J. set Al-'Ijliyyah, the little Italian greyhound, gently onto the floor, then began to rummage in her notes. They were haphazard, scrawled onto the backs of envelopes, theatre programmes, and long sheets of blank newsprint that Stoker used for his sketches, but J. J. insisted she knew precisely where to find exactly what she wanted, and in a very few seconds she unearthed a tourist map of London parks. She studied the scribbles over Hyde Park and nodded. "*Solanum dulcamara*. Commonly known as bittersweet or bitter nightshade. And the meaning," she said triumphantly, "is death."

"It was a threat on his life in botanical form," Mornaday said. "Just like the wolfsbane."

"Precisely," Stoker agreed. "And Harkness took it seriously enough to take his own life rather than wait for death to come to him."

"Why not just flee the country?" Mornaday queried.

"How could he?" J. J. put in. "His father controlled the purse strings, and he had a wife and family. If he left without them, it would expose them to terrific scandal, but how could he go with them lacking the resources to start a new life? He must have felt cornered. Leaving would have opened his family to the shame of abandonment, and staying would have meant—at least in his imagination—a grisly death like Quincey's. The only solution was to take the bull by the horns, as it were. Far better to end it all, knowing his father would invariably use his influence to see that the death was ruled an accident and his children would carry no stain upon their name."

"There is also the possibility that he knew something significant about Quincey's death—perhaps the exact circumstances in which it occurred." I turned to Mornaday. "You said his widow described his state of mind just prior to his death as one of increasing distress. Perhaps something more than just the death of his friend preyed upon him."

"Harkness was the one with the interest in the occult," J. J. said suddenly. "What if he were the one who introduced Quincey to the Harpocrates Society? If that secret cabal were responsible for Quincey's death, Harkness must have felt in some measure responsible."

"We cannot presume that the society is responsible," Mornaday began.

The rest of us greeted this statement with an assortment of scornful noises.

"Of course they are!" J. J. protested. "Unless you believe it is possible that *two* groups of people are haring around London pretending to be vampires."

"The society members study folklore and superstition," he returned, brandishing his woolly egg at her. "There is no reason to believe the members play at being vampires, apart from Ruthven, and furthermore—oh, damnation and hellfire!" He shook his hand, but the egg remained firmly fixed. "I've only gone and stitched it to my bloody cuff." He bent to worry the threads with his teeth.

"I do not like coincidences," I said firmly. "And two unrelated vampires would be an unthinkable coincidence. I believe Stoker will agree with me that one vampire is quite enough for any investigation."

"He is not a vampire," Stoker replied in a tone of acute boredom.

"I am speaking of the identity he assumes, not his actual state," I corrected. "Regardless, Harkness was suffering after the death of Quincey. He had just lost his best friend in dreadful circumstances, and the fact that he received a threat means he knew something about the murder."

"That is a tautological nightmare of a scenario," Stoker offered.

I shrugged. "It is the only inference that makes sense of the facts. We may conclude that Harkness feared being murdered, because he took the death threat so seriously, he flung himself off the balcony."

"Of course," Stoker said slowly, "one must wonder why—if Harkness knew something of significance regarding Quincey's death, namely the identity of the killer—he did not go to the police and reveal all."

"Surely, beloved," I answered, "he feared the publicity. Harkness was a man of prominent name and respectable reputation. For any gentleman to become involved with the police in any capacity is considered disgraceful. To do so in the course of a murder investigation? Unthinkable."

"Thank you for that," Mornaday said dryly.

"You yourself said Sir Ranulph treated you like a dustman," J. J. reminded him. "It does make perfect sense that a man so high in the instep as Jameson Harkness would rather throw himself onto the flagstones than have any dealings with the police that would expose him to public scandal."

Stoker tipped his head thoughtfully. "The question is what they mean to do now." His hand moved in lazy circles as he petted Nut, the little hound that liked to curl onto his lap, her nose tucked firmly under his arm.

"Come again?" Mornaday said.

"Let us suppose that some members of the Harpocrates Society did murder Quincey. Harkness knew something of it and was pressed to remain silent under threat of death. Instead, he removed himself from the equation permanently. What now?"

We fell silent, pondering the question.

"Carry on as usual?" J. J. suggested. "They have what they want—Quincey dead and Harkness silenced."

"Possibly," Stoker conceded. "But why did they want Quincey dead in the first place? What offence could he have committed, and how was it so significant that they would rather see him dead?"

The others continued to discuss the matter, throwing out increasingly outlandish notions for the reason for killing Quincey, but my gaze had fallen upon a file J. J. had left atop the stack she had been working her way through. It was the material on Horace Von Hilsing, and I retrieved it, returning to my chair with my little Italian greyhound Al-'Ijliyyah cuddled under one arm. To Huxley's obvious disgust, I fed her bits of jellied chicken as I flicked through the cuttings. I had not made a careful study of them the first time—there were quite a few, as befitted a man of Von Hilsing's prominence—but as I studied them, I felt the clockwork gears of my mind click into motion.

"Of course!" I cried. Al-'Ijliyyah leapt from my lap and dove under my chair. I should have to make it up to her later, but this was no time for modest expression. I waved the cutting I had just discovered.

"What is it?" Stoker inquired.

"The Mortlake Jewel," I said. I held the illustration out for his perusal. "Do you recognise it?"

"Ought I?" He leant forwards, shaking his head, then paused. "Wait. *Wait.*"

"Yes," I said, knowing he had leapt to precisely the same conclusion as I.

"God, they are doing it again," J. J. said to Mornaday.

"So tiresome," he agreed. "Would you care to tell the rest of us what this is about? Use your words."

"The Mortlake Jewel," I repeated, passing the cutting to J. J. "One of Horace Von Hilsing's most prized and priceless possessions. It is believed to have been created for Queen Elizabeth I in consultation with her physician, John Dee of Mortlake. She wore it for a painting, then gave it to Dee in thanks for his service."

"It features an emerald the size of a plover's egg," J. J. said. "Why on earth would Good Queen Bess of Ye Jolly Olde England give her doctor such a prize?"

"Because he was not just her physician," I told her. "He was an astrologer and a skilled alchemist."

"Alchemist? The lads that try to turn things to gold?" Mornaday asked.

"Among other things," Stoker added. "Many of them were obsessed with the question of immortality. Dee among them."

I resumed the thread of the narrative. "The Mortlake Jewel remained in his family for some years before passing to the Cotton family, and then it vanished. There is reportedly a curse attached to it."

"My god," J. J. said, skimming the rest of the cutting. "It is said to have passed through the hands of Peter the Great's son—tortured to death, a Portuguese noblewoman—also tortured, and Emperor Maximilian. Not tortured, but I should think death by firing squad not exactly a day in the park. It has survived shipwreck and other disasters. Apparently, Horace Von Hilsing dared not wear the jewel, but kept it safely locked away."

"Locked away until someone stole it," Stoker suggested.

"Seward Johnson, perhaps?" I guessed. I turned to the others. "We saw this very jewel on the voluptuous bosom of none other than Lord Ruthven's female companion, the witch Asphodel."

"And you think Johnson stole it from Von Hilsing for them?" Mornaday asked.

"What other explanation could there be?" I demanded.

"I can think of seven," Mornaday replied. "Von Hilsing might have sold it to Ruthven. He might have made Asphodel a loan of it. She might have been wearing a good copy." He had been counting the possibilities off on his fingers, but I stopped him at the third.

"Asphodel's jewel was genuine," I said. "I have some little experience of emeralds thanks to a winter spent in the jungles of Colombia. Paste ones never have the right fire, but this one did. A very curious and old-fashioned cut as well, not to mention the enamel work."

"So it was authentic," Mornaday allowed. "That does not mean it was stolen."

The rest of us looked at him with pitying expressions.

"How is it that the one policeman in the room has the highest opinion of human nature? You are all a pack of cynics," he protested.

"We have simply seen a bit more of the world than you have," I told him kindly.

"Ruthven makes a good show of prosperity, but he could not run to the purchase of the Mortlake," Stoker added. "If Asphodel wore the real jewel, it was come by nefarious means. And Von Hilsing is presently on the Continent. It is the perfect opportunity for Johnson to steal the jewel and deliver it to Ruthven and Asphodel."

"Provided the jewel was kept at the house in Steel Square," Mornaday countered. "Surely Von Hilsing would have given the thing to his bank for safekeeping."

"Not likely," J. J. replied. "Von Hilsing is famously mistrustful of banks. He prefers to keep his treasures where he can see them. It is far more plausible that he kept the jewel at the house in Steel Square. And there would be no call for him to take it with him to the Continent."

"Particularly not as it would mean taking it aboard a ferry for the Channel crossing," I added. "There is a superstition about the Mortlake Jewel and seagoing vessels."

"He has been gone for some days according to Johnson," Stoker added. "That would give him plenty of time to access the safe if he needed to break into it."

"Or perhaps Von Hilsing has enough trust in Johnson that he simply gave him the combination," J. J. said. "He might have matters of business to which Johnson needs to attend in his absence."

Mornaday sat up. "Very well. We will contact Von Hilsing and ask."

"How?" Stoker prodded. "Do you have a forwarding address for Von Hilsing? Johnson said he was in Deauville, but that hardly narrows the matter down. And we cannot exactly ask Johnson where his employer might be found."

"We do not need to," I said. "We can easily discover his whereabouts for ourselves."

"How do you propose to do that?" Mornaday demanded.

"Johnson must be writing to him. Ergo, there must be an address at the house in Steel Square."

Mornaday guffawed and even J. J. looked amused. "Do you really expect Johnson just to give that information to you?" Mornaday asked. "He will know you suspect him of the theft before you've even got the words out of your mouth."

"He does not have to give us the information," I replied loftily. "I have something else in mind entirely." Despite his best efforts, Mornaday got nothing more from me. In my experience, it is best not to confess to a crime before one commits it.

CHAPTER 26

This was not, the attentive reader will recall, the first time Stoker and I had had cause to enter a house unlawfully. But in this case, the ends most decidedly justified the means. Who cares for a bit of broken window glass when a crime is to be solved! Although, it occurred to me only after we had applied ourselves to forcing our way into the garden door, we might have chosen a window that did not consist of a rather fine set of stained glass panels. They depicted the goddesses Flora and Fauna accompanied by the symbols of their domains. Both were tall and wearing elegant draperies, Flora wreathed in blossom while Fauna was surrounded by all manner of wild and docile creatures brought to heel. Stoker gained ingress through a particularly pretty pane featuring a swan.

"Pity," I murmured as he gathered the glass feathers into a neat pile.

"You said time was of the essence," he reminded me coldly.

"It is," I assured him. "But there is no need to enter like Visigoths. We are modern and civilised Europeans."

"I doubt Von Hilsing will see it that way when Johnson informs him of the damage," he whispered back. We had remained in the back garden for more than an hour, watching the lights in the downstairs extinguish one by one until the house was shrouded in darkness. Secreted under the shrubbery, we had watched Johnson leave—quite correctly—through the rear door, locking the house carefully behind himself. We waited a further half an hour lest he return for some forgotten purpose, then crept forwards, shaking life back into our limbs as we embarked upon our escapade.

Once the glass was breached, Stoker turned sideways, slipping nimbly as an eel through the panel, an astonishing feat for a man so fully muscled as he. I followed, running into the impenetrable hardness of his back as he paused, waiting in the darkness. The stench of fresh paint was still present, making me wonder precisely how many rooms were meant to be redecorated while the master of the house was away.

"What are we doing?" I inquired in a whisper. I could see nothing at all, not so much as a suggestion of the dimensions of the room or its furnishings.

"Close your eyes," he instructed.

Stoker moved away, his feet passing almost noiselessly over the carpet. Only by listening intently could I detect the slide of his soles as he walked. A moment later, there was the soft susurration of taffeta curtain panels being slid apart, and I opened my eyes. A shaft of moonlight shone into the room. It was diffused by the leaves of the garden, shedding a silvery glow onto the carpet, but now I could make out the shapes of the furniture. A heavy round table stood in the center of the room. It was set with a single chair of tufted upholstery, a tall crystal candelabra taking pride of place in the centre of the table. A dozen other chairs were lined against the walls, awaiting guests, I imagined. But that sole chair at the table was lonely, I thought, standing in solitary splendour.

A finger to his lips, Stoker slid his other hand into mine, and we moved forward as one. The floor was marble, so there were no creaking floorboards to fear, and so long as we walked slowly and with care, we were silent as shadows, wraiths that haunted the mansion of the millionaire.

There were no lamps lit anywhere in the house, and in the great foyer, the long windows were hung with thick curtains of heavy velvet. But above them were transom windows, undraped and permitting just enough moonlight to show us the way. Stoker moved towards the study, and I shook my head, pointing upwards.

I could see the arch of his brow in the gloom, but I pointed again, more emphatically, and when I turned towards the staircase, he followed. It had been constructed for an entrance, that staircase, for grandeur and hospitality. One could easily imagine a hostess draped in pearls and duchesse satin directing her guests towards the vintage champagne. Or perhaps a bride, descending on her father's arm, her train sweeping elegantly behind her. Instead the steps had been laid with newspaper, each tread carefully covered to protect the pale marble.

"I do not like this," Stoker muttered behind me. There were noises in the house—the soft ticking of the clocks, almost but not quite synchronous—and the unmistakable tiny patter of mouse feet behind the walls. But no human sounds made themselves known, and we continued on, pausing at the top of the staircase to choose which of the half-dozen doors we should try.

"His suite would be the first," Stoker murmured in my ear. "It will overlook the garden and be quieter than the rest."

I nodded and we moved together to unlatch the door. It opened onto a sort of sitting room, the walls lined with bookshelves filled to groaning. I went to the window to make certain the thick curtains were tightly pulled. "Those will not admit a crack of light," I whispered. "I think we might dare a candle."

He nodded, and I reached into my pocket for a box of vestas. When I had struck one and lit a candle, the room revealed itself in detail. There was a fireplace of dark green marble, heavily veined, and beside it sat a deep armchair—just the one. This was no place for convivial entertaining of intimate friends. It was a solitary aerie, the room of a recluse who admitted no one to his private pleasures. The most surprising thing about the room was not the number of books but the fact that each had been bound in matching green kid, the covers stamped in gold with Horace Von Hilsing's initials.

"You cannot be serious," Stoker said as he pulled one free from the shelf. "He has bound copies of magazines to read. This one is numbers of *Punch* from twenty years ago."

"What an odd little man," I said, taking out a volume of my own. "This one is a textbook from a school in Massachusetts. It is inscribed with his name in a child's handwriting, but it has the same binding as the others."

"He has bound everything," Stoker said, showing me a set of essays from a secondary school. "Everything he touched, it seems, reprinted into a matched set. God, the cost of it all."

"And no one to share it with," I said, suddenly fiercely glad that I was not alone in the world. I could not imagine owning such wealth and being so impoverished that I could not call a single person my friend, much less my soul's twin as I had in Stoker.

I shook myself and carried on, searching the desk for some indication of exactly where on the Continent Horace Von Hilsing might be found. There was a blotter, the page fresh and untouched. I skimmed it lightly with a pencil, but no markings showed through. The drawers were empty save for a dull paper knife and a sheaf of writing paper, not the heavy, embossed sort used for correspondence, but only the rough sheets for sketching out one's thoughts before composing a letter.

"The desk has been cleared," I told Stoker.

"There is nothing of note here," he said, rising from the armchair. He had been searching its cushions, no doubt in hopes of finding secrets.

He paused and looked around. "The room is rather dirty," he observed, drawing a finger across the mantel. "It hasn't been dusted in some time."

"Von Hilsing is abroad," I reminded him.

"The room ought either to be properly dusted or the furniture shrouded in sheets," he said severely. "That is how things are done in great houses. This is slipshod. And very curious. I suspect Von Hilsing would not care to know his things are being cared for so cavalierly in his absence."

He was lost in thought, no doubt pondering cobwebs in the corners, so I moved to the connecting door which led, I surmised, to the bedroom. I did not expect to find much of significance in there, but it was against my principles to leave stones unturned.

I opened the door and paused on the threshold, regarding the enormous four-poster bed draped in green silk. "Stoker, I do not think Mr. Von Hilsing will be much put out by dust on the mantel."

"Hm?" His voice was distracted. "Why so?"

I did not take my eyes from the slight figure propped up in the bed. "Because I believe he has been dead for quite some time."

CHAPTER 27

Stoker and I stood for a long moment in the doorway, regarding the unfortunate Mr. Von Hilsing. Or what remained of him. There was no point in attempting revivification. He had clearly been dead for some few weeks, and the warmth of the house had done him no favours.

"I wonder we did not notice the odour before," I said, covering my nose with my hand. At such close quarters the stench of mouldering flesh was unmistakable.

Stoker retrieved one of his enormous red bandanna handkerchiefs and offered it wordlessly to me. I took it and tied it bandit-style around the lower half of my face as he extracted a peppermint pastille from the tin in his pocket and sucked it hard. He disappeared for a moment into the adjoining dressing room, and I returned to the study, taking a slow tour about the space to see if anything had gone undetected.

I had nearly finished, when I espied a handful of ash left in the fireplace. The hearth had been swept, but this last bit must still have been burning when the room was tidied. I knelt swiftly, taking up the poker to sift through the ashes for anything of significance. Paper had been burnt—quite a bit of it, it seemed. All of it had been reduced to so much sooty grey fluff, useless for my purposes. I grumbled as I turned over the last bit, scattering it to powder.

"Is it too much to ask for a clue?"

And just then I saw it—a tiny banner of charred paper stuck to the iron grate. It was fragile as a butterfly's wing and I dared not attempt to lift it. Instead, I contorted myself so that my head was fully inside the fireplace. I brought with me a candle, the brave flame of it brightening my little cave just enough to read the scrap of burnt paper.

Greville.

"We do not know of any Grevilles," I muttered. "That is not at all helpful."

With that, the ruined shred disintegrated, falling to ash. All trace of it was now lost. I backed out of the fireplace, wiping away any sooty smudges as Stoker called to me.

"I am quite fine where I am," I told him. If the bedroom boasted a corpse, I was reluctant to see what horrors the dressing room might harbour.

"You ought to see this," he insisted.

I held my breath and joined him in the dressing room. "Does the name 'Greville' mean anything to you?" I asked.

"Nothing," he replied in a tone of some distraction.

"I found it on a scrap of paper, burnt in the study fireplace. But without context, I cannot say if it is significant or not. Botheration."

"Look at this room," Stoker urged.

Unlike the darkly sumptuous bedroom and the elegant study, the dressing room was a space devoted to a solitary purpose—the health and maintenance of the body. Ranked against the walls were a series of machines and apparatuses suited to a gymnasium, climbing bars and racks of dumbbells in assorted weights. A trapeze had been bolted to the ceiling, and tumbling mats were neatly stacked in one corner. An enormous and intricately calibrated weighing machine stood on one wall, and a series of pencilled inscriptions on the pale paint showed where Von Hilsing had weighed himself each day.

"It never varies by more than four ounces," I said, marvelling. Stoker had opened the tall cupboard on the opposite wall, which was crammed with bottles and jars and packets of every description.

"Grooming aids and health tonics," he said. "Most of which I suspect are nothing more than a bit of coloured water and some flavourings." He opened one and took a tentative sip. "Rosemary and honey. Rather tasty that but pointless except to ease a bit of sore throat, as would this slippery elm. A dozen bottles of various preparations all promising a fine head of hair. Peppermint and ginger preparations for stomach ailments. And few things here for the teeth—oil of clove and an embrocation of thyme, pumice toothpaste from Italy. Ah!" He dove into the cabinet, emerging with a bottle of mentholated goose fat, which he rubbed liberally beneath his nose.

"How did you know he would have that?" I asked, applying a touch of the stuff under my makeshift mask.

"Every hypochondriac keeps a fully stocked chest of medicaments," he replied. Armed against the smell, he approached the bed, studying Von Hilsing's recumbent form. He poked and prodded for several minutes whilst I kept to my post. At one point he returned to the dressing room for nail clippers and made as if to pare a bit of fingernail from the corpse, but he straightened with an exclamation of surprise.

"Christ and seven saints, the whole nail just came off," he said. He wrapped the fingernail in a bit of paper and stuffed it into his pocket as I turned away.

"Veronica," Stoker said in a voice that rumbled with suppressed laughter, "are you finding this queasy-making?"

"Not at all," I assured him. "I am acting as guard so we are not surprised by the miscreants who have left Mr. Von Hilsing in this state."

"Hm." He might have carried on tweaking my nose, but he had

apparently concluded his brief attempt at a post-mortem. He came to where I stood, taking tiny sips out of my flask of aguardiente and breathing through my mouth.

I offered the flask, and he took a deep draught. "God, that is a nasty business."

I regarded him with surprise. "I should have thought you inured to this sort of thing."

"*This* sort of thing? No, Veronica. I have had precious little experience in examining the half-desiccated bodies of elderly American recluses."

"But you deal with animals," I pointed out. "Humans are hardly different."

"And I seldom deal with shreds of rotting flesh," he said, taking another pull on the flask. "The smell is so far inside my nose, I think I shall never get it out."

I retrieved the flask and replaced it under my skirt. "Let us get out into the fresh air, and you can tell me what you have discovered. There is nothing left to be learnt here."

He did as I suggested, and in a very few minutes we had passed through the mews door again and into the square, both of us breathing happily of the cool night air.

"Coal smoke, horse shit, and rotting garbage," he said, inhaling deeply. "Heaven."

We walked until we reached a bench, secluded in the shadows of a spreading oak. A convenient little shrubbery hid the bench from passersby, and we sat gratefully.

"Is it odd that I am hungry?" he asked. "Starving actually."

I rummaged in my pocket for a packet of greaseproof paper I had secured for just such an event. I handed it over, and he applied himself to the ham sandwich inside with gusto. "You are a goddess amongst women," he said through lusty bites. "Deserving of the most devoted worship. Although you forgot the mustard."

"Next time we plan on discovering a rotting corpse, I shall pack a proper picnic," I assured him.

He grinned at the sarcasm, popping the last morsel into his mouth with a sigh of pleasure. "I could eat a dozen more, but that helps, my love. Now, as to what I discovered, you will understand that I was able to undertake only the most cursory examination. A thorough post-mortem would be required in order to formally establish the cause of death—"

I held up a hand. "Stoker. I am no court of law, and we will have no quibbling. The cause, I beg you."

"Poison," he said promptly.

I blinked. "Poison? Just like that? So decisive and certain are you?"

"Absolutely. He was a gentleman of mature years, yes, but like most who are nervous of their physical health, he was in fine fettle. Apart from tinctures and tonics for hair growth and the tin of goose grease which anyone would keep for remedying the odd cold, he had precious little in that chest of medicines—nothing that would suggest underlying health concerns. Treatments for the occasional sore throat or bit of dyspepsia, but nothing significant. No preparations for the heart or liver, nothing for the lungs. He may have been obsessed with his bodily well-being, but there was not a single suggestion of actual ill health. He was slender and well muscled and would have liked better teeth, that is all."

"His heart might have attacked him," I said dubiously.

"Might," Stoker stressed. "But such things are uncommon in men who are not corpulent and intemperate in their habits. Von Hilsing was abstemious, remember. He ate sparingly of a vegetarian diet and drank nothing at all except milk sent in from his own cows. He could afford the best doctors. He might have lived another thirty years or more.

Besides which," he added, "if he had expired of natural causes, why would his staff not alert his doctor? His family?"

I considered this a moment. A breeze had sprung up, rustling the leaves and sending their heady green scent aloft. Something lushly sweet was blooming nearby, and with the stars winking to life under that benevolent moon, the night might have been a romantic one indeed. Stoker's hand had dropped to my neck, where his fingers were making lazy circles against my skin. It was an absent-minded gesture, one born of unthinking affection, but coupled with that perfumed air, I found myself growing rather warm.

"Are you quite all right?" Stoker asked.

"Entirely," I assured him. "And I know exactly why someone would not carry the news of Von Hilsing's death to his next of kin. If you preserve the fiction of his life, you may carry on with his affairs of business, provided you can forge his letters well enough."

Stoker nodded, the fingers circling even more slowly. "You needn't even forge the letters—a mere signature would do. Most men of his ilk do not write their own letters. His correspondents would be accustomed to seeing Seward Johnson's handwriting instead of Von Hilsing's."

"All Johnson need do is scribble a signature he doubtless had time enough to perfect after years in Von Hilsing's employ. By such a stratagem, Johnson could take over the man's entire life!"

"And Von Hilsing needn't have died naturally for such a thing," Stoker pointed out. "In fact, it rather suggests poisoning as a likelier occurrence. Even with the considerable effects of decomposition, I noted that Von Hilsing's skin was darker, thickened, and the skin of the palms and soles of the feet were toughened. Furthermore, he had remedies for sore throat and indigestion in his cabinet of medicaments. Alone, they are common treatments anyone might have for minor ailments, but a troubled stomach and persistent sore throat, coupled with the changes to his skin, are classic signs of arsenical poisoning. To be certain, I have taken the fingernail that dropped off for testing. Come. I am eager to set the experiment."

He rose from the bench, removing his caressing hand, and I felt a sudden rush of cool air where the warmth of his flesh had sustained me.

"Very well," I said in resignation. A lady might have appetites, but they must never supersede justice, I reflected.

Once back at the Belvedere, Stoker cleared away several stacks of Wardian cases to make room for his investigations. I glanced idly at the shrouded corner. "Wouldn't it be easier to do this in your part of the workspace?"

Only the tiniest twitch of his mouth betrayed his unease with the question. "Not at all. The specimen I am working on is delicate. I cannot take the chance of damaging the scales."

Scales! When only the day before he had made reference to fur. I could not imagine what benighted sort of creature he was wrestling if it had both scales and fur, but I was burning to know.

Before I could task him further on the subject, he had gathered his equipment and set to work, assembling a rudimentary form of Marsh test. Unlike many poisons which were still undetectable in the human body, arsenic had been successfully identified by a procedure developed by James Marsh in 1836. He had built upon the work of several German physicians in the previous century, but it was Marsh's definitive analysis which served to isolate that most convenient and treacherous of toxins. Used by incalculable numbers of villains to dastardly effect, arsenic was the very queen of poisons. Until the Arsenic Act, passed nearly half a century previous, it had been readily available from any chemist's shop, a friendly solution to the problem of an abusive husband or aging parent who would not obligingly pass from this mortal coil. So popular was it that it had been known as "inheritance powder," and one shuddered to imagine how many people had been hastened to their ends by its deadly powers. A pinch in a cup of tea would be enough to see off the hardiest soul, and the effects were often mistaken for cholera. Both wreaked unpleasant havoc in the bowels, and if a doctor were not astute enough to detect the telltale garlic stench from the effluvia of an arsenic patient, the death would most likely be attributed to natural causes.

Even the introduction of the Arsenic Act merely blunted the demand, for it only required chemists to keep a record of purchasers, and there were any number of legitimate uses for the stuff. Poisoners learnt to be more cautious. Rather than slaying their victims through acute poisoning—administering one fatal dose which progresses rapidly from violent digestive unwellness to cessation of cardiac activity—the crafty killer chose to murder through chronic poisoning, the doses administered incrementally over a longer period of time, thus weakening the victim until one last pinch tipped them into immortality. This latter approach left distinctive traces upon the body, traces Stoker had already identified in the corpse of Von Hilsing. The skin itself would change as the poison was absorbed, giving rise to the darkened appearance and thickening skin Stoker had noted, as well as causing the painful throat and unbalanced stomach for which Von Hilsing had obviously procured the usual remedies. The case might not have stood a barrister's scrutiny in one of Her Majesty's courts of law, but it was enough to persuade me—provided the Marsh test on the fingernail was conclusive.

Stoker was busy about his test tubes and flasks and an early Faraday burner he had unearthed from a crate of laboratory equipment donated to the Rosemorran Collection by a scientific widow. (It was not as elegant as that developed by Bunsen some years later, but it was near at hand and surprisingly effective.) Stoker provided a running commentary of his efforts, explaining the chemical properties of the zinc and acid he had added to a flask. He handed me a pair of wide, tempered spectacles to wear and donned a pair himself. "Do not take these off," he cautioned. "Now, if arsenic is present in the fingernail, it will be isolated in the form of arsine gas. Once ignited, the gas will leave traces of—"

"Ignited?" I asked. But before I could query him further, he had bent to his work, and a pretty little jet of flame erupted. (I have often observed that most men, however grown, never lose the rather boyish enthusiasm for fire. This was no less true of Stoker. Any attempts on my part to deal with the rather temperamental Swedish stove were always met with firm resistance.)

Stoker had reached for a china bowl and held it up as the flame burst forth. When the little fire had died away, he looked into the bowl, grinning. "There we are." He pointed to the smudge inside, black but with a curious, silvery quality. It shimmered in the light of the Faraday lamp.

"Arsenic?" I asked.

He looked persuaded, but with a scientist's caution, he temporised. "I cannot swear to it. I have isolated this substance and it *appears* to be arsenic, but until it is compared to a control, it is still only a theory. Wait here."

I did as instructed, admiring the lustrous sheen of the substance in the bowl until he returned with a second bowl and a sheet of flypaper. He repeated the experiment, snipping bits of the flypaper into a fresh flask with a new complement of zinc and acid.

"The flypaper is impregnated with arsenic," he explained. "If this specimen matches the other, then we shall know for certain."

Again there was a pretty rush of flame and a sooty deposit left on the inside of a china bowl. It looked identical to the first to the naked and untrained eye—namely, mine—but Stoker carried on, carefully scraping a sample from each and depositing them onto glass slides. These were slid under the lens of his microscope, an ancient and unwieldy thing, but suitable for our purposes.

He moved the slides back and forth, comparing them several times until he sat back with a wide smile.

"Arsenic," he pronounced at last.

"You are certain?"

He waved me to his chair, and I peered through the scope. "They look identical to me, but I am no chemist," I said.

"Neither am I, but there were one or two things I picked up on the *Luna*," he told me, invoking the name of the ship to which he'd been assigned during his time in the Navy as surgeon's mate. "The surgeon was an amateur chemist by way of a hobby. He used to smear all sorts of nasty things onto slides and make me look at them. And he was forever blowing things up—not a habit calculated to endear him to the captain. The skipper forbade him from doing any experiments which were not absolutely necessary to the health and well-being of the crew, but before that, the surgeon taught me how to do the Marsh test. He said it might come in useful one day, and by god it has."

"What now?" I asked.

He carefully wrapped the slides into two pieces of brown paper, labelling them with a grease pencil. "These ought to go to Mornaday. Along with the news of Von Hilsing's death."

"Agreed," I said slowly.

Stoker quirked a brow heavenwards. "Agreed except for what? I can hear hesitation in your tone, Veronica. Surely you do not mean to conceal this death. We have established it is unnatural. Von Hilsing was murdered."

"And his murderer ought to be brought to justice," I said in emollient tones. "Just perhaps not tonight."

Stoker folded his arms over the breadth of his chest. The gesture was not, I believe, intended to divert me from my purpose, but it very nearly did. The development of his pectoral and biceps muscles was admirable to the point of distraction. "Go on."

"It did occur to me that if we take this matter directly to Mornaday, questions might be asked. Awkward ones," I said.

"Awkward ones?"

"Yes, like 'Why did you break into a millionaire's mansion?' and 'Were you planning to steal anything?'"

"Of course we weren't there to bloody steal," Stoker thundered.

"You know that, and I know that, and we might even be able to persuade Mornaday of that, but what of his superiors? You must admit, dearest, it does look rather suspicious that we forced entry—quite illegally—into the abode of an American millionaire and now he is dead."

"That is not our fault! Besides which, I have just established that he was poisoned over a long period of time. Arsenic is not stored in the fingernails from a single acute dose."

"Yes," I agreed soothingly. "But it might take some time to bring Scotland Yard around to our way of thinking. Once news of Von Hilsing's death is known, the press will descend like vultures. Our British newspapers are bad enough, but just consider, dearest—"

"The Americans," he said hoarsely. His face had gone very white, and he slumped into a chair. "It will be awful. They will accuse us of terrible things, and they shall do so ungrammatically."

"Indeed. Now, I do not mean we should keep this from Mornaday indefinitely. I have perfect faith that the murderer will be brought to justice in due course, but in the immediate future, it is we who will be imperilled. Scotland Yard, if you will consider our personal experience with that organisation, require a little time and some guidance to find the correct solution to such mysteries. They are easily distracted—like magpies with a bit of gimcrack glitter. I do not wish to be glitter, Stoker, distracting professional detectives from their official duties. And I should most assuredly not care for incarceration, however temporary."

"And it mightn't be temporary," he agreed. "Even if they are eventually persuaded that we had nothing to do with Von Hilsing's death, we are certainly guilty of trespassing on his property."

"Far worse," I reminded him. "You could reasonably be charged with desecration of a corpse—you stole his fingernail."

"For the purposes of science!" he countered indignantly.

"I do not think Scotland Yard care very much about science, my heart. It requires thought and comprehension."

He threw his hands up in resignation. "What do you suggest, then?"

"As I have noted, the hour is late. A good night's sleep should be our first order of business. After that, a conference with J. J. to discuss the best means of bringing Seward Johnson to justice."

A slow smile spread over his features. "Then you agree Johnson is our villain?"

"I do not concede that he is the murderer," I said with as much equanimity as I could muster. "But he must be involved in some capacity. Even the greatest dullard could not fail to notice his employer in such a state."

"Even now you will not admit to losing our wager?" he teased.

"I am not convinced I *have* won it," I maintained. "Johnson may be merely an accomplice."

"To whom? You are thinking of Ruthven, of course," he said.

I made no reply. Something was tickling the back of my mind, a pesky little mosquito of a thought which darted in to buzz annoyingly and then flitted away again before I could capture it. I could only hope to find it properly within my grasp before the killer struck again.

CHAPTER 28

As expected, a solid eight hours of repose had a restorative effect. I said nothing to J. J. of our discovery of the previous night—largely because she was not to be found. I looked into the Bavarian folly before retiring and found her snoring loudly enough to wake the dead. In the morning, she had risen before I woke, and it was clear she had availed herself of the Roman bathhouse, disappearing before I arrived. There were telltale traces of her occupation of the little temple. She had helped herself to my things, leaving behind a cake of luxurious French soap to dissolve into a puddle and my towel crumpled and damp. But even my imperfect ablutions could not quell my rising spirits. Stoker and I were agreed that Seward Johnson must play a villain's part in this little drama, but I could not see him as the director of the play. That would require a surer hand, a greater imagination. I had no evidence for my suspicions; I could call it only intuition. And without evidence to support it, there was little point in raising the possibility, but I was suddenly uncomfortable with the notion of keeping our adventure from Mornaday any longer than necessary.

I breakfasted alone to the sounds of Stoker hard at work in his curtained workspace, loud sea chanties punctuated with banging and the occasional profanity. His mood was as buoyant as mine, it seemed, and when J. J. finally appeared, Mornaday hard upon her heels, we had each put in a solid morning's work at our respective tasks. Given our activities the night before, I was not best pleased to see Mornaday, and from Stoker's expression, I gathered I was not alone.

"We didn't expect you," Stoker told him flatly.

"I need to be kept abreast of any developments," Mornaday replied loftily.

We mounted the winding stair to the snuggery, J. J. carrying the little male Galápagos tortoise which seemed to have adopted her. Huxley the bulldog, who does not as a rule care for Testudines, gave it a sniff and then turned his back to stalk away on his little bandy-legs, clearly aggrieved.

"I am sorry about Huxley, but this fellow will keep following me about," J. J. said, settling her newfound friend onto a cushion beside her. She pulled a handful of lettuce from her pocket and began to feed him little titbits as we talked.

I cleared my throat and began, addressing my remarks to no one in particular, but careful not to look Mornaday in the eye. "Stoker and I paid a visit to Horace Von Hilsing last night to see if we could discover a forwarding address, a place to direct our queries about the Mortlake Jewel."

"Von Hilsing is dead," Stoker said abruptly. "Poisoned. We believe it was arsenic, administered over a period of time in several small doses considering the fact that the poison was present in Von Hilsing's fingernail, which I confirmed via the Marsh test."

Mornaday's mouth gaped as Stoker finished. He closed it and it gaped again. I turned to Stoker. "You ought to have broken it more gently. He looks rather like a landed carp struggling to breathe."

"He looks like something," Stoker agreed.

J. J. shoved an entire pocketful of lettuce at the tortoise and brought out her notebook. She licked the tip of her pencil and began to write furiously.

"You . . . wait now, I am still trying to understand," Mornaday began. "You went to Von Hilsing's house and . . . what? Broke in? Is that the first of your crimes?"

"The first of many," I told him. "I should add that we did damage a piece of rather nice stained glass to gain entry. But that is the limit of the physical destruction we committed."

"Oh, good. I am so glad," he said, his brows lowering. "I should have hated if you mussed the carpets."

"Do not be churlish," I remonstrated. "We did you a service, Mornaday. We went where you cannot, and we discovered what you would never have—namely, Horace Von Hilsing, dead in his bed."

"Dead in his bed!" Mornaday stuffed a fist into his mouth as his complexion purpled. He withdrew it a moment later, forcing the words through gritted teeth. "You went upstairs. To the bedroom of the fourth-richest man in the world. An American, no less. It will be a diplomatic incident. They will blame me." He thrust his hands into his hair, clutching hard.

"Don't do that," I urged. "It is terribly damaging to the follicles, you know, and you really haven't enough hair to spare." He made a strangled noise in his throat and calmed himself with a visible effort. I went on. "In due course, you can be the one to present the case to your superiors, but surely your first priority is to apprehend the murderer and hand him over to justice as a fait accompli."

Mornaday skewered me with a look. "What the devil do you mean?"

"When Stoker and I first called upon Seward Johnson, there were packed cases in the house in Steel Square—" I broke off, casting my mind back to the moment we entered the darkened hall the previous night, the vast, empty echo of the place.

Stoker picked up the thread of the narrative. "Johnson told us the cases were for Von Hilsing, but when he told us that, Von Hilsing must have already been dead upstairs."

"The cases are now absent," I added. "They must have been Johnson's and not Von Hilsing's at all. His departure must be imminent! Mornaday, you will want to check all of the steamship offices and train stations."

His eyes goggled. "All of them? For a passenger named Johnson?"

I shrugged. "There is little point in attempting to find him in his present circumstances. If he is clever, and I suspect he is, he has moved into some middling sort of genteel hotel until it is time to board his ship. That will be your last chance to apprehend him."

Mornaday swore a streak of profanity so fluent it would have done Stoker proud. He left, slamming the door of the Belvedere behind him for good measure.

"He is inordinately out of sorts," J. J. observed.

"Because he has only the slenderest of threads and it is up to him to pluck it," I replied.

As soon as Mornaday departed, Stoker removed himself to his work, taking refuge in his secret project whilst I set to cleaning a recently acquired tray of albino specimens of *Cyaniris semiargus*. It was painstaking and delicate work, requiring perfectly focused attention and the better part of the day. J. J. had taken herself off to parts unknown, and Stoker was still hard at work on his mysterious trophy when I finished. I longed for company, but he had made it quite clear that interruptions would not be welcome, as his efforts had reached a critical juncture.

With J. J. still absent and Stoker unavailable, I decided to pay a visit to my favourite place of respite, the Hippolyta Club. What inspiration I drew from within its walls! The moment my gaze fell upon the brass plaque outside the door bearing its blazing motto—ALIS VOLAT PROPRIIS—my spirits rose. I greeted the porter, Hetty, at the front desk, pausing a moment to exchange a bit of informative discussion with her. (A lesser person might call this gossip, but Hetty and I were interested only in the accomplishments of fellow members and spent practically no time at all discussing a proposed member who had been discovered in the broom cupboard with one of the maids.)

I took myself upstairs to the smoking room and, mindful that I had missed luncheon entirely, enjoyed a plate of sandwiches and a pot of tea. Refreshed, I settled in with a violet cigarette and a glass of whisky as I read through the latest issue of the club journal, *Hippolyta Speaks*. There were the usual notes on recent expeditions, biographical sketches of featured members, essays on the rights of women, and appeals for support for ongoing projects. My favourite feature was to be found on the back page, the exchanges of private messages, usually in some form of intriguing code. To reach it, I had to flick through the advertisements, everything from cold creams to fishing reels—all that a lady explorer might require.

Just as I paged past an advertisement for steamships, I saw it, a single word that demanded my attention because I had so recently seen it on the scrap of paper in the house in Steel Square.

Greville.

Throwing down the journal, I drained my whisky, stubbed out my fragrant cigarette, and made my way out to the street, where I quickly hailed a cab. I ought to have called at the Belvedere for Stoker, but impatience burnt within me. The leads in this investigation had been maddeningly opaque, and here at last was a clue that required immediate attention. I was straining at the lead like a bloodhound on the scent of a fox.

I instructed the driver to carry me to the offices of the Belleville steamship line. While not as luxurious as the Cunard or White Star ships, the Belleville liners offered very comfortable accommodations, if their advertisements in the newspapers were to be believed. It was a little flourish of theirs that every ship under their flag bore a name ending in "-ville," a conceit of the founder of the line, Sir Emory Belleville. And that was why a single word found on a mere scrap of paper had led me to this moment.

Greville. It was a name that might have meant anything, jotted on the spur of the moment as an aide-mémoire. I had connected it to nothing whatsoever until I had seen the advertisement, a discreet notice of the launching of a new flagship, the HMS *Belleville*, and listed below, all of her sister ships. Tucked neatly halfway down the alphabetical group—the HMS *Greville*.

It was a slender thing, this certainty of mine, but the closer we drew to the offices of the Belleville Line, the stronger it grew. I leapt out of the cab as I tossed a coin to the cabman. Inside the Belleville offices, the air was stuffy thanks to the windows, tightly shut against any fresh air, and the press of people. Dozens were there, purchasing tickets, inquiring about passage, and generally making nuisances of themselves. The clerks looked harried and hurried, so I waited, counting slowly to a hundred in Cantonese, then again in Farsi, and again in Arabic. I had nearly resorted to counting in French when at last a young man of depressed countenance beckoned me to his window.

"Yes, madam?" He had the animation and charm of an incontinent basset hound, but I smiled sadly at him from under my lashes.

"Good afternoon," I said in a low, confiding voice. "I wish to inquire about passage on the *Greville*."

"She is nearly full. The only available berths are in steerage," he said in dull monotone.

"I do not wish to travel," I amended hastily. "I wish to see the passenger list."

He stirred a little at this, looking livelier. "Madam, that is not—"

"My husband, I believe, has booked passage on the *Greville*. She sets sail tomorrow, does she not?"

"Yes, but—"

"He did not secure passage for me," I said in a tone of wounded dignity. "I think he means to abandon me. And our children."

"Children?" A flicker of pity kindled in his gaze.

"All seven of them."

"Seven! I can hardly blame him," he muttered. "It is against—"

"I beg you," I said, laying a hand to his sleeve. "Please. If he leaves, the children will starve. Even little Peter. He has a bad leg, you know. And baby Millicent has the whooping cough. And the staggers." I do not say that I fluttered my lashes pleadingly, but the astute reader may assume it. Perhaps it was this, or perhaps it was the thought of the seven ailing children who would surely starve without their feckless papa, but the clerk sighed.

"I think you will find the staggers is an ailment confined to cattle, madam," he informed me. I began to protest, but he raised a hand in surrender. "It is against the rules, but I cannot begin to care," he said, shoving a ledger towards me. "You may have one minute to peruse as I step away to make a cup of tea. When I return, the ledger will be closed and you will have gone, agreed?"

"Agreed." I fairly snatched the ledger from him, running my finger down the passenger list. Halfway down the page, I saw it. Seward Johnson, travelling in a first-class cabin on the next crossing from Southampton to New York with stops in Ireland and Nova Scotia.

"Excelsior!" I whispered in exultation. "I have you now, you blackguard." But before I could enjoy my triumph properly, I saw the next name on the list.

And that changed everything.

CHAPTER 29

I returned to the Belvedere as speedily as the teeming streets would permit. I had expected to encounter Stoker hard at work on his project, but he was nowhere to be found. He had left a note for me—if one can reasonably call a few words scribbled on the back of a piece of paper still sticky with gingerbread crumbs and stuck to the wall with a boning knife a note. I plucked it free and spent a good few minutes deciphering the squiggles Stoker had made with the pencil stub he habitually carried in his pocket.

Gone to see abt walrus was what I finally interpreted. I screwed the paper up and tossed it to the dogs to play with. I wanted nothing more than to discuss my findings with Stoker, and his absence was a source of considerable irritation. I decided to do a little housekeeping whilst I awaited his return, but as I busied myself tidying the Belvedere, I could not help but feel a mounting sense of something amiss. It was nothing so strong as premonition; the gentle reader must not believe I am blessed with supernatural gifts. Say rather that it was a flutter of intuition that brushed my face with gentle wings. And as I worked, tamping pages of manuscripts and dusting assorted dead things, the delicate prickling turned into outright buzzing.

"Drat the man," I muttered to the caryatid I was dusting. "Where the devil has he got himself to?"

It occurred to me, in light of our previous detectival adventures which had so often resulted in bodily injury to Stoker, that he might once more be in danger. I had no logical reason, at this point, to think so. His absence might well have been perfectly legitimate. He had been obsessed with the walrus for some months, and he had apparently been given a golden opportunity to express his opinions on the matter forcefully and to the people who might actually listen. It was little wonder he had left so precipitately.

And yet. Unable to dismiss the notion of an imperilled Stoker, I cleaned all the harder for perhaps half an hour more, then threw down my dusters. It was entirely possible that the walrus had been so much bait to lure him from his aerie for some nefarious purpose.

I pushed the thought from my mind and moved purposefully towards the area Stoker had curtained off from prying eyes. I had no business there; it was a violation of Stoker's privacy as both a gentleman and a scholar. It was *unthinkable* to trespass upon his work.

So, I gave it not a moment's consideration but simply strode up to the curtain and yanked it aside with a firm tug. What lay beyond was so entirely unexpected that I could not quite believe my eyes. I surveyed the creature he had been working on with the frankest astonishment, and I made a mental note to have a robust discussion with Stoker upon the subject the first moment it was possible.

"Oh, my very stars," said a juvenile voice behind me. I knew who it was before I turned.

"Lady Rose," I said repressively to Lord Rosemorran's youngest and most wayward child, "you are not permitted in the Belvedere without either my or Stoker's express permission."

She was looking past me with rapt attention fixed upon the trophy

Stoker had been working upon in secret. "I want it," she said, moving forwards, hands outstretched.

"Absolutely not. You are not to touch it," I said, catching her around the waist and dragging her backwards. "Your hands are *green*."

"Not forever," she assured me. "But I was putting dye into Arthur's hair tonic, and I may have spilt a bit."

"Lady Rose," I said, biting back my rising temper, "I do not have time, nor do I care to inquire, why you are torturing your brother by dyeing his hair green."

"What if I pay you to let me touch it?" she asked craftily. She reached into her pocket where, no doubt, all sorts of grubby treasures resided. She extracted something and extended her hand, opening her palm to show me an item that glittered. A coin.

It was unmistakably the guinea that Stoker and I had been trading back and forth for the better part of three years. It had been minted in the time of George III, and the old king's nose had been greatly worn away through the ninety-odd years it had been in circulation. I ran my fingers over the familiar profile, a sudden chill clutching at my heart, for Stoker would never have been careless with the coin, representing as it did the many adventures we had embarked upon together. Hardly an investigation had passed that we had not wagered it upon the outcome, the winner gleefully taking it in turn to keep the coin safe until the next time it should be risked. If he had lost it, it was because something had happened to him. Or *someone*.

And I had a terrible, gnawing suspicion I knew exactly who it might have been.

"Where did you find that coin?" I demanded.

"On the kerb outside," she said in a tone so docile one might almost imagine her a sweet and tractable child. It would be, I hope I have persuaded the astute reader, a fatal mistake. "Stoker dropped it when he was getting into the carriage with the lady."

"The lady? What lady?" To my knowledge all of the parties associated with the walrus debacle were men of the stuffiest and most turgid variety. "Did she have black hair? Dressed a trifle outlandishly?"

She nodded, peering around me to look once more at Stoker's work in progress. "Can I ride it?"

"Most definitely not," I told her. I put a quelling hand to her shoulder to steer her out of the area and back towards my desk. I paused to collect a few items I suspected I should need in the course of my next activities—a waterproof container of vestas, a selection of blades, and my handy cheese wire, coiled neatly into a tin box that used to hold humbugs. I blessed the fact that I was wearing my hunting costume, for I would never have dared to take the time to change. My flat boots were the perfect footwear, and the skirt concealed my narrow trousers, lending an appearance of propriety to an ensemble suited to scaling Mont Blanc herself. I stuffed a few more items into my pockets including a paper twist of Stoker's favourite honeycomb in case he should be in need of sustenance when I found him. My flask of aguardiente was freshly filled, and I was as equipped for the endeavour as I should ever be. I clapped my hat onto my head, spearing it with the sharpest of my hatpins, Lady Rose's eyes round with interest as she watched.

"You are leaving when I do, and I am locking the door behind me," I warned her. "I must discover where they have taken Stoker." I only wished I knew whether they were taking him to the house or to Highgate. The delay in choosing wrongly could mean the difference between life and death for him, I realised with a pang so sharp it nearly drove me to my knees.

"I know where he has gone," Lady Rose said with a matter-of-fact insouciance she might have been discussing hair ribbons.

I knelt and took her shoulders in my hands, none too gently. "Lady Rose, tell me where."

She tipped her head, considering her price, the little felon. "I want a postcard."

I blinked at her. "A postcard?"

"From Hampton Court Palace. They sell postcards with ghosts on them. Nanny told me, and I want one for my collection."

Lady Rose, following in her forebears' august footsteps, had decided to indulge her own acquisitive instincts and begin assembling favoured articles for purposes of display. Unlike her kinsmen, her collection tended towards the macabre, no doubt in part due to her experiences with an Anatomical Venus during our last investigation.*

"Your collection?" If a person could breathe fire, I believe I might have done so. I know it took an herculean effort not to shake the child, but I merely gripped her tighter and forced my voice to calmness. It has always been my belief that one should never strike nor shout at a child, although I would have happily made an exception long enough to drag Lady Rose to the pond by her pigtails and toss her into the duckweed.

But whilst such actions might assuage my frustration, they were certain to cause more problems in the end as well as delay me further. "Very well. A postcard. With a ghost. From Hampton Court."

"Do you promise?" The eyes narrowed as they met mine.

"I do."

She spat into her hand and held it out for mine. "Swear to it."

"Adults do not spit," I told her.

"Father does when he has a chicken bone," she began.

I may have lifted her off her feet the merest bit, but she kicked me hard upon the shin, and I released her at once. "You have my word," I ground out through gritted teeth. "Now, where has Stoker gone?"

"Highgate," she said, inspecting her lurid green fingernails. "I heard the lady call out to the driver as they got into the carriage."

"Thank heaven for that," I breathed. I resisted the urge to pat her on the head. (The last time I had done so, my hand had come away with an

---

* *A Grave Robbery*

unpleasant stickiness I found nearly impossible to wash free.) "Excellent work, Rose." I ushered her from the Belvedere then, locking up as I had promised.

She lingered upon the doorstep, her jaw set in a mulish expression as she blocked my path. "Mind you bring me the *best* postcard you can find. Perhaps you ought to bring two and I can choose my favorite."

"I will bring you a dozen, you little demon, if you get out of my way,"

She stepped aside, still regarding me suspiciously. "Where are you going?" she demanded.

"To Highgate Cemetery, of course," I said with conviction. "Stoker is in need of a rescue."

CHAPTER 30

Although Lord Rosemorran had kindly made over to us the use of his carriage—when not wanted by a member of the family—as a perquisite of our employment, I did not stop at the mews on my flight from Bishop's Folly. If horses were already harnessed, it meant the carriage was wanted, and if they were not, it would take far too long to arrange. Instead, after returning to Lady Rose long enough to instruct her firmly to send J. J. and Mornaday after me the second they appeared at Bishop's Folly, I charged through the door in the garden wall and onto the pavement, throwing a hand into the air as I issued a piercing whistle.

Instantly, a hansom drew to the kerb, and the wheels had not yet ceased to turn before I hurtled inside, shouting directions to the cabman. I promised him an exorbitant sum for the fastest possible trip to Swain's Lane, and as he sprang the horses, I was flung against the seat. I grabbed at the strap and held on for dear life, having recourse to use it to keep my balance more than once. I dared not look at my watch, but I felt the seconds tick past with every beat of the pulse in my throat. Stoker and I had faced danger before. In the course of our endeavours, he had been variously shot, stabbed, punched, drowned, immolated, and poisoned. (In the interest of accuracy, I must admit that not all of these assaults were received at the hands of villains. At least one had been inflicted by his brother Tiberius, and I myself had been responsible for two of them.) And prior to our meeting, he had been attacked and nearly killed by a particularly nasty jaguar in the Amazonian jungles. (His response to this—which I share now in case an unfortunate reader should find themselves in a similar position—was to slowly force his fisted hand past the fangs of the beast and down into its gullet, effectively smothering it. This takes a good deal of strength and considerable time, so do not attempt if you are in a hurry is my advice.) But Stoker had survived each of these precarities thanks to his own robust constitution and some unexpectedly good luck. It had long been my fear that one day his luck would run out.

Such were my unhappy thoughts as I was hurtled through the darkening streets of London. The hour was late and not many folk were yet abroad, a piece of good fortune as our way was less impeded than it might have been. Still, there were too many stops and delays for my liking—including a particularly vexing interlude where we were forced to halt for more than a quarter of an hour while an overturned milk cart was righted. By the time we swung into Swain's Lane, my nerves were slightly taut, I will admit. I had been clasping my hands together, and as I scooped coins out of my pocket for the driver, I saw that my nails had left bloody little half-moon indentions in the flesh of my palm. This would not do. If I were to rescue Stoker, I would require all of my faculties about me. I took a deep draught of aguardiente, grateful for the rasping burn of it from throat to stomach. I replaced the flask under my skirt and surveyed the situation. The tall gates were shut and locked, it being a few minutes after sunset, and I saw no means of illumination. Beyond the gates, all was shifting darkness, shadows that parted and moved and came together again, endlessly forming and re-forming in some malignant blackness that seemed to whisper and murmur although no breeze moved the air.

There was no help for it. I should have to scale the barrier. I chose a spot deep in shadow to conceal my presence from any passersby, put my booted foot between two rails of the iron fence, and began to climb.

At once, a soft sigh moved through the trees.

"There are no such things as ghosts," I muttered as I turned my attention once more to the fence. It was higher than expected and with few proper footholds, but by wedging my feet tightly apart and exerting considerable effort with my shoulders and arms, I was able to inch my way up the bars. At the top, I swung one leg over, settling neatly between two of the high spikes that ran in a forbidding row along the length of the fence. It had doubtless been put there to serve as deterrent as much as embellishment, for there was no simple way to descend from its height with those tall iron teeth ready to carve into one's flesh—a point brought home to me when my skirt snagged on one as I prepared to lower myself down. I had managed perhaps two feet of my descent on the inside of the fence when my movements were sharply—and somewhat painfully—arrested. The sudden stop caused me to lose my grip, and I slipped from the fence, swinging gently out into the air. I looked up to find my skirt tightly wrapped about a spike, the fabric all that stood between my person and a fall of some greater height than I would have chosen. The moon had risen by then, shedding a fitful silver light onto the scene, casting long, eerie shadows.

"There are no such things as ghosts," I repeated—more in hopes I might come to believe it than in any real conviction. A scientist must keep an open mind about such things, I have always maintained. But being able to firmly discount phantoms as existing solely in the realm of fantasy would have been a consolation as the soft wind moaned woefully in my ears and the shrubberies sighed in despair.

It occurred to me that it might have been prudent to wait for some sort of support in my mission. Mornaday would have been the obvious choice, but even J. J. might have proven herself useful under these particular circumstances. I swayed back and forth a few times, much like an aged cheese in the window of an Italian grocer, as I considered my options.

I had not yet settled on a course of action when the situation was taken out of my hands. In short, the fabric of my skirt gave up its valiant effort and parted with an audible rip. Luckily, it did so slowly enough that I was lowered with a series of awkward jerks towards the mossy ground beneath. The last bit of ruffle might have held, but I shifted my weight, and this too tore, dropping me neatly onto Mr. Bevan Strangeways, or at least onto what was left of him. His grave was newish, I realised, for grass had not yet covered the mound of dirt, and it was something of a morass of mud into which I had fallen face down. The gravestone, clearly installed quite recently, was sharply incised with his dates of birth and death.

"1801 to 1889. A very good innings, sir," I said, saluting him as I rose from his place of repose and wiped the worst of the mud from my eyes. My efforts to tidy myself were in vain. Mud caked my clothes, and I could feel a mask of it hardening upon my face. My hair had come loose from its pins through my exertions, leaving it in a tangled snarl liberally coated in more mud. My skirt was beyond repair, the back of it completely open, so I removed it altogether, grateful for the fact that I had worn trousers underneath, even if they were a little too inclined to cling to my form with indecent tenacity. I dropped the skirt onto Mr. Strangeways and began to pick my way through the cemetery, heading towards the spot where we had found the remnants of whatever unholy rites Asphodel had performed.

I dared not light a vesta, so I was dependent upon the moon's capricious light. Sometimes it provided welcome shadows, concealing me as I moved. At others, it left me thoroughly exposed. It seemed a hundred eyes watched my progress through the cemetery, and more than once I stopped to take my bearings.

It was during one of these pauses that I first heard it—a sound barely louder than the susurration of the wind in the treetops but with a curious rhythm, a chanting of sorts. "Voices," I murmured. But what were they saying? I could not make it out, but I was encouraged by the fact that the presence of other people meant Lady Rose's intelligence was correct. It was only at that moment that I realised the significance of the date, a slender scrap of information I had unearthed in my researches. It was the thirtieth of April, the feast of Saint Walpurga. It was, amongst Germanic peoples, the most important night of the year for witches—the night when they mounted their brooms and flew away to commune with the devil himself.

I skirted the Circle of Lebanon, eased my way down the Egyptian Avenue, and emerged behind a handy bit of concealing shrubbery. The chanting was louder here, but still unintelligible. I kept to the shadows of the bushes, working around the area Asphodel had chosen for her ceremony. I looked about more than once, hoping to spy a caretaker or guard I might despatch to go for help, but there was no one. We had already surmised that Asphodel and Ruthven would need to bribe the cemetery staff to conduct their little gatherings, and this was proof of it. As I drew near, I could see the glow of the torches, and the sound of the chants rose, loud enough to send owls and nightjars scattering.

I stopped behind a handy pleurant, one of the tall weeping memorial figures wrapped in stone draperies. It concealed me from view, offering me a place to observe without being detected. As I anticipated, a group had assembled, each of them heavily shrouded in dark woollen cloaks with deep hoods and sleeves that fell well below their hands. They looked like monks from a mediaeval manuscript, illustrated in shadow-black ink. They stood in a loose circle, half a dozen of them holding torches which flared up into the night sky. In the centre stood Asphodel, also garbed in a black hooded robe, but hers had been embellished with a sheen, the neckline cut low enough to show off the pendant she wore—the Mortlake Jewel. It glowed against her skin, the flames of the torches sparking fire into the heart of the gemstones. It glittered as she moved, and the shifting light made it seem almost alive, a thing that existed apart from Asphodel, a thing that carried a knowledge of its own.

The makeshift altar was in use again, set with black candles and fresh heaps of ebony salt. Beside them sat several flacons and bottles, and Asphodel mixed these in a pewter pitcher, murmuring incantations as the others continued to chant. I looked for Ruthven, but if he was there, he was dressed like the others, his identity concealed by the long hooded robe. I turned back to Asphodel, watching in interest as she stirred her mixtures together into a potion of sorts, using a long slender bone—the femur of a dog, I suspected.

When she had finished, she raised her arms heavenwards, calling down gods whose names have long been forgot. Then, with a smile, she moved among the gathered crowd, offering them the pitcher. One by one, they took the pitcher beneath their hoods, drinking from its inky depths.

"Drink," she urged. "For tonight I share with you the sacred potion that enables me to fly. Drink of it and feel yourself liberated, my friends. Fly with me!"

It was the most ludicrous of claims. To begin with, the flying ointment of witches was historically just that—an *ointment.* It was applied to the skin and gave the sensation of flight, among other hallucinations. I racked my brain to recall the exact ingredients. The trouble was that there were numerous receipts in folklore—including Francis Bacon's insistence that it contained grease made from boiling up juveniles. (I highly doubted Asphodel had been popping children into her cookpot. I had smelt nothing of the sort in their house, and cooking human flesh is notoriously odiferous.) However, the rest of the ingredients were all to be found in her conservatory. Wolfsbane, belladonna, others of the nightshade family—all with hallucinatory compounds.

But of course, that was her aim, I realised. To create an atmosphere of unreality, to induce flights of fancy, perhaps to coax her acolytes into misbehaviours they would scarcely recall the next day. She needn't administer the traditional embrocation. Any herbal concoction would do, provided it contained enough of the appropriate substances to persuade the partakers that they had experienced something beyond the explicable. It would heighten her powers, drawing out their confidence. But if I was correct, it was also intended to provide her with a magnificent exit.

Asphodel finished her rounds, pouring out the last of the libation onto the altar stone. The chants—some questionable Latin and a very rude phrase or two in ancient Greek, if my interpretive skills were up to the job—had trailed off as the participants began to fall under the sway of the potion.

"Feel yourselves surrender to the call of the night," she crooned. "Give way to your impulses." The group did as they were bade, some breaking off to stretch out on the graves and watch the passage of the stars, others climbing the nearest tree. One enterprising soul scaled a mausoleum, tipping his head back to bay at the moon in what can only be described as a thoroughly unnecessary fashion. Several others merely remained by the altar stone, hoods thrown back as they swayed on their feet, staring glassily into the middle distance. Whatever she had given them, they were well and truly foxed.

After several minutes of such goings-on, Asphodel clapped her hands, drawing their attention back to her. She raised her arms, her pale flesh glowing in the moonlight, shadows dancing malevolently over her face. At a gesture from her, two of the hooded figures moved forwards out of a place of concealment, a third held between them. They all wore gloves, long gauntlets which concealed their flesh, and their hoods were pulled low, obscuring their features. The flanking pair supported the third fellow until they reached the altar stone, where they laid him out, and when they did, his hood fell back, and my heart seemed no longer to beat.

Stoker. His features were relaxed in an expression of perfect repose, his limbs loose. He was unconscious, and as I watched, they pulled the robe away, baring his throat.

"Tonight we offer up a sacrifice, the great gift of life and blood that will ensure all of you will enjoy eternity. A fortnight ago, we gave the life's blood of one of our number on the night of the dark of the moon—tonight we seal the pact. The circle is complete, and you will go forth under the veil of immortality."

She raised her hand and I saw a dagger, thin and sharp, glittering in the torchlight. I did not pause to consider my options, for in truth, there was only one: stop Asphodel, whatever the cost.

Stepping onto the nearest gravestone, I launched myself into the air with a banshee wail that would have struck terror into the heart of a sober man—and there were precious few of those in Highgate Cemetery that night. Several of them began to weep openly, and one clapped his hands to his eyes, screaming, "Demon!" I realised then that my appearance was only stoking the pandemonium. From my trousered legs to mud-encrusted face, I was a fearsome sight to behold, particularly as I kept my mouth agape, shrieking Irish curses into their faces as I leapt from gravestone to gravestone on my way to Stoker.

But I was a second too late. The blade swung down, driving straight for Stoker's heart. I screamed, a great inhuman cry of pain and disbelief and rage, all of the torments of hell rising in my voice as the dagger plunged to do its terrible work. At the sound of my cry, Asphodel looked up sharply, dagger still gripped in her hand. But she stared in confusion from the knife to me and back again, for it was lodged in Stoker's chest, the lethal point of it stuck fast somehow, but it had not penetrated his heart.

The delay borne of her shock afforded me enough time to cross the clearing and make one final jump, hurtling myself over Stoker's recumbent form and directly into Asphodel's midsection. I bowled her over, onto her back, landing much harder than I had upon Mornaday, for all of the wind was knocked from her lungs and she lay, making a terrible, gasping moan as she struggled for breath.

My sudden and shocking appearance might have alarmed the acolytes, but it was the sight of Asphodel, robbed of her power and writhing—whilst gasping out a few coarse imprecations—that seemed to rattle them the most. They scattered then, tripping over their robes as they fled. Asphodel and Ruthven had apparently schooled them to obey but not to defend, for they could not get away quickly enough, some of them running headlong into statues and monuments as they ran.

I shoved myself off her, careful to plant a foot on her solar plexus as I did so. I meant to rescue Stoker, but I saw to my relief he was already sitting up, locked in some sort of embrace with one of the two hooded figures that had laid him on the gravestone altar.

"You were unconscious, damn you," huffed the hooded man—or Hegarty, I should say, for as he spoke, his hood fell back and his face was revealed. He grappled with Stoker for a moment, and I saw that Stoker's wits were still a little fuddled, for otherwise he would have shaken off Hegarty as easily as a lion will dash a cub from his back. He swung his head from side to side to clear it, and when he realised Hegarty was attempting to subdue him, he issued a backhanded blow that sent Hegarty reeling, nose pouring blood.

"You've broken it!" Hegarty wailed, clapping his hands over his unfortunate nose.

"I'll do a damned sight more if you don't move," Stoker said, rising from the altar stone with his hands curling into fists. He paused, noticing the dagger still lodged in his chest. "What in the name of seven hells?" He wrenched it free and tossed it aside as Asphodel pushed herself to her knees, one arm surrounding Hegarty.

"Go now—leave us in peace," she begged.

"Leave you!" I was sorely tempted to jab her with the business end of a minuten for suggesting such a thing. "You will face justice for your murders."

She emitted a low moan of pain and continued to cling to Hegarty. Stoker climbed to his feet—a trifle unsteadily—and I decided later it was this momentary lapse of strength which emboldened Seward Johnson.

For of course, he was the second hooded man. He had hung back in the shadows—and all I have related took place over the course of no more than half a minute—but at the sight of Stoker marshalling his strength, Johnson must have realised he had only one chance to seize control of the situation. He was not meant for brawling, but then a man with a gun does not have to be good in a fight.

He raised his arm, the little revolver emerging from the heavy folds of his sleeves.

"That is quite enough, thank you," he said, his voice underpinned with a note of steel I had not heard before. Hegarty sagged against Asphodel, and she helped him to his feet.

"Go," Johnson told us, jerking the revolver in the direction of the nearest crypt.

In other circumstances, we might have thwarted him by the simple means of each leaping in a different direction. He could not, after all, shoot us both simultaneously. But Stoker was still weaving a little, and I would do nothing that might endanger him. I had no idea if Johnson were practised at taking people hostage, but it is never a wise notion to argue with a man holding a gun, I have always said.

"Single file," he ordered. "Miss Speedwell, you will follow Mr. Templeton-Vane." It was a well-considered move. With my own body as a buffer between them, it ensured Stoker would attempt nothing heroic at the possible risk to my person. And Johnson was careful to keep a short distance between us, far enough that he would have ample time to shoot me should I decide to launch myself at him.

Our options were, at the moment, limited—something Stoker agreed with, for he turned his head and murmured to me, "Do as he says. We will get free later."

"Unless he shoots us first," I countered.

"Miss Speedwell, I beg you, do not force my hand," Johnson said politely.

His tone was even, but his hand trembled, and it occurred to me that—in spite of my instinct to launch an attack upon him—he was unpredictable, and upsetting him further would not be our best strategy. Instead, I followed Stoker into the crypt. It was a narrow thing, just a short walkway between two broad shelves, each holding a coffin. The whole thing was fashioned of pale, creamy marble, embellished as lavishly as a cake with scrolls and cherubs and flowers. An enormous urn held long stems of roses, once red perhaps but now faded, the petals brittle as parchment in death. At the far end of the crypt was a small iron door set into the marble floor. It had been stood open, and through it I could see a staircase.

"Down, please," Johnson said. We obeyed this as well, and I could tell from the sprightliness of Stoker's step that he was assessing the situation with the same practised eye as I.

The short flight of stairs led to a subterranean chamber, an undercrypt, this one far nastier than the building above. Here the coffins had been exposed to damp, the walls running with trickling water. The air smelt thickly of mould—and bone, I fancied.

Stoker and I moved into the undercrypt, herded forwards by Johnson and his little gun. The chamber was lined with stone, and if he discharged his weapon here, not only would the noise be deafening, the ricochet would be too dangerous to risk.

He pushed us to the furthest reaches of the room. Behind him, Hegarty and Asphodel followed. Hegarty's nose still streamed gore, and Asphodel had a murderous glint in her eye. Johnson was by far the most reasonable of the trio.

I thought.

But he turned his head slightly to address Hegarty. "Miles, I think you know we shall have to kill them."

He had the grace to sound regretful, and I wondered if he might be swayed from his position. Hegarty at least opposed him. He staggered a step or two nearer, leaving Asphodel at the foot of the stairs. He put a hand to Johnson's shoulder. "I do not think so, Seward. Can we not simply leave them here? It would take them ages to get out if they are able to make an escape at all. And we shall all be away by then."

His voice was gentle—persuasive, even. But I could see Johnson was undeterred.

"You may be too softhearted," he said to Hegarty. He turned towards us and lifted the gun a little straighter.

Stoker immediately thrust me behind him, but I was not prepared to let such an attempt at heroism stand without making an effort of my own.

I ducked under Stoker's arm, emerging to face Johnson. Stoker growled a little, but I ignored him, locking eyes with our potential killer, pinning him in place. "Are your colleagues aware that you have made plans to abandon them? I know that you mean to run, and not to the Continent," I said to him. "I have been to the Belleville offices."

"Oh." He breathed out the single syllable in an exhalation of perfect resignation.

"That is not new information," Asphodel said dismissively from her post at the foot of the stairs. "We knew he intended to leave. Now that we have what we wanted, he is free to go with his share—to New York, wherever he chooses. Meanwhile, Miles and I will remove ourselves to the Continent, won't we, darling?"

Her eyes were gleaming as she revelled in her triumph, and for a moment, I permitted it. I knew how hard the next revelation would be for her to hear, and so I allowed her one last minute to nurse her illusions.

Then I turned to Miles Hegarty. "But that isn't right, is it? Because Seward Johnson did not book passage to New York for just himself. You mean to go with him."

Asphodel's lips parted scornfully. "Don't be stupid. Miles and I are leaving tomorrow for Paris and thence to Marseille. We say good-bye to Johnson here. Tonight." But the more she talked, the clearer it became that she was trying to convince herself. Her eyes never left her lover's face, but he could not meet her gaze. "Miles. Look at me."

It took him a long moment before he could do as she ordered, and when he finally looked her fully in the face, she gave a moan of pain like a wounded animal. "I am sorry," he whispered. "I never meant for this to happen."

"Never meant—" Her eyes were wild as she looked from him to Johnson and back again. "You intended to leave me. Did you think to take our share, *my* share?" she demanded.

Miles raised his hands in protest. "No, no, of course not! I was going to leave you everything that was due you—and mine as well. I insisted to Seward upon it."

"Then why—" she broke off in mystification.

"Because they are in love," I said simply. "Is that not correct, Ruthven? Your book in the dressing room. It was an indifferent translation of *The Iliad*, not one any true scholar would choose. But it was marked at a particularly warm passage about the devotion of Achilles and Patroclus. True love."

"No," Asphodel said, shaking her head. "It cannot be." But even as she said the words, I saw the dawning realisation on her face.

Misery stamped itself upon Miles's features. "I am sorry, Asphodel. I know this comes as a blow to you."

"A blow? No, a blow is a solitary thing. One can survive a blow. This is an annihilation," she managed tightly. "How long have you been planning this?"

"Since before Maurice Quincey died," Stoker put in. "That is why he had to die, wasn't it? He discovered the plan for the two of you to run away together and had to be silenced." I stared at him in astonishment.

"You knew they planned to leave together? How?"

"George," he said simply. "I set him to do surveillance on Johnson, and he told me he'd seen him at the Belleville offices. Belleville only does transatlantic crossings, so he had to be booking passage for America. Before I could tell you, they called," he said with a nod towards Asphodel and Ruthven. "They sent a note claiming to be representatives of the Pinniped Society in need of my services for that cursed walrus."

"And you believed them!" I protested.

"Of course I bloody well didn't," he said scornfully. "What sort of cotton-witted bumpkin do you take me for? It was obviously a trap. But I realised that if Johnson was planning to leave, I had no choice but to go with them in order to force a confrontation."

"If we might—" Johnson put in.

"No, we may not!" I turned back to Stoker. "Have you no sense of self-preservation whatsoever? Of all of the moronic—"

"Enough!" Asphodel roared.

"Very well," Stoker replied. "You want to return to the topic at hand. We were explaining how we realised these two planned to abandon you. Do you want more of the details?"

"Like how Jameson Harkness had to be warned in case Quincey, his best friend, had confided anything to him before his death," I added. That much was a guess, but it was a good one. The arrow struck home.

The pair of murderous lovers looked abashed. No doubt they had never anticipated being held accountable for their crimes—or for their planned abandonment of Asphodel. Hegarty made a gesture of conciliation towards her, but she remained motionless, implacable.

"It all got so out of hand," he said piteously. "We were so careful and then Quincey, *bloody Quincey*, happened upon us. We had come so far already, we could not simply walk away. He wanted money for his silence, far more than we had. We promised him the Mortlake Jewel. But then Seward pointed out it would never be enough. Quincey would always come back until the well had been drained dry. We could not take the chance of living like that. So we made a plan to leave. But I insisted the jewel go to you, my dear girl. As a means of starting you off in your new life."

Asphodel's fingers went to the jewel at her throat. "This was always meant to be a gift of farewell?"

Miles held out his hands. "My darling, I am so sorry. But you will be happy again, I know it."

She ignored him and moved towards Seward Johnson, removing the jewel from around her neck as she came near. She placed it into his hands. "I do not want it," she said evenly. "I want nothing at all. Except revenge." She whispered these last two words into his ear as she struck out suddenly with her fist. Johnson gave a little cry, and when she pulled away, we saw the blood pooling around the slender dagger in his throat.

"No!" Miles Hegarty gave a great cry of despair and leapt to catch Johnson as he fell. Johnson gaped and gawped, his mouth moving though no sound issued forth. He gripped Hegarty's hand in his own, his gaze full of sorrow and something else. Regret, perhaps? For the lives they had ruined, their own included.

Hegarty turned to us, desperate and despairing. "Help him, I beg you! Send for help!"

"He is beyond help," Stoker told him gently. And even as he said it,

Johnson's eyes took on a faraway look, the light dying away as surely as the last star shutters itself at the dawn.

"But—" Hegarty looked back at his beloved, at the warm, spreading ruddy pool covering them both. Suddenly, he rose to his feet with a roar of grief, arms outstretched, hands curled into claws. "I will kill you!" He staggered towards Asphodel, but she snatched the jewel from the floor and grabbed the revolver that had slipped from Johnson's grasp. She raised it as she leapt backwards, as quickly as a scalded cat. She scrambled up the stairs, keeping the revolver trained upon Hegarty, until she reached the top. Without a backwards glance, she dropped the iron door down into place. Then the quick scrape of the key in the lock, and it was done. We were trapped with a dead murderer and his accomplice. And it was a very long time until morning.

CHAPTER 31

Stoker and I exchanged glances, both of us understanding instinctively that we must proceed with all caution if we were to emerge from our current predicament alive. The air was not quite as foul as I thought at first, and I looked up, spying a grille set into the ceiling in the corner. Through it, fresh air flowed. At least we would not suffocate here, I decided.

Stoker noticed the direction of my gaze. "Bolted," he mouthed, and I realised he had already assessed this as a means of egress and found it lacking. We should have to wait to be rescued, and whilst we waited, we should have to engage with Miles Hegarty, a proven murderer, who now had nothing to lose from adding to his roster of victims. In fact, he would have been wise indeed to do away with us if he meant to pursue a scheme of revenge against his inamorata. I eyed him warily as he sat, completely poleaxed by the loss of his beloved. He seemed broken, but I trusted him as much as I would a cornered cobra, which is to say, very little and with great reluctance.

Stoker, with his usual innate courtesy, removed one of his enormous red bandanna handkerchiefs from his pocket and draped it gracefully over Johnson's face, concealing the emptiness of those blank, staring eyes.

"Thank you," Hegarty said. "Thank you."

"He deserves dignity," Stoker said simply. "The dead always do."

Hegarty gave him a bitter smile. "Unlike Von Hilsing, you mean. God, it was a nasty business, leaving him in that house. But what else were we to do? Burying him in his garden seemed worse. At least in the house, he will be discovered in due course and he can be buried. It was the most decent thing we could think of to finish an indecent act."

I cocked my head as I looked at him. "Shall we call you Ruthven? Or should we dispense with the deceit, Mr. Hegarty?"

His brows rose a little in surprise. "Ah, the book in my dressing room. I thought you had moved it. But you were looking at the stamp inside, were you not? Clever. I presume you paid a visit to the school?"

"They told us nothing at Little Saints. But we met Professor Badlesmere. He said you were a teacher there once. He described your tenure as unsettling."

"It seems a century past and yet a second ago," he said dreamily. "It started as parlour tricks, the attempts at mesmerism. Gullible little fools," he said, but without heat. "I treated the boys kindly because I thought it could make a favourable impression upon their fathers. Schoolmasters, as you might imagine, collect precious little in the way of remuneration. And I have always had a fondness for nice things." Without seeming to know what he was doing, he stroked the fabric of his own sleeve, his fingertips moving along the weft of the silk.

"But you were asked to leave," Stoker said. "Pressed your luck too far?"

"Something like that. I like to think I would have left of my own accord, but of course, I would like to think that, wouldn't I?" He paused, sighing. His gaze fell to his beloved and he reached for Johnson's body, rocking him slightly as a mother will a child.

"What happened? After you left Little Saints," I asked.

He shrugged. "I hardly remember. None of it was important. I tutored privately, took other positions in other schools. It all seemed so terribly dull, so pointless. And then I met Asphodel. And then—" He paused, his gaze dropping to the corpse he cradled. "He was the one who persuaded me we could make something of the—of Ruthven."

"You think of him as something apart from yourself?" I was intrigued. "Like a sort of character you created?"

"As much as if I'd been in a pantomime," he replied. "There was none of it that was real. But it was a way to gain influence over a very particular sort of person."

"Disaffected young men," Stoker said.

"It was a truth I learnt whilst teaching. Boys want someone to look up to, a focus for their aspirations. And if they cannot have that, they want someone to fear. Ruthven gave them both."

"So you established the Harpocrates Society to attract—what? Easy marks?" Stoker said.

"Seekers," Hegarty corrected. "We wanted those who believed there was more to the world than toiling away in the service of others. We found clerks and secretaries and other young men who were firmly under the thumbs of their elders, men who stifled and suffocated them. And we promised them something better."

"Eternal life?" I could not help the derision in my tone.

"Yes," he replied with a touch of indignation. "We had to dazzle them. Promising them riches or fame was a shallow and silly business. But the sheer theatricality of what we offered—the possibility to live forever. It was bewitching."

"It was daft," Stoker retorted.

"You would be surprised what people can persuade themselves to believe," Hegarty said mildly.

"Like curses," I put in. "Quincey must have believed he was cursed—he wore a Romany witch's charm against harm. And Harkness was so credulous all it took was a scrap of a dried plant to make him destroy himself."

Hegarty shrugged. "He was an unhappy young man. His wife does not love him, he is held under his father's thumb. He claimed he came to the society for learning occult secrets, but he came for escape. They all did."

"You gave them the illusion they could be free of their problems," I pressed. "But what did you take?"

"Money, mostly," he said with an openness I had not expected. With Johnson dead and his secrets exposed, the fight seemed to have gone out of him. "They sold their trinkets. Sometimes they stole things from employers or miserly parents. Sometimes they did favours, such as arranging the lease of the house or making a tailor's bill disappear. And sometimes they paid us in secrets, information we could use."

"All of this theatricality," I said with a gesture towards his robes. "And all the while you were just common blackmailers promising your accomplices the secrets to eternal life."

"Surely only the most gullible, grass-witted, nonsensical fools would have believed you for a moment," Stoker said.

"But that was the point, was it not?" I asked Hegarty. "Anyone clever or careful enough to see through your charade was someone you could not have manipulated into doing your bidding. You set yourself up as a vampire and Asphodel as a witch because you needed people who would believe in you."

His tone was flat when he spoke, his face expressionless. "Yes, that was the point. There were one or two sceptics, but they did not last long. We weeded them out very carefully, keeping only those who were suggestible, those who would succumb to our encouragements. We presented it all very logically, of course. History tells us there were witches—we have the records of those who were burnt. Who is to say they did not actually cast spells and fly upon their brooms? And in the mountain villages of Europe, vampires are feared even today. Are they creatures of fantasy and folklore? Only a fool would be so quick to dismiss the idea. All we had to do was dangle the possibility in front of them and see who snapped like a carp at a bit of bait."

I raised a new point. "How did you explain the need for Quincey's death to Asphodel? How did you persuade her to send the wolfsbane to Harkness?"

"Seward was unlucky. He thought to steal the jewel from Von Hilsing's safe and abscond to greener pastures after the old fellow left for America, but Quincey would not wait. So Seward removed it from the safe, and in the act, he was surprised by Von Hilsing. He struck him a blow, and it killed the poor man. Accidentally." His voice broke, and he put the back of his hand to his eyes, dashing away quick tears. "Sorry," he muttered.

Stoker and I exchanged glances.

"Mr. Hegarty, I am afraid that is not true," I said. "Von Hilsing's death was not an accident."

He blinked furiously. "Of course it was. Seward told me that is what happened, just as I have told you."

"Von Hilsing died of arsenical poisoning," Stoker told him. "I ran the tests myself."

"That is not possible—unless, maybe he was desperate, maybe he stirred up a quick dose just to finish him off," he babbled, grasping at anything to make the truth more palatable.

"It was *chronic* arsenical poisoning," Stoker said firmly. "Johnson had been working at killing his employer for quite some time."

"Nothing about this was sudden or accidental," I added. "Johnson meant to kill Von Hilsing, but if he was willing to let Asphodel have the jewel, then that theft was not the purpose of murdering his employer."

Hegarty swallowed hard a few times before finding his voice. "He said we would go to New York, then immediately travel to Canada, where no one knew Von Hilsing personally. I was supposed to impersonate him, take money from his accounts. And then we would disappear. South America, he said. It would be easy to reinvent ourselves, and even when Von Hilsing's body was discovered, there would be no reason to connect him to Miles Hegarty. Seward would be suspected, but he said it would be a simple matter to make it seem he had disappeared into the Canadian wilderness. With new identities, we would be free—and rich. He used to talk about such things when we first—" He paused to rub his face. "He used to imagine Von Hilsing would die and leave him a bequest which would set him up for good. He painted such a pretty picture of us together, the life we would lead. I never really thought he meant it. He knew I cared for Asphodel, but he wore me down. He kept saying she was an anchor upon me, unworthy of my affection."

Poor foolish Asphodel, I thought. Putting her trust into baneful men who had planned to cast her off like so much rubbish. And then I realised that if the pair of them had escaped as planned, it would have been an easy thing for Johnson to send an anonymous message to the police, telling them of Asphodel's whereabouts and of the death of Von Hilsing. A dead millionaire and a woman skilled in poisons in possession of his stolen property? She would have been hanged before the year was out, victim and scapegoat in one fell swoop.

Hegarty went on. "And then Quincey found us together, Seward and I. And it all just happened so fast. Seward was so calm, so controlled about it all. He seemed two steps ahead, making all of the decisions for me."

"Perhaps because he knew it was coming," Stoker suggested.

Hegarty's head snapped up. "What do you mean?"

"Just that if Johnson had been poisoning Von Hilsing and dreaming of a future with you, what better way to ensure it than to make certain Quincey found you together and exposed your relationship?" Stoker said. "Asphodel finding out about your love affair would have forced your hand, brought everything to a head. Being discovered would have meant the end of the endless, torturous waiting for you to choose him."

"Perhaps," I told him, as gently as I could, "Johnson was not a character in your little drama. Perhaps he was the puppet master all along."

At those frank words, Miles Hegarty put his head down upon Johnson's breast and began to sob, deep, soul-rending cries that sounded as if the world itself were ending. And for Miles Hegarty, it had.

We were there only another quarter of an hour before I heard the "hallos" of approaching voices.

"Down here!" I called.

A bobbing light came near, then the face of Mornaday appeared at the grate.

"Good lord, however did you find us?" I asked.

Another face appeared, bobbing into view. "Hallo, miss!"

"George, it is past your bedtime," I said firmly.

"I know, miss, but Mr. Stoker sent me with Miss Butterfield as soon as them villains came for him," he explained.

"'Those' villains, George," I corrected.

J. J. peered through the grate. "How the devil do we get you out?"

"There is a door down here, but it is bolted from the outside, and no doubt Asphodel has taken the key," Stoker replied.

There was a bit of scrabbling and thumping, and several minutes passed before their faces appeared again at the grating above. "You were right," J. J. said. "No key to be found, and this seems by far the easier way in. Several of the bars are rotted through."

"Move aside," Mornaday said, lifting up a handy bit of gravestone. He struck at the bars several times before they began to break, showering the stone room with flakes of rust and bits of decaying iron. At last the grate itself gave way, crashing to the floor with a clatter loud enough to have roused the dead.

"Bit disrespectful," J. J. admonished as Mornaday lifted the grate away. She held his legs as he leant down and reached for my hands. I climbed up, toes slipping on the chilly, waterlogged stones. I emerged, drawing in great breaths of sweet night air. I turned to give a hand to Stoker, but he was standing over Hegarty and Johnson.

"It is time to go," he told Hegarty, putting a hand to the fellow's shoulder. Hegarty had been silent after his fit of melancholia had subsided, lying flat atop Johnson's body. At Stoker's touch, he rolled onto his back, his eyes open and unblinking.

"Mother of god!" Stoker exclaimed. He looked up at the three of us, moonlight silvering his face like a pagan god in his prime. "He is dead."

In the golden lamplight, we could now see the black pool of blood beneath him, a slender rivulet still flowing from his thigh. Stoker shook his head. "He has slit his femoral artery. A quick and silent death."

"And his last trick," I said. "I suspect he collected the dagger you threw aside and kept it on his person."

Stoker hauled himself up the wall and out onto the grass of the cemetery. "It is better this way," I went on. "He would not have wanted to go on without Johnson. It is rather romantic, really. If one overlooks the fact that they were homicidal criminals."

Stoker put an arm about me, and I ducked my head to his chest, marvelling again at the fate which had brought this man, so perfectly matched to me in every way, into my life. In moving, my face brushed against the slit the dagger had left in his shirt.

"How was it that Asphodel's dagger did not kill you?" I asked. "She struck directly at your heart."

He grinned and pulled the neck of his shirt aside. There, luminous and fairly glowing, lay the hagstone he had been given by Magda for his protection. “The tip of the dagger caught in the hole,” he said. “If it hadn’t—”

I put a silencing hand to his lips. “Do not even whisper it. I cannot bear the thought that she might have taken you from me, that murderous witch.”

Mornaday pushed his bowler to the back of his head. “What was that you said?”

I dropped the grate back into place and dusted my hands. “Come along, Mornaday. It is a long story and we have all the time to tell it.”

CHAPTER 32

In the end, we did not gather that night to discuss the case. Stoker was still suffering the effects of his drugging, and the rest of us were feeling the various aches and bruises that were the mementoes of our adventure. We parted at Bishop's Folly, George to sleep in the stable block, Mornaday to his lodgings with a promise to return the next day, Stoker to his temple, J. J. to her Bavarian folly—now free of pests—and I to my little chapel. Vespertine joined me, and I left him slumbering on the tiny sofa as I moved behind the screen to wash and change out of my hunting costume. It was streaked with mud and assorted other substances, so I left it in a heap to be attended by the maids and wrapped myself in a dressing gown of velvet patchwork, shaking out my hair and giving a sigh of relief that all had come out well in the end.

"Are you quite finished?" came a voice from the other side of the screen. "Only I have a train to catch shortly."

I stepped out to find Asphodel, sitting on the sofa, Vespertine tucked comfortably alongside.

"Forgive me," I said evenly. "I did not realise you were waiting. Would you care for a drink?"

"Whisky," she said. I poured a glass for each of us and poked up the fire. She watched me closely as I moved.

"You seem remarkably poised," she observed. "And not at all shocked that I have come."

"I would put it at mildly surprised," I admitted. "I thought it a possibility, but if I had regarded it as probable, I would have sent out for sandwiches."

To my surprise she laughed, a warm, rich sound. I said nothing more. She had come to me, and it was for her to start the conversation. Instead, I held my silence, sipping the whisky and listening to the soft crackle of the fire.

She rolled the glass between her palms, studying the play of light in the amber depths of the liquor. "I believe that sometime soon—a day or two at most—I will think of what has happened in these last few hours and I will become inconsolable, hysterical even. But for now, I can speak calmly. And I would like to talk about it."

"You believe I am the proper audience for your confession?"

"Confession! Well, they do say it is good for the soul. And to whom else shall I unburden myself, hm? You have wrecked my life, picked it up and shaken it to pieces, and now I think it only fair that you hear the truth of it."

"Very well," I said, settling myself more comfortably. "Go on."

She grinned bitterly. "Do not think of it as a confession. Think of it as a cautionary tale. You believe you would have been cleverer, in my position. I know you do. But it happened by inches, not all at once. And you can learn to tolerate anything if it creeps up slowly. That's what Johnson was—a slow, creeping thing that stole the love of my life from me."

She sat back, one hand stroking Vespertine. I made a note to have a stern discussion with that dog about loyalty, but he seemed to give her some comfort, for she kept a steady pace, petting him as she talked. "We were down to our last few shillings when we met Johnson. I say 'we' but it was Miles who met him first. It was in a dreadful, grubby little gin palace in Whitechapel. I was reading palms for ha'pennies, and Miles was nursing a glass of blue ruin. We had always talked of going abroad, trying our luck elsewhere, but we could never quite manage to scrape together the fare."

"Miles was a tutor," I said quietly. "Had he left his profession?"

She nodded. "He used to try his little tricks on his pupils—a bit of mesmerism, nothing serious. He would make the boys take things for him, as a lark, he told them. But then he would sell them on and pocket the proceeds. It worked, after a fashion. Because Miles himself never stole anything, he was not caught in the act of pilfering. The only true risk was in selling property that did not belong to him. So he only asked for small trinkets and modest sums of money. It brought him a little extra brass, but nothing much."

"You cannot make a person behave contrary to their own character under hypnosis," I replied.

Asphodel's smile was small and sour. "You have correctly identified the flaw in Miles's little schemes. The lads who were not averse to a bit of thieving would bring him the odd pound note from their fathers' note-cases or a bit of pretty china he could pawn. But occasionally he met with a boy who refused. He was always able to pass it off as a joke, but in his last post, the child told him no and reported Miles to his father. He was turned out the same night. Without references."

"And a tutor without references—"

"Might as well be a dustman," she finished. "No one wants a person of dubious character shaping young minds."

"For good reason," I murmured.

She waved an airy hand. "It was a bit of petty theft."

We would not see eye to eye upon the matter, meaning there was little point in pursuing that path. "So, you were at a low ebb when you met Johnson," I prompted.

She nodded. "Do you know, of all the things that are curious about this business, all the questions I have that will never be answered, the one that puzzles me the most is why Horace Von Hilsing's private secretary went all the way to Whitechapel for a glass of cheap gin. I never asked why he was there that night, but I can tell you, when I walked over to where he was sitting with Miles, he turned and looked at me and I felt it."

"It?"

"The shiversome feeling when someone walks over your grave. Fate had a hand in that night, I am certain of it. Johnson and Miles had arranged to meet again, and I tried to put an end to it. I told Miles I didn't like him, thought he was too lofty for the likes of us, but that wasn't why. I'd seen his palm, you see. And I knew he meant death for us."

She fell silent for a long moment, her hand still moving along Vespertine's fur, as slow and steady as a metronome. When she resumed her narrative, her voice was quieter, huskier. "But Miles would hear nothing against him. He liked Johnson. It was the air of poshness about him. Miles and I both grew up poor, you see. Oh, his poverty was the genteel sort—a father with a head for stories and lungs thick with consumption. My parents were third-rate players in the most broke-down theatres in the provinces. They taught me how to get by on my wits and with a bit of showmanship. But where I learnt to despise my 'betters,'" —her mouth twisted on the word—"Miles could never quite get past being awed by them. The bits and bobs he stole were to get something of his own back, but he could never bring himself to really commit to the part. He could have taken far more off them if he had tried."

She looked ruefully into her glass. "One good sip left. But I won't trouble you for more. I would enjoy a little oblivion, but I've business to attend to tonight, and I need a clear head." She peered up at me with a furrowed brow. "Where was I?"

"You and Miles had just met Johnson. You were unimpressed."

Her laugh was the short, sharp bark of a fox. "'Unimpressed'! Oh, you do have a droll wit, Miss Speedwell. I will grant you that. 'Unimpressed' indeed. I knew he was a devil, but he hid it so well behind those pleasant manners and that mouth that wouldn't melt butter. It wasn't long before Miles told him about his little japes with the boys—the tricks of mesmerism and so on. And it was Johnson who suggested how he could make the whole thing bigger, bigger than he had ever dreamed."

"The Harpocrates Society," I said.

She pointed to me and winked. "Got it in one, my clever girl. Johnson saw at once that Miles's tricks could be used on a much grander scale. He explained it with one word—'Archimedes.'"

I puzzled over this for a second, then snapped my fingers. "Of course! 'Give me a lever long enough and a fulcrum on which to place it, and I shall rule the world.' You needed only a bit of information to serve as a lever, and you could make anyone dance to your tune."

"Precisely. Miles had told Johnson about how he had persuaded a few of the more gullible lads at one of his schools that he was a vampire. He thought Johnson would have a good laugh, but I saw the gears turning. If any of us were not human, it was Johnson. If you were to split him open, you'd find nothing but mechanics and crankshafts inside. Anyway, he told Miles that assuming the identity of a mysterious vampire was just the thing to set the society apart. Rich people, exclusive people, they want something more than money. They want power, and there is no greater power than to thwart death. We began by hinting at mysteries and rituals and matters beyond their ken. Miles told them that we had known one another for centuries, and they believed. They believed because they *wanted* to believe."

"And possibly because you dosed their tea?" I suggested politely.

She gave another sharp bark of laughter. "Oh, my dear! It was the easiest part I ever played. A bit of kohl around the eyes and a few dramatic gestures with a trick teapot. Suddenly, there I am, a four-hundred-year-old witch helping to keep a vampire alive. And they lapped it up, every last one of them! Not a speck of common sense amongst them." She put her head back against the cushion of the chair, her expression thoughtful. "It was Johnson's idea to go after Harkness and Quincey—they'd bullied him terribly at school. They thought it was all great fun, of course. Their sort always think casual cruelty is just a very good joke and that schoolboy japes do not matter in the real world. Johnson saw a chance to get his own back at them. He pretended all was forgiven and forgot, and they lapped it like cream." She gave me a jaded smile. "You know why they were so susceptible to our little machinations? They were second sons and ripe for being singled out, told they were special. It was Johnson who spotted that. He was one himself. He said he'd never got past the resentment of everything going to his elder brother, and Miles saw the sense in it. Second sons who were already aggrieved were an easy target, ripe as plums for the picking, they were. We played upon the sense of injury, that somehow fate had been unkind in not putting them first in the queue. I never failed to be astonished at how entitled they were, thinking that somehow, because they were gently born and male, the world owed them even more. Not one of them understood they had already struck gold compared to the rest of us." She paused and her eyes met mine. "You have felt that sting, have you not? The lash of the whip because we are female and therefore lesser? Most women do not. They carry on, content to be silent accomplices in their own subjugation."

"You played second fiddle to Miles Hegarty willingly enough," I pointed out.

Her smile was mirthless. "Oh, and I will regret it until I die, believe me. I allowed myself to be a pawn in his games instead of setting the rules myself. Of course, I did not know it at the time. That was his true gift, Miss Speedwell. Many people are manipulative enough to coax you into doing what they want—how many can convince you that it is your idea? It is only now that I have thought back that I understand it was Miles who created the character of Asphodel. He conjured and cajoled until she was precisely what he wanted her to be. My hair is not even black," she said with a brittle laugh. "I played the part he wanted, and I thought myself lucky because he loved me. There is no fool so great as one who connives at her own destruction."

I said nothing and her gaze sharpened. "I suppose you think I have received my just deserts."

"I think you have been betrayed," I told her honestly.

Her eyes shimmered, but no tears fell. She cleared her throat. "Thank you for that. Most women in your position would no doubt succumb to the temptation to gloat, even if only a little."

"I am not most women."

"Well, you have possibly too high an opinion of yourself, and that would be tiresome after a while, but I think under different circumstances, we might have been something a little less than enemies."

"But never quite friends," I added.

"Never," she agreed. But she smiled when she said it. After a moment, the smile faded. "Perhaps if I had had a friend, she might have counselled me to abandon Miles when I had the chance."

"Would you have listened?"

"Of course not. What woman wants to look in the mirror being held up to her and see a fool? But I knew. I refused to think about it. I would not acknowledge it, not even to myself, but I knew what was happening."

"Miles and Seward Johnson?" I asked gently.

She nodded. "They were always shutting themselves away, having whispered conversations that broke off as soon as I appeared. I wanted to believe it was business, but I saw the way they looked at one another, and—" She broke off, pressing her lips together until they went white. "I thought it was a passing fancy, some sickness in the blood, a fever that would break if only I could hold my ground. So I stayed. And I shut my eyes, and I pretended none of it was happening. Perhaps I was right. Perhaps he would have come back to me in the end, broken things off."

I said nothing to this, but it occurred to me that a woman who thought she could be content with castoff emotions was a woman who was not entirely honest with herself. I realised then that she had left before Hegarty's final, desperate act, and I steeled myself to tell her.

"Would you have had him back?" I asked gently.

"No!" The word was spat like a curse. "He does not deserve my love. I have left him, and I wish never to see him again so long as I walk upon this earth."

"Then you will not," I told her simply. I put another question to her. "It was Quincey, was it not? When he found them together, that must have set everything in motion."

She nodded again. "Yes. He threatened to tell the rest of the society, to expose them as—well, you know the word. I do not have to say it."

"But surely they did not tell you this at the time. You seemed truly astonished at the revelation of their affection," I said.

"It was never acknowledged," she said fiercely. "That is how I was able to pretend it did not happen, *was* not happening. They told me Quincey had discovered some financial irregularities and was threatening to go to the authorities about it. I chose to believe them, and of course they were cautious enough never to let me speak to Quincey alone. They explained that he demanded money for his silence, but there was precious little to give him. It was Johnson's idea to steal the Mortlake Jewel from his employer."

"A pointless thing if Quincey could not sell it," I remarked.

She shrugged. "Quincey was greedy and stupid. The jewel would have fobbed him off, at least long enough for us to get away."

"But you did not get away," I reminded her. "You chose to kill Quincey instead."

"Not me!" she protested. Vespertine stirred at her shrillness, and it was a long moment before Asphodel collected herself. "Not me," she repeated with stubborn calm. "At least, it was not my idea. Miles and Johnson came to me and said they had had an idea for a sort of ritual to persuade the society of Miles's powers."

"And yours?" I suggested.

"And mine. They noted that the moon would be dark, a perfect time to enact a ceremony, one that would bind the society in a way we had never dared attempt before."

"Had you performed rituals before this?"

"A few times. Mostly on All Hallows' Eve or a full moon. We did them at Highgate so as to set the right atmosphere. It was very effective," she added with the fleeting smile of a showman. "And the society members wanted to believe. All it took was a few black candles and a bit of mangled Latin, and they were seeing spirits behind every gravestone. Then I would give them a cupful of tea with my special herbs. The rest of the night would be oblivion. They would wake in various places with fractured memories of what they had seen and done. It was a simple thing to make them believe whatever we wanted." She paused. "Those nights also gave us the opportunity to suggest that they had done things—unforgivable things."

"And were thus open to a bit of gentle blackmail," I finished.

She bristled. "Nothing as crude as that, I assure you. We never asked directly for money to keep our silence. But we conjured shame in them, and shame is a powerful motivation. It bound them to us as the keepers of their secrets. And once they had tasted true deviltry, they were so much easier to manage. We had only to hint at something we needed, some bit of information or little favour, and they were only too happy to oblige."

A sudden thought struck me. "And by involving them in Quincey's murder, you made accomplices of them all. How exactly did you do it?

Drug him with your accursed teapot? Then drag him to the cemetery for some unholy rites made up on the spot?"

"Something like that," she told me. "Then Miles and Johnson handled the rest."

I noted her delicacy in not describing the gruesome scene which must have followed—Quincey laid out upon the stone, his blood drained away as the others watched in—what? Horror? Fascination?

"The puncture in his neck was made after death," I remarked. "To simulate the attack of a vampire. How did you drain his blood away? The wounds in the throat were too small."

"His femoral artery," she explained, her expression amused. "My grandmother was a healer and taught me a thing or two about the body. I knew that if Quincey were nicked in just the right spot, it would pour out of him and the black of his trousers would hide the fact of it in the gloom of the cemetery. It was a simple enough matter to have a basin behind the stone to catch most of the blood. I poured it away later, down into the sewers."

"Why bother? The others had witnessed the death."

"They had seen an unconscious man laid upon the stone. We danced and chanted, being very free with certain libations that heightened the experience and fuddled the senses. After some time, Miles bent over Quincey, shielding him from view. When he rose, there was a small pair of punctures on Quincey's throat and he was clearly dead. Hey, presto! A vampire has slain a victim in full view of the society."

I shook my head slowly. "There is no greater deviltry than murder, and by killing Quincey in front of the rest of the society, they became your co-conspirators."

She smiled thinly. "It was a stroke of inspiration. Eliminate the threat to us and simultaneously tie others to us even more securely. We knew Quincey's family would never permit the story of his murder to be made public, and the s ace seemed even more ominous to the society members, as if we v able to draw a veil over the matter, to influence the great and goo keep the death secret. They were happy to believe that and we wer y to let them."

"But t kness presented a problem," I said.

"He urice Quincey's closest friend. I dosed him heavily at the sta ritual, so his memories were only fragments, jagged pieces , half remembered at best. I . . ." She paused and seemed to g ength. "I told Miles to put a bit of Quincey's blood into h. When he woke, he had the taste of blood upon his lips."

Ha I stared at her in horror.

my finest moment," she acknowledged. "But it meant would never tell anyone what had happened that night— not his family. He was not certain if he had had a hand in th, if somehow Miles's supposed powers had been given to le was nearly demented by the thought. He shut himself up would not return to the society, but Miles and Johnson night eventually break down, become desperate enough to thorities."

the envelope on the morning of his death—wolfsbane and ."

as only meant to ensure his silence," she said.

ell, it certainly succeeded on that score," I replied dryly.

I am sorry for his death," she returned. "Truly. But how was I to ow he would choose that path?"

"How were you to know? Human decency, perhaps? Or is that one power you lack?"

"I deserve that," she said. "I knew you would not be kind. I think I wanted to be held accountable by you. To pay my penance."

"I'll grant no absolution," I warned her. "That is beyond me."

"I will never receive absolution for the things I've ne. It is far too late for that."

She fell silent again, her hands gripping each other v, the pale flesh corded with tension.

"After Harkness died, you must have known that you hoice but to flee."

"Yes. Miles and I were supposed to go to France. Johr would go to New York. He planned to travel there for a little then make his way to the Argentine with a new identity. I wa I thought it meant I was going to have Miles to myself again. A a little while. They had mentioned meeting up again in Buen But a million things could have happened in the meantime. I h I *believed* we could be rid of him at last."

"And Stoker? You were prepared to take his life tonight. Why?

Her smile was thin. "If I had meant for him to die, he would no live. It was a stratagem to strike terror, nothing more. To frighten away from coming after us once we had fled."

"Why invite us into your lair in the first place?" I demanded.

"That was Miles's doing, to discover what you knew about us. A dangerous game, but he thought he could dazzle you with his little tricks. He discovered at the Danse Macabre that the pair of you were incorruptible. He ought to have left well enough alone," she added with some bitterness.

I changed tack.

"You must have known Von Hilsing was dead. How else could Johnson have got his hands on the Mortlake Jewel?"

She made an abrupt gesture of dismissal. "No! He said that Von Hilsing had gone travelling and he had taken the jewel from the safe. So long as Johnson left before Von Hilsing returned and discovered the jewel was missing, he could make his escape. I thought the old fellow was alive, you must believe me."

"There are already enough deaths at your door. I wonder that you will not claim this one," I told her.

"Because I did not know. Believe me or not, that is your right. I thought the jewel had been stolen outright. Johnson told me he could not travel with it in case Von Hilsing returned and discovered the theft. He would send detectives after Johnson, and he could not be found with the jewel or he would be arrested. So he gave it to me, for safekeeping and a sort of peace offering, he said."

I felt my lip curl in scorn. "You are not that stupid, Asphodel! Surely you must have seen that he meant for you to be found with it and arrested for the theft yourself."

"I see that now," she said, biting off each word. "But at the time—"

"At the time you were blinded by your own greed."

"It is a very pretty jewel," she said with a ghost of her old vivacity. She reached into her bag and withdrew a small bundle of black velvet tied with a silk ribbon. She laid it on the table between us.

"I'll not be lumbered with it for exactly the reason you say—it is a poisoned chalice. The minute some copper finds it on me, I'll have the noose around my neck, and I'd rather not."

"So you mean to leave it with me!"

"You will ensure it returns to Von Hilsing's estate," she said, rising to her feet. "Or you will throw it in the Thames. Or perhaps you will keep it. It is a grave temptation."

"Where are you going?" I demanded.

"Away, vanishing into the night like any good witch," she told me.

"I could report you," I told her.

Her expression was pitying as she buttoned her coat. "My dear Miss Speedwell, you do not even know my name."

With that, she squared her shoulders, opened the door, and disappeared into the darkness beyond.

CHAPTER 33

The next day, Mornaday arrived, joining us in the Belvedere for a comprehensive discussion of the previous night's events over tea and scones—a discussion which was progressively less cordial as the details were revealed.

Stoker was other than pleased that I had heard Asphodel out.

"You let her stay without summoning help? May I remind you that she is a murderer, Veronica?"

"Says the man who got into a carriage with her and allowed himself to be dosed into being a human sacrifice," I muttered.

"That is beside the point—"

Before Stoker could warm to his theme, Mornaday broke in.

"You let Asphodel escape," he raged. "I have two dead men at Highgate Cemetery and a woman on the run. I shall need to call in reinforcements from the Yard."

"How will you find her?" Stoker asked placidly. "She is of average height and weight. I suspect she will have put on a wig, either brown or grey to help her to blend in. No doubt she will have assumed nondescript, respectable clothing. She would be a particularly elusive needle in a distinctly enormous haystack. She might go anywhere in the world."

"No corner of this earth is safe from the eagle eye of British justice," Mornaday replied loftily.

"The earth is round, Mornaday," I reminded him. "And you cannot begin to find her if you do not even know her name. I should point out that 'Asphodel' is a pseudonym, a *nom d'occulte*, as it were."

He stared at me for several seconds, then swung his gaze to Stoker, and back again, fairly pop-eyed with rage. He turned to J. J. "Do you countenance this?"

"Of course," she said with a serene smile. "It makes for a much better story."

All the while that Stoker and I had been detailing the results of our investigation, J. J. had been scribbling in her own peculiar version of shorthand, her pencil flying over the pages of her notebook. Mornaday snatched at it, but J. J. retrieved the book with a wounded look.

"Just because they did not share with you the most essential elements of the case before they solved it, do not take your ill temper out on me, little man," she advised.

"You cannot write that. Print a single word, and I'll have you clapped in irons," he warned. He jammed his bowler back onto his head and prepared to leave.

"Do not be angry," I soothed. "You are, after all, the one who will solve the mystery behind the deaths of Jameson Harkness and Maurice Quincey. And you have two dead bodies to present to the Yard. I should think they would be grateful."

I suspected only the presence of his hat prevented him from tearing at his hair.

"Harkness's and Quincey's deaths are closed. I cannot reopen those cases even if I wanted to. As for these two bodies, I cannot begin to suggest that the son of a prominent diplomatic family was engaged in a highly illegal romantic affair with another man. My hands are tied."

I thought for a second. "No, but you can give them Horace Von Hilsing."

His eyes narrowed, a fox on the trail of a tender rabbit. "Go on."

"Say you were passing Steel Square and noticed something amiss—like a broken window in the back garden. Naturally, being a man of the law and knowing the importance of Von Hilsing, you investigated, only to discover his dead body. You can even suggest the possibility of arsenic poisoning. Stoker can tell you what details of his appearance would raise that suspicion."

Mornaday's nostrils flared gently. "I know what signs of arsenic poisoning are, Veronica." But I could tell he was warming to the notion.

"Furthermore, you could be the one who points out that the Mortlake Jewel is missing from the premises," J. J. added.

"And it could be your eagle eye that lights upon a scrap of paper in the fireplace that falls to ash—a scrap bearing the word 'Greville,'" Stoker put in. "Leading you to suspect Johnson was the culprit and that he meant to flee. Then when Johnson and Hegarty's bodies are discovered, it will seem as if they were merely jewel thieves engaged in a criminal conspiracy, particularly when a quick inquiry at the steamship offices reveals they had booked passage together. There needn't be any suggestion of a romantic relationship between them."

Mornaday considered this, his countenance brightening considerably. "I would be something of a hero at the Yard," he mused.

J. J. emitted a sound of frustration. "It will not work. How is Mornaday supposed to account for the fact that the supposed jewel thieves are dead? Who will have murdered them if Asphodel is not implicated?"

"A quarrel between co-conspirators," I said promptly. "One of them took the jewel, intending to double-cross the other. They quarrelled and things got out of hand. As proof of that tidy little theory, you have two dead bodies and the spoils of their crimes."

"And Asphodel?" Stoker asked. "J. J. is right. Her absence is suspicious. How does her disappearance fit into your tale?"

Mornaday's smile was sharp with cynicism. "My dear Stoker, no one at the Yard will much care what has become of a woman if I have a pair of jewel thieves who murdered a millionaire in hand. She is insignificant to their inquiries." He turned to J. J. "I am off to Steel Square to 'discover' the body of Horace Von Hilsing. If you happen to be passing when Special Branch descend, you can scoop the story. That ought to get your superiors at the *Harbinger* to take you back on board."

"The *Harbinger*?" Her tone was frankly scornful as she snatched up her hat and clapped it onto her head. "I will write it as a freelancer and sell it to the highest bidder. 'The Mysterious Death of the American Millionaire Recluse' will be the making of me!"

"Wait," Mornaday said, stopping so short that J. J. ran into the back of him. "A bit of grit in the oyster that we haven't considered: I haven't actually *got* the jewel."

"In point of fact, you do," I said. I reached into my pocket.

I opened my hand, and the jewel lay on my palm, cool and luscious and alive, it seemed, with movement flickering in the depths of those remarkable stones. The four of us stared, mesmerised by the cold fire in its heart. The central emerald was dazzling, almost too perfect to be real, and was surrounded by sapphires that somehow deepened the sea-swept hues of the green gem. Beyond the sapphires, rubies or spinels—something rich and bloodred—circled a pure white diamond. All of this was set in a plate of gold, heavy and ornately embellished with enamelled figures of dancing skeletons and winged skulls.

"Remarkable," Stoker breathed.

J. J. was already sketching the thing into her notebook whilst Mornaday's hand reached to take it.

"I shall make certain this is found with our jewel thieves," he said.

Stoker arched a brow at him, and Mornaday bristled. "I promise. No funny business."

"A thing like that could fetch a fortune," J. J. said longingly. "It could change a man's life. Or a woman's."

"Or it could cut it short," I reminded her. "It is said to be cursed."

J. J. snorted. "There are no such things as curses."

"Perhaps not," I said. "But vampires are not supposed to exist either, and we found one."

Stoker rolled his eyes heavenwards. "Veronica—"

I held up a hand. "You mistake me, dearest. I do not claim that Ruthven—Hegarty, that is—was an immortal creature who lived off the blood of others. But he hounded Harkness to death by means of the threat he sent, and he did, in point of fact, drain the actual lifeblood from Quincey. He survived by extracting the will to live out of his victims. In that sense, you must concede, he was most definitely a vampire."

"I will allow it," he said graciously.

I dimpled at him. "Excellent. In that case, I believe you owe me a guinea."

CHAPTER 34

After the other two had taken their leave, Stoker and I remained in the snuggery, dogs curled at our feet—apart from Vespertine, who decided my feet would make an especially nice bed.

"Now you come back, traitor," Stoker chided him. "You do realise you were consorting with a murderess last night."

"Would we, in fairness, call her a murderess?" I asked. Stoker lay sprawled upon an ancient Turkey carpet, the silk pile worn clean away in places. Huxley the bulldog had pushed Nut quietly out of the way to nuzzle against Stoker's thigh and was noisily worrying a juicy lamb bone.

"She provided the poisons, even if she did not always know their intended use," he said. "Let us call her at least an accomplice."

"She was not the author of the plot," I reminded him. "She was a . . . a supporting player in their little tragedy."

He snorted. "I think Maurice Quincey would consider her to have taken a leading role. Remember the *putsi* he carried—a charm of protection against witches. He was afraid of her. And he made demands of Ruthven and Johnson, not her."

"Because they had access to Von Hilsing's wealth!" I protested. "What could Asphodel have given him?"

Stoker shook his head, his thick black hair shining in the lamplight. "He said nothing to Asphodel because I think that was the point of the blackmail. I would wager the threat he held over their heads was not to go to the authorities—it was to tell Asphodel of what he had seen transpire between Ruthven and Johnson."

"Wager?" I perked up.

Stoker rose and lifted me to my feet, placing his thumb under my chin and tipping my face up to his. "You already have the guinea. But next time? Double or nothing."

[The interlude that followed bears no relevance to the investigation of this ghastly case and is therefore redacted.]

When the fire had died down and the air was filled with the assorted gentle snores of our pets, the first watercolour shadows of the gloaming settling over the gardens, Stoker and I finally rose. Hand in hand we descended the stairs to the ground floor of the Belvedere.

"I think I shall ask Tiberius to arrange a dinner for the Brisbanes," I told him as we walked. "They might be interested in knowing how it all turned out."

"If we must," Stoker said with a pained expression. "So long as you promise there will be no dancing afterwards."

"I promise."

We had come to the bottom of the stairs, and he turned as if to leave, but I paused, canting my head, brows raised.

"What is it?" he asked sleepily.

"There is one more mystery to unravel, my love," I told him. I turned towards the private workspace he had created. He made no attempt to dissuade me; Stoker is far too familiar with my ways to mistake the situation when defeat is at hand. He followed me with a sigh as I tugged the concealing tarpaulins free, revealing the project at which he had been labouring so diligently.

"I presume there is a reasonable explanation for this," I began politely.

"Veronica, there is, I assure you."

"I do hope so. Given that you were so entirely dismissive of the possibility that vampires might exist, you can, I am certain, comprehend my astonishment to find you working on *this*." I sketched a dramatic gesture with my arm, encompassing all of the creature that loomed above us.

"Now, that is an entirely different matter," he began.

"Is it? Is it indeed? Pray, do explain how one creature from myth is an idea so ludicrous that you will not even consider the possibility of its existence, but another is such a reasonable notion that you are happy to create one?"

"It seemed a good idea at the time," he muttered.

"Stoker, it is a *unicorn*."

"Yes, yes, it is," he said, and a light of something that must have been pride kindled in his eyes. "A rather good one, I think."

"Rather good" was a tremendous exercise in understatement. The creature was stupendous. In illustrations from fairy stories, such beasts are rendered the size of large deer or perhaps ponies. But Stoker did nothing by halves. This specimen had had its origins in a draught horse of monumental proportions, measuring nineteen hands at least. Its coat was snowy white, the mane and tail rippling in silken waves that glinted with silver threads he had skillfully interwoven with the animal's natural hair. The hooves, enormous things the size of dinner plates, had been leafed in silver and burnished to shimmer in the light.

But none of these embellishments compared to the magnificence of the horn. Set neatly in the centre of the brow, it shimmered like mother-of-pearl, spiralling to a lethal-looking point. It was proportional to the rest of the body, rising some three feet into the air.

"The horse was a Percheron, I suppose," I remarked.

He nodded. "From a farmer in Belgium. It died quite suddenly during a thunderstorm, and the owner did not have the heart to burn him, as he was so beautiful. He wanted him put to a greater use."

"And the horn?" I asked.

"The tusk of a narwhal. An antique I purchased at auction. It wanted a bit of polishing, but it was remarkably straight."

I circled the specimen, taking it in from all sides. It had been posed in a rearing position, its weight balanced precariously yet perfectly on its hind legs, the forelegs raised in a suggestion of a salute. The eyes were dark with a watchful gleam, as if daring the viewer to venture closer. The effect was one of danger and beauty and power that was held in check, but only lightly. Come near and risk being crushed, it seemed to say.

I rounded back to where Stoker stood, watching me intently.

"It is magnificent," I told him truthfully. "Who is it for?"

"The Duke of Albany. Do you know him?"

I furrowed my brow, trying to place the name. "The peer who has been in the newspapers, agitating for Scottish independence?"

"That is the one," he said with a grin. "He is rabid on the subject, almost to the point of treason. Tiberius had him to dinner and Albany mentioned he wanted a very particular commission—one he was prepared to pay handsomely for. Tiberius put me forward for the job."

"And a handsome one you have made of it," I remarked, looking again to the unicorn. "It seems a trifle large, even for the home of a duke."

"Oh, he doesn't mean to keep it at his home," he said. "Albany has purchased a warehouse in Rotherhithe that he means to convert to a club for like-minded Scotsmen. It shall have pride of place there because the unicorn is the symbol of Scotland herself."

"How very fitting," I said. I reached for his hand. "The work is exquisite. You ought to be very proud."

"I am, rather," he said. He squeezed my hand in return, then dropped it to replace the tarpaulins, shrouding the beautiful image in darkness once again. "I have only a few minor details to finish, and then he will be ready for collection. Once the duke has settled his bill, of course."

He finished tucking the unicorn away from sight, then extinguished the work lamps. From high above, a shaft of morning light pierced the gloom of the Belvedere, illuminating him like a Renaissance painting.

"What do you mean to do with the money?" I asked, brushing an errant lock of witch-black hair away from his brow.

He slipped his arms about my waist, moving his mouth to my ear. "Well, usually a commission is enough to buy some books or a new coat when mine is threadbare, but this one is a little more significant."

"Shall you buy two coats?" I teased. If my voice was a little breathless, it was only because his lips had begun to trace a slow path from the curve of my ear to my collarbone, then back again.

He did not answer for a long moment, preferring to bend his attention to other tasks, and when he had finished, I was far more breathless, as was he.

"I thought," he said slowly, tipping my face up so that he could see it better, "that it might be a worthwhile thing to use the commission for a trip."

I blinked. "A trip? What sort of trip?"

"The Templeton-Vane-Speedwell Expedition has a rather nice ring to it," he said, his lush mouth curving into an inviting smile.

"Expedition to *where*?" I demanded, poking him sharply in the chest with my index finger.

"Wherever we decide. Someplace that has butterflies for you and something of interest to me. I am partial to fossils, you know."

"I do know," I said, reaching up on tiptoe to express my enthusiasm in a way he was certain to appreciate. When I had kissed him as thoroughly as a man has ever been kissed, I pressed my forehead to his, my arms still looped about his neck. "And I know something else."

"What is that, my incomparable, adorable Veronica?"

"That the Speedwell-Templeton-Vane Expedition has a much better sound."

He opened his mouth to argue, but I stopped it with another kiss. I felt the laughter rumbling in his chest, and when he lifted me off my feet, it seemed for just a moment that I had taken wing. Justice had been served, albeit imperfectly, but the man I loved beyond all others was safe and sound, and we were to embark—at long last!—upon an expedition of our own. Excelsior!

Note in the Rosemorran Collection: The Mortlake Jewel

Pendant of solid gold embellished with enamelled figures and symbols such as silver-white skeletons believed to represent the danse macabre as well as other alchemical and allegorical images. Small yellow and white bouquets have been identified as blossoms of immortelle interspersed with white roses, both flowers representing immortality. The images are set around a central stone, an emerald weighing approximately fifty-five carats. Known as "the jewel of kings," the emerald has associations with royalty and eternal life. The reverse features tiny diamonds set in constellations and is inscribed with the Italian quote "E quindi uscimmo a riverder le stelle." (Translation: "And thence we came forth to see again the stars.") Around the edge of the pendant are several mottoes inscribed in Latin, French, and Middle English. Debate continues as to whether these are incantations or prayers. Whilst most of the images elude specific interpretation, the pendant is generally believed by scholars to celebrate immortality.

Likely commissioned in the mid-fifteenth century, the

piece is of possibly English or French design. It first appears in the historical record in 1631 in the will of Sir Robert Cotton, who purchased many of the effects of John Dee of Mortlake, astronomer and alchemist to Queen Elizabeth I. He identified it as being called "The Mortlake Jewel," indicating it had once been in Dee's possession. The pendant passed through the Cotton line until it was eventually sold, and its whereabouts cannot be incontrovertibly verified until it surfaced in the possession of eccentric American millionaire Horace Von Hilsing. (Rumoured owners of the pendant are Alexei Petrovich, tsarevitch of Russia, tortured to death on the order of his father, Emperor Peter the Great; Marchioness Leonor de Távora, Portuguese noblewoman, tortured and executed for the attempted assassination of King Joseph I of Portugal; Emperor Maximilian of Mexico, deposed and assassinated in 1867.) The jewel was said to have been purchased by Maximilian from the estate of Estefania García de Teruel (wife of Canadian millionaire Hilliard Steen), lost in the explosion of the *Sultana* in 1865. Because of its association with so many owners who suffered tragic and violent deaths, the pendant was said to be cursed, and Mr. Von Hilsing was careful never to wear the jewel, in hopes of circumventing any ill luck.

In spite of his precautions, Horace Von Hilsing was murdered in London in April of 1890 and the jewel stolen. It was later retrieved by detectives at Scotland Yard and restored to his estate, passing eventually to his niece, Mrs. Elizabeth Fortescue-Beale of New Haven, Connecticut, in the United States. Mindful of the pendant's rumoured curse, Mrs. Fortescue-Beale declined to take possession of the jewel and donated it to the Rosemorran Collection, where it is currently in storage awaiting permanent display.

Dated: September 21, 1890
Signed: V. Speedwell, Curator

[Further information may be found in the private memoirs of the curator.]

AUTHOR'S NOTE

In writing of vampires, it is difficult to overstate the contribution of Bram Stoker to the genre and therefore impossible to resist tweaking his nose just a bit. (See Veronica's note at the beginning.) Careful readers will note the inspiration of character names in *A Ghastly Catastrophe* from characters in *Dracula*. These are used in a spirit of homage with tongue firmly planted in cheek. But while Bram Stoker receives the lion's share of credit for popularizing the vampire, he certainly did not invent it. The undead were among the occult topics discussed in the writings of the scholar William of Newburgh in the twelfth century, and medieval villagers in Wharram Percy in Yorkshire took care to bury several corpses after burning and dismembering the bodies—a sure sign they were concerned the dead might walk again.

In *Dracula*, Stoker might have created a brooding, even romantic figure in the vampire, but he was not the first to do so. John Polidori—with a nod to history's most problematic friend, Lord Byron—gives us the first louchely sexy revenant in "The Vampyre." And Sheridan Le Fanu's Carmilla is so alluring she is able to work her wiles on unsuspecting virgins, extracting their essence to keep herself eternally youthful. Intriguingly, the name of Ruthven runs like a thread through vampire fiction. First appearing in Lady Caroline Lamb's *Glenarvon*, it was given to an avatar of Lord Byron who was not a vampire at all. But when, a few years later, Polidori needed a name for his bloodsucking aristocrat, he reached no further than the epithet Lady Caroline had given their mutual frenemy. Thus, the image of the privileged revenant was born, and for the rest of the nineteenth century, the vampire would evolve from horrifying monster to glamorous seducer. John Stagg, Byron, Samuel Taylor Coleridge, James Malcolm Rymer, Paul Féval—all took a stab (no stake joke intended) at writing about one of folklore's most fascinating figures. Forever alive and forever alone, the vampire is unique, rousing our fears as well as our sympathy. Without the certainty of death, how can life have meaning? And how can we not pity a creature forced to watch everyone they love age and die as they trudge on, year after year, centuries dawning and passing away as the vampire forever endures without real connection, without redemption, without hope.

When writing *A Ghastly Catastrophe*, I wanted to include the panic surrounding the death of Mercy Brown, a suspected vampire from Exeter, Rhode Island. Dead at nineteen from tuberculosis, Brown was believed to have risen from her grave to exact a terrible revenge upon her family, drawing the life force from her brother, Edwin, until he hovered on the brink of death. Her heart and liver were burnt and the ashes mixed into water for Edwin to drink. The cure, such as it was, failed, and Edwin died two months later. The reason I could not include it is that it occurred in 1892, a full two years after Veronica and Stoker embark upon their investigation into their purported vampire. The Brown case is a tragic one, not least because it illustrates one of the most enduring suspicions about vampires—that they exist by first attacking those they loved the most in life.

One final note: I have written about vampires before. In 2010, *The Dead Travel Fast*, my only Gothic novel, was published. In researching that book, I was able to secure an interlibrary loan for *The Land Beyond the Forest*, a very same edition of the book Bram Stoker used for his own research on Transylvania in writing *Dracula*. In combing through historical records, I also encountered a news story about a village a hundred miles from Bucharest where the inhabitants, fearing a vampire walked among them, dug up a corpse, tore out its heart, burnt it to ashes, and mixed it with water to give to his relatives to protect them from his evil. The police intervened, threatening charges against the villagers for desecrating the grave, but those involved were unrepentant, claiming the ritual was necessary for their survival.

The year was 2004.

Some things—like vampires—never die.

ACKNOWLEDGMENTS

The terror of writing acknowledgments never ceases—mostly because of the ever-present dread of forgetting someone wonderful who very much deserves their name in print. If this is you, I hope you will accept an abject apology and a cocktail the next time we meet.

Here are the folks who deserve bouquets of heartfelt thanks and showers of accolades for all they do:

My friends and family—otherwise known as THE VILLAGE because it takes a lot of people to keep me going. Especially big bouquets to Jen and Laurie for being such amazing cheerleaders while I do extremely hard things.

The Berkley team of Ivan Held, Jean-Marie Hudson, Christine Ball, Craig Burke, Tom Colgan, Claire Zion, Loren Jaggers, Jessica Mangicaro, Annie Odders, Tara O'Connor, Tawanna Sullivan, Anthony Ramondo, Jennifer Lynes, and every single person in the editorial, marketing, art, PR, production, and sales departments. Veronica simply would not be possible without the various enchantments of my editor, Michelle Vega. An extra round of applause to Angelina Krahn for a truly extraordinary copyedit.

The audiobook production team, with special thanks to Angèle Masters and Amber Beard.

My agent, Pam Hopkins, for almost thirty years (!) of the absolute best representation on either side of the Mississippi.

My entertainment agents at William Morris, Sanjana Seelam and Nicole Weinroth; my online team at Writerspace; and my literary attorney, Paula Breen.

All of the booksellers, librarians, reviewers, fellow readers and writers, book clubs, and social media book folks. Thank you for everything.